Ligh

CW01674209

by Ke

A Nebula Radian Publication
© Kevin Elliott 2020
ISBN 978-1-9163885-0-5

Dedicated to Bill Moulford

'There is a single light of science, and to brighten it anywhere is to brighten it everywhere'

Issac Asimov

Contents

Chapter 1: ask the wrong question

Had her lookout tree escaped the sickness? The ferns choking the bank were still a slick green, and Phos scrambled through the bracken to slap her hands over the elm's bark. She sniffed and retched: her tree wafted out the same outhouse stench as the others. What had looked like gnarled bark churned into stinking pulp under her palms. The trunk still soared upward to shoulder over the other elms, but the fingerholds she'd used to haul herself into the rustling canopy of leaves had collapsed into streaks of mush. Dad watched from the path.

Her memories of climbing stayed fresh. Phos's hands had gripped the twisted branches wrapping the tree's topmost perch, and she had watched the tops of other trees flutter in the breeze as her patch of forest stretched ahead and down to follow the tunnel's curve. To eveward, the forest gave way to rolling grassland. She'd spent hours watching donkey carts trundle across the silvery tracework of paths, a web connecting each village, Leester to Belhander and on to Drostalic, knots of whitewashed cottages settled along their tunnel's base. On clear days, the world walls had made haze-mellowed slabs of pale blue to left and right, each fifteen miles away. The side road curled up the shallow start of the northern world wall's slope to touch

Lostaramir's flax fields, and more villages studded the grassland further ahead until her world curved down to sweep below the horizon.

Some days she imagined everyone living inside a hollow cartwheel, but whatever force pulled you to the ground pulled you towards the wheel's hub; walk a thousand miles along the tunnel's downward curve, and you still stamped across grass.

Now the elm's bark sloughed away, and the trunk's damp reek left her reeling. Dad frowned, and she pushed herself away from the lookout tree and wiped slime from her hands. Her boots sank into the mud. She coughed and tugged her feet free before tramping back to Dad, who waited with crossed arms on the school path. Hoofprints and wheel ruts chopped through the sludge – carts had hauled cured leather from Belhander village or fish from Drostalic's river – and daylight knifed through the forest to scatter shadows ahead. Dad might lend her a drill: she had to know why the wood rotted.

Bad smells lurked everywhere, and school stank worst of all. When had chalk dust started to stink of lies? Three years ago she'd strained forward as teachers had chalked out trees and plants before writing names underneath, and she'd inhaled their dust. Each squeak of chalk had sparked memories of day-long walks when she'd explored the overgrown paths snaking around her village's forest; sap and resin scents had tempted her into the darkness with promises of deeper secrets. But promises failed, and schooldays had withered into mouldy exercises. Cooking, cleaning, memorising scribbled lists that dragged her away from real learning – lists were like looking at food rather than eating it. Didn't she deserve answers at thirteen?

'I've decided,' Phos said.

'You're desperate for this detention?'

'There'll be no detention: he'll shout and get back to teaching.'

Dad chuckled. 'Grump hates questions, and you still plan to interrupt him?'

'Listening tells me nothing.'

'That's why you never listen.'

'Teachers don't teach.' Phos snatched a tumbling leaf from the air, and the wizened brown shell crumbled between her fingers. Twigs bowed under her feet as they rotted in the forest's half-light, and she squatted beside a slime-covered puddle. What had sent this wave of sickness into her village? Were the crops already rotting in the farms clustered around Leester?

Hushed rumours had trickled from Ferstus and villages past the moor to dawnward. She'd not believed them, but three weeks ago an ashen-faced cart driver had whispered stories of dying trees while handing her a withered elm leaf, and now decay tainted her wood.

Did carts carry the sickness, or was it birds or winds? Climbing trees had let her believe she was escaping the world, but now her illusions rotted; she'd never climb her lookout tree again or watch daylight stroke the shallow hills to eveward.

Dad tapped her shoulder, and she rose to follow him along the path. They inched together along the grass verges. Her neck prickled as a damp breeze scuttled past. She'd used scissors to stop her hair nagging her face, which was against the rules for girls, but today's plans meant trouble no matter what. She'd clutched the coppery hairs in her fist and thought of wires before tossing them into the evening wind.

Phos chewed a fingernail and glanced at the canopy of branches. Was this morning darker than usual? 'How can they say the world never changes when there's change everywhere?'

Dad gripped her tunic sleeve to shepherd her around a puddle. 'Would you argue if Grump said water was wet?'

'You taught yourself; you said school was hopeless. The teachers sit at their desks and dream up new stories.'

'Say that in class, and you'll earn a week's detention. And keep up: being late doesn't suit you.' Dad ran his hand over his head. His fine hair plastered itself to his scalp as raindrops glistened on his coat.

‘I don’t need escorting,’ Phos said.

‘The roads aren’t safe now.’

‘I’m best alone.’

A branch had crashed over their path, and Phos dashed forward to ferret through a clump of leaves. She plucked a seed and brandished it at Dad, and her tunic strained at her shoulder though it had fitted fine last month.

‘Trees come from seeds, and plants too, and you said I came from a seed.’

‘I remember our conversation; you knew more than me.’

‘Here’s a story I worked out: plant a seed and water it, and the tree grows to escape the seed. I escaped the womb and so did you. If we imagine this world as a womb, tell me why we can’t escape? Might help us avoid the filth sweeping in from dawnward.’

‘Our world isn’t a seed or a womb, and we can’t escape anywhere. No reason to escape.’

‘I want more than baking and scrubbing. School doesn’t even allow questions.’

Dad smiled. ‘Dress as a boy and sneak into metalwork classes.’

She flicked the seed at him, but it tumbled into the mud. Phos had handled acorns, ideas for trees, tiny plans bundled into a nut, but the handling sparked questions. Who had written the elm’s instructions?

Who had drawn the designs for the leaves and set out their colours? Who told poppies to cluster, and why did gorse bushes have thorns? And why had the trees started to stink?

They hiked forward, and a grassy clearing appeared on their left, where the village carpenter had built his one-room home: a moss-covered shack with bowed wooden walls. The door twitched in the breeze. Dad knocked before stepping inside, and Phos followed, but the fireplace was cold. Leaves scuttered over the earth floor, and two chairs had toppled in the gloom.

Dad frowned. 'I've work for him. Where's he gone?'

'He's off searching for a seed.'

Dad snorted and stepped outside. 'Every time I meet your teachers, there's the same story. Can you avoid trouble for one day? Stop blocking kitchen chimneys.'

Phos slouched behind. 'I wanted to see how smoke behaves indoors.'

'And what did you learn?'

'Smoke floats and smoked pastries taste yucky.'

Her trousers didn't reach her boots any more, and mud daubed her ankles; Phos wasn't fussed but Dad winced. Light shuddered through the forest from behind, and the crossroads waited ahead. The other children would clump together while waiting for school, and they'd stopped bothering her with gossip months ago, so she'd have time to think out her question. She'd only get one, and she'd never hear a direct answer, but Grump's reaction might speak: if spittle flew from his lips, she'd have prodded a sensitive spot. School would complain again, but her parents always managed.

They reached the crossroads, where thirty children milled about beside the school path, and Dad sighed. 'Remember me telling you about the museum city to dawnward?'

'Morzenthal, past Ferstus village. You promised to take me.'

'I grubbed through their archives four years back; the books might keep you quiet for a time. The priests haven't cleared out Morzenthal's libraries yet, and the exhibits might answer some of your questions.'

'Any priests there?'

'Priests hate the place: it makes their cathedral cities look like a village, and it's older than anything they've built. They can't hide it, so they've scrubbed it from the maps.'

'You never said who built it.'

'No one knows. We'll go soon, but for now think twice before questioning your teachers – you've had enough warnings.'

'I'll think, then ask.'

'I'd meet you after school, but there's no telling how long your detention will take. Don't goad your teachers, and don't walk back alone – you can fake being pleasant.' A burst of rain broke the silence. They hugged, and he gave her a thin smile before striding towards Leester village. She almost understood his work, even if being female meant she'd never touch money. Running back home was a choice, but so was breaking school rules.

Outside the school, she lingered beside the decaying scatter of buildings. Moss slathered the brown walls of the seniors' hut, and a bored junior had scratched a crude face into the green fuzz. The thatch covering the juniors' classroom had sagged overnight. As she stepped forward, an adult barged into her from behind, and black robes raced past – a priest. She skidded over the gravel, but her legs jittered like a colt's to hold her upright.

Priests didn't have masters; they saw everything, and the guards were their teeth. Run to the world walls, and they'd still find you. Proper escape meant piercing those stone barriers, but everyone told her that was impossible. Teachers said their world was a tunnel looping around to meet itself, like a wheel, and for once their words smelt true; their faces puffed up with gloating when they said there was only rock outside.

Sometimes she'd imagine future days when she'd find a village full of girls working to understand how the world fitted together. She scowled: dreams were torment. No girl escaped the dark cloud of marriage, and she'd learn nothing but cooking and cleaning for a drunk. Mum had been spectacularly lucky finding Dad, but Phos knew not to trust luck. Even the word *wife* sounded like swearing, and how many wives died giving birth?

School time, and she filed in with the chattering girls to their cabbage-bestenched red-brick cavern of a kitchen. They'd cleared the blankets she'd jammed into the chimney, but her soot marks still decorated the brickwork. Pots clashed against cutlery, and Phos hammered her fists into her dough. Why did dough need folding? She'd not waste her question on cookery, but learning might mean escape and burrowing through the world walls.

Lunch came, but the bread's bitter taint left her gagging. The kitchen staff stared down her complaint as half-eaten apples teetered beside the counter, and Phos stumbled into the thin air outside to stare at the distant stone curve of the northern world wall. In this light, it looked like a wave threatening to crash into her.

The tunnel's wall rose fifteen miles away. It bowed out in the middle before curving over her head into the vault, a rocky ceiling beyond anyone's reach. A bank of cloud now hid the southern wall, but her cage was complete: walk forward or backwards, and you'd be an ant scrambling along the bottom of an immense pipe. Walk with a wall on each side, and you'd skirt village after village as their ring arched back to meet itself. Phos had heard of people walking the ring in a two-year slog, but teachers tried to silence the stories.

The sun's arch coated their tunnel's rocky top and sides – a narrow band of scorching light crawling eveward like a bracelet sliding down an arm. Teachers scolded you for staring, but Phos looked dawnward and shielded her eyes. Last month, she'd walked north and climbed the lower slope of the world wall. She'd struggled upward through the stunted grass until the incline had stopped her, but the grey stone had still loomed over her head, and her neck had ached from the staring. At noon the sun's arch had passed above, and shadows had fluttered around her feet, but even the lowest part of the glowing arch had hung far beyond reach, far up the cliff face. Teachers said the sun's arch was there to light your work, and she'd asked if it had always slid over the walls and who had built it and how it worked, but those adult mouths clamped shut.

The bell thudded out for the afternoon's lessons, and the other children slouched classward. Phos scrambled into the seniors' low-slung timber classroom – if first, she could choose her seat. Oak beams stretched over the stained plaster ceiling, and she darted to the warped back bench. Three weeks ago someone had carved the words 'Lanky bitch Phos' here, and her fingers stroked the crude letters. Chalk dust tickled her nose, and white powder coated the pot plant on the teacher's table as two boys grappled with poles to open skylights. The two girls beside her argued about their nearest cathedral city.

'It's not Torzene – that's a monastery.'

'Not any more. Dad said they're building a new cathedral there, past Ferstus, past the moor. They're rounding up all the carpenters and roofers.'

'That's never true. Torzene isn't….'

Silence fell in a heartbeat, and she smelt Grump's entrance: their teacher walked without sound, but he probably bathed in chalk dust between lessons. Phos glared as he prowled past towards his desk. His fingers sinewed around a stick of chalk and, without words, his stick-like arms scratched out a section of their world. Forty minutes of religious lecture before he'd burn her time with prayers.

A sudden crash rang out behind, and Phos turned as two black-robed priests kicked the door open to bustle inside. Whispers rippled around their classroom, and Grump swung around with his mouth agape as the pair swaggered to the front before sitting with crossed arms. Grump's white eyebrows stayed firm, but his chalk stub quivered a fraction, and after several heartbeats, he jittered back to his blackboard and continued drawing. She'd rock her foot soon to make the floorboards squeak at the front.

The ceiling had sagged since yesterday, and the damp patch at the front had spread. Did one cause the other? Grump finished shading his drawing and stepped back before launching into his well-worn syllables, words reminding everyone how their world had never changed. She'd only get one question, and he'd kick her into detention right after the final word fell from her lips, but doing nothing meant mouldering.

If nothing ever changed, why did apples rot in the orchards, why did the elms stink, and why did every blackberry make her gag? Now Grump mumbled the words that pushed bile into her mouth, words to stamp the right attitude into their minds, a picture of their world marooned in an endless sea of rock, a tiny wheel of life encased in darkness. Did priests see themselves as jailers?

Phos unfolded her legs and stood. 'Why are you so sure nothing changes?'

Dust swallowed her words as every student twisted to face her, but Phos folded her arms – being the only copperhead made standing out easy. Grump's mouth hung open, and his head rocked a fraction as he glanced at the priests, but they stared back at him. His face flushed crimson, and he reached under his desk to pluck out his cane.

'Come forward. Face the class, and raise your left palm up.'

Had she misheard? No one got caned. Boys had stolen wheels from the school's cart without being caned. Astonished murmurs and gasps rippled across the benches, but Phos looked ahead and Grump's watery blue eyes locked on to hers. She stood and walked towards him, and her arm obeyed as the others fell silent. For one moment nothing moved, but his bleached rod rose and hung above her arm for a heartbeat before Grump's spindly arm writhed downward, and one instant of blur became an agony of fire lashing her hand. Her eyes snapped shut, and breath whistled through her mouth as her body lurched forward. Now her eyes wouldn't open, and pain scalded her palm as her body locked itself.

'Stand up and raise your left hand.' The words sounded as if they'd drifted miles, but fury coloured his voice. If she stayed bent over, he'd slash her back, or those priests would seize her wrists.

Phos inched upward as breath seeped back into her chest, and she raised her arm. His second stroke splashed more fire across her fingers. The third left her teetering and sweating. Her classroom turned grey, but she locked her knees and waited. Grump's mouth hovered beside Phos's ear as his whisper wormed through her.

'The world never changes. It has always worked this way and will continue in this fashion forever. Will you question me again?'

Madness dressed as punishment. She imagined snatching his cane and screaming back a volley of words before running into the forest. No. He'd cuff her to the ground or cane her face. Phos blinked, and her head nodded before she clamped her hand under her arm and shuffled back to her bench. She'd found Grump's delicate spot. Questions about their world scared teachers, and priests terrified teachers enough to turn detentions into canings, but could this knowledge be used?

Gree and his burly friends stared open-mouthed. She'd not planned to impress troublemakers, but she nodded back. Grump's cane scraped the blackboard as words leaked again from his mouth. Fatigued syllables described villages and woods snuggling the tunnel's floor. He stepped back, and his cane scratched his drawing.

The other children stayed silent.

'Without beginning and without end, these limits define us, and we embrace our bonds as our walls embrace us. We must revere hunger because hunger reveals our limits, and our limits create our souls.'

Phos shivered.

Everyone faced forward for the words of dismissal, but the priests stood to bracket Grump and murmur into his ear. Grump stared at Phos, and his lips whispered her name, Dad's name, Mum's name, all captured with a priest's twitching pencil, and their teacher forced a smile onto his face before following the invaders outside. Once the door slammed, the boys stood and bustled towards their woodwork lesson. Most glanced her way as they passed, and Gree winked and gazed at her. Most boys marked the girls out of ten, even those who couldn't count, and she was used to coming near the bottom, so his thick-lipped smirking made another puzzle.

'You want anything, Phos? Leaves for the pain?'

She shook her head. Even if Grump had flounced off, she'd never give a teacher an easy win, and her lips stayed shut as she sat with the other girls for embroidery. Three angry streaks striped her hand, and she fumbled the needle. Their teacher fussed until she saw the welts. Her neighbour had talent; her threads pierced linen to weave a crimson rose over black cloth.

Ask a question and earn a caning. She might ask other teachers, but what if the priests scared them too? A single tear rolled over one cheek, but she wiped it clear.

Could you learn by asking questions of nature?

Plants told stories by budding and flowering, and she'd asked how plants knew when to grow their leaves, what instructions lurked inside seeds and stems. Dad hadn't known, and he'd shouted when she'd torn a rose apart; the shreds in her hand had taught her nothing. But throw seeds onto bare earth and they'd bring life, so she'd keep watching.

Outside and home time, the sun's arch had crept eveward, and the other girls jostled past her to rush home before the evening winds. A strangled chittering screeched from above, but the scratching branches were empty. Phos stumbled back through the growing shadows to the school courtyard while nursing her palm. She'd struggle to hide the welts from Mum, and she'd never conceal the passion she'd hatched in the priests.

Feet pattered behind, and she turned as the blacksmith's son, Mitch, gangled towards her – all limb and scuttle. He'd ripped his shirt last week, and no one had sewn the tear; ribs showed on his flanks, and his wispy hair had matted into fawn-coloured clumps.

'You all right? No question deserves a caning.'

'Depends on the question,' Phos said.

'You sounded angry, and I've never seen anyone angry with Grump before. Were you testing him?'

Phos glanced back towards the school. 'I'll test everything. Now I know priests frighten teachers, and teachers want to hide the past.'

'You're making your own lessons.'

'Perhaps that's the way, seeing as school teaches nothing.'

'Watch out for those priests: they're swarming the villages.' Mitch darted forward, and his feet skimmed over the mud.

The chapel's stone pyramid squatted at the courtyard's far edge. In this twilight, the door made a grey gash, but a reluctant dribble of lantern light sneaked out, along with adult voices. If priests caught her loitering, they'd grab her, but she dawdled past.

Each village held the same pyramid, and each bustled with priests who swaddled themselves in black robes. Each village had its own garb: scratchy leather jerkins for Belhander, linen tunics for Leester, swirling blue robes for Pulgro's riverside fishers, stooping in their stilt houses, but however far you travelled, the priests all sweated inside those satiny uniforms. Who told priests how to dress?

Phos listened but heard only a whispered voice smothered with hissing tones. She crept back to the crossroads and along the school path. Dad had told her not to walk back alone, but she'd learn more by breaking rules.

Ideas came: she'd retrace those day-long treks she'd taken through the forest around her village to seek new sorts of flowers and berries, or look for another pair of those trees that grew into each other; anything to make sense. One villager might hoard an ancient book with clues about a hidden cave, or she might hear whispers of hidden towns around the ring where priests never stepped. She'd press Dad for a Morzenthal visit. Seeing the past or reading forbidden books might uncover hints of some forgotten escape route – help her become more than a wife. Everyone flinched when priests walked past, so if priests were scared of Morzenthal, she should carry her questions there. What caused those tangled thickets of wild bracken she'd seen by her house? Why did nameless plants appear beside this road? Why had so many animals turned savage? Had her world grown from a single seed?

Her own questions left her mind spinning, and Phos paused as pools of shadow spread across her path. Her questions would fill books, but she'd never find enough answers. Lies often sounded like truth, so how could she sift true from false?

Her lookout tree rotted further up the path. From its top she'd imagined herself hovering over Leester's forest, but she'd never poke her head above the ceiling of leaves again. She'd never heard of anyone escaping marriage; even Dad, with his patient answers, couldn't see any way out. Black thoughts circled her mind, as painful as the throbbing welts scarring her hand – did priests wait at home?

Chapter 2: cider without a glass

Caliper's roomswayed and the floor creaked as his windmill waited for the evening winds, but he'd stay to relish these last few quiet moments. Enough buttery daylight trickled through his two windows to let him plonk bread and cheese on his table; he had space for his cider flagon and that tinker's jar. The cogwheels twitched behind him, and sawdust still spiced the air from those new gear teeth. Scratches covered his hands, but he'd eat now and share with the fly buzzing above his head. His table wobbled and creaked as his backside spread over the tiny wicker chair.

Cider foamed and amber bubbles frothed against the tinker's blackened jar. All twist and sag it was, but the beaker still held drink. The tinker from Belhander village had tossed the thing, but Caliper wasted nothing. Pour cider, beer, water, tea, even piss in there, and the liquid fitted no matter its class – almost like the jar gave orders.

The cider had strength, and for all its kinks, the beaker held a decent swallow. After two gulps he saw himself as the cider. He'd fill a huge glass, sure, but half-pints always left him chuckling. The priests rabbited on about nature designing everything, and if they were right, nature must have designed his belly: a place to rest his jar.

Caliper knew he could swear for two minutes without repeating; curse words coiled inside him night and day, but he only ever spat them out when alone. Sure, he'd imagine himself spitting fire over the priests, but their long words and black robes made him bottle his fury inside his guts. He'd bend around their orders and do their bidding without argue. Like his cider. Afterwards he'd grind his teeth and hate the weakness sloshing inside him, but he'd do nothing but drink his booze and flick cider drops off his beard.

There stood his trouble; strength only came when he sat alone. No one would sit beside him tonight; no one ever did, but with luck he'd not be alone.

Two futures beckoned. Both were threats, but they were threats of different flavours. One route meant some class of safety: grind the grain brought by Leester's villagers and deliver their flour. Money would trickle in, and he'd receive blessings and invites to festivals, and he'd keep his belly stuffed. That path was certain; a thousand millers had trodden it before, but his mind never stopped reckoning the second path.

If he mulled over that route, he'd see a narrow trail winding through a wolf-haunted forest crammed with thorns and sudden snarling jaws. Even if he survived the windmill's fall, there'd be screaming fury in the faces of the chasing priests and guards, and people talked of starving brigands prowling the forest between Leester's farms and the southern world wall. Caliper had tens of reasons to stay a miller and only one to take the second road – Christina's road.

Sunset tinted the wooden beams and bricks, but memories of Christina's face roamed across his mind. Full lips, a bold sweep of nose and those rounded eyes he always lost himself in: her face gave him courage to walk with danger. He'd borrow her strength and become cider without a glass, and stop obeying those sneering priests.

Too many friends had fallen silent. Carpenters and stonemasons vanished for weeks and returned with downcast faces; fear sealed their lips and stories went unspoken. His stonemason friend Turllog kept snarling back at the black robes, spurning their orders with fresh swear words, but the priests kept dropping words in his ear, sentences wrapped around unspoken threats. Turllog's wife had found his body behind their cottage in Ferstus. The priests had never tried hauling Caliper away. Perhaps their plans didn't need millers, but rebellion had begun to smoulder in his chest that day, and if he let Christina's words enter his heart the flames would burst into life.

Shadows stroked his windows, and for one heartbeat the eveward treetops bit notches from the distant bow of light, but the sun's arch dipped below the horizon, and darkness flooded his room. Above him the rafters and stolen lanterns faded into the roof's black pitch, and Caliper fumbled under his table to pull out a candle. It popped and fizzed. Had he grabbed a special? No, he held a normal candle, just a rotten one, like most things these days. If any guards caught him, they'd knock his teeth out, but he'd not drink in darkness.

He'd sweated deep into the nights to carve out Christina's changes, sweated whenever his body had obeyed him. Sometimes fear had frozen his hands, and on those nights he'd crawled under his bedding sacks to hate the coward inside. He'd learned how cider might coax him back into chiselling those curved gear teeth she'd drawn, and he'd strung up those flowing windmill sails with their curves and slats shaped like a bird's wing, but fear still shook his hands. When the cider wasn't enough, he'd tell himself he could rip out the new gears and hide the sails and keep clear from the second path, and that had kept his hands turning, carving Christina's designs into sweeping arcs of wood and canvas. Yesterday he'd hoisted the new sails into place.

Now the night for choosing was here, and Christina's sails fluttered while waiting for the evening winds. She'd said they'd bite the wind better than the old. His body wanted the safety of staying a miller, but his mind wanted more, wanted to plunge into

Christina's journey. Didn't a man need danger to live? Grey hairs threaded through his beard, so how long could he keep slinging flour bags into carts?

Caliper drained his jar and shook out the last few drops before slamming it onto the table. His cooking pots glinted in the yellow flicker, but they could stay dangling from the wall hooks: if he found the strength tonight he'd not need them again.

He stood and tugged the wires chaining the lanterns, all linked to the brass box she'd had him steal from a church. Each visit had seen Christina guiding him through her changes. He'd not understood them all, but he'd followed her, and now he'd wait for the winds.

Yesterday he'd nudged his reforged windmill into running at quarter pace, and his home's sullen chatter had become a slick pulse, a hushed murmur of oiled speed that boiled dust from the ceiling. His lanterns had glimmered for a minute before fading, and Christina had said running the windmill at full speed would spew light across the countryside, enough for her to see with whatever class of eyes she had. Those new gears would also rip his home apart, which meant he'd have beaten his body, and the coward's choice wouldn't be a choice any more: he'd have burned the safety out of his life. Hanging up his patched overalls and apron might celebrate the change, but he'd no other clothes.

The outside light faded as the vault shaded to

grey, and his windmill twitched under the evening winds like an old man grumbling before work. Rats had been trouble, but he'd not seen one for months.

The bricks behind the cogwheels twisted and warped, and the mortar wove itself into a net of curves. Cider or Christina? His dawnward walls shuddered and stretched like molten glass – she always made his world dance. Fog billowed before him before writhing into Christina's face. The cogwheels behind her stayed visible as the watery smoke curdled to form her shoulders. Her lower body would fill his downstairs space, and plumes of mist settled around her head. Shoulder-length hair twitched in a breeze he couldn't feel.

Breath surged through his mouth. 'It's yourself.'

Christina's voice slid into his head; her lips parted, but they never fitted her words.

'Is your signal ready, Caliper?'

'You still need my light?'

Ripples quivered over her face like a reflection thrown on water. 'I tried everything, but I cannot see your location: my eyes differ from yours, and much here has broken.'

How long would her image stay this time? Her light bathed his room and glinted from his copper pots. Anyone outside would see him stand, but he'd not care. 'You've not told me how wind becomes light.'

'I'll explain later.'

'These winds are your man, and they're coming, and your lanterns are ready.'

'Once they glow, I'll place you on my map, but right now I cannot tell your location.'

'I do this, and the church will chase me without stopping for breath.'

Christina blinked, and her face faded for a heartbeat before returning. 'You can stop; slow your windmill and remain as you are.'

'And we'll never meet.'

'You've decided?' Her eyes wavered, and her face tilted sideways a fraction. Did light dazzle him, or were tears streaming across her cheeks?

'Decided long ago, so I did. You'll see where I live, and you'll guide me. I've no return once your winds wake the windmill.' Christina never appeared for long, but would the cider glowing in his stomach help him destroy the windmill?

Again ripples swelled over her image, but she raised her hand, and her misty fingers hovered a half-inch above his cheek. 'Ensure you're outside and head dawnward. I am sorry about your windmill, but I need an immense amount of light. I can't stay; it remains your decision, but we must meet.'

'You should stay, Christina, and feel our wind here.'

‘Too much fails, and….’ Scratches hid her face for a heartbeat before her features reappeared. ‘…I know you’ve strength for this. I must….’ Her image faded, and his space snapped back into its old shape, bricks swaddled in mortar, battered pots hanging on hooks. Sweat trickled over his brow, and he slumped back onto his wicker chair to guzzle the bread and cheese he’d slapped on his table, mouldier than usual, but if he wolfed it fast enough, there’d be no noticing. Some joker had given him a comb once, and it had made a decent toothpick, but he’d snapped it last year.

She wasn’t a dream; that was sure. Dreams changed each night, and the same smile always danced over Christina’s misty eyes. Christina was real, though maybe there’d be different flavours of real – flavours no priest ever mentioned. His journey might teach him.

He’d have a few more heartbeats of flickering candlelight before the winds. Timbers quivered and temptation nagged: if he threw enough cloth into the gears, he’d stay with his flour sacks and keep mumbling through church services and be a miller with warm bedding and the full belly. Christina’s face haunted him. If he failed to take her path, colour would drain from his world.

He lit two more candles, and fresh winds brushed his cheek. The gears behind clattered into life, and his sails strained into motion. His floor bucked as the cogwheels jammed and the sails groaned. Splintering sounds came, and Caliper choked back his swearing as he knelt to peer at the gears. A tooth had sprung from its socket to clog the wheel, and Caliper fished a mallet from his apron.

If he knocked the tooth back into place, he'd start Christina's journey; if he stayed his hand, he'd stay a miller. A final battle, and now his hand wouldn't move, but he gulped air and closed his eyes as the floor throbbed. Memories of Christina's floating hair came as if she'd stroked his mind, memories of Turllog's beer-soaked stories, and Caliper grinned before smacking the tooth into its socket.

Life rocked the floor as gears snapped, and Caliper jumped back. Sails snared wind, and ruddy shadows flickered over his walls and ceiling. The lanterns drank wind and spat it back out as light, which grew brighter each moment. No return – his mind had won, and he'd carve the sky with radiance.

The windmill screamed as its beams splintered and the lanterns flared violet-white. Each new gust spattered shadows everywhere, and streams of dust poured from the roof as cracks ripped through his floor. Had he stayed too long? He hurtled down the stairs. This illegal light meant rebirth, and he snatched up his backpack before striding out to gulp air, tart and fresh after the dust. Sails swooped six feet above as violet light spilled over the hillock ahead. The surrounding trees became shimmering fingers of light, and the crashing sounds made him wince, but he climbed.

Light flooded past him as he reached the peak. Caliper glanced behind. His home had become a screaming pillar of brilliance. Sheaves of resin paper glowed red before shredding from the tower. Blasphemy never needed half measures. Speed blurred his sails as their canvas ripped, and the windmill rocked like a trapped animal scrabbling for escape. One lantern fell and shattered while others swayed, and the tower's left side roared and collapsed as broken timbers spewed out. The remains slumped forward. A grit-coloured growl would be the grindstone escaping, and a sail broke loose to hurtle upward before fluttering back to crash into the forest. Only a single spar stayed upright, a spur scratching the night. Church and Christina, both would see.

The crashing faded, and his light guttered to red and black. Dense thuds slapped the earth as his windmill's wooden bones plummeted into the trees. The windmill would have lasted centuries, but he'd killed it, along with his miller's life, and this victory smelt of brick dust and scorched resin. Fighting himself was hard labour; he wanted to fling himself onto the ground and sleep, even though he'd not used his muscles, but Caliper shook moisture from his overalls before striding down the hillock and away from the wreckage. He'd sniff out Ferstus village in the dark. His path hummed with risk, but each step meant making his own light.

The church would come screaming from all directions towards his windmill's corpse, and he had to wrap himself in the night's silence. If he didn't escape their fists and knives his journey would end in a church cell.

Chapter 3: dawn comes early

Phos's eyes snapped open as streams of silver light slid through her bedroom shutters and lapped across her wardrobe and hammock. Her framed drawings of the world glimmered in the broken night, and Phos leaped up to slap her bare feet onto the wooden floor. This light flickered with a silent pulse, and she flung her shutters open.

Change had come. A needle of shining energy shimmered in the dawnward forest, and violet-laced rays flared across swathes of trees. Ghostly echoes drifted through the night air to hint at clanking and shattering, and Phos stared as the radiance ebbed and flowed. In a single heartbeat, the distant windmill juddered and folded; light winked out to let the velvet darkness flow back. Tart air stung her lips. Light had shocked the forest beside Stormaze Hill into a breathless silence.

Warmth might linger under her blankets, but she'd never sleep now. Was this an accident? Flames needed guarding, but the light had shown rhythm, and its violet tinges reminded her of the lanterns paraded on holy nights. Priests said light made a rare gift, but here someone had splashed it like water. The windmill – she'd seen the windmill burst into life – she'd wandered near three years ago to watch its sails snap and billow in the wind, and the rhythm had calmed her, but there'd been no lanterns: churchmen demanded workers manage with daylight whatever their job.

Churchmen would swarm the site and hide any secrets, but could she get there first? She imagined tiny cogwheels working inside a caterpillar as it wove itself into a butterfly. Change would teach more than questions, and Phos's fingers traced the welts on her palm. Hadn't her question changed Grump?

Dad had warned her of starving gangs roving Leester's forest at night, but some decisions made themselves. Phos had spent last evening chewing her fingernails as Mum darned socks; each pop of sparks from the hearth fire had made her jump with thoughts of priests, but no one had shown. Sometimes she worried too much; escaping marriage meant embracing risks.

Phos fumbled in her wardrobe. She piled on layers and thick boots, and grubbed at the back for her liramic cloak. It still breathed out a faint blue-green wash, and she draped it over her shoulders.

She'd slip through the hedge past their garden before turning right to sneak through the wood. The snagging branches might slow her, but they'd give cover. There'd be a few rushed minutes to explore the windmill, and she'd be back before dawn.

Her bedroom door swung open, and she left it

ajar. The stairs would creak, and she'd wake Dad and face endless questions, so she draped her tummy over the banister and lifted her feet to slide as faint shadows pirouetted across the plaster walls. Her boots made a soft landing on the polished hallway floor, and she faced her granddad's portrait. Dad's shoes rested underneath.

Outside, and Phos ducked from the flower basket dangling above the front door as the chill wind gnawed her neck. Her cloak gave out glimmer enough to show the stones set into their garden path, and she reached the main road and glanced both ways before turning right. Her soft boots meant less noise. A hedge loomed on her left, and a hovering square of night marked where children had worn the hedge away.

She eased herself through the gap and wrapped the cloak tighter as she climbed into the wood. Her feet tapped out a path over the snaking roots. After ten steps her eyes picked up a green tinge of tree light trickling over the soil, brighter than normal, as if the flaring windmill had woken the forest. Soft moss appeared underfoot, and she gripped a liss tree's trunk for balance; the spongy bark yielded under her touch, and pepper and lemon scents drifted past. They'd grow rich as the night deepened, and one day she'd learn if trees talked through scents.

Twigs snapped behind as people thrashed

towards her through bracken, and Phos ducked behind a tree trunk as her trousers creaked. Two dim figures approached in ragged clothes with heads down to snuffle for food, and one scythed the ferns with a blade. Phos crouched and choked back a cough. The couple glanced her way before stumbling north.

She'd hidden behind a young liss tree. Its bark was dim, but the moss grudged out enough pale blue-green glow to reveal her to any searching priests or guards. Phos scuttled between saplings and held her breath. A small clearing stood before her, where a long branch arched from one tree into its neighbour like a light blue ribbon riding the night. A perfect curve and an invitation to stand between trees and pretend she stood inside a tiny slice of the world. This space needed avoiding now, but she'd played here years ago. The north and south trees bowed the same way as the world walls, and the branch looked the same width as the sun's arch, though the arch was huge. It had set hours ago, gone eveward to light other lands, a band of radiance riding over the walls and vault. Teachers called it the sun's arch, but what sort of name was Sun?

Belhander, with its stinking tanneries, Lostaramir and its flax fields nestling beside the northern world wall, the twin villages Drostalic and Pulgro, each saw the sun's arch later than Leester. To dawnward, Ferstus squatted in its swamp as if cringing from the moor beyond. Ferstus had the sun's arch before Leester, though nothing would ever dry the village out.

Today's arch had looked the same as yesterday's, but one afternoon she'd traced circles in the dirt outside Dad's greenhouse. People took two years to walk the ring, and the sun's arch didn't move much faster than a human, so it couldn't ever return by dawn. Did copies of the arch chase each other, and did the spaces in between create nights? Her questions had left her friends giggling.

A moth the size of her face trembled beside her head for a heartbeat, and ahead the trees petered out. The windmill stood alone on a hillside, so she needed caution. Phos dawdled and searched for more wandering figures as thoughts raced through her. What had turned the ancient windmill into that wonderful figure of light, the dancer in the evening sky?

Pattering sounds drifted from leaves as slim strokes of rain brushed her cheeks, and Phos raised her hood without breaking stride. Peaty scents drowned the pepper and lemon notes, and trunks surfaced from the night, wooden ghosts wrapped in blue threads of branches. She glanced back, and her footprints glowed on the grass to make a trail for anyone to follow. Her cloak sighed out more glimmer as liramic grass crunched underfoot – her cloth remembered being woven.

What had brought the storm of silver light? Had a rebel priest ripped open the world? She'd heard stories of ghosts, giant women built from clouds, women bringing madness. Had one struck here?

Darkness stretched past the last trees, though the liramic grass carpeting the windmill's hill doled out a dim green wash. Other eyes might see her climb, but she'd arrived before anyone else. Silence sat heavy on the hill, and a single pole shimmered in the dim light, but the windmill didn't show, and where were the sails? Shouldn't the grass's light show canvas?

A dark patch snatched her gaze leftward, where a tangle of wooden beams blocked the grass's sheen. The windmill must have shattered into a tumble of blocks and boards before strewing itself over the hill, and the pole marked a single survivor. Rafters showed higher up the slope, and a curl of stiff paper crunched under her foot – resin paper. They nailed resin paper over plaster to fend off rain. A sail sat mangled into a spewed-out knot of wood and canvas; the cloth stayed taut in places but flapped elsewhere. No burning smells, so there'd been no fire.

Phos lifted a spar and the wood snapped. Twisting it backwards showed bright metal spots where nails reflected light. The timber smelt fresh – three days ago this had been a tree, so someone had been busy.

What could she recover before the priests blundered close? Phos edged towards a grey bulk half her height. The grindstone had burst free and rolled before toppling. Ten more steps took her to the hill's crest, where three beams still scratched upward The stench of scorched wood left her sneezing as her foot struck a wooden wheel with teeth surrounding the outside, and she bent to run her hands over the still-warm wood. Brick walls had collapsed to leave stumps, and a dangling metallic thread stroked her hand.

She'd need to run in five minutes, but this place handed her a thousand questions, and maybe answers if she stayed.

Voices below – men talking. Phos bundled her cloak under a scrap of canvas and shook raindrops from her hands. Her older footprints had faded into dim smears, and there was enough darkness to let her creep towards another wrecked sail on her left. Phos squatted beside the sodden fabric to lift the sail over her head, and damp grass soaked her backside as water dripped down her neck. The church hired anyone, even those whose minds loafed in taverns, so she'd not run. Night made men lazy, and they'd chatter about the windmill.

Orders punched the air, and three bright lights showed through the coarse fabric – handheld lanterns. One man barked out a command.

'Scour this place. I want the miller.'

Glass crunched underfoot, and Phos shivered before holding her breath. Larger churches boasted windows, but never windmills, so what else used glass? One man's voice boomed out.

'Lanterns, Sergeant. There were ten or more strung out – there's the light we saw.'

'It's deliberate?'

'No doubt. Church lanterns too, but no idea how he got so many.'

'How'd he light them? You find any batteries?'

Phos gulped. What were batteries?

'We're looking, but I've seen batteries work; their light stays the same, and this changed. Bright, dim, bright, different each second. And wind gusts that way, so….'

'That's enough.' The sergeant rasped out a cough. 'Keep looking.'

A late gust lifted Phos's sail. She clenched her teeth and gripped the canvas.

'Any fire?'

'Not a spark. Your miller had resin paper stuck outside. All torn off now, but it's full of small tears, like someone was working up to a bigger rip. Fire wouldn't leave a scrap.'

'Search the ground and check those sails.'

Feet approached behind her, and Phos closed her eyes. What would happen to her parents if these men uncovered her? What words could touch these guards? Her limbs froze, but the men's words fermented a delicious brew of knowledge, and she'd not miss one word.

'What we got here?'

Two hands grabbed her arms to wrench her backwards and upward. Hands clutched her waist. She shrieked as canvas ripped from her fingers and her feet scrabbled over grass. The guard lifted her and spun her around; leather rasped her cheek in a whirling instant of dizziness. His face was a brawl of stale beer and sweat.

Men gathered with waiting beards and greasy tunics.

'I'm sure you've got a great story.' The sergeant's voice dropped to a murmur. Phos tried staring back, but her body flinched and her gaze fell to the left. The man squatted until her feet touched ground, but his hands still belted her waist.

'What's your name?'

'Phos.'

'Not old enough for your second syllable, which is more reason to stay in bed. Where d'you live when you're not playing at ghosts?'

Words jammed in her throat. What were their plans? What about Mum and Dad?

'Who tucks you in at night? Where's your parents?'

'They're near Leester village.'

'There's a start. Next question is, why this night-time ramble?' Another guard pushed his lantern towards her face, and Phos screwed up her eyes. 'What got you out of bed?'

'Same thing that pushed you out of bed!' Phos clamped her lips shut. These weren't teachers, and they weren't acting or pretending to be angry. Nothing made sense now, and screams boiled inside, but a smile teetered onto the sergeant's face, and his hands slackened. Could she dish out the words they wanted and rush home before dawn? Leave learning for another night?

'The windmill lit up and I couldn't sleep,' Phos said.

'Night-time isn't a safe time any more. How d'you squeeze through the wood?'

The guards had wrecked their night vision, so her liramic cloak might stay hidden. 'I've been here in daylight. I like woods.'

'Good for playing in, aren't they? You got here before us, Phos, so big question: what did you see?'

'Not much.' She lowered her head: the sergeant's breath stank of rotten egg. 'I came five minutes before you.'

'See the miller? Tall guy, all beard and belly?'

She shook her head. These guards didn't need to

hear the few words she'd shared with him months ago.

The sergeant rubbed a finger against his eye. 'It's too late, Phos, and no one should be out – especially not girls your age. We'll walk you back to your house and wake your parents.'

'They won't need waking.'

'I'm sure you don't want us to wake anyone, but—'

A hard drumming ripped through the night, and the sergeant stood and gripped his belt. The rhythm slowed before stopping. The guards all faced downhill, so could she escape to wear the night again? Lantern light dribbled over the grassy slope. Below, an animal showed – four long legs and bigger than any dog, its long head reared back as if laughing. A single black-robed figure stood beside it and coiled ropes around his arm. She'd seen pictures of horses, but this living animal left her gasping. Spittle darted through air as the horse shook its head, and one foot pawed the ground.

The priest whispered into the horse's ear before turning, and his robes parted. Crimson flashed inside the top of his cloak. Phos stared as the man lumbered upward. His skin was smooth and pasty, and his full red lips made a puckered scar against the puffy bag of his face. He stared at her with his lips fixed into a half smile before glancing at the men.

'Where's your leader?'

'That's me, sir,' the sergeant said, standing upright. 'We were patrolling and saw lights blazing.'

'You left your route without instruction?' A young voice greased with confidence. He hauled himself uphill without trouble and crouched one foot away from Phos. His pudgy fingers stretched out to stroke a lock of her hair.

'Sir, we'd never seen the like, and we wanted to catch the man what's responsible. The miller's gone, but there's this girl.'

'She can give me the pleasure of her company.'

'We found her hiding under a sail. Didn't touch nothing; she's just curious.'

'Curiosity? That needs attention.' The officer's lips parted, and he drew his hand back. Phos's head wouldn't move, and she couldn't stop staring at his black eyes. Danger hurled her onward like a leaf in a storm, but here stood a chance to visit Torzene and watch priests at work. Did this officer own books? Wasn't Torzene almost on the road to Morzenthal?

The sergeant coughed. 'We planned to take her home, sir, to let her parents know she's safe.'

'Thinking again, Sergeant? We'll have plenty to discuss back at Torzene.' His dark robe creaked as he stood, and crimson shimmered again inside the top quarter of his cloak. 'Return to your route. Tell nobody about this site. Discuss nothing among yourselves. She comes with me.'

'Sir, she's young, and her parents will be frantic if they—'

'I will tell her parents. Discuss nothing.'

Phos hugged her knees, but she kept staring at the priest's wan face. His eyes and nose looked lost inside his swollen cheeks, but the guards clustered around him. His fingers brushed her cheek. She shivered: she'd tasted freedom with her night-time ramble, but now she'd become a prisoner.

The priest grinned at her. 'Are you cold?'

She nodded.

'I have an extra cloak. When did you last travel by horse?'

Chapter 4: glimmers in the night

His hand clamped Phos's shoulder, and he guided her downward as the guards followed. She imagined Mum staring at her empty bed.

The horse stamped its front legs, and steam billowed from the animal's nostrils as it cocked its head to watch her. She stroked the horse's flank, and sweat pooled around her fingers, but the priest's hands clasped her waist to hoist her upward. Her stomach churned until she found herself perched on a leather seat covering the horse's back – hard and slippery under her trousers.

'Let's keep you warm,' the priest said, handing up a woollen cloak, which she draped around her shoulders. He swung up behind, and his hands wrapped around her sides as his thighs clamped hers; she winced as he arranged leather straps to surround her and link himself with the horse's leashed head. Weren't these called reins?

The priest recited orders, instructions for gripping and following the horse's motion, and he flicked his wrists. His horse tossed its head before launching into a run. Slabs of muscle quivered under her seat, and the road blurred as his hands caught her again to bulk out his words about moving with the horse. Phos fitted her breathing to the bounce, and her hands tangled themselves into the horse's mane. What was the smell? Hay and sweat churned with manure?

The surrounding wood smouldered with alien colours as the horse galloped: dull orange gleams mixed with distant red flecks. Each heartbeat drove her further from her parents, and she remembered the stories her teachers had fed her: they'd grimaced while burbling about hazards from strangers, and they'd dished out plans for running and shouting. Right now Phos did neither, but she imagined Mum screaming as the horse's hooves kept drumming.

They passed into a fog bank, and sourness wreathed the air as pale shadows of houses flitted past before hurtling behind them.

Each new moment made a lesson, and new questions flocked through her mind as she relaxed. Sleep stalked her, and she forced her eyes open. The juddering made focusing hard, but the priest's lanterns picked out ghostly birch trunks in the distance. A dim glow to the sides suggested the land curving up to become the world wall. She gripped the horse's mane with both hands as her nose streamed, and the horse hammered on as frosty air flowed past.

He squeezed his legs against her, and she remembered how he'd scared those guards without trying. Why this endless ride? What plans fermented in his mind?

Pink and grey filaments slid onto the vault ahead, an early dawn as the sun's arch drew near. Or was it *a* sun's arch? She hoped to walk the whole ring one day and have the world curve underfoot as she marched forward, so this journey might make a rehearsal.

Her body jerked – had she snatched a few heartbeats of sleep?

Grey light blurred over a bleak moor, and the northern world wall showed streaks of orange at its top. Phos slipped leftward before the priest's arms hauled her body back against his chest.

'Not far now.' He tugged his ropes, and Phos leaned forward as they slowed into a wide turn. Gravel scattered below; they'd found a path weaving up a hill, and a crumbling stone embankment appeared on her left, capped by wooden cabins and untidy heaps of planks. Dark green creepers smothered the buttery stone.

A gap showed in the wall ahead: a gate with two sentries. The priest slowed his horse into a walk to swap words with the guards before ambling inside and into a muddy courtyard. Creepers slid over these walls too, and fresh timberwork capped the creamy stone. Boxy rooms creaked in the breeze as two men hammered nails into a floor, and more labourers stormed, swearing, from a doorway. The church had stacked three storeys of wooden cubicles onto the older stones, like children playing with blocks. Ropes strained against groaning beams, and Phos thought of rushed homework.

To her left, two carts rested beneath a pole carrying a broken lantern at its top. Unused barrels and scythes piled against a wall to her right, but ahead sat a grassy field festering with huts. One twisted and collapsed as she watched. Wind squalled against her face, and Phos retched – were they building a village by starting with tannery smells? The sun's arch limped above the stone, but the mud still clung to the colour of night.

Her parents would notice her missing cloak; they'd search the wood and find nothing, and they'd hammer on neighbours' doors. Fear would choke them; fear she'd created. Yesterday's caning had ended in moments, but punishment here might last weeks.

The officer dismounted and reached for her. So far his words had stayed soft, but maybe he wanted her quiet. Adults never wanted you vomiting over them, and she kept her eyes open as he helped her down; mud swallowed her boots. Torzene was nothing like a village: she'd always known centuries-old houses with age-buckled walls; this place had sprouted almost overnight like an artificial toadstool, and toadstools hatched sickness.

The priest faced her and smiled; his lips looked like a gash in a rubber ball, and sweat dotted his face.

'Welcome to Torzene. We need breakfast, don't we?' His hand stroked her shoulder, and she flinched before letting him shepherd her through a doorway and into the buttery-stone building. Moss doled out beige glimmers inside, but Phos blinked in the murk. Embers of light bathed a corner, and the priest nudged her forward until a cell appeared on their right, where three guards hunched over a smoky fire. The officer paused before entering and pointed at Phos.

'We have a visitor, so can we rustle up breakfast?'

'We've eaten our rations, sir. You might try the mess, but they're short too.'

The priest stared back, but the guard never moved, and again his hand gripped her shoulder. He shoved her further down the mildewed corridor and into a small room.

A dull glow trickled through a skylight over three chairs and a lopsided table. Papers towered beside a sprawl of box files. A shelf held a teapot and several cups, and damp stained one wall. He owned a model world, a braided wire ring suspended by threads from a wooden frame. Two coils of thin rope dangled from hooks on the back wall. Tape wrapped a bundle of five books, and three handheld lanterns with used candles sat on his desk.

'You work at night?'

'Aren't you the observant one? And that's why you're here. Please sit.'

Phos rested her hands on her lap and clamped her lips together.

The officer unclasped his cloak and fussed over its folding before hanging the fabric in a wardrobe.

'My name's Rastersen. I'm tasked to watch this area for problems, though I'm climbing the stair soon.' He paused and sat. 'Your name?'

'Phos.'

A flicker of surprise. 'One syllable? When's your second due?'

'Three months.'

'Phos, one syllable. Very good, Phos.' Air wheezed past his lips as he played with her name, and his fingers flicked through a ledger.

'You must come from Leester. Tell me of your parents.'

'Grasteller, my father, is a money counter. Shelaker, my mother.' Phos paused. 'They don't know I'm here.'

Rastersen wrote; his letters were too small to read, and after a few words his quill hovered above the page. 'I've heard fine things of Grasteller. You left no note?'

'I planned to return before dawn.'

Rastersen smiled. 'You saw the windmill's light from your house. Did the lights ever change?'

She'd seen the connection. A gust of wind had followed each of the windmill's sudden flares as if wind had become light. Phos knew wind took time travelling and light didn't, but girls shouldn't know that, and she blushed.

'Lights came and went – bright and dim.'

Rastersen licked his lower lip as he studied her face. 'Was there a pattern?'

'No.' Phos let her mouth hang open.

'Are you sure?'

Phos stayed silent. Why had Rastersen demanded silence from the sergeant's men?

The priest smiled. 'Why is your hand marked?'

She'd learned to keep lies rare, but the truth held danger. 'I was late for school too often.'

More questions sidled from his lips, and Phos ladled out vague answers as she tried to keep her voice level – the knowledge she'd wrung from the world should stay hidden.

Rastersen slouched back in his chair.

She still remembered Quiss. He'd sauntered into school early and smashed a tiny glass window. She'd gasped – glass was precious – but he'd sorted through shards until he'd found one he wanted. He'd grunted and pocketed the fragment before grinning at her, and she'd kept quiet.

Outside at lunch, he'd held his shard beside a paper scrap. Light had twisted through glass and dashed over his sheet until smoke and a tiny flame had appeared. She'd smiled, and he'd shown her how turning the glass scrunched the light up and how smaller spots were more burny. Again, she'd kept quiet.

Did Rastersen believe her? Why had he carried her here? Would he tell her parents? Phos quivered.

Quiss had been desperate to show others, and their teachers had heard. They'd hauled him away with one teacher gripping his wrist as Quiss threw her a panic-stuffed glance. No one had mentioned him again, and all the lists shrank by one. She missed the way he'd never left their world alone. He'd turned light into fire, and she'd seen wind become light, and now Rastersen had all day to pry at her thoughts.

The priests knew she asked questions; if they knew the breathless bliss she earned each time she solved a problem she'd never see the sun's arch again. Marriage might feel like a prison, but she'd heard of real prisons: windowless cells heaving with spiders.

Rastersen smiled. 'Your curiosity is enough to spill you from your comfortable hammock and into the night, and you know enough to hide your learning.'

Phos remembered climbing trees and stepping

onto a branch: she'd gradually applied her weight until the wood's weakness had unfurled in a heartbeat of snapping and plummeting, and Rastersen's questions would keep coming until she broke. The damp walls seemed to close in around her.

Two sets of footsteps sounded behind, and Phos turned as two priests strode inside. Rastersen surged to his feet. The taller newcomer was a thin stick of a body capped by baldness, with crimson lining half his cloak. He glanced at her.

'Another child, Rastersen? Where is this one from?' Long vowels, thought Phos: wealth, power and strength.

Rastersen blushed. 'The dawnward Leester windmill collapsed, sir, and the guards found her under the wreckage, and—'

'Attend to your duties, Rastersen. You are not tasked with examining commoners. Leave the detection of talent to your superiors. Girl, will you stand?'

Phos stood.

'Your name?'

The shorter priest stared.

'Phos.'

'One syllable, Rastersen? Do you believe the talent would appear in such a girl? Return her, and resume your duties.'

Again the elder priest glanced at her as if she

was grit in his routine. Rastersen nodded once.

'We will check, Rastersen. With you, we always check.'

The short priest frowned. 'You're not detaining the girl? She's seen our preparations.'

'Soon thousands will see. One early girl makes no difference, and besides, her absence will stir her village into action. Return her untouched.'

Their orders hung in the air after they'd left, and Rastersen slouched as a sigh whistled through his lips.

'You had the intelligence to hide your intellect, and few children show your insight; imagine the stories and learning we might have shared.' He smiled, and Phos relaxed as the skylight brightened: her parents would dish out a month of extra chores, but she'd be home.

'There's much those two don't know, Phos. For instance…' Rastersen pointed at his desk lanterns, and two heartbeats later the candles lit.

Phos gasped. 'How…how did you do that?'

'Aren't you young ladies told to win yourselves a husband? Why this interest, Phos? Why are you blushing?'

Phos closed her mouth.

'Our elders grumble when we reveal exploits outside the priesthood, but there's a keen mind under your hair, and you deserve more. I can show you their workings, but it takes time. Don't fret: I'll find you.'

Her mouth felt dry. A door to an immense store of knowledge had creaked open, but she'd watched schoolboys set worms on hooks to bait fish.

'You've more of these…exploits? And the priests mentioned talent.'

He gazed at her. 'Care to take tea?'

Rastersen poured water from a flask into his glazed teapot and lifted a tiny bag from an inlaid lacquer box. He dropped the pouch into the water and closed his eyes before wrapping his hand around the vessel. Lemon and pine scents wafted out as the teapot steamed, and Phos sat in silence.

The tea burst over her tongue with a fruit-laden sweetness. The priest watched her drink but said nothing. Afterwards he stood and donned his cloak, and she followed without thinking. Again his fingers pressed through her tunic as they drifted outside into the muddy courtyard. Three labourers heaved a cart against a stack of barrels but turned their heads away as she passed.

Rastersen prodded her away from the main gate and into the hut-strewn space she'd glimpsed earlier. Someone had vomited a village onto a field of wiry grass. Shoddy huts sat beside stables, shelters and open-air ranges mixed with forges. In the distance, a jagged, half-finished timber fence wrapped the false hamlet;

three gangs of labourers hauled planks upward as she watched. Rastersen strode forward with bristle and regrown passion.

'You've not told me how you lit those candles,' Phos said. 'What's this village doing without people?'

A squat brick hut without shutters sat next to a stable with two famished horses. The bricks looked smoked, almost black, and muddy ground surrounded the hut's walls.

'Listen, Phos, you have a lesson.'

She followed and skidded on mud as Rastersen stood outside a bolted iron slab of a door. His puffy face swung towards her. 'I'll return you to Leester, but don't breathe one word about your time here or meeting me. Why not tell Mum you were out berrying – you like berries?'

Phos stayed silent.

His hand stretched out and clasped her elbow. 'I don't want you to meet the people inside, but talk and they will find you, and you'll become another job.' His eyes fixed on hers, and his fingers squeezed; the man had the strength to hold her here, and perhaps strength to disobey the senior priests.

'Shall we listen?'

Rastersen wrenched at an iron bolt and tugged the door open to uncover a tiny chamber holding another door. He gestured her inside and stood behind to cup her waist with his hands.

A thin scream leaked out, a weary plea without words that shuddered into Phos's mind – a young woman in agony. Gabbled words came, pleading mixed with despair.

'She talked.' He squeezed her waist, and Phos's arms froze. 'Your youth means nothing. Living far away means nothing. Playing dumb means nothing. I'll try to protect you, but you must rely on me for help: I can protect you from those inside.' His hands slipped away, and Phos's vision turned grey as she stumbled forward.

'How about going home? You've been a very lucky girl, and as your parents' house overlooks the windmill, I'll always know how to find you. We'll talk again.'

His mention of home left her nodding, and he led her towards the stables. Daylight felt thin, and sweat chilled her skin as bile surged inside – what had ripped the scream from the woman's body? Candles and screams and danger fought against learning; Rastersen pulled and pushed at the same time.

She'd had no choices since being discovered at the windmill. Questions swarmed around her, but questions alone weren't enough for learning; she needed answers too. Even if Rastersen let her go, could she trust herself not to trot back here and learn those exploits? Had he read enough of her mind to shape her curiosity into a noose?

***

Twigs splintered under Caliper's feet, and a branch snagged his apron before snapping. The air stank like a latrine, and cobwebs clotted over his beard. These forest trees had glowed well, but now only the faintest blue tinge limped out, and he stumbled over a pile of muck. He paused and held his breath, but only heard a distant owl's hoots.

Speed and silence were friends now. He'd creep through these dark, wooded paths and avoid the guards until Christina breathed at his ear again. His windmill's corpse rested silently behind him. One day, he'd dredge up enough courage to revisit the site.

He'd tried to imagine Christina's home, but only ever saw her cloudlike figure scurrying across a ruined castle that dripped with moss. Christina never had words to describe where she was; he'd chosen dawnward as a direction without knowing if that was right, and the need to move burnt inside him. Right now she'd stand in her home and pin his position on whatever class of map she used. She'd find the right time to reforge their link. She only came when he was alone, so he had to avoid the guards. Mostly her voice stayed level, but some days grief cracked her words.

Their first meeting had carved out this path for him. He'd heard ghost stories at school: boys swapped hushed fables of a female giant gliding through walls before trying to speak. Everyone agreed listening brought madness, but the stories had dried up once he'd left school, and he'd almost forgotten the tales.

Three months ago he'd rested upstairs as owls hooted through the night's chill, and the spectral image of a woman's head had drifted through his windmill. Terror had almost thrown him into the night, but he'd stayed – even then he'd sought different roads. She'd flowed like a misty waterfall towering above him, and the image had flickered as if trying to decide between blurry and sharp. The face had smiled and held eye contact as she spoke. At first he'd only heard noise: each word had started on one tone but ended on another, as if the figure played with sound. After two breathless minutes, Caliper had recognised broken words, and even sentences.

She'd dropped to his level – perhaps she'd crouched – and her face had hovered inches away as fresh phrases drifted into his mind: a single word repeated, her name, Christina. He'd pointed at himself and spoken, and afterwards he'd named everything she touched. Christina's memory was perfect. The first time he'd mouthed her name, he'd imagined his jaw would crack, but she'd repeated herself until he'd mastered those tongue-curling sounds – three syllables. He'd thought they were the same age, but she'd laughed and said her name didn't work that way.

Should he be ashamed for having a girlfriend with a body you could see through? Christina was twice his height, and the strangeness meant he'd never shared his story. Each time she appeared, her face became sharper, the lips and nose a touch fuller, as if she'd learned how to appear, and until now she'd always returned.

Walk in darkness these days, and you became a crook, but pedlars found a way: tools wore out or pots broke, and pedlars skulked between villages with goods and whispered stories, so Caliper had matted grime over his overalls and stuffed trinkets into his backpack.

Twigs snapped ahead, and the distant owl fell silent.

If he stayed unseen for long enough, Christina would find him. He'd grab that thought: she always returned. If he gave her time, she'd show him the way as if she'd given him those candles.

Christina hadn't heard of candles, but he'd choked back his surprise and explained their nature. They'd visited Leester's henge, and she'd taught him how to use its stones as a forge, where they'd fashioned candles together.

'You're grinning, Caliper.'

‘I’m after more.’ He’d rubbed his neck and recalled boyhood dreams; there’d be no harm in the asking. ‘Candles last hours, but they’re dim. Can they be brighter?’

She’d smiled. Yes, she could make special ones that burned like a hundred candles while scrunching their life into thirty heartbeats. Christina had made the specials, and he’d wrapped them in a separate paper roll, since he’d no way of telling what tools he’d need.

A lantern flickered through the trees, and Caliper ducked. Two guards advanced and their pace quickened. He’d never outrun them: their feet punched through undergrowth, and shadows raced around the forest; he’d no chance to shelter under ferns. A voice rasped from the darkness.

‘Who’s there?’

A wiry face surfaced from the gloom and waited for Caliper’s words as a burly younger guard hulked in the shadows. Metal badges glinted on their leather jerkins.

‘Officers, can I help?’

‘What you doing?’

‘Just a pedlar aiming for Ferstus village by dawn. Yesterday at Leester; not bad trading, but we’re always after greener grass.’

‘A stinking pedlar.’ The thickset guard lunged forward to ram his stick against Caliper’s belly.

‘Whatever he’s carrying, there’s no night roving allowed. Darkness ends the day, and dark’s for sleep. We’ll arrest him.’

Arrest meant priests and questions shouted in a cell, and Christina wouldn’t come. The burly youngster bustled behind him. Caliper focused on the older man’s grizzled face, but the young guard’s hand tugged his elbow from behind. ‘I’ll take my thumbs to his eyes and make it night forever. What you peddling?’

The older officer shoved his face against Caliper’s. ‘Get him to the Ferstus guardhouse, and see what they make of him. Check his pack.’ The younger man tugged Caliper’s backpack from his shoulders.

Caliper glanced at the battered lantern in the older officer’s hand and its sulking stub of candle. Guards chased crooks all hours, but priests never doled out enough candles, and the need for sleep glazed the older officer’s eyes.

‘We always want glow, don’t we?’ Caliper said. ‘Just a few candles, scraps of light for evenings; sometimes work outlasts the day.’

The young guard spewed out more church words. ‘“Light scours; light blemishes; light carries evil to the eye.”’

A sigh drifted from the smaller officer. Some saw nature and religion everywhere, but others spent more time living; no surprise the older guy held the lantern. 'Manage it, do you, Jero? You manage a whole night without glimmer?'

'I use what I need, but night's meant to be dark.'

'Look what I'm carrying, Jero. Can we work in the dark? There's lots of law, lots of "meant tos" and "should bes" all lined up and waiting. "Meant to" won't finish our job, so let's worry about what's important.' The older man lifted his lantern. 'Still, let's see these candles.'

Caliper swung his pack down and pulled oilskin away to reveal his normal candles.

'What are those below?'

Caliper hesitated but opened his pack of special candles and fished out two waxy cylinders. The guard held them beside his lantern and ran his thumb over the wick, and Caliper stopped himself from wincing.

'Feels weird,' the officer said. 'You dunk them in oil, or what?'

'My dad peddled; said it stopped them crumbling. Dunno about that, but I enjoy sticking with the old.'

'Tradition, eh? How many oily candles you got?'

'A dozen.'

The guard's lined face broke into a smile. 'You shouldn't carry that many. Why don't we take the lot and arrest you anyways?'

'Ah, but think where I got those.' Caliper squatted beside his bag. 'I'll visit Ferstus village tomorrow with more. Same next day; it mounts up.'

'Tomorrow?' The older guard squinted at Caliper; the younger hissed, but a single glare silenced him.

'At dusk by Ferstus crossroads.'

'Well, three's a lucky number.'

Caliper held back a sigh: an extra candle made an easy bribe. He'd have enjoyed watching the guards light these candles, but he'd bought safety, and he'd keep alive his dream of seeing Christina. The candles vanished inside the guard's tunic.

'Ferstus by dawn, eh?'

'Going right there,' Caliper replied. The younger guard glared, but Caliper ambled dawnward. Truth mixed well with an occasional lie, but next time he'd try comedy.

Sweat chilled his body: like a tightrope walk, every step on this journey had to end well. There'd be guards he'd never bribe and brigands he couldn't fight. One slip or one bad dice roll, and Christina's face would stay forever a drifting ghost, and he'd rot alone the rest of his days.

Chapter 5: truth carries a knife

Wisps of smoke curled up from the kitchen range, and Phos sat at the table and stared at the copper pans hanging from the crazed plaster walls. Mum gripped her sleeve, but Phos wouldn't turn towards her even when Mum's clammy fingertips brushed her cheeks. She'd already glanced at those watery eyes and their tears, and the unfairness choked her. Not her fault that taking two steps outside had snared her into a wild journey where promises of learning had blurred into threats of torture. Why should nudging limits injure others?

Mum had dressed in sash and belted tunic as if heading for church. Worry had drained the smile from Dad's face, and he stood beside the range with his bony fingers clutching his waistcoat. The morning's freshness had faded into this middle-aged day where light wheezed through the kitchen shutters.

Rastersen had dropped her half a mile away, and she'd scrambled home. Now she had to flesh out her story. Phos pressed her lips together: if her parents learned about the priest's sweated threats they'd scream for help, and he'd know she'd talked – the woman's cries still seethed through her mind.

'I've said I'm fine, Mum, so don't worry.' Sunlight glinted over the spice jars on the shelf above the door, and the kindling stacked in the corner wafted out resin scents. Phos turned and wrapped her fingers around Mum's wrists before drawing them to the table; her story needed to make them parents again. Other villagers must have seen the windmill's lights or stumbled over wreckage, so did Rastersen plan to silence others, and had he talked with those priests from school?

Mum's hands skittered back to Phos's hair and pressed against her cheeks. 'You're our only child, Phos, so what sent you charging through the night? When we found your empty hammock….'

'I've gone before and I've always returned.'

'Last time you appeared before breakfast; today you missed lunch.'

'Still under a day.'

'I wanted to search Leester, but what would everyone say? "Shelaker hoards junk but can't keep her daughter safe." Did you think how they'd talk?' Mum leaped up and rushed to the workspace to wipe a cloth over plates without looking. Fake housework, a dance driven by anger, and Phos waited.

'Neighbours talk. They always talk. They run to church the instant they see strangeness.'

Whitewashed walls loomed above Phos; those splodges on the ceiling looked like leering faces, and Mum slammed a plate and cutlery before her. Her parents knew she twisted words – they'd listen for gaps – but the truth would hurt them all. She still felt Rastersen's hands pressing against her chest, and his demand for quiet still rang in her ears.

'What possessed you, Phos?' Dad's voice kept quiet, his eyes hard and unblinking. 'The last few harvests have been appalling. There are starving people wandering outside, and starving twists your mind. Meet them, and you'll be a way for them to forget hunger.... I can't....'

If Dad was too squeamish to finish his sentences, Rastersen's threats would destroy him. She'd not ignore the priest's warning, but a halfway path might wait for her; half-truths might help her avoid secrets while restoring her parents' calm.

'Did you see the windmill?'

Mum glared. 'You disappear, so you think I'll rush out to check the windmill? You mad girl.'

'Last night it lit up like a church service, and light leaked through my shutters.'

Mum stared into her eyes as Phos's story flowed. Reciting details from her forest walk was easy, and Phos added memories from earlier walks to spin her fiction. This story saw her hiding from churchmen before spending hours reading books scattered among the wreckage.

Mum sniffed. 'Where's your cloak?'

'Left it under a sail.'

'You didn't pick it up when you returned?'

A single shake of her head, but Phos winced inside: details snapped at her words, and Mum's eyes stayed motionless. Questions followed about the books, but Phos had sneaked enough looks at church volumes to knit her ideas into the story. Dad shifted in his seat.

'I wanted to check the dawnward windmill, as it's not far.' Phos's fantasy pranced through the wood's far side; she'd rambled there weeks ago while needing time on her own, and the path had faded to let stalks burst through the gravel and snare her feet. Paths often died these days.

'You shouldn't spend so long on your own, Phos – you'll reach womanhood soon, and people will think you're—'

'Men, women, people can talk as they please. I followed the southern path.'

'So you reached the waterwheel near school?' Mum stopped blinking and her voice strengthened.

'Yes.'

'I looked for you there this morning.'

Dad drew a long breath, perhaps air to start a sentence.

Phos kept still, but her mind lurched. Why had she assumed her parents would stay home?

Mum leaned forward. 'Was the watermill's

wheel turning?'

Phos blushed. There was always maintenance, and she'd never know what Mum had noticed. Turning or not turning, she tried to choose, but her lips stayed shut as her story withered.

Thirteen was too young to weave a story that wouldn't unravel, and how could she avoid becoming a wife when adults could twist her into lying? The quiet of her parents' kitchen blurred her memories of Rastersen's bloated face, and Phos stared at the rush mat beside the sink.

'This isn't you, Phos, is it?' Dad sat beside her. 'Outright lying is always your last choice. We'll protect you from threats, but if threats are making you lie, you must talk.'

Phos stayed silent, and Dad took her left hand.

'Remember when Lith threatened you at school and kept pulling your hair? You were small.'

Phos nodded.

'We never told you, but their parents needed a loan to keep their farm running. I was lead counter, and at first I refused. Her father stared, his mouth open, and he pleaded. He kept thinking of his next meal, and once he understood what being a victim felt like, I told him about you. Afterwards I gave him the loan, and they spoke to Lith.'

'And she left my hair alone.'

Rastersen was an overgrown boy, and perhaps he'd lied about hunting her. Were scared people more likely to obey? The earth-brown tiles under her feet had cracked, but they still fitted together; blows and threats shouldn't change your nature. She'd have to mention Rastersen, but opening her lips meant she needed to seal theirs. Other fears teemed through her mind: would he visit her house, and could she resist the lure of his exploits?

Phos hung her head and remembered last night's capture and her ride. She'd need to tell everything or her parents would winkle the truth from her, but she had to hear them promise to stay silent. She silently cursed the miller and his shimmering rays of light; he'd led her into this swamp of lies.

***

Caliper's eyes watered. Ferstus scraped his nostrils and no arguing, but seeing Christina meant braving the stink. Marshes each side forced the world through this village, and travellers dumped their rubbish here. Today an extra taint shredded the air – rancid cat vomit, maybe – and Caliper breathed through his mouth as he slogged along the dirt track.

Two-storeyed thatched cottages huddled either side. Their shutters should have opened at dawn, but everything stayed closed, and silence throttled the air.

Two cats waited beside the front door of a burnt-out cottage, and Caliper's foot crunched against a broken fiddle.

He fought off sleep; his eyes smarted as the sun's arch appeared, and he staggered past the outlying houses.

Where was Christina? Had she seen his signal? He'd eyeballed trees and leaves, expecting the greenery to distort itself, but there'd been nothing. She should speak before he reached the vast moor beyond this village, sweeping miles of waterlogged wilderness where he'd need direction.

Dawn lurched over Ferstus. Dingy alleys dribbled out a few villagers who stared at him, and cauldrons holding yesterday's fat lurked below fish-head-covered carts. Two shoeless women squeaked water from a well as a boy dragged a braying donkey through mud. A hunchbacked herbalist struggled with her shutters and glared his way before rushing into her shop. He could treat wounds or spill secrets about pain-easing herbs, but he'd stay quiet.

Ferstus used to bustle, with children chasing each other around the shops lining the main road, but now cottages stood empty, and windows without shutters left eyeless sockets facing the central street. Caliper's eyes closed themselves, and his body teetered before he jerked himself upright.

There on his right, a refuge: a cottage's scorched shell with resin paper gummed across its punctured roof. He stepped inside and onto a small reed mat. Puddles pockmarked the muddy floor; a toy bear sprawled on a broken plate; a bed had been upturned and legs hacked from a table; and marks showed where pots had sat. This cottage should house six, so what had happened? Caliper flipped the bed upright and ruffled the bedclothes; he'd soak his body in dreams before stomping dawnward. Fatigue meant he'd not worry over the mud-smeared blankets, but would Christina's arrival wake him?

Dreams: his body rose through billowing clouds as his eyes peered through mist and hunted for castles.

A hard jolt threw Caliper back into the stench as a hand slapped him awake.

'Get your thieving arse up, you lazy beggar.' A guard's face snarled six inches above him, all screaming teeth and hair. 'There's work here – not dossing time.' The guard grabbed Caliper's overalls and pulled, but the guard's fingers were spindly, and Caliper stayed in bed.

'Get working, or I'll call my mates.'

'You do that.' Caliper eased himself up to tower over the guard. The mud on his face cracked as he yawned. One slap would knock the guard out, but guards never worked alone, and a slicker escape route might appear later.

'Pedlar, eh? Not any more: you'll build our barn.'

'You'll want a builder.' Caliper hauled on his backpack.

'You're a builder now, so come this way.'

Outside and early afternoon, and a tight squad of men stamped past – two black-robed priests with fluttering hoods led four guards. A trio of elderly women wandered across the road but looked away. His guard snarled and gripped his wrist. Caliper broke his grip but followed down the road as two guards watched from behind. Christina never appeared unless he was single: he had to ditch his new friends and find some class of distraction or wait for the blanket of darkness.

They arrived at the Ferstus crossroads, where he'd offered to meet yesterday's night guards. Most fieldworkers should have left for the fields hours ago, but they flocked here: ploughmen, seedmen and swineherds swarmed underneath a towering timber frame. Crude cuts of green wood strained against ropes and jumbled knots, and nails covered the earth. A monster barn, a freak; he couldn't stop staring at the joints, even though staring brought danger. Design meant scripture as holy as any book; he'd handled scrolls showing allowed designs for nails and planks, and the church sent priests scuttling to new buildings to make sure builders followed the old plans. Fresh doors and shutters had to match ancient recipes.

Here carpenters had been forced into blasphemy: they'd wrenched down five or six houses to clear space for this mangled skeleton.

Orders pierced the afternoon air as priests goaded workers into hoisting beams. Labourers snatched and strained at tangled ropes, and three men hammered away while perched on rafters. Two men fought over a mallet while a priest screamed at workers heaving at a wheelbarrow.

His guard caught his arm. 'Get your muscles on these ropes. We're watching, so no mistakes.' Two priests shadowed Caliper as he joined the crew.

Memories of apprentice work flooded back, and he nudged the other workers into steady rhythms: his strength needed hoarding, which meant holding back without letting the guards suspect. After a few words, his team fell into the flow he wanted.

He could manage this act, but Christina wouldn't appear among these sweating workers, and these guards expected trouble, so staging an accident would be hard. He ruffled his hands through a box of nails and listened as two priests stared upward.

'That'll never hold – your gap's too big.'

'We'll cover it.'

'That gap needs filling, not hiding.'

'No time – we've three days.'

'Saying that won't hold it up – if it collapses at mealtimes....'

Caliper stopped fiddling. Old buildings stayed up because they copied those standing for centuries, so what had maddened the church into creating this nightmare? He'd heard rumours of larger buildings changing shape if the church willed it, but Caliper had scoffed, and this wreckage exposed the lie.

The priest rubbed his hands. 'We finish in three days so Torzene gets its workers.'

Hadn't he visited Torzene? A single-storey stone-built monastery capping a hill, with monks who ate nothing and bought less. Were the real builders already at Torzene, knocking up another wooden monster?

A Leester priest wandered past, and Caliper jerked away. Priests could travel but not millers, and this cleric knew him. Caliper hit the ground and scrabbled in the dirt for nails as priest feet stamped beside his hands. His pedlar disguise would only last an instant. Was the cleric waiting for him to rise? Another bunch of nails showed to his left, and Caliper picked them up and held his breath until the feet left.

Lanterns dotted the ground, so they planned on working after nightfall. Caliper knelt and rummaged out three of his special candles. He glanced around and popped off the lantern caps to swap the candles inside for his specials; the stolen candles fitted inside his apron. Focus enough, and your crimes looked like work.

Two churchmen interrogated a labourer about weights, but their questions confused the man. Another worker sneaked into the dusk, but two guards clubbed him down and screamed the other labourers back to work. Nightfall would bring the guards he'd tricked last night, and if they'd used his candles….

Workers heaved in tables and hung kettles over fire pans that sat beside stacks of firewood. Someone planned a canteen for the whole village, but why? People bought meat and vegetables to cook as they liked; you had taverns for anyone wanting to buy dinner and drink beer in the glow of a fire they'd not had to light. Would that end with everyone corralled inside this bloated pigsty? Not good, not if priests were cooking. Flagons of broth arrived, and workers dived for food as Caliper shared words with a silver-haired worker.

'Want stew?'

'You're a strong one,' the worker said.

Caliper shrugged. 'Not as strong as I was.'

'Pulled you off fieldwork, did they?'

Caliper nodded.

'I'm a cooper – always have been. They come

up yesterday and told me to work here, but I've no idea what I'm doing half the time.'

The cooper's spindly body was hopeless for building work, but Caliper showed him how to make hoisting easier – he crouched when the Leester priest passed. The sun's arch drifted eveward, and darkness pooled around the skewed framework. The workers above draped canvas sheets over the topmost beams, and his crew jeered as light faded.

A young clergyman lit a spill, and Caliper stared at the tampered lanterns while pretending to untangle ropes. He'd asked Christina for a delay before the candles showed their quality, and the third candle had lit when his first sprang into life. Incandescent sparks stormed from the lantern's top to screech and cascade over a wooden trellis. The burning flecks scattered sideways before veering up again, and everyone fell silent. His second candle ignited and slammed the lantern's cap away, and again white fire spewed upward, missing the beams to rise thirty yards. The last candle took longer to catch, but the lantern shattered; his candle toppled and skittered backwards to spray out a fan of brilliant white glitter. Several priests ran shouting and screaming, and the churchman with the glowing spill stood agape as the labourers stared, and a handful sniggered. Even chuckling at priests held danger, but he'd carved out enough distraction to let him slip into the night.

Would Christina see his candlelit signal? Tomorrow he'd reach the moor past Ferstus and wait for her image. Memories of her beautiful strangeness came unasked – her full lips and rounded eyes meant she never felt distant, though he'd never stop worrying.

No one followed. His grimy overalls merged with the twilight as his path trickled past Ferstus's silent houses and into the deep night. Daylight's last dregs bounced from the vault, and the dying glow should help him find another abandoned cottage or hedge: he needed to stay dry, so he'd share with the birds while waiting for Christina.

She had to come soon, or he'd wander without direction over the barren moor ahead, drift without food or clean water. Where were her words? Had she abandoned him?

Chapter 6: learning doesn't need schooling

Dad hadn't lit the kitchen fire, and a chill lingered in the morning air. Mum's absence further froze the room; her bedroom door stayed closed despite the fresh day. Phos stepped onto the kitchen's tiles but cringed at the cold and slipped on her boots.

Dad struggled through breakfast with clipped sentences; he kept his back to her as he stuffed fruit inside breakfast rolls. She ate without speaking, and words piled up inside, but she'd let them fester. The rolls vanished. She pushed her plate away, and Dad paused before drawing up his stool to perch beside her.

'Your mother's still upset. Take yourself to school, and we'll talk this evening: we need extra rules.'

'Remember Rastersen? If he hears I've spoken—'

'We'll talk this evening.'

'You must stay quiet—'

'This evening, Phos. Wait until evening.'

They walked outside and paused by their front door. She blinked under the hazy light. Were there extra words to seal Dad's lips and lock her story away, or would another round of pleading help? Beyond her control; she hugged him and left.

School was a starved dog yelping in panic.

Teachers rushed lessons while glancing at their doors; no food arrived for lunch, and late afternoon saw them locked inside the seniors' class without a tutor. The same dark walls and wooden ceiling beams surrounded her, though the boys worked on new desk graffiti. Phos sat back as rumours sprouted, gossip about teachers working the fields and food turning poisonous.

Home time passed, and chatter changed into complaints. Two boys kicked at the walls to knock out an escape, but their door rattled, and a junior teacher burst inside to order them home before darting off.

Outside, and school stood empty as leaves rattled past her face. The sun's arch slid eveward to wrap shadows around her body. Phos caught up with two girls and mentioned the windmill to them, but they said nothing. She mumbled goodbye without watching them leave.

School made a ripped storybook where only crusts of knowledge survived; scraps of learning that made no sense. Priests had stripped books from the library before her birth, and those left only held directions for becoming a wife – cooking and cleaning, or handling drunken husbands – so those whispered tales of women winning church roles must be false.

Two years ago she'd sat in her garden and gazed upward while hiding the sun's arch behind sheets. The vault wasn't smooth: tiny shadows shrank as the arch crept forward, and lengthened afterwards, and shadows always pointed away from the sun's arch. Next day, she'd sculpted model hills over a plank; she'd been young enough to play with mud, and she'd brought two dolls as cover. A mirror had reflected arch light, and twisting the mirror had moved shadows enough to prove her idea of upside-down hills covering the vault. Phos had asked her teachers if anyone lived there, and she'd earned a detention. Now change had come, and questions earned a caning.

Dad had smiled at her game; he'd known her mind, and tonight she'd run through ideas for learning with him – anything to have him talk again. She might run chores for older villagers while sneaking glances at their books or rifle through teachers' desks after they'd left.

Phos meandered home with reluctant limbs. Was Mum still angry? She wasn't at the door to their house, and darkness veiled their windows. Inside, a silent twilight gripped the hall. Even yesterday Mum had scurried and tidied, but now Phos's footsteps broke the stillness. Unseen hands had ripped down her granddad's portrait. Cooking pots and ladles dotted the kitchen table, and a potato-filled pan sat beside the range. Phos choked; the dying fire left their kitchen lifeless, and Phos rushed through her house, the lounge, her parents' bedroom, her own room.

No sound except her own throaty gasping. Was this revenge? Mum knew how to scold, but this trick was beyond her. Explanation lurked somewhere, and Phos rifled her wardrobe and cabinets and chests of drawers, but only her parents were missing. Had Rastersen's hands rummaged through her wardrobe? Wind rattled the shutters – shouldn't Dad be home?

Priests knew where she lived. Her mind raced: *Find light, food, warmth; keep alive; get out and hide.* Her parents' bedroom held candles, and the kitchen range might cough out an ember.

Noise, heavy thuds and splintering shook the house, and feet slammed into the front door until it crashed open. Boots rang out and jars smashed. Men ripped out drawers and snickered. Phos peeked through her door and crept downstairs, wincing at the creaking. A metal pan flew out of the kitchen and across the hallway, but she stopped herself looking into the kitchen. What if she darted through the door's wreckage? She reached the foot of the stairs, and swear words rang out. One man shouted about searching upstairs. Phos stepped into the hallway and faced the ruined front door.

A roar burst from behind and Phos cringed, but the two invaders argued. Were others waiting beyond the door? She choked on bile, but she'd not glance back, and she wove through the door's remains. Her head jerked as the hanging basket snared her hair, and she clamped her mouth shut – the front door was visible from the kitchen.

Phos reached back and gripped the basket before jerking her head forward. Blinding pain screwed over her scalp, but she was free. She muffled a gasp before sprinting over Dad's garden and into a thicket of trees, and she looked back as violet-white lanterns scuttled through the kitchen.

These guards might check the forest, but her home was a certain trap. She'd idled away tens of afternoons with dreams of running away, but parents meant food and warmth. Images of playing games with dolls jostled against thoughts of begging priests for food and shelter. Phos had ignored Mum's gentle nagging about finding a husband, but if she relied on the church for food, they'd do more than nag.

If the invaders left, she might slip inside and search for essentials and scratch out a tiny world for herself deep in the forest; a few days' thinking time. Phos watched their lanterns, and her hand clutched a branch, but it squelched into a stinking mass of rot as flies scattered out. She fell backwards, and the soaked undergrowth drenched her trousers.

Tears came unasked; Phos needed silence, but she could only damp herself into a snivelling whine. Nothing made sense. Questions without answers thumped through her mind, and violent shudders swept her body. She threw herself onto the ground and sobbed once before falling silent. Darkness flooded through the forest, and she retched again. Tears returned as memories of Mum and Dad's faces drifted past.

There'd been homework; perhaps she'd invent an excuse for not doing it.

***

The moor's wiry grass snagged his feet. A horse had stamped hoofprints into the mud. Caliper trudged towards a woollen scarf, a slash of brilliant red lying on the soggy turf. The moor's low hills looked like dollops of mud in the distance. Rain clouds brooded above his head as the damp chill seeped through his boots. Christina had said her city crowned a hill; he'd meandered up two slopes but backed down after finding barren stains of dead grass at their tops.

He'd searched an abandoned warehouse; it had been dry, but priests would scour the village, so he'd shunted his body out to scratch up a few hours of sleep under a hedge. Sure, he'd dreamed of guards and knives, nightmares to slap him from sleep and leave him gasping in the night, but he'd dodged their hunting, and he risked a smile.

Caliper had nowhere to store regrets: staying a miller after his beard had wilted into grey meant a slow death as his muscles withered, but without a home he was naked and shivering. Where was Christina? Was she repairing devices he'd never understand, fighting enemies she'd never mentioned, or had she always planned to forget him? Was the old pattern repeating?

The story repeated every year, like a cracked cartwheel thudding against mud. He'd visit a market or harvest dance and see the smiles and dancing eyes of a young woman, and they'd swap a few words, and that night he'd dream of future embraces. Plans would ferment: ideas of buying a small house in Leester village, where he'd plant crops; he'd almost hear laughing children.

Dreams would fade. Silence would come, or polite excuses for absence, and the young woman would disappear from her usual paths. Caliper's careful letters would go unanswered, and he'd lie awake through empty nights as failure churned through his mind. New women came, but always hope faded into silence: the flower never blossomed. Changing clothes and posture made no difference, and after enough repeats, his failure felt as certain as nightfall. Rocks always fell; winter always followed summer; and he'd always stay single.

Christina was different: a splash of ice water on a sweltering day. She always returned and listened and asked questions, and hope had simmered. These last few months he'd let himself dream again, but now stillness returned.

The priest had mentioned Torzene, and he remembered a monastery perched on a hill beside the northern world wall. There'd been a henge halfway between Ferstus and Torzene, and Christina often took shape at the henges.

Caliper's path led across a shallow ditch holding brown water. He leaped over the stream, but muck splashed his trousers. He stumbled but kept walking.

Stones nudged above the sodden horizon ahead, like an unfinished circle of teeth sunk into the grassy plain. The grass surrounding the stones made a green velvet disc in the wasteland – a splash of welcome colour. Even close up the standing stones looked like rock, but he stroked the mossless surface and warmth seeped into his fingers. They might have been solid blocks centuries ago, but time had scoured channels down their sides.

Caliper raised his hood against the rain and winced as water soaked his beard. He'd spewed last time he'd used the monoliths, and sickness had greyed his vision for days, but the standing stones let him scout the land: his body would stay here while his mind roved the hills and sought Christina's home. Caliper placed his hands on the stone, and warmth bathed his palms as he closed his eyes and rested his forehead against the rock.

This lurch was only a gentle nudge, so maybe tiredness fended off the worst shocks. New visions flooded his mind. His body leaned against the stone as dust sleeted from the rock, and images came of blades of grass trembling as their roots stretched through soil. Caliper trickled his vision over to a small elm wood thirty feet away, and focused on a single branch, a single leaf; the greenery inhaled one kind of air and breathed out another. His vision drifted towards the ground's moss; the plants were hungry enough to climb the trees' knotted trunks, and worms forged themselves into tight bundles of energy to coil through the earth.

Caliper pushed his sight above the trees. Three birds plumed out red and purple trails between the topmost branches as their tiny hearts pumped blood through their veins – Christina said all bodies worked this way. He'd no time to play: pain laced through his mind despite the shimmering visions, and the trees fell back as he twisted his sight forward – this was more exploring memory than seeing. A winding track drifted through the grass, and another wood rose into view. Dried-out trees wheezed at the air as sap stuttered through their trunks. Nausea crashed over him; his sight turned black for a heartbeat, but now he moved without thought. He'd become a passenger. His vision hurtled onto a rolling grass plain, and the track passed on his left. Far ahead, the plain swept up into the northern world wall until the thin grass faded into grey rock.

Grass blurred underneath as his vision rushed past a jagged rock sticking up like a bleached tooth. Ahead, the horizon juddered, and a rip tore through his vision as the world wall behind appeared to stretch. Was this Torzene? Caliper heaved his mind towards the breach, and he found the gravel-covered path he'd once climbed to the monastery. Beside it ran a buttery stone wall, and the black rip fluttered above. White-hot needles of pain scraped his body, but he forced his sight on and upward – Torzene crested a hill, as did Christina's city.

No warning. Caliper's vision shattered into blinding shards as agony shredded his body. He fell and crashed onto rock and screamed inside as his blood choked him. Grey mist foamed before blackness swept over him – darker than any nightmare.

***

Light came to Caliper as a flickering beam the colour of daylight, but damp gnawed half his face, and a shrill ringing left him deaf. His left arm was a lump of dead flesh, and he'd spewed over the grass.

Someone called his name. Few called him anything these days, and Caliper grunted before rolling over.

Christina hovered three feet above him, lying flat in the air. Her lips moved as his name rolled through his mind, and he glimpsed the stony vault through her body. Caliper bathed in her presence as he waited for the pain to fade, but Christina's face crawled with worry.

'Caliper, can you still understand me?'

'I…I wanted to see the monastery.'

'Monastery? I don't know that name.' Christina's voice sounded hollow, as if blown by wind for hundreds of yards.

'It's not a name, it's a building….' He paused: thirst burned his throat. 'I used the henge to see you – I wanted to peek ahead.'

'My controllers didn't configure the surveying program for new constructions.'

New words skittered past each time he spoke with Christina, and one day he'd learn what they meant. 'You found me. Did you catch my windmill's light?'

Christina's head shimmered. 'I learned your location. Walk dawnward for three days, and we'll meet, but angry people hunt you with dogs.'

'You heard them chatter about me?'

'Your brain has a unique signature, and if you raise fear in others, their minds hold traces of yours. Time is short, Caliper.'

'You owe me a thousand answers, so you do,

and I'm sure you're squatting on ten thousand stories, but I'd welcome the drop of water.'

'I made you new supplies. Can you follow me?'

Caliper's ribs creaked as he stood. 'Everything works, though I've fierce pain.'

Christina's watery image winked out, and all twelve feet of her body reappeared, standing now; her sandalled feet hovered four inches above the turf. She glided towards another stone, with a silver bag sitting at its base. Inside, his hands brushed candles of both types, rope, loaves, cheese and a small beer bottle. He uncorked it, but the acrid gunk inside left him gagging.

'You'll never make a brewer.'

'There's water too.'

More rummaging in the bag brought him a glass water bottle and a set of tools looking as if she'd carved them from a hunk of iron.

'I felt you wake the henge, Caliper, and I've not sensed that before. You've three days' dawnward walk left, but you must stay hidden, and you must hurry.'

'I've visited Torzene; it's never three days off.' Caliper stared up at her face; mist had never sculpted itself into such elegance: her billowing robe hinted at her figure. Even though she was made of mist, he couldn't stop his staring – perhaps you only ever saw perfection when you fell in love. If he found her for real he'd never want the looking away.

'What blinded me?'

'The surveying program examines growth in trees and grass, but it's not calibrated for new buildings.'

'So Torzene's being rebuilt.'

'I sense people gathering three hours' walk from you, but this Torzene must be the wrong place; you must avoid it. Walk three days dawnward, and bring others if you can.'

'You want others?' He tried reading Christina's face but only saw a patient calm. Would they not share moments alone?

'I'll explain when we meet, but we must meet. This connection will fail in moments, so stay safe and bring friends.'

Christina's image froze and faded; a few folds of her robe hung like ribbons in the air before vanishing. What could others bring? Was she planning a contest, or did she need assistants? He scowled.

Caliper stared dawnward to trace out a path; the wood he'd seen sat a touch north of dawnward, and the track beyond led to Torzene, so Christina must have misread the distance. Had another of her machines broken?

His hand brushed a stone's gnarled surface; he'd known ladders to creak and break underneath to pitch him sprawling over earth, but he'd never blamed the ladder, and he'd not blame whatever contraptions crouched inside these stones. Perhaps Christina hoped he'd find someone with hidden knowledge. They might have read one of those books with painted pictures, or skills might dance in their fingers, skill to work these stones well.

The sun's arch clung against the world walls like a barrel's hoop; if he nudged north, he'd reach Torzene by early afternoon. The thicket of elm trees made a start, and Caliper's feet padded over the emerald grass.

Bark had sloughed from trunks to expose wan patches of pulp, and the leaves had crisped into an early autumn's gold as Caliper strode forward. There'd be comfort with the right thoughts; he'd dream of Christina's arms, and an embrace, and her words whispering in his ear and her fingers wrapping his. He pictured a silver thread winding between them, a thread growing shorter with every step so no one could say they weren't connected.

Doubt still nagged his heart and his pace slowed. Why did she want others – did she think him lacking?

Chapter 7: you'll take the darkest path

Grey light elbowed Phos awake, and she rolled over. Twigs snapped, and mould stink left her retching. The branches above throttled daylight into drab slices, enough to let her glimpse her house; brown muck slathered her tunic, and leaves clung to her hair as she sat up. Her left foot stayed numb, and her fingers still reeked of the rotten stick she'd grasped.

A few minutes before dawn. Had those invaders camped overnight in her kitchen? The house looked like an anvil resting on grass, but the shutters stayed dark. Hunger left her giddy, and she crept into the back garden and towards the shattered front door before listening. No sound. She stepped into the gloom, and her muddied boots skidded on the polished floor before tangling with a wrecked picture frame. Shafts of daylight trickled through the kitchen shutters, enough to show gold and crimson streaks of powder splashed over the tiles. The thugs had smashed the spice jars above the door and ripped the drawers from the dresser.

Phos slunk upstairs. They'd slashed her hammock and bedclothes, and forced open her trunk to rip her dolls apart. She clamped her mouth shut and knelt to run her hands over the remains of her knitted figures. For each doll, she listed a classmate who might house her, but her hands froze: calling someone a friend never stopped them running to priests. Two or three days' hiding in the forest might give her time to learn and ask the right questions. Had guards seized other parents, or had her school question summoned these invaders? Each question spawned a clutch of possible answers, but how could she winkle out any truth?

She could push furniture back into place and sweep up the crockery shards, but the guards had stripped her house and scattered Dad's books over his bedroom floor. She scooped the volumes back, but gaps remained on the shelves like broken teeth. A single sheet wafted out, a sketched circle wrapped by a maze, with Dad's writing crawling around the image of Morzenthal, the museum city far to dawnward. Coins littered the floor.

Mum's fragrance lingered, and sitting beside Dad's books bathed her in the musty richness of words, but those scents would fade. Phos rose and walked back to her bedroom to stuff the one surviving red-haired doll inside her backpack.

Outside, and she walked with bowed head towards Dad's blackwood shed and wrestled the door open. He'd bought stacks of crocks for repotting plants, but the men had shattered each pot; green streaks of plant life wound around clay shards. The air was heavy with peat, and she remembered Dad saying how shifting plants into bigger pots let them grow. Now she needed her own world, one large enough to let her mature – no schoolgirl could survive alone.

Phos walked on but saw nothing. Trees passed by in a haze of moss-covered bark as she paced forward. Had other schoolchildren escaped the guards, and would they seek familiar places? Had they seen her parents?

The elms' sour taint shook her from her thoughts; she'd reached the school path. Too open. Phos backed into the forest on her left and picked her way through the tree trunks. She stopped every few moments to listen, but drizzle rattled the papery leaves. She'd sneak into school and hunt ledgers and diaries: some teacher might have recorded orders, and the priests should have finished their arresting by now.

Phos crept past the crossroads, glancing around her each moment until she reached the school's southern fence. One section had buckled, and she squeezed through the wooden slats. Inside, an empty cart waited beside the bakery, and the playing fields stood deserted. A pair of child's trousers sat beside a slashed-open football. No boys racing around the fields and no chattering girls, just leaves scudding over damp grass.

She sidled into the main hall, and her boots clomped over the wooden floor to echo over the walls. Someone had hauled trestle tables into a corner, and guards had kicked down a cupboard door.

Embroidery samples littered the juniors' floor, though cloaks still hung up at the back. Inky puddles pooled over the floorboards, and Phos imagined she heard pens drying out. Invaders had rifled the teacher's desk and seized the registers, so she'd never squeeze any story from this wreckage.

Phos stepped back outside, and a bony hand grabbed her shoulder. She froze. Had they seized the others this way? No words, just pressure gripping her shoulder. Phos turned to face the blacksmith's son, Mitch, all messy hair and ripped shirt and muddy face. The stolen day had left him pale and panting; snot ran from his nose. He pulled his hand back and pressed it against the wall.

'When did you arrive, Mitch?'

'H-half an hour ago. I came late and found the writing room. All the dictation books finish mid-sentence.'

'Who told Grump to stop?'

'They looted his desk,' Mitch said.

'What happened to you?'

'Dad left before I woke. I stayed home, but he never came back. Since Mum died….' His voice faded, and he stared downward.

'So you were very late?'

'I've no food. Can we try the storeroom?'

Violence had smashed the storeroom's lock, and Phos pulled the wooden door open. Raiders had trampled loaves and boulmer fruit into the soil, but enough remained on the racks. Mitch ripped a chunk from a loaf and crammed it into his mouth.

Phos waited. 'Did you see anything yesterday afternoon?'

'I skipped school after lunch 'cause I wanted to avoid Gree's gang, but this crowd marched past on the Ferstus road with a priest at the front and two guards behind – all shout and shove. No idea why you'd visit Ferstus.'

'Ah, but the road doesn't stop there.'

'Can we work out what they want? Why not check the chapel? There're books and a hundred scrolls inside – sneeze, and the priests write it down.'

'It's not prayer day till tomorrow; they'll have locked it.'

'Days don't count no more, and nor do locks.'

Today she'd agree with Mitch. He led her past the quiet stone of the kitchen block and its garden with its straggling elm saplings. He stooped to touch an upended wheelbarrow, where black soil spilled over grass. Stand anywhere in the school, and the chapel's peak showed, but most children stayed clear: prayer days meant sermons in the clammy air and shuffling past that week's book while mumbling answers to questions.

The door sat recessed two inches into the pyramid's stone walls; the grey iron swallowed daylight. No lock showed, but Mitch pulled out a leather bundle.

'I always wanted to crack this – those spare locks Dad brought home were too easy.' Mitch unrolled his leather and slid two prongs into a metal ridge.

'That's not where the key goes,' Phos said.

'That key's for show, so keep quiet.'

A door banged in the distance, and leaves skittered as Mitch bent over the door and muttered until a click snapped through the air.

'Try the door now.'

She glanced behind, but they were still alone. Phos pushed, and the huge slab swung open without creaking. Inside, daylight dribbled over scrolls stacked against a wall, and a glass bookcase trapped a set of leather books. The incense still stank. Copper rods and glass tubes sat in one corner, and the buttery stone walls tapered together to fit at the top. No villager had shaped these blocks, so did the church own secret gangs of brilliant stonemasons?

She'd take days to read these scrolls, so she needed the right question. Guards had arrested Mum and Dad yesterday, so where would priests store fresh papers? She opened a few scrolls to check dates and blushed: they were in date order. The newest documents sat to her left, but her hand refused to move.

Mitch reached past her and unrolled one scroll. 'There's the newest paper, but what are your parents called?'

Phos recited names as if praying, and Mitch used one hand to steady the roll before running a finger down the list.

'These are Leester names and jobs,' he said. 'My dad's here but not Mum, so it's new. Can't see your parents, but this leads to a second scroll.'

Phos closed her eyes as Mitch rustled out a new roll.

'They wrote a special list yesterday, a short one.' Mitch paused. 'Your parents are here, and so are you. There're priest letters above. Can we ask a priest to translate?'

'Let me.' She'd relished learning the scratchy priest alphabet, but she'd known enough to keep her success quiet; now Mitch needed to know. A few moments' concentration revealed the words.

Priority cases: relocate to Torzene immediately.

'What's Torzene, and when did you learn priest letters?'

Her voice wavered as she told Mitch the story. Memories of Dad's stories left her reeling – she'd give anything to hear another of his warnings. Was travelling to Torzene her only choice? Plans had smouldered in Rastersen's eyes, and she'd seen his hands fondle his ropes. The priests' keep rested on dozens of dark cells.

No choice. She owed her parents everything. She'd try to enter Torzene unseen, try to avoid Rastersen's hands. Mitch might help her skirt roads and find overgrown footpaths, but the priests were hunting, and they knew the paths as well as he did.

***

Mist swirled around Caliper and hid the track sulking on his left. Every few minutes he'd spot streaks of beige gravel, and he'd trundle rightward over the sodden grass for the hiding.

Mist was worse than bathing: damp overalls pinched his thighs, and a tear ran up his back. He'd fallen earlier, and half his face throbbed, but he'd not rest. Christina's warnings of priests and dogs stuffed his mind, and he pushed his aching legs into hopping over a ditch. Did water hanker after ground to make wet clothes heavy? Caliper fired swear words into the fog, but cursing never helped a single man.

He was sure Torzene was Christina's home, but he had to sidestep the guards and keep the track just visible as he shortened the thread between them.

Footsteps rattled from the road, and Caliper

wheeled around and crouched as movement ghosted through fog: a crowd four abreast with a stout priest leading. Shouts rang out. The words stank of orders as the mist thinned, and Caliper scuttled back to hide. Ten yards of crouch and slide brought him to a single standing stone twice his size. His hands touched rock, and fleeting warmth stroked his palm as he scampered for its far side.

Caliper peered out. The crowd still showed; two guards walked behind, and one shoved a teenage girl forward as the prisoners flinched. There stumbled Sirella the baker, a man who never missed church days; Leester's cobbler lurched beside him with a bloodied scalp.

'Pick up the pace: we're running late.'

These people would reach Torzene inside an hour, and other roving prisons would follow, so how could he slip inside? Caliper slumped against the stone. Everything directed him here – the priests and his vision and Christina's words – but what use was direction when Torzene crawled with scowling guards?

Fog swallowed the snake of prisoners as they marched ahead, and silence returned as water dripped off his hood. His fingers sponged into the standing stone, which pulsed out a faint heat, a scrap of warmth in the waterlogged day. If he closed his eyes here Christina might help him inside.

This time his nausea only whispered as his sight switched, but the grass reappeared in his mind like a circle of vivid green surrounding a blinding white stone. He'd not send his vision roving again, but he could wait and stare at the glowing turf.

Mist puckered as blades of grass spiralled into the air to form a net. A thick knot of fog swelled from the centre, and shades of grey unfolded themselves into a ghostly robed woman with shoulder-length hair. Long sleeves hung from her arms as her head tilted.

'You have the wrong destination, Caliper. I see where you're headed, but its inhabitants hunt you.'

'Every where's the wrong place for me, but I'm sure you're at Torzene – it caps a hill.'

'This world's full of hills.' Christina glanced leftward as if checking. She raised her hand, and her fingers disappeared.

'You don't measure our world so well – that's for sure – so maybe you're not elsewhere.'

'I see distances well, Caliper; I'm not wrong. Patrols stalk you across this moor. Try to enter Torzene, and they'll catch you. Even your current position is perilous. I can help.'

'The mist hides me.'

'Mist won't last. Head south half a day before travelling dawnward, and two days' walk will unite us, but I must distract the church to keep you alive.'

Christina's body shimmered. 'Torzene looks like a child's fort; I see rooms stacked on rooms without new foundations or regard for stresses, and warnings cover my displays.'

What were displays? Caliper ran his hand through his hair.

'Metal bolts hold timbers together, but if we remove them, the building will crumple under gravity. The patrolling guards will rush to help, and you can escape this area.'

'What's gravity? Ah, don't mind with the explaining; staying safe sounds grand.'

Her face stayed alien in its misty beauty, and her generous lips meant he'd never read her expression, but a smile dawdled on her face.

'Caliper, my change needs your permission.'

'Eh?'

'I never received the gift of free will, but your words let me act on my thoughts. Give me permission to invoke this change, and change will protect you.'

'What can I do?'

'These alterations will take several minutes, but you'll hear the collapse. Stay beside your stone until the path clears.' Again her ghostly blue eyes fixed him. 'Do you give me permission?'

'I do.'

Christina closed her eyes and bowed her head a

fraction. Her image froze for three heartbeats before she flicked back into her standing pose, and her sleeves wafted in a breeze he couldn't feel.

'Torzene will fall, Caliper. Wait before walking, and find me in the city above the hill.'

Her figure turned pure white for an instant before fading into a set of ripples chasing each other through the air, and Caliper breathed out. *Enough with the stone-seeing.* He opened his eyes.

Drab grass and grey stone surrounded him, but a spectre of movement danced through the mist ahead, and Caliper rested against his stone. Was mist spinning? His path had been sure, but now he shivered. Did he hear dogs barking? Would he feel their teeth?

Chapter 8: both silence and noise mean danger

Rastersen's horse had stormed over this path, but their journey was a slow plod: the earth caked her boots and her legs ached. The Ferstus road rambled past a birch forest, and the slits in the ghostly white bark looked like half-opened eyes, but the right side opened onto a set of pasture fields carpeting a shallow set of rolling hills; the southern world wall showed as a distant band of blue haze. Dandelions had broken through the gravel, and thistles sprouted from the verges.

Mitch had found a tunic that fitted him beside the road, and she'd splashed water across his face to ease away the mud. She glanced behind at him. Torzene bristled with locks, so she'd never manage alone, and he'd promised to follow if she darted beneath the trees.

'Follow me, Mitch. Keep close.'

'Is it Torzene we're heading for?'

Phos nodded. Mitch's heartbeat might hypnotise him; she tweaked her backpack straps and fiddled with a rip in her trousers before marching beside the boy. Pools of shadow grew over the broken road as the sun's arch glided eveward, and Phos asked Mitch to keep watch behind; the boy stayed sure-footed even when walking backwards. Three horses without riders hurtled past, and she'd expected their riders to come chasing, but the path stayed empty in the fading light.

Each step brought her parents closer. Phos tried to recall Torzene's layout to work out where to search, but memories of the mud and creaking huts left her twitching: images of Rastersen's gash-like mouth reared up in her mind.

Night fell, and Phos led Mitch into the birch forest; a liss tree draped spindly branches across her face. The turf here was spongy and dry, and their backpacks made pillows as they camped. Owls punctured the silence with drawn-out hoots. She lay on the ground and yawned as she listened to their cries, but any pattern stayed buried.

Lantern light trickled over the trees as two horsemen cantered towards Leester, but Phos had hidden well, and night returned. They snatched four hours' sleep to rise before dawn. Pale gold slashes streamed over the vault, and Mitch stood to scrape sleep from his eyes.

'Do we have to visit Ferstus?'

'Yes, unless you plan to wade through bogs. We sneak through before any guards wake.'

Ferstus's rancid-fat stench had attacked her throat when she'd raced through on Rastersen's horse, and now they had to scuttle through the reek. The first whiffs came when they were half a mile away; a faint touch of grease grew into a stink like boiling vomit.

Mitch's eyes streamed as they entered the main

street. Two-storey wattle-and-daub cottages slouched each side. Ahead, guards milled around a horse, and Phos hauled Mitch into a burnt cottage, where charred furniture sat on a puddled mud floor under a broken ceiling. Someone had wrestled a bed from the chaos. Had the guards carted Ferstus's workers off to Torzene?

'Move through, Mitch, and try the back door.'

Outside sat a scrap of rough turf. Ahead, the land sank into an immense bog. Flat islands of dark grass capped rippling brown water, but the smell had settled into a rotten-yeast flavour. A narrow path slid behind these cottages, and tinsel strings wormed where neighbours had seen boundaries. They sneaked past tens of silent shutters as daylight began to flow over the gardens. Phos expected their trespass to brew up shouts, but no one appeared.

Brick houses now, where short wooden fences claimed a slice of back garden. Easy to hop over, but ahead a six-foot blackwood fence stretched from house to bog, and the planks resisted Mitch's kicks.

'Some people never share,' he said.

'Here.' Phos opened the back door of the house before the fence and stepped inside. Whitewashed walls stood behind polished wooden furniture, and an oil painting covered one wall, showing two young girls posing before smiling parents. Two baskets stuffed with lilies sat on a polished dresser; a petal had fallen from the baskets.

Phos held her breath. What would she tell the owners if they appeared? Daylight stroked through the shutters, but the living room stayed silent.

Mitch coughed. 'Perhaps they have lanterns we can borrow.'

'Let's search.'

Stairs creaked as Mitch climbed and Phos followed. His body tensed as he reached the top, and she looked over his shoulder into a child's bedroom. Faded blue rugs covered the floor, and a toy pram sat against a wall. On the far side, twin hammocks clasped two seven-year-old girls, and Phos slipped past Mitch – even youngsters knew stories.

Garlands of knitted dolls and animals surrounded the girls – twins, maybe, with silvery hair arranged into ringlets. Both wore pale blue dresses. Were they sleeping? Ribbons of daylight streamed through the bedroom shutters.

Phos touched the nearest girl's sleeve, but neither girl moved. Their arms stayed folded over their chests, and Phos watched for signs of breathing or movement in the toys covering their bodies. Nothing. Mum had said you'd struggle to tell the difference between a sleeping child and one who had died.

Mitch rested his fingers on a girl's neck, and he stooped to breathe air.

'Hours old, but there's lethewort.'

'The sleeping draught?' Phos shivered.

'Enough helps you dream; too much makes a final gift. The toys and hair, it's all arranged; you'll not move for the love here, but what makes killing the kindest choice? Their parents must be in the other bedroom.'

'Do we need to check?'

'They'd learned something, and they couldn't let their girls face the future,' Mitch said.

Phos's limbs wouldn't shift; her gaze locked onto the nearest twin. What had the girl seen in her last moments? Had her parents' faces given anything away?

Phos struggled back and glanced at the ballerina dolls balanced on a cabinet, then at a small wall mirror, everything free from dust.

They walked into a larger room, facing the street. Two slim, silver-haired adults lay face up on a spotless bed. The male's cream waistcoat matched the woman's tunic, and her crimson sash was tight and creaseless. A bedside table held a black flask and two elegant glasses. This couple would never stop holding hands.

Almost enough to explain the silence, but what sights lurked elsewhere? Had other deaths lacked this peace?

Mitch's voice scratched out. 'Still plan to visit

Torzene?'

'Sneak in, not visit.'

'That's our best option?'

'Parents, Mitch; I told you.'

'Didn't your caning teach you? We need limits.'

'I don't.' She paused. She'd never survive Torzene without Mitch's talents. 'The badness at Torzene will spread, and going there means we'll see it early, so we can react.'

'And we'll get it worse. Best you travel alone.'

'They'll never expect us at Torzene, so it may be the safest place.'

'Breaking into prison, that's very Phos.'

'We might find your dad.'

'That's what scares me – even in prison he'll spend all day shouting. Best we split up.'

Phos faced him. 'I won't stop you running off, but the guards reach everywhere.'

Mitch glared.

'Together we have a better chance: our skills fit and Torzene has locks,' Phos said.

Mitch's hand hovered an inch above the woman's cheek. 'Let's not argue here. At least let's leave Ferstus.'

'I've always thought tomorrow should improve on today, so let's start there. You're right about leaving.'

Downstairs, Phos peered through the front door. The house looked over Ferstus's main square and onto a line of thatched cottages, but men had ripped down houses to punch a hole in the village. An unfinished barn squatted where they'd been, a deformed wooden skeleton scorched on one side. Tools littered the barn's base, saws, hammers, pots and pans scrambled together. Fire pans hid underneath sooty tarpaulins, and Mitch uncovered a cauldron.

'They build and they cook; then they stop, so what happened?'

'Keep moving, Mitch, or people will see.' Phos guided him through a muck-filled alley winding between two cottages and out onto Ferstus's north side. A patchwork of flower gardens ran out from the backs of the cottages; their splashes of red and blue made a barrier against the bog's brown water. Mist still lingered, but they could skirt the houses here and travel dawnward.

Mitch stared back towards Leester.

'We need to make sense, Mitch: if we know the church's heart we might predict their next move.'

'Yes, being arrested will teach us loads.'

'I've seen Torzene; there's a huge courtyard at the back, and they're still building its fence, so we'll slip inside and listen.'

'Listen to what?' Mitch tugged at a mist-soaked

frond.

'Words about my parents or where Leester people have gone and what Torzene's for, and most important, we find out why.'

'Always with the questions, Phos, but you'll never know which answers are right.'

'It's a start.'

'It's madness – you'll stand out, and the guards will grab you. There'll be no food at Torzene, but the Leester forest has blackberries and mushrooms.'

'Not when winter comes.'

'We split here. I'll hole up in the forests; the guards will stop hunting soon.'

'The trees are sick and getting worse, and what if fruit stops growing?'

'Always this chatter about change, Phos.'

'Everything changes if you wait long enough, and everything starts somewhere.' Phos paused. 'I kept running one idea past Dad. Trees and plants have seeds, so why not our world?'

Mitch's hand stopped pulling at the frond. 'Everything sprouted from a seed, did it? Everything we see and touch and eat?'

'Has to come from somewhere.'

'Everything? Flowers, bees, birds, rocks, air, leaves, houses, churches, caterpillars and carrots, more bees, cats and dogs and your scrawny arse all popped from this baby seed, did they? One the size of your brain?'

'It's a way of thinking, Mitch.'

'You're not safe, you're half-mad. You look like a scarecrow, but you do entertain.'

'Let's stick together. I need you for lock picking and sneaking, and you need me for…well…you need me…end of sentence.'

'A single seed for the whole world? Did your man Rastersen tell you this?'

'Shut up, Mitch.'

'What made your seed, and what plant spat it out?'

'Shut up, will you?'

'No, messing with your brain is fun. I'll stick with you for a bit. Not long, mind.'

'Just shut up.'

They walked eveward, and Ferstus's houses gave way to cabbage fields. The dawnward road snaked onward, a muddy scar to pierce the fields and slide through the straggling grass and reach the moor beyond the village.

She'd keep the moor's road on her right, keep it just visible. The damp fog brought extra cover, but she still felt Rastersen's hands curling around her waist. Phos hefted two blankets from her backpack and handed one to Mitch.

Hours passed, and Mitch fell silent as their boots thudded over the soaking grass. They kept a steady rhythm as the day advanced, and Phos kept nudging Mitch away from the road.

Time to imagine Torzene's purpose: did priests want loggers to keep carpenters busy and blacksmiths to forge horseshoes? Perhaps Dad was there to organise the money, but they'd tossed Dad's ledgers over his floor and scattered coins everywhere.

Footsteps thudded through the fog, and Phos crouched before peeking at the road. Twenty people, a packed formation four abreast, and a cloaked priest at the head, with two club-waving guards behind. Dim shadows without faces and too distant to see her parents, but she stared.

'Head down,' hissed Mitch.

Words slid through the greasy air, and she caught the word 'schedule'. The priest glanced her way, and a dim crimson flashed underneath his cloak. Phos froze, and Mitch gripped her waist to haul her onto the ground.

The group's footsteps held their pace, and once they'd faded she raised her head. This mist might vanish in a heartbeat, so she should stay further from the road.

'That was your man, wasn't it? Your knees jammed.'

Three, four breaths, and she sat up and looked around. Phos squinted as a flurry of wind uncovered a tooth-like silhouette ahead: the squared blocks of Torzene's lashed-together timberwork scratched the foggy sky.

'Swing north, and we'll circle towards the rear courtyard.'

'That's best, is it?'

'Easiest way in: the back courtyard is huge, and the fence is all gaps.' Teachers said trees took decades to grow, so you could only cut down a handful each year, and there sat another rule the priests had shattered.

Phos stopped. They'd heard nothing since the prisoners had vanished, but now several sharp cracks rang through the chilled air. Torzene's battlements appeared ahead but quivered before sliding forward and shattering to scatter a framework of beams into the air. Two spars snapped, and a section of wall drooped and collapsed. A corner tower sank and vomited out timbers and sheets of plaster, and the whole front tipped forward and dissolved into billowing clouds of dust. Roaring filled her ears as Torzene crumbled.

Change had touched this place as it had touched her and her parents; violence threatened every corner of her world. A single falling beam would shatter her body, would shatter her parents' skulls.

***

The grey mist enveloping Caliper faded, and more grass showed every moment. He crouched beside the standing stone and stared forward with one hand pressed into the waterlogged turf.

Christina had tricked agreement from his lips; she'd read him like a book and scribbled in his margins. Why had she asked him to bring others? Why hadn't he thought of Torzene's prisoners? Was he cider in her glass?

A tooth-like pattern formed in the air ahead where the church had rammed a vast wooden cap onto the ancient monastery of Torzene, and boxy pillars and rooms stood to shape a wall facing him like a fist. The stone foundation sat on a shallow hill, and guards loitered by the front entrance.

Caliper hid behind the stone and screwed up his eyes, trying to remember Christina's words and the shapes her lips had created. She was right: this ramshackle fortress wasn't her home. He'd have questions for her, but her words had stopped him rotting with the wheat at his windmill, so her thoughts should still live in his heart, and he'd skulk back to her henge before heading dawnward.

Splintering timber noises crunched through the air, and Caliper peeked around the stone. The fortress reared into view as mist faded, a vast wolf jaw shaking with fury. The leftmost wooden tower twisted and collapsed to spill out timbers as the decay spread, and those topmost cubicles slid forward as the front sagged to drag the timberwork down.

Was his mind adding sound, or did he hear screaming? Christina's work, beautiful and dreadful all at once. He'd not forget his labouring over the windmill's sails, but Christina's power made him feel like a child waving a toy hammer at a blacksmith.

Torzene had become a rolling bank of filth that spat splintered planks and dust over the slope below. A single wooden block of a room burst from the cloud before tumbling over the ground, and plasterboard sheets surged out as dust seethed. Two bodies like floppy dolls smacked over the wreckage while broken tables and rugs cascaded over the earth.

High officers always grabbed the high-up offices, and he'd never regret any levelling, but if they'd dragged Leester families here there'd be more than upper-class bruises. Shouts and screams scraped through the haze. His blurted words, his permission – his fault.

Caliper ran forward: the few scraps of medicine he'd stolen might ease these pains. At least he'd search the old monastery stones for the injured and undo a crumb of the pain he'd caused.

Chapter 9: destruction breeds change

Mitch's hands clasped Phos's waist and dragged her back into the long grass. The impact winded her, but she raised her head and gazed at the destruction ripping through Torzene. Dust heaved out as screams curdled the air. Damage spread into the fence running behind; the barrier collapsed inwards, and its posts pointed at the fake village.

'We'll explore,' Phos said.

'Will we? Can't we let this settle?'

'Chaos, Mitch; no one will expect trespassers.'

They skirted the wreckage to reach the fence, and the screams died into a burbled wail as the dust cleared. Leaden clouds loitered above. Spars had tumbled like kindling over the older stone base, and ripped shreds of tarpaulin flapped through the air as two wiry guards hauled a body from beneath a beam.

The fence had collapsed into a shifting pile of broken stakes and planks. Mitch helped her climb. Inside, a fringe of trampled moor grass surrounded a sea of crude huts. A gaggle of ten-year-old boys ran towards them and yelled but veered away to scramble over the fence's wreckage.

Acrid smoke clawed coughs from Phos's chest, but she strode on and peered inside the nearest windowless shack, six feet high with a flat roof and bare earth floor. The rough-cut timber smelt fresh. An elderly couple sheltered in the next doorway and held hands while staring at her. Ahead, tens of similar shoddy huts pocked the mud.

Mitch glanced back. 'How do we find your parents?'

'Search the old part: it's made of stone, so priests will stuff paperwork there.'

'It'll be full of guards.'

'There's children everywhere, and we'll blend in so long as we act like we belong.'

Their path wound past a trio of bruised labourers squatting on the grass while holding their heads; one peeled a jerkin from a body. White sheets danced through the air, pages of escaping words. One flittered past, and her hand reached up, but she stepped back: she'd collect pages later with Dad.

Four guards raced past her and hauled a workman to his feet before shunting him against a hut. Their barked questions cowed the labourer into a closed-eyed panic, but the guards ran out of questions and let the labourer fall to his knees.

Mitch tapped her shoulder. 'Stop staring. Shouldn't we hunt for your parents?'

'We are.'

'You're not – you're thinking.'

'The prisoners entered through the front. Priests

love taking names, so let's check the ledgers in their offices.'

'Blundering inside church rooms is safe, is it?'

'Smile, Mitch; you might confuse them.'

Several rows of boxy cabins still rested above the stone building like stumps of broken teeth. The violence had stripped away their fronts to stamp a doll's-house design onto Torzene's carcass. Timbers teetered like twigs above the rooms, and guards rushed to wrestle desks from the edge.

There sat Rastersen's brick hut, and she kept her head down while darting towards the monastery. Two guards ran across the slush, and she turned her face away – she'd watched birds from her bedroom, and they always flitted between stillness and flight to avoid cats.

'Try to look scruffy,' Phos said.

'You're ahead of me.'

Three dingy huts stood between them and the squat stone building.

'If we wait for—' Phos squawked as a hand seized her wrist and yanked her body around. A guard's bearded scowl glared at her.

'What you doing? Where you going?'

'We're looking for our parents, sir. Everyone ran after the shaking, but we got lost.'

'Don't come here: the monastery is for

processing adults. What's your village?'

'Leester, sir.'

'Leester? You stinking runts, get back. Your huts are that way. Get near the monastery again, and I'll slap you.'

Phos faked a smile and nodded before walking away from the monastery, and Mitch followed. She'd walk the wrong way for a minute to colour in her lie.

'You fibber,' Mitch said.

'Always go where you're not wanted.'

'Can we find disguises, like cloaks or new tunics? And the monastery's middle is swarming with guards, so can we try the sides?'

'Let's keep looking.'

They stepped over broken timbers, and Phos dished out a hunk of bread to two five-year-olds waiting beside an empty wagon. She glanced back; the forest of huts hid the monastery, and the guard had vanished, so she circled around and hugged the northern fence. The mud here only showed two tracks of footprints.

Phos suggested Mitch keep watch behind as she crept forward, and they reached the ancient building. Age had gnawed the flinty stone, but ahead a dark passage burrowed into the building.

'Inside, quick.' Water dripped on her head as an earthy taste crawled inside her nose, and wall moss gripped mortar to make a faint glowing net behind the bricks. Damage had hammered through the ceiling; lanterns and firewood littered the floor; and a door had shaken free to teeter against the far wall.

Phos stepped into a dim, low-ceilinged cellar reeking of yeast. A stack of barrels had burst open, and beer puddled the floor to lap against wheels of cheese. Soil-filled trays held coiled green vegetables she couldn't name, and a jumble of wood filled one corner.

'That was a chair, but some nutter's stolen the screws,' Mitch said.

'Didn't the rooms above use screws? If the screws all vanish, everything crunches together.'

'Like the door: I know those hinges, and you can't get the bolts out without breaking wood, but there're no bolts and no damage.'

Heavy footsteps echoed from the corridor. Had the bearded guard returned? Phos turned towards the doorway and held her breath.

A hulking labourer wearing tattered overalls walked inside. Grey hairs grizzled his beard. He wiped his hands on a grease-smeared apron tied around his waist, and rips showed in his sleeves, though a huge leather backpack fitted him well.

'Are yous hurt?' His voice burred through the air.

Phos shook her head. 'Were you inside when

everything collapsed?'

'I…I was outside, so I didn't see nothing.' He stepped inside and checked the door hinges.

Mitch stepped forward. 'What happened to the bolts?'

'The metal's gone and the front's crumpled, and now there're holes everywhere. There're two guards down the corridor, but they didn't survive – best not go that way.'

He looked away, but guilt had smouldered in his eyes. He was choosing his words, and memories flared inside Phos. 'You're the miller…. Your windmill ripped itself apart…. What happened? Did you wreck this place too?'

The miller smiled. 'I can't vanish metal.'

'But you knew the bolts had gone…and what brought you here? What made your windmill light up?'

'Someone your age should answer questions.'

'School's closed,' Phos said.

'So you're taking control?'

'What's your name?'

'Cal.'

'What do you mean you're called Cal? Are you thirteen?'

'Caliper – I don't use age syllables.' His feet tapped a beer puddle.

'You don't. Everyone else does but you don't.

Did you forget about ageing?'

'No. I got drunk at twelve, and when I sobered up, I looked this way. Happy?'

Phos grinned and leaned against the wall.

'Let's start again,' Caliper said. 'What's your name?'

'Phos. My second syllable comes in three months, and here's Mitch. We school at Leester. Did guards force you inside?'

'No. I saw a crowd lugged here, but the place collapsed, so I came to help. I'll not stay.'

'Why follow the villagers? Who were you chasing?'

He paused. 'I thought a friend lived here, but….'

'You've still not said why your windmill wrecked itself.'

'New sails, Phos, and new designs to capture wind and shove its energy into lanterns. My friend needed to notice.'

Questions screamed inside her: what designs, and where had he found lanterns, and who was this friend? Her mouth opened, but no words came, and her neck hairs prickled as a smile waited on Caliper's face. One question squeaked out. 'Did you smash this place too?'

'My turn for the questions,' Caliper said. 'I'd ask for two questions, like you, but that'd make a question, so tell me, where are your parents?'

'No idea.' Mitch's voice quivered. 'They're building a new village outside, but Phos wanted to search here first.'

'Don't hang around – the evening wind will trash this place. Shouldn't you head back to Leester?'

'You know why this building crumpled, don't you?'

Caliper whipped a knife from his apron and whittled out a chunk of cheese from a wheel. He took one bite and slid the rest into his apron pocket. 'You'd not believe me.'

Phos rattled through her own story as Caliper rummaged through stacks of potted plants and ran his hands over a cloth roll. Once she'd finished, he stood and faced her.

'I saw people dragged from Leester, but you escaped. Was that luck?'

Mitch shook his head. 'We were late for school, so we missed the "getting arrested" class.'

'I never expected this much damage.' Caliper stroked the door.

'You expected damage?'

'I came to patch wounds. There's months of bandaging work here, but I've someone to meet.'

'We want to find our parents.'

'We're all looking, aren't we? We'll step outside

and find priests to dodge.'

They followed Caliper into the afternoon's smoky light, but both priests and guards had vanished, and an elderly couple helped each other across the mud. Far off, a crowd swarmed around a burning hut.

'I'm trying to fit this together, but everything keeps changing,' Phos said.

'We're all befuddled, but try thinking who gains. We saw people gathered, which reminds me of harvest time. Scythe wheat, and you've ten thousand stalks, but you'll not take each stalk to your mill; you bale the lot and haul a wagonload of bales. Those people were being baled.'

'A harvest of people?'

'All about control, Phos. I reckon you're right to say your parents are here, but we've chaos now, and a chance to write our own rules. I'm leaving tomorrow, but today I'll help find your mum and dad. Just go easy with the questions.'

Caliper wandered towards a hut with a crushed wall and ran his fingers over a small handcart. He flicked his hand, and the cart toppled onto its side.

Mitch leaned over to Phos. 'Shall we follow him?'

Torzene's rubble needed shifting, but would the miller's strength shackle her? Questions brought canings now; priests broke orders to scare young girls while parents vanished. Caliper hadn't explained himself; secrets writhed inside him. Were his words a disguise?

***

Thin rain fell, and Caliper's boots roughed up a peaty scent from the old monastery gardens – did herbs have ghosts? Caliper raised his hood as the girl strode inside a hut and rummaged through crates, and her copper hair twitched as those long limbs fidgeted. She heaved out a set of blankets before tipping the crate on its side and kneeling to paw through the box. She was all awkward gangle, as if puberty had sneaked up on her.

Phos's shoulders slumped. She stumbled from the hut and stood head bowed before glancing at him. 'I need to find my parents, Caliper, but where? I thought there'd be documents.'

Mitch rubbed his nose. 'There're five hundred huts here, easy, so if Caliper's leaving tomorrow….'

Caliper stood in front of Phos. 'What brought you to Torzene?'

'We found a journal in a chapel, which listed our names in priest letters, and they saw my parents as special. They searched our house and smashed jars and cut up my dolls – no idea what they wanted, but….' Phos turned her head away.

Caliper stepped forward but stopped: a fumbled

hug helped no one. Light drained from the vault, and it was too late to strike dawnward today, but tonight he'd reach out to build some comfort.

'Look for sticks and cloth,' Caliper said. 'I don't suppose you're taught the healing?'

'Healing's illegal.'

'Ah, that's only words. The church won't ban healing until it bans accidents, and there's reeper cloth roll against that barrel, so tear it into strips as wide as your wrist.'

'Officers!' Phos and Mitch ducked behind a crate, but Caliper slouched and ambled towards a dark grey brick hut. Two guards led four brown horses towards the shack, and strings of orders rang out. Four priests mounted before cantering dawnward. The other clergymen and guards swapped words with their heads down against the drizzle, and after a few moments they followed the horses. A flurry of loose pages swirled behind the tramping men and fluttered into the clouds.

'Clears our way, and now yous can come out,' Caliper said.

'Can we search inside the brick hut?' Phos's voice trembled. 'That place was important to them.'

'You've been there before?'

She nodded. 'I…. They used this shack…. They didn't let me go inside, but they wanted me to hear a woman screaming.'

Villagers had blackened the air around him with a thousand stories. He'd not believed the half of them, but pain showed in Phos's eyes even as her lips sealed shut. Rot festered in crops and plants, and he'd seen fungus crack open oak trees, so perhaps all this poison sprouted from the church.

'You're sure you want to see? Face too much horror and you'll not sleep.'

'If Dad had something they wanted, they'd have brought him here.'

'You should think twice.'

'I've thought a thousand times, and I need to know.'

Caliper might drown himself in the cider, but this girl's passion kept her rushing; she'd face her own fear to find her parents while he lacked the words to defy a single priest. He followed her to an iron slab, an outer door. It creaked as Caliper tugged it open. Inside, a tiny inner space held another door. Mitch stood behind Caliper.

'Do I keep going, Phos?'

She nodded.

The inner door squealed open, and stagnant air snuffled at his face as light drizzled from tiny skylights. Glimmer enough to show tangled metalwork woven around a naked body and pinning it against a chair. Dried blood streaked the man's chest, and Caliper swept his arm back to block Phos's sight.

'Let me see. Let me see!' Phos dashed forward and stared at the body's face, and her hand stroked the body's arm as she moaned. 'Dad's friend.'

Caliper cursed himself without words: no one could stop the girl learning, but he should find her a gentler path and help her hold back – no one grew up in a day.

'Priests get impatient,' Mitch said.

Two bloodstained chairs faced the wall, surrounded by the iron restraints used on animals, and blood had spattered over the wooden floor. Caliper watched as Phos kneaded the body's hand. A book learner's hand. Most likely Phos's dad had the same smooth fingers, so should he shepherd her outside for the comfort?

'He brought me presents….' Phos gripped the irons. 'Why didn't this metal vanish?'

Was she distracting herself? If distraction helped, he might mention his talking to a woman built from mist and water.

'There's a passage further on,' Mitch said.

Phos paused for a heartbeat before lurching towards Mitch, and Caliper forced himself onward, but his overalls caught on a metal prong and ripped. The passageway tunnelled into a cramped office where three books, a rope and a brass rod sat on a narrow desk.

'There're Dad's books, and that's his.' Phos snatched the rod. A sob escaped her lips, but she held the tube up to a skylight and twisted one end. The tube lengthened. 'Still works.'

'What works?'

She pocketed the tube and the rope. 'It shows faraway things like they're closer. I'll show you later.'

A hundred years of careful handling had smoothed the book's edges. Hymnals, verses for church services, and older than any book he'd seen. They'd fit into his backpack.

'Want me to take those?'

Phos blinked before nodding.

'Let's keep searching.' A drawer offered papers and a heavy rubber-coated rod. His thumb touched a button, and brilliant white light sprayed against the ceiling – his thumb jerked away, and the light vanished.

Mitch whistled. 'Torches, handheld lanterns. We're not supposed to see those.'

'We're not supposed to own candles, so we'll take it. Anything else we need?'

'I need air,' Phos said.

The sun's arch had slid eveward, and labourers had battered down a row of shacks to fuel campfires. Lost children latched on to bereaved parents to forge new families, and squeals capered across the false village. Ahead, people toasted bread and made soup at a forge.

Distant cries pealed out from behind, and Phos stopped fidgeting. One moment of silence passed before she wheeled around.

'That's Mum's voice, behind us.' Phos loped back towards the ancient monastery.

'Watch for guards, Phos.'

The cries rang out again from one of the surviving rooms on the monastery roof. No telling which doorway in the old monastery led upstairs, but roof timbers had spilled into a ramshackle ramp, and Phos tugged at a plank as Mitch drew up beside her.

'Mitch, I've seen you climb. Can you find your way up with this rope?'

The boy tapped a beam with his foot. One leap, and he ran upward and stretched his arms out before jumping onto a steeper plank and tilting his body. Another jump and another rush forward – he almost reached the top, but wood snapped. Mitch leaped rightward and his body twisted. His feet caught another spar, and he scampered onto the roof.

'He's good. Let's charge people to watch,' Caliper said.

Mitch disappeared for a few heartbeats, but his rope writhed towards them, a black line against the fading light. Phos took it and climbed onto the monastery roof without trouble, but the beams groaned underneath Caliper, and gripping the rope turned his knuckles white. He stumbled onto the roof.

Shadows pooled everywhere, and the surviving walls made a maze of fences rattling in the wind, but those cries had stopped. Phos heaved at one of the wooden panels, but her passion outstripped her strength. Caliper reached out and twisted the wall to open a gap, and she pounced forward with Mitch.

'Careful, Phos; stay together.'

Centuries of weather had chipped chunks from the flat roof, and Torzene's collapse had gouged fresh channels; slabs rocked under his feet. He'd not squeeze through the gap he'd opened, but some obstacles only lived in your mind, and Caliper gripped the crushed wall's underside and pulled until it popped free from the stone.

Three women sat with bruised faces and torn clothes. Rope tied their hands to a bench behind them. Phos cradled a woman's head, and their foreheads rested against each other while Mitch fussed at their restraints. This had been a hall for meetings or feasts, but chaos had stripped the ceiling away, and two bodies filled a far corner beside a huge table. Their entwined cloaks left him staring; the priests wouldn't approve of the blood staining the plaster or the slashed tapestries.

The women turned, their faces sodden with dread, but their gaze flickered over his clothes, and they relaxed.

'Mum, you know our miller, Caliper. He helped us.'

'Yes, hello, Caliper.' Her face was fresh with tears, and a livid bruise wrapped her jaw. Phos's red hair tangled with her mother's long black tresses, and she spent a moment untangling herself.

'Hello, Shelaker. What happened?'

'They tied us here hours ago. I didn't believe I'd see sky again until this shaking. The whole building twisted, and our roof slid right away. Do you have water?'

'Here, take it slow.' A gash ran along her lower leg, but Caliper's reeper cloth stopped the blood.

'We wanted rain for drinking, but you came. What happened here, Phos?'

'Caliper happened, but he's not talking.'

Caliper stood and corked his water bottle. Still the wrong time to mention Christina; he'd not want to scare the girl, but he'd play with thoughts of bringing Phos to Christina. Fading daylight meant evening winds, and tomorrow's light would bring more priests, so he needed haste, and he still had damage to heal.

'I'll cut your bindings,' Caliper said. 'How did your priests die?'

'There were five, and two wanted to feed us.' Shelaker took a deep breath. 'The others said the plan didn't have spare food.'

'The plan?' Caliper fished Christina's tools from his backpack and set his knife to cut their bindings.

'They told us to eat less. Everything measured, and no growing extra or saving food for feasts. One of them said nothing mattered long-term.' Shelaker faced her neighbour. 'What was the phrase?'

'"Hard landing." We didn't understand but they argued. The room shook and twisted, and they screamed and fought. They killed the two who didn't want the hard landing.'

'Hardly a fight: those hard-landing priests brought knives,' Shelaker said.

'It's the shock: it breeds anger.' Caliper stripped away the binding twine. 'That's you free, but keep rubbing your wrists. I'll have you clear soon, Shelaker, since everything's rotten.'

'We found Dad's telescope and books inside a brick hut, but do you know where he's gone?'

'I've not seen him since we arrived, but keep looking.'

'Don't worry.' Phos kissed her mother's forehead.

The twine wrapping Shelaker's wrists snapped, and the woman cradled her jaw before heaving herself upward to clasp Caliper's shoulders.

'Thank you, Caliper. Where do we search?'

'You're hurt and need rest, so leave the looking to us, but we must leave the roof before the evening winds.' Caliper sliced through the last woman's bindings and handed over a water bottle before brushing plaster from their shoulders.

'Mum, there're a sea of empty huts below; Leester people might have their own area. We'll find Dad.' She whispered in her mum's ear and smiled before glancing at Caliper.

Wind buffeted them as they stepped onto the roof. Below, huts spread out into the gloom. One distant fire had spread into a shack, and its flickering light scattered shadows through the village. Caliper layered beams from roof to ground to ease the women's route, and they crept downward while clutching Mitch's rope.

'They'll look like other villagers,' Caliper said.

Phos stayed silent before facing him. 'The priests heard me ask a question at school, and afterwards they singled my parents out, so can questions cause damage?'

Caliper watched Phos's mum and her friends pick their way over rubble. 'The church wants control, but it'll get nothing until we lose our strength, and this place is meant to weaken us.'

'They built this place to control?'

'I knew Torzene as a monastery where good

men harmed no one, but now priests are building a prison. The priests have been binding people tighter and tighter these last few years till no one breathes without their say – can't grow this; got to let guards check your tools – and now those rules have spawned this place. It's slow-spreading, like the rotting fields, but everything's there.'

'I still need to find Dad.'

'There's wind to avoid, but I'll help.'

He'd dream of Christina tonight, that was sure, but while he stayed awake, he'd help the girl. Churchmen had written the girl's name in their priest letters, and those scratching runes always smelt of secrets and trouble. If she came with him to Christina, the guards would come screaming, but helping Phos find her dad might ease a chunk of his guilt, like rubbing dock leaves after you'd touched a nettle. He'd no room for caution now: if he ignored the girl's spirit he'd suffer.

Chapter 10: the words of stepping out

Shadows swallowed Mum's figure. Raindrops spattered against Phos's face, and she raised her tunic collar before walking to the eveward roof edge. Clouds hid the sun's arch, and the moor stretched into the distance while the shattered remains of Torzene's rooms lay scattered over the slope. Splinters needled her palms; hugging Mum had let her ignore the pain, but now it flowed back.

Mitch and Caliper stood behind her.

'You'll think you've seen the last priest, but one more always slopes out of the woodwork, so we stay sharp,' Caliper said.

Mitch sneezed. 'Your dad had illegal books, so the high priests would have words for him, and they work high up.'

'It's a right scrap they have on fighting for the higher rooms. "Climbing the stair," they say.'

'And now there's no upstairs 'cause the top rooms fell forward, and they're smashed.' Mitch pointed forward.

Skewed and broken plasterboard sheets caught the wind on the moor below, and scraps of resin paper blew past. Below, half a dozen rooms clung together like battered dice. Two bodies slumped over the moor like broken puppets, and Phos shivered.

'We've steps leading down,' Caliper said. 'Want to search those cabins?'

Phos nodded. What nightmares did those broken rooms hide, and why hadn't they found Dad? She'd cross them off her list before searching the monastery. Stale grey light doused the world wall on her right as shadows grew around her.

Caliper took the stairs two at a time and kicked a box out of his path before skidding onto the road below the monastery. The miller's hands blended skill with passion – he'd bandaged Mum's leg without fuss or trouble – and Phos followed him onto the moor.

Several cubicles had survived the fall. The closest one was a half-crushed box open to the air on one side. Caliper grabbed his torch.

'Everyone will see,' Mitch said.

'We're visible now.'

'Priests will think we're other priests, and they'll come running.'

'I'll handle them.'

Phos rested her hand against a battered wall and waited as Caliper draped cloth over the torch's head. He walked to the open end and snapped on the light.

Loose paper and tapestries curled around a table's broken legs, and silvery goblets rested on the dark grass. A dagger pierced the soil. Nothing else showed, and Phos rested her eyes.

Another tumbled room sat further down the slope. A doorway had survived but now sat horizontal. Caliper glanced at her and gripped the door before heaving it up like a flap to flood the inside with light, and rays shone through the cube's gaps.

Words wouldn't come, so she waited as Caliper's head nudged inside. His gaze fixed on the far corner, and his head stayed still. At last he turned back to her. 'Don't go in there.'

'Is it a body?'

'I'll not lie: they've cut his throat and tied his hands, but there's no way your eyes should see this.'

'What does he look like?'

Caliper fell silent.

'You can't keep me out,' Phos said. She stood beside Caliper, and he jabbed his arm out to block her from the doorway, but she gripped his sleeve. 'Can you describe him?'

'You want the knowing?'

Phos nodded.

'There's fine blonde hair on him, and good clothes, and he wears a waistcoat.'

Phos knew other men with similar hair, and money counters liked their waistcoats, but what did finding the two together mean? She dashed to a corner. They'd stitched the walls together with rope, but the fall had sliced through the cords, and she wrestled back a plasterboard sheet.

'No, Phos. Stay.'

The plasterboard snapped as Caliper let his torchlight die. She scurried through the gap, and enough light crept into the shattered cubicle to show a body on grass – half-covered by a crumpled reed mat. Blood matted half the hair, and for a heartbeat, the darkness let her hope she'd found a stranger, but her eyes lingered. There were the hooked nose and thin lips he'd given her, and those blonde eyebrows he'd always fussed over. She'd grown up with this face. He'd bathed her and read stories and scolded her and coaxed her through illness. Silent now, his thin lips pressed together, and his eyes stayed closed.

Death had drained a quality she couldn't name to leave this cold mask of a face. Phos's gaze veered to the scar ripped across his throat, a dark red invasion, and an end to the shelter he'd always offered. Rough cords bound his wrists to his belt while blood soaked his shirt and waistcoat.

Phos's fingers raised themselves to her throat. Were any guards watching? Had anyone seen her squeeze inside this broken room? She slid her hands under his waistcoat to learn if his warmth tarried there, but she felt nothing, and tears fell from her cheeks to leave icy trails she'd never forget. What had their last shared words been? Time might let her remember, but for now speech wouldn't come.

Caliper and Mitch opened the gap. Phos unclasped her fingers from Dad's chest and stroked his cheek before standing. Her red-headed doll sat in her backpack, and part of her demanded she leave it here, but her hands stayed to wrap Dad's face.

'I can say the words,' Caliper said. 'I'll never make a priest, but I've heard the words of parting.'

Phos wiped her eyes. 'Later. Those are church words, and the church killed him. Find much else?'

'I've not looked, so should I keep looking?'

'I need to know where this started. I need…I need another room.'

Caliper flicked on his torch and stared at the far wall before hoisting it into the air. Phos and Mitch followed towards the next heap of broken timber, where three walls still held together to shape a corner huddling in twilight. Blinking didn't stop her remembering Dad, but she'd keep moving.

Tens of books had spilled over mud here, and shattered chairs filled the corner. A framed mirror still clasped the wall.

'Any plans, Phos?'

She bent to scoop a book from the muck and angled its spine towards Caliper's light. *Herbs for Medicine*, illegal enough to make her gasp. She'd never concentrate now, but she'd savour these words later and remember Dad by learning.

'I spent ages watching for change, but now nothing stays still.'

'Let's take a couple,' he said. 'They're heavy, so choose—'

Shouts from behind, and Phos swung around as a dark figure crashed into Caliper. The miller staggered before twisting to face his attacker, but his torch smashed onto the floor to fling shadows over the walls. Leather tunic and belt; the guard bellowed and punched Caliper's face, and their arms locked.

The guard screamed. 'Ma'am, this way! Villagers.'

Caliper's leg buckled, and he slammed against the earth. The guard pounced on Caliper's chest and grabbed his neck.

Phos froze as part of her wanted to run screaming into the night. If she smashed the mirror shards might come, but guards always laced daggers into their jackets. The guard bent over Caliper's face and roared. What had Dad seen in his last moments? Caliper scrabbled at the priest's wrists, but his grip slipped, and Mitch stood still.

Another figure loomed from darkness: a hooded and cloaked priest.

'Some help here, ma'am.'

The priest tossed back the hood. There stood a

slim woman with an age-stroked face and hooked nose. A slick of grey hair coated her scalp. She plucked a small dagger from her belt and rested her free hand on the guard's shoulder before slicing her blade across his throat.

One heartbeat of stillness passed before the guard's hands snapped against his neck, and he gurgled out a scream as blood spattered over Caliper's chest. The woman stepped back with the blade balanced in her wiry fingers. The guard fell backwards and slumped over the grass, and the woman's lined face broke into a gentle smile as she sheathed her dagger.

'Caliper. Lovely to meet you at last. Reading about you wasn't the same.' Her words sounded as if a sculptor had carved each syllable, and her eyes darted over Phos and Mitch. 'I don't believe anyone's introduced us, so excuse me one moment.' She twirled to the mirror and flicked back a strand of grey hair. A ring with a black jewel sat on one finger, and shimmering crimson cloth lined her entire cloak.

'There. Where were we? Introductions, yes. I am Frinelia, and I apologise for my ex-colleague's rudeness. We had differences of opinion, though I believe they're now resolved.' Her boot tapped the guard's skull. 'Aren't they?'

Phos closed her mouth. Here stood a female priest of the highest rank, a smiling killer who'd read about Caliper, and the four-syllable name rattled around Phos's mind.

Frinelia smiled while finding out their names. 'I would enjoy your company in my cell. Rank entitled me to a high room, but I prefer keeping contact with the ground, and for once I chose well. Can you walk with us, Caliper?'

The miller struggled upright. 'I should thank you, but you're a priest.'

'I left the priesthood long ago, but the church never knew, and I kept the cloak.' Frinelia flicked a speck of dust from her sleeve as she waited for his reply.

Caliper picked up his torch. 'Can I trust you?'

'Should the tiny matter of my saving your life prove insufficient, I can alter my wardrobe.' Frinelia flicked her cloak from her shoulders, and for an instant, their broken room turned rosy.

'Disrobe, and you're still a priest.'

Frinelia held the cloak before her and let its hem brush the ground. Her eyes closed as she mouthed words. The grass shimmered, and Frinelia's cloth glistened before flaring into a forest of red and orange streaks to flicker like fire without heat. Flames ate half the cloak before Frinelia opened her eyes. Her hands opened, and fire gulped down the remaining cloth before winking out. Dusty streaks rose through the air.

Caliper stared. 'Who have you talked to?'

'Your exploits caused quite the stir in the church, and as we share talents we should talk.'

The miller slipped his torch into his blood-soaked apron and winced. 'Learn that at priest school, did you?'

Dust still hovered in the air. Was this a cousin of Rastersen's candle trick? Had this woman shared a teacher with Caliper, and why wasn't he surprised at the cloak's burning?

Frinelia didn't waver. 'One question remains, Caliper, one crucial query: how do you take your tea?'

***

The pale lantern in Frinelia's cell struggled against night. Age-chipped stone loomed on four sides. Caliper smelt roses, and threadbare tapestries hung from two walls while Frinelia's cot rested above a thick black rug, and guards must have dragged in a trunk and a table. Books and crockery littered the floor beside the shards of a smashed mirror, while three wooden heaps had been chairs.

Frinelia touched the lantern, and the glimmer grew to show a body sprawled in a corner.

The priestess smiled and pointed at the corpse. 'I prefer walking my clients to their resting place before their passing, but we must grasp opportunities as they arise. Could you porter for me?'

'A friend?'

'A friend of your attacker; a puppeteer.'

'You're killing entertainers?'

'Not quite. It's our term for a certain group. Tea before explanations.'

Still warm, the body had the spotless skin of a young man, and Caliper carried him several yards before laying him on grass and smoothing his hair; no telling what lies others had fed him. Ahead, cooking fires flared between huts, and cheers rang out as a ring of dancers linked arms around a pile of burning clothes.

Laughter might mean there'd be no priests left except this uncloaked woman who'd read his secrets, a smiling killer who'd saved his life but kept her dagger. Was she hiding a spare cloak?

Caliper headed back as Phos and Frinelia rigged a tattered sheet over their doorway.

Phos's fingers twitched. 'Mum needs telling, so can we find her?'

'Certainly, though I'd advise waiting till dawn.' Frinelia draped a blanket over a box before kneeling beside a fireplace and heating water in a battered tin. Mitch stacked her books in neat piles as Phos sagged onto the rug – her hands trembled.

Caliper sat before her and held out her dad's

hymnal, and she paused before taking the book and stroking it.

'Remember the church words of bearing?'

Her reedy voice quivered as she recited. '"Strong the family of one child, weaker the family of two, weakest of all the family of weeds and dregs."'

'It says that now, but your dad's book is older than me and tells a different story.' Caliper teased the book open and pointed. '"Give birth to the future, and let your seed bear witness to the passage of the years."'

'Those aren't the words.'

'Those were the words.'

Phos's body shivered as her fingers darted through the pages. 'Who wrote this?'

Caliper shrugged. 'Ask our priestess. They say nothing changes, but now you've proof they're lying. Your dad knew the hymns had changed, though I suppose fear sealed his lips.'

Frinelia poured boiling water into a teapot, and Caliper winced. Was she brewing one of those damp flower teas?

'Even the quietest people have stories,' Frinelia said. 'I should hear yours, but you deserve mine, so let's start there.' She lobbed her dagger onto the table – its blade was clean. 'Our miller noticed the changes.'

'Stinking grain and rotten wheat?'

Frinelia nodded and wrapped a shawl around her

shoulders. 'Orchards stand bare, and berries wither on the vine; vegetables rot before they ripen, and animals fight over scraps.'

'And fighting spreads our way.' Caliper perched on the cot. Had Frinelia heard of ghosts, and would a sane man mention women made of mist? Christina's plea festered inside him, but he stayed silent.

Frinelia sat on her trunk. 'Walk the world's length, and you'll see the same story: whole stretches of our ring stand barren, and each year more land falls into famine; streams become bitter, and blackberries poison children. Nature is dying.'

Phos glanced up. 'You said nature never changes.'

'We said enough to stop panic, and until now we scraped together enough food.'

'Until now, but the decay spreads, so what's next?'

Mitch arranged the surviving crockery into squares.

'Tell couples to have fewer children,' Caliper said.

Frinelia bowed her head. 'We changed those sermons in my youth, but words and unenforceable laws weren't enough; we required new directions.'

'You tried controlling food.'

'Hard times breed hard choices. We tried

cooking moss and bark, but nothing worked, and failure led to desperation, and desperation spawned puppeteers.'

'You mentioned them. Who are they?'

'I'll need tea before describing them, but let Mitch pour.'

Caliper cradled his tiny cup and sipped, the tea too delicate to wake his tongue.

Frinelia stared upward. 'Some are content to let others live as they please. Surround them with people dancing in different ways or eating peculiar foods or wearing strange clothes, and they'll smile or ask polite questions. But others fret at differences; they'll say there's one correct way to carry out each action, one correct way to dress or behave or talk. They'll force people into uniforms or demand everyone eats at the same time or prays in the same position. They're easy to disgust; they're always scrubbing. I often wonder why. Perhaps, at the core, there's a desire to control and manipulate; some find joy in seeing others dance to their tune. Maybe they sense an emptiness inside themselves, and controlling the world is how they know they exist.'

'Puppeteers,' Caliper said.

'My friends wanted a gentle decline where fresh laws made births rare. Our population would dwindle until it matched the food supply. Only a scattering of villages in fertile areas would remain, and the pain of seeing empty cradles might be tempered by hope for nature's recovery.'

Frinelia drained her tea. Her neck glistened under firelight as she refilled her tiny cup, and Caliper waited as moths jittered against the doorway's sheet.

'The puppeteers accused us of weakness and sloth. They sneered and called us soft landers.'

'They wanted the hard landing,' Phos said.

'Who have you talked to?'

'Many people.'

'You learn well.' Frinelia cradled her cup in her palm. 'Puppeteers preferred to invite death. At first our urge to stay human made us reject their ideas, but our first plans failed, and panic spread. The puppeteers learned how to scare people and threatened disaster if people didn't obey their commands. People obeyed.'

Caliper scratched his ear. Had Christina seen a thousand murders while staying silent?

Frinelia stood and stretched. Her hands sought the base of her spine. 'The bad areas saw controls and rationing and harsh laws, and spies sprouted like toadstools. No one disputed the need for new laws, but the puppeteers saw those laws as roads.'

'Flies to horse shit,' Mitch said.

'What a lovely boy. The puppeteers forced more limits onto families, not to help the world but to control it.'

'Did yous keep shifting my tools?'

Frinelia nodded. 'Puppeteers use fear – use it so well I suspect they terrify themselves. One morning I stood before a map that charted a swathe of our ring. The puppeteer leader swept his hands over drawings of villages and towns, and uttered two words: "Remove them." Even the other puppeteers shuddered, but orders stink of strength, and chaos makes toughness erotic. I suggested testing our policies on a small village, but action carries its own romance, and action made the church regard its own people as burdens.'

'Can't be,' Mitch said. 'People would have complained.'

'They did complain, right until they were silenced.'

Phos rocked back. 'Where did everyone go?'

'Camps like Torzene. Rooms at the top where the mighty watched their property, and one vast eating area to confine the families we used to help. Set mealtimes, with thinner soup each day, and spies listening everywhere.' The fire popped, and Frinelia flexed her neck as the figures on her tapestries seemed to shimmer.

'But people still needed feeding.'

'Puppeteers waited until the new routines became habit and people became weak. The fences closed. People stayed inside but no food entered. Illness became disease, and the church waited until the crying stopped, waited for the hard landing. Puppeteers saw soft landers as a threat, and they spewed fear through our ranks and terrorised my people into silence. The plans rolled forward like an immense cartwheel, and the villages around Torzene would have emptied, but our miller came. Caliper, your destruction makes my learning look like a child's burbling – I should applaud.'

'Why d'you think I'm to blame?'

'Who else, Caliper? Your work carries its own signature. Four hours ago I imagined our fight lost, but in a single heartbeat you transformed my world. Mortar rained from my ceiling; you destroyed my chairs and broke cherished crockery, threw me against the ground and bruised me where I cannot reach, but you kindled hope. Don't let us hope without reason; say how you destroyed Torzene.'

'You can't stay silent,' Phos said.

Could he explain without mentioning Christina? He stared at the floor. Frinelia brought light to his confusion, and Phos's passion would help him punch through obstacles, but one whiff of madness and they'd abandon him.

'You'll not believe me.'

'I never believed Torzene would fall, so don't

fret; the unbelievable keeps happening.' Frinelia gestured for his words.

Caliper leaned back, and the cot creaked as he braced himself for jeers.

'I heard stories at school, and I'm sure you did too: your ghost, the tall woman who comes at night and tries to speak. The world shows through her.'

Frinelia's mouth hung open. 'The eidolon – you witnessed the eidolon?'

'We spoke; it was ages before we understood each other.'

Frinelia's mouth stayed open. She had good teeth.

Caliper grinned. 'You said a name there.'

'The eidolon. We've records of sightings, but you've spoken? Scholars spend half their lives picking over tiny details of her appearances, but I've never….' Her voice faded.

Mitch stared at Frinelia. 'What's an eidolon?'

'Older than our learning and beyond any book; people map sightings and try predicting her next appearance, but in truth we understand nothing.'

'So there's only one? Am I special?'

Frinelia coughed. 'We only see one at a time, but if she's alone, she moves like lightning, and many believe she ignores distance. You've talked with the eidolon?'

'We've chatted.'

'Chatted? Our best minds can't communicate, but you've chatted?' Frinelia rocked on the trunk. 'People said you'd stolen books; we knew you'd learned exploits, and one member of my team thought you talked into air. I should sift through wreckage for your file. You'd enjoy the read. Can you two speak now?'

'She comes when she pleases, but being near the henges works best.'

'Many scholars thought the henges attracted her.'

Phos stood. 'Why destroy Torzene if you didn't know about this hard landing?'

'The choice was mine, but Christina handed me the tools,' Caliper said.

'Chris…Christina?' Frinelia struggled with the sounds. 'You know her name?'

'We shared names.' No need to wait for Frinelia's recovery. 'She wanted a signal, so she showed me the making of light. Fresh sails and new teeth for the gear wheels, with lanterns nicked from churches, and it all made a grand show, since her eyes pick up the special light your lanterns splash out. Christina made the candles I used at Ferstus.'

'You sparked that riot?'

'We're a pair, but I only ever see her image, and

she wants to meet me for real, though her sight's strange, which makes the finding hard. I stumbled across Torzene, and those swarming guards meant danger, so she suggested a diversion, and that's this wreckage. Christina wanted to steal metal, the nails and screws and such, and she needed my permission to go about the stealing.' Caliper gazed at the fire and chewed his lip. 'Never thought I'd see the end of the breaking and crumpling; if I saved anyone it was an accident.'

'I won't forget you saving Mum,' Phos said.

Mitch stared. 'So is Christina human or ghost?'

'No one ever told me what they mean by *ghost*, but there's thinking each time we meet, and it's not all mine, so she's human enough.'

No laughing or sneering, not yet; perhaps they'd make a group. He'd keep talking.

'You're best saying she's human but different: her name doesn't get longer with age, and she'll use words I've never known, while she can't follow my simplest sayings. The tricks…. What was your word, Frinelia? She taught me plenty, but I imagine she holds the best back.'

Frinelia glided to the doorway and peered past the sheet. 'Exploits. Learning them is supremely expensive, but I paid in ways most churchmen couldn't, and I gathered many. I kept moving to leave my past behind, and at each new abode, my talent, my armoury of exploits, brought me a decent status.'

Phos fidgeted. Was she blushing? 'We can learn from… What did you call her?'

'Christina.'

'Such a funny name. How did you learn these exploits?'

Caliper shrugged. 'I grew up with some, and a handful slid into my dreams, but Christina taught me more. How to make trees glow or grub up weeds or tell vines to clamber over a trellis overnight.'

'How do you use them?'

'Empty your mind, and picture your wants before rolling words through your mind, and you'll feel threads spool from your fingers to do your work. Here's one.' Caliper grabbed a blanket from the cot and closed his eyes. It snapped into a rigid square, and he let it clatter to the floor.

'Not seen that one before, Caliper – we must compare. Mine are mere tricks. You saw me burn cloth, and I can break pots and cups; fine for impressing newcomers, but Caliper's talent leaves me shaking. It's late; sleep will let us ponder, and I have blankets untouched by any miller. Tomorrow Torzene will crawl with priests, but for now I'll mention a place dawnward of us, a museum city where half the scholars scrabble for clues concerning the eidolon. A handful claim they've seen her drift through walls.'

Phos choked on her tea. She stared at Caliper but stayed silent.

Caliper's mouth felt dry, his tongue papery. 'Is it above a hill?'

'Yes. Yes, it is,' Frinelia said. 'How did you know?'

'I'll explain later.'

Phos and Mitch shared the cot, while Frinelia laid a pillow on the floor. Caliper snuffed out the lantern to let the night drift inside, and he lay by their curtain to block the entrance. He'd relax with the breeze: for the first time he'd mentioned Christina to others, and no one would call him mad for saying those words. He'd learned an extra scatter of details about his ghost, and he might even dream of his path to her home. There'd be nightmares too, priests and their guards rising from the wreckage, sharp knives in the darkness to stop him reaching Christina. He stared into the darkness as he remembered Christina asking him to bring friends – another nightmare to handle.

Chapter 11: towards your second syllable

Phos awoke into the bitter dark of Frinelia's cell. Dad had smiled in her dreams, but now she remembered the savage gash torn through his throat. She drew Frinelia's musty blankets around her face and screwed up her eyes: the next bout of sleep might show his face again. But the minutes passed, and Caliper's rasping snores echoed over the stone walls. She blinked and sat upright.

She'd seen Caliper work the lantern, and she set it glowing over Frinelia's books to form a puddle of yellow light while Mitch brought her a blanket. The tapestry figures loomed above, creamy-white characters with bulbous heads and enormous backpacks roaming a grey desert, and her fingers flicked over the stained and patched spines of Frinelia's books. Even under lantern light, the pages were amber with age. One volume held etchings of birds frozen in mid-air with writing flowing around their wings, and others showed plants with sliced-open stems and petals.

Phos ran her palm over a stack of books; stories of her world's origins might crouch inside, or even an image of her world seed. She tiled the stone floor with open volumes, but each picture spawned questions. Why were wrens so small? Why did owls have eyes on the front of their heads? Why did birds come from eggs? One page showed acorns looking like a ball in a cup, fatter than those she'd played with – were these older versions?

Frinelia's breathing stayed slow, and maybe secrets lurked underneath her silvery hair. The lantern faded, and a delicate radiance rose from Frinelia's ancient tunic, like a memory of Phos's cloak, a faded whisper of liramic's blue-and-green dance.

Sleep nagged her after hours of squinting, and she returned to her cot. At first her dreams stayed gentle; dolls capered around her hands, but Dad's spindly figure reappeared with a face stiffened by sadness, and her dolls crumbled as he shuffled backwards into fog. Again her eyes opened.

She'd find Mum and slip away to rebuild a family with her new friends; Mitch had mentioned people surviving in forests, and Frinelia's books described food. Everyone left home once their second syllable had rooted, boys after learning their trade, and girls once they'd dredged up a husband, and the hymnals held words of stepping to colour in the boundary – she'd secretly learned them when her school had become a cage.

Her idea withered in her mind. Guards would prowl through the forests, and the trees were already dying, so living without a family at thirteen was a cruel fantasy.

Phos stayed awake as daylight trickled through the doorway. Mitch curled beside her with his hand draped over her shoulder, and Frinelia lay face up with closed eyes as Caliper snored. Her stomach rumbled as chill air numbed her fingers.

Enough dawn to return to Frinelia's books. One volume held a long paper strip folded over and glued into the front. Phos prised the yellowing leaves apart and held her breath as she pulled. Fold after fold unpicked itself as she paced backwards, and a faint mustiness breathed out from the creases.

A long picture, a faded drawing of her world, with the world walls inked along the edges, and the artist had etched in five yards of careful detail.

Frinelia's voice drifted out. 'That's a small section, Phos, but it shows our location and destination. A friend wanted to map the entire ring with a thousand volumes, but the church stopped him.'

'I must find Mum, but let's take it.'

Frinelia sat up. 'I can't believe I'm saying this, but we'll cut those pages out. Be quick: the priests will return today.'

Phos stared at the faint ink. People had walked the ring and returned with stories of eveward grasslands petering into deserts. Struggle past, and rich jungle waited, which led into ice-scraped mountains and a vast sea stretching wall to wall. Beyond sat the Outland:

glass mountains criss-crossed with ravines. Keep going, and the pattern repeated in reverse, and you'd finish where you started, with a thousand bruises.

She wanted to watch daylight trickle through the Outland's rocks, but her friends had laughed. Her story had made Dad smile, and he'd drawn a circle on a precious scrap of paper. He'd marked their home before curving his pencil to the far side, at least a year's journey. She had a reply: quarries grubbed stone from earth; she'd shape a huge pit and scramble down her tunnel to the Outland, though she couldn't work out what happened halfway. Again he'd grinned: digging one mile would take her whole life. He'd recited the story her teachers had fed her – like a ring, their world had no beginning. Phos had argued change happened when plants grew, but Dad's patience had worn her down.

She'd taken the drawing to bed, a circle for her world, and sketched sea and mountains alongside desert and forests before scratching in her version of the Outland's glass. Sleep had taken her, and her dream had seen her tunnel struggle through air and towards the world's vault before burrowing into the outside world.

Teachers claimed those rocks went on forever, but she'd not believe them; she'd keep her dream of rising and running her hands over the vault's unknown surface.

Now she trembled beside those silent books as her breath fogged the air and cold leached through her boots. Caliper snorted himself awake and jerked upright as daylight touched him, and Frinelia rose to pour water into a basin.

'Your tunic, Frinelia, is it liramic?'

The priestess ran her hand over her chest. 'My daughter harvested and wove the cloth.'

'You've a daughter?'

'Had. She was your age when the fever came.'

'I'm sorry… I….'

'Don't apologise. I should remember her more. Can I tell you the story?'

Phos nodded.

'I remember cradling her as the fever burned, and I'll never forget her last breath fading on my cheek. Afterwards I sat as priests mumbled about harmony and nature's plans, and anger burned through me like molten iron, but I kept my face calm and my hands steady, even when I heard stories of healing machines reserved for high priests.'

'You're a high priest.'

'I am now, or maybe I should say I'm good at acting. My daughter's last breath set me climbing the stair, and each step became a monument to my daughter.' Frinelia clasped her hands together. 'Revenge makes a strange fuel; I've never felt tired, but

I never enjoyed success. I kept wanting more – another promotion to hit the church harder, another exploit – but I'd have waited forever if Caliper hadn't arrived with his strange learning.' She faced the miller and smiled. 'I gained strength to burn my cloth, and if he shares his knowledge our fight may continue.'

Caliper looked at his hands. Timbers crashed and tumbled outside – was there running?

'We must leave,' Frinelia said. 'The horsemen will have reached their local keep, and they'll return with others.'

Pain gripped Phos's chest. 'We can't leave until I've found Mum; we'll hide if we need.'

'Be quick. Once she's found, we should aim for the museum city to dawnward.'

Caliper picked up a blanket. 'What's this city called?'

'Morzenthal,' Frinelia said.

Phos remembered the name falling from Dad's lips and the hushed tones in his voice.

'Our world swarms with guards and clerics, but it's the one place they avoid,' Frinelia said. 'Decades ago it was a home for retired priests, and the elderly still arrive, but now Morzenthal is a home for different thoughts. Priests who can't stomach the church's thinking, commoners with extraordinary powers, misfits and adventurers of the mind, each outsider changes Morzenthal and shifts it further from orthodoxy. We're out of the way and without power, so the church usually ignores us, though I've known priests to hammer on our gates with questions for our archivists. We play at being absent-minded librarians, which eases their prying. If you value curiosity over control you may enjoy the place.'

'What questions do the priests have?'

'Crop histories, plans for antique machines or ancient maps, questions that leave us cringing even though we smile outwardly. We bottle knowledge too dangerous to store elsewhere, and too useful to destroy.'

'You said it's a museum.'

'An outer ring is crammed with exhibits and models and relics that move as if alive, and I'm sure the exhibits enjoy terrorising trespassers; the unwary die each year.'

Phos's eyebrows rose. 'The exhibits can think?'

'Good question. You should decide for yourself, but the carousel's exhibits learned survival by fighting each other, so that area is perilous.'

'You're sure Morzenthal's safe?' Mitch pulled on his backpack.

Frinelia slid a slim book from a stack. 'It's not safe, but it is the safest place.'

'So, who lives in the rest of the city?'

‘On occasion, you’ll meet someone too old to work the fields and too frail to fight, but whose mind still seethes with skills. They’ve learned how people think. They give orders that sound nothing like orders, and they’ve united at Morzenthal.’

‘There’re more like you? You should have warned us.’

‘No one is quite like me; one pleasure of age is knowing you’re unique. I often waited there while my past faded, and many there see me as middle-aged.’

‘You’re not middle-aged: you never grew up with those wrinkles.’ Mitch grinned.

‘Aren’t you the charmer?’ Frinelia handed Caliper three books.

Dad had died at Torzene, but he’d lived in Morzenthal, and dust from his breath might still drift in its halls. They might scratch out new lives in this museum city, or cook meals together while poring over books, and she’d learn without teachers.

‘Let’s find my mum and bring her.’

Caliper gathered food and water bottles as Phos shivered, but a hunk of bread quelled her hunger, and she stared at him.

‘Yesterday you asked if Morzenthal stood on a hill. What made you ask?’

‘Christina won’t know our place names, but she wanted us to meet, and she noticed the light I ground out, and learned enough to whisper directions.' Caliper looked past her. '"My city sits atop a hill," she said.' His eyes fixed her for a moment. 'She told me to bring friends as well, though I don't know if she meant you.'

Frinelia packed a small bag and glanced around before smiling. Her hand brushed the door's sheet aside. 'Head dawnward: if your mother found the Leester villagers she should be at the far fence.'

Phos blinked in the light and struggled to keep up as Caliper and Frinelia strode forward. Mud and sawdust everywhere; clay caked her tunic, and ahead two half-naked men wrestled beside a smoking cauldron as others cheered.

Caliper picked a yellow weed from the ground and stuffed it into his apron. 'Why were your people raising that barn at Ferstus? Shoddy work, that was.'

'Chaos, Caliper. Many churchmen fight for control, and each seeks to stamp his own desires onto the world. One group wanted a small Torzene in each village, though I understand some miller upset their plans.'

'Chaos is fun.'

Stragglers hid as they threaded past huts, and the stringy grass grew longer here. People streamed through gaps knocked into the ramshackle fence, and ragged children eyed them before darting away. Caliper doled out reeper cloth to a young woman with a gashed arm, and three ten-year-old boys followed them for a few paces until Frinelia stared back.

The priestess jarred to a halt and urged them into an empty hut smelling of soap before holding up her arms for silence. Phos waited in the gloom as her boots crunched on the ruddy soil underfoot, and she glanced at Frinelia. Shadows flickered outside; a priest and two leather-clad guards strolled past, and Frinelia recoiled before letting a slow sigh escape her lips.

She stepped outside and Phos followed, but the three figures had waited for them. Rastersen's bulk hovered a few feet away – his black cloak was smeared with grey – and two guards stood behind with folded arms and scowls, bookends to Rastersen's jowly grin.

'Here's what used to be a priest, and my curious young lady from the windmill.' He plucked a rope from his belt.

'Show due respect, Rastersen; do not dare ignore my rank.'

'A cloakless officer has no rank.'

'I remember you begging to keep your cloak while we discussed your inability to follow the simplest order.'

Rastersen grinned. 'You burned your cloak and treated commoners to church secrets.' His gaze glided to Phos. 'Maybe you should ask the priestess questions; ask what benefit she seeks from your presence, what risks she will have you endure. Remember those children you took charge of, Frinelia, back in Adastran? Were their bodies recovered, and what did you tell their parents?'

Rastersen's eyes snapped back to Phos and held her like glue – shouldn't her body obey orders? Frinelia's hand gripped her shoulder.

'Does Frinelia aim to test the terrors outside Torzene on your body?'

'Always threatening children,' Frinelia said. 'Afraid adults will fight back?'

'Success comes when you specialise: a craftsman always beats a dabbler, and my guards add richness to my promise. Let's discuss your treason. After your imprisonment, Phos and I can discuss her future career; these changes will open doors for us both.'

Caliper swung his backpack to the ground and reached inside. 'You're ignoring Mitch and me.'

'Keep walking, miller, and take your boy.'

Caliper gripped a candle and pinched the wick. 'These work better at night, but you'll not want the waiting.'

Phos couldn't breathe.

Rastersen snorted. 'Candles? Are you mocking me?'

'Me? Mock? Never.'

'What the…?'

Caliper pointed the candle at a guard. One heartbeat passed before fiery sparks ripped through air to splash against the man's face. Screams rang out, and the guard crashed backwards. Caliper flicked the flaming spray towards Rastersen, and the priest tumbled sideways and hit the earth before curling up. The last guard stood open-mouthed for a heartbeat before darting into the forest of sheds.

Frinelia stared. 'Caliper, what have you…?'

A few final sparks sputtered from the candle, and Caliper lobbed the stump at Rastersen's slick hair. The priest's cloak smoked as he sobbed. The fallen guard didn't move, and Frinelia knelt beside him. 'Still breathing; no idea if he'll see again, but, Caliper, those talents keep coming.' Phos glanced at Rastersen's quaking body.

'You knew his plans; you saw how he looked.'

'I've no criticism: you've saved us. But we've decisions to make.'

'Decisions?'

'I can silence the priest.' Frinelia touched her belt.

'That's your decision?'

'Other priests called me the Cleaner, but not for any dusting talent.'

Rastersen rolled onto his back and groaned. His

eyes stayed shut while his head lolled back, and breath flooded into Phos's lungs.

'Leave him, Frinelia,' she said. 'He's snot and vomit.'

'You're sure?'

'Phos and I are sure.' Caliper squatted on Rastersen's chest and tapped out a smouldering ember on the priest's shoulder. 'Listen, fat boy. Two weeks back I burned my hand on a special candle; they're bastard painful, but I didn't roll around shrieking like a baby.' He shunted forward and gripped Rastersen's throat, and the priest's eyes stayed shut. 'You people gave Phos nightmares, but she's still standing, so without other people's muscle, you're.... What was it, Phos?'

'Snot and vomit.'

'There're some pretty words. You've been thrashed by a girl, so don't think stealing other people's strength makes you strong. That guard who ran off is telling his mates how you cried, so if you see us coming, head the other way – I've plenty candles left.' Caliper flicked Rastersen's ear before standing. 'There's enough; we'll find Phos's mum.'

Rastersen's eyes flicked open to peer at the vault, but his blubbery face stayed still. His stare had wrapped icy chains around her body, but her legs answered her now, and she stepped back; perhaps her second syllable would help her resist more. Rastersen heaved himself onto his side before staggering eveward.

'Torzene's a wounded beast, Phos, so you'll stay sharp.' He grinned and patted her shoulder, and her eyes closed as she felt herself imagining a rising sea and swirling black cloaks flooding the rolling hills. Morzenthal might stand as an island, a single peak of freedom.

Frinelia coughed. 'You've met Rastersen before?'

Phos explained, and the priestess nodded while strolling onward.

'Both Rastersen's parents were full officers, like me. I remember him as a boy of wide-eyed questions and smiles. He loved reading, but that wasn't what priests did; his parents scolded him into the seminary.'

'Should have left him with his books,' Mitch said.

'Apprentice priests are quick to sort out their ranks: you torment others or you're tormented, and Rastersen was bottom of the heap. They'd dangle him naked over the altar before services, or force wine down his throat when he was due to read, or slip ferrets into his bed at night. He was never priest material, and now he's a left foot in a right-footed shoe, all ambition without talent. If he'd chosen his own path....' Frinelia fell silent. 'Perhaps he's trying to remember those book-filled days from before his second syllable.'

'When he owned his future,' Phos said. 'He's been looking for people with talent; he wants more exploits, but does he expect me to grub them up?'

'It's possible; he wants others to work for him.'

Phos frowned. 'I'll ask my own questions.'

Two men kicked planks from a hut beside the fence and threw the wood onto a huge stack to prepare for the evening. A group of women in shawls knitted beside a cart but stopped to watch Frinelia as she glided forward.

'There're brewers from Leester.' Phos pointed at a couple holding hands and sitting with bowed heads outside a hut. She touched the husband's shoulder, and he winced before lifting his face. Red eyes blinked among his bruises.

'Have you seen my mother, Shelaker? She was with two women.'

The brewer pointed dawnward at a hut with liramic petals lacing the doorway, and Phos dodged a handcart as she ran forward.

Silence inside, and two women knelt beside a figure laid on a stack of blankets, but Mum's tunic and sash were unmissable.

'Mum? It's Phos.' Her hand curled around to touch the tears on Mum's cheek.

'You came?'

'I'll not leave.'

'Your father…I stayed, but my friends searched through the night and found his body.'

Phos held Mum's hand as she inched through the story. Her eyes were bloodshot, and she'd chewed her fingernails to the quick. Their tears eased, and they dried each other's faces as Caliper entered with hot water. Frinelia hesitated before producing a tiny cloth bag and making tea to spice their shack with a fragrance halfway between lemon and pine.

Shelaker fell silent and stared at her cup while tweaking her sash. 'Is this frangista?'

'Difficult to obtain, but people praise its soothing qualities, so let us rest before facing future challenges.'

They drank in silence, and Mum's trembling faded as she eased out a smile.

Frinelia's fingers tapped the hut's wall. 'I regret the need to press people, but time passes, and the church will seek to restore Torzene's status as a prison.'

'Best we return home, Phos: it's the best place to remember your father.'

Phos imagined herself meandering home to remember Dad's insane stories, sitting beside the fireplace, where she'd listened to them, reading his books and eating from plates he'd once grasped, but he'd not be there. A family was a cradle, even one without a father, but a cradle was both protection and prison, and avoiding change meant not growing. She'd seen hulking men cling to their parents long after their third syllable had arrived, wolfing down mother's food and cowering inside their tiny world, afraid to learn – a plant stuffed in too small a pot. Phos never knew what happened once their parents died. Rastersen knew where she lived, so perhaps she should have asked Frinelia for cleaning.

'There's a safer place dawnward,' Phos said. 'Dad's been there, and there won't be any priests.'

Mum shook her head. 'I need to give watch in our home: we shared laughter there. Give me a week, Phos; come with me, and we'll wander the forest paths we took. Shouldn't we say goodbye together?'

Frinelia sighed. 'The church will expect people to head home.'

Mum paused before speaking. 'What's this place called?'

'Morzenthal. Dad had books.'

'The museum city?'

'Frinelia's an exhibit,' Mitch said.

'Many thanks, Mitch. The church tries to avoid the place, and it won't expect us to travel there. You'd be welcome; they have space for several villages, even if their food defies description.'

'I'll return to Leester, Phos, and say the words of passing. We built our home ourselves, and you were born there. Doesn't that count?'

'Mum, it's not safe!'

'I can't grieve in a museum. Come with me, and we'll hide in the forest until the priests forget.'

'They won't forget; they'll track you with dogs,' Frinelia said.

'I'll bring pepper,' Mum said. 'They searched our house when they seized us, and they'll not expect anyone to go where they've searched.'

Phos had stopped arguing with Mum years ago: like night followed day, each argument had its counter. Phos's fingers twitched. She'd remember Dad by hunting the words he'd jotted in Morzenthal's books; her fingers might trace over his writing, or the city's dust could hold a trace of his skin. She'd breach the carousel, experience enough, and her second syllable might write itself without a priest's words.

Caliper and Frinelia whispered together for a moment. The miller sat beside Mum and touched her shoulder. 'There's a path between the world wall and Leester's forest that's too stony for horses, so you'll not see churchmen. Stick to the woods when you travel; they'll have combed my windmill's wreckage, so it might mean safety, and it's near your house, isn't it, Phos?'

‘Don’t delay, Mum, and bring your friends.’ They clasped hands before switching into a tense hug. Mum’s oakmoss scent lingered in the chaos, and Phos buried her nose in her neck. Even the plants poisoned people now so she’d spend a few heartbeats here in safety. Morzenthal might be safer than Torzene, but the museum city reeked of danger, and what if the men there knew Rastersen?

No point in worrying - Phos only had one destination, and leaving this shack started her journey. The miller and the priestess would help, but she’d need to pack years of experience into the next few days.

One last squeeze. For an instant, their heartbeats matched, but they pulled apart to face each other.

‘Find the way, Phos. I’ll meet you at Morzenthal.’

Chapter 12: what do you mean by *horse*?

Phos stomped past Caliper and her feet punched the springy turf as if trying to stamp through the soil. She slapped her hand against a wooden stump and heaved through a narrow gap in Torzene's fence. Caliper slouched behind, and a few villagers tore planks away while others straggled outside and milled over the moor's edge.

The dawnward lands stretched ahead, and grassland clung to the landscape like a velvet cloth; steep valleys crinkled across distant rolling hills. Hints of lavender bathed the air, and the green carpet shaded to blue as the grass stalks rippled under wind. A distant forest lined the southern horizon with shadow.

Frinelia pointed south and dawnward. 'Morzenthal's in that direction, and there's a shallow valley we can't yet see, but once we cross we'll reach forest before evening. We'll stick together and keep an easy pace.'

This group's talent might impress Christina, and he'd try to hold them together. Caliper strolled towards Mitch: priests and their guards meant danger on this exposed moor, and Torzene's destruction meant they'd be in arresting mood, so he'd need everyone's skills until they reached the forest's cover.

'You're not wanting to find your dad? He should

be in Torzene.'

'I saw him three huts away from Phos's mum, but he didn't see me.'

'You didn't say hello?'

Mitch's head stayed lowered. 'I wasn't the son he wanted. He always had me fetch and carry, and I can do better. I'm not sure parents are safe now.' He glanced up at Caliper. Mud streaked his face. 'Besides, I want to see Phos's face when she learns there's no world seed.'

Caliper frowned. 'World seed?'

'Phos thinks everything sprouted from an acorn. Plants, animals, hills, rivers, all spewed from a nut. Don't you, Phos?'

The girl paused before stamping forward again to jog down a slope.

'She's too silly for me,' Mitch said.

Caliper sighed. 'If this world sprang from a nut, I wasn't around, so I'm not knowing world seeds. Go watch Phos doesn't trip.'

The girl halted and swung back.

'Sneer as you want, Mitch, but there're always more questions. If there wasn't a world seed, where did everything come from? And, Frinelia, our people break their backs at work; I've known fishermen lose fingers in nets and seen labourers crushed by falling beams, so why hide this learning?' Her fists clenched. 'Do you know how our world started?'

'Might not have been any start,' Mitch said. 'Our world's a ring, and rings don't have starts.'

Frinelia kept silent and splayed her hands out for balance as she edged down their gentle slope.

Phos folded her arms. 'Your hymns have us singing how nature stays perfect, but you made us sing lies every week. Are you sure there's nothing outside our world?'

'Here we go. Let's search her for stupid questions,' Mitch said.

'I'm not ancient enough to remember so far back.' Frinelia glanced at her feet. 'I've heard ten thousand arguments, and our own stories confused us. I never knew if we ever said anything original or wanted to keep our mouths moving. But I had a friend who studied ancient documents. We talked by lamplight for hours and explored every way of thinking, but his mind always returned to the question of our origins. I wish you'd met him.'

Caliper glanced behind; a few figures struggled through the fence, but hiking down the hill threw Torzene's wreckage out of sight.

Frinelia eased herself down the incline. 'My friend gathered pages from antique books. Many were forgeries, but he insisted a handful were genuine. He broke into derelict monasteries with forgotten libraries and spent hours dissecting flowers and seeds, and once I found him hammering rocks into shards. He'd go without meals to visit elders, and travel for weeks at the rumour of a book. And he whispered of a time a thousand generations ago, a time beyond any story or song. He said he'd found stories of tiny machines flowing through plants and soil. Everything too small to see, but these machines helped trees and greenery in their growing and acted like minuscule looms or cogwheels or carts. I suspected he'd brewed up his ideas before finding evidence to fit, but his eyes gleamed when he talked.'

Mitch pouted. 'If he couldn't see them, how did he know these machines existed?'

'He never truly knew, but he believed. We watched other priests burn books and threaten commoners, and we hid what written matter we found in the cellars and roofs of ruined monasteries. One night we turned our lanterns low and stitched his discovered pages together with our drawings to rebuild a book; he showed me pictures of flying metal birds and animals built from corkscrews and gears, breathing trees, and fish that linked with each other. He thought these machines might take our orders, and he taught me two exploits that he said they'd understand. I couldn't make them work, but spirit flared in his eyes as he described what should happen. The next day he vanished.'

Phos paused. 'A friend?'

'Yes, a good friend. We'll search through Morzenthal's documents; fragments of his writing have survived, and your young eyes may notice evidence we miss.'

Phos stared ahead as if remembering, before darting forward to pick long blades of grass capped with tiny yellow petals.

Caliper smiled. 'Souvenirs?'

'Liramic. I had a liramic cloak. Weave the cloth right, and it glows.' Phos paused and glanced at Frinelia, and the priestess nodded. The girl tied one stalk into a loop and threaded another through the circle, and her fingers danced to knit a chain. Pressure thrummed in Caliper's fingers; liramic always beckoned the exploits, but he'd wait.

'Busy hands, busy mind.' Phos stopped walking and focused on her weaving fingers.

Frinelia edged closer. 'Here's an exploit – can I borrow your necklace?' Frinelia plucked the chain from Phos's hands and held one end in each hand before raising it above her head and closing her eyes. The yellow blooms trembled, and the chain vibrated into a blur that expanded into a sheet a yard long and glistened like mist. Frinelia's gnarled hands twisted, and the fluttering stopped. Now her fingers gripped the top corners of a net built from yellow threads, and she tossed the mesh upward six inches before catching it one-handed. 'Fishermen would have killed to make nets this way, and to answer your earlier question, Phos, my church wanted people working when they weren't asleep.'

Phos held out her hand. 'Can I see the net?'

Frinelia lobbed the lattice at Phos, but Caliper snatched it from the air and dangled it from his little finger. Pressure throbbed across his palm as if he held back a stream, and his eyes shut themselves as unseen threads sprouted from his fingertips.

'What are you…?'

His eyes opened, and Phos's net hovered before him for a heartbeat before flaring into an eye-watering lattice of fire that drifted upward without sound. The glare winked out to leave fine ash drifting downward, and he smelt charred straw.

'Where's my necklace?'

'I'll buy you a new one if we pass a flower seller.'

'Did Christina teach you this?'

Caliper nodded. 'This was the first. She talked and I didn't understand, but when she finished, I had fresh memories I hadn't earned.'

'Have you used this before?'

'Not around other people, no.'

‘I’ve seen it,’ Frinelia said. ‘Never learned it myself, but it’s called Fire Rising, and most say it’s our strongest exploit. And here’s our miller making it brighter than ever – we must talk.’

‘Most things are useful,’ Phos said. ‘Plants become clothes or food, and any animals you can’t eat make good workers, so were these exploits designed?’

Frinelia adjusted her shawl. ‘The world isn’t a puzzle with elegant answers, and there’s always a mess to manage, especially at Morzenthal.’

‘Was all the city built at once?’

‘Parts look older than others. A few stone floors show wear from centuries of strolling feet, but most appear new, and people say walls and rooms move when nobody’s watching.’

Frinelia grimaced and pressed her hands into her back as she shuffled towards a small copse of liss trees at the valley’s bottom. ‘In the spirit of staying alive we should share exploits.’

‘A contest?’

‘Not at all, Caliper: a demonstration. We reveal exploits in turns. Here’s my first.’

She closed her eyes, and her face wrinkled as she strode downhill. Blue-green footprints glimmered behind her for a few heartbeats. She turned and smiled. ‘You tell grass it’s liramic, though it works better at night.’

'Riders!' Mitch pointed dawnward.

Caliper turned. Four horsemen rode over the moor's dawnward horizon and into their valley. They were minutes away, but the riders swerved towards them and broke into a gallop.

'Churchmen, and we'll not outrun horses,' Frinelia said. 'Leave words to me.'

'Ah, but it's my turn to share an exploit.' Ten strides took Caliper to a liss tree, and he sunk his fingers into its gnarled bark as dangling branches scratched his head.

'Let me manage them, Caliper.'

The horses gobbled up the distance, and their hooves pounded like drums. Caliper stared at their pulsing legs; the intricate scurrying left his eyes watering, but the essence of speed was clear.

The priest's yelling flowed over the wind. 'Stay where you are.'

'Caliper!' Terror poisoned Phos's voice.

He faced the tree and let his breathing match the horses' rhythms. His palms vibrated as if his fingertips were seeping into the tree. Caliper's eyes closed themselves, and new pictures swarmed into his mind, hazy images of his body hunched over the tree trunk as leaves swirled over his shoulders. Phos's shouts dissolved into hisses and crackles as pain sliced at his fingers.

The bark swallowed his thoughts, and his eyes opened. Above, the tree's branches had stiffened to stand out from the trunk like skewers stuck into a log, and energy rattled through their limbs.

The riders slowed and prepared to dismount. Harsh splintering sounds burst out above as the branches snapped from the trunk and crashed downward before squirming and binding together. One stick slapped his shoulder before softening to slither into the mass piling up behind, and he turned to watch.

The branches glided and knotted themselves into a seething mob of black worms, and four columns coiled upward from the pile. New branches sprouted from the top of the columns and linked to form a cloudlike body balancing on pillars, and both ends of the cloud swelled outwards. One side grew into a skeleton model of a horse's head, and the other a tail, a pulsing memory of a horse.

Leaves rushed inwards to plaster the beast in green and orange, and a tremor shivered across his horse's body as its eyeless head flailed through the air. Again splintering rang out as the horse's legs snapped free from their carpet of black branches. His beast strutted forward five yards and tossed its head. Its body tensed for a moment before charging the four priests on horseback. They recoiled and scrabbled at their reins, and their horses whinnied before scattering across the grassland, and one man screamed while clutching his saddle.

His branches had sewn themselves into imitations of throbbing slabs of muscle, and leaves trailed behind Caliper's horse as it galloped. Two of the flesh horses bolted forward with their clinging riders. One rider slipped sideways but scrabbled upright as Caliper's beast capered around its prey.

The priests fled eveward and scattered up the valley's slope, and his horse broke into the loping gait he'd seen in sheepdogs, snapping and swerving to force the men away. The five vanished over the hill's brow, and Caliper flicked dust from his shoulder.

The others stared at him, and Mitch picked up a broken branch to tap it against the grass.

'Let's see, Frinelia. Your glowing footsteps against my horse. Fancy another contest?'

Frinelia's mouth stayed open, but Phos looked ravenous. 'Where was that from?'

'Christina said trees took orders, and I wanted to try things out.'

'Did she say what would happen?'

'Not so much. She'll teach the skill, but leave you to explore its uses.' A few amber leaves drifted past his face, and the puddle of remaining branches creaked.

Frinelia swallowed. 'I've never heard the

faintest whisper of this. If I had one tenth of your…well…. Imagination has a place, but let's focus on our situation. What will these men tell their masters?'

'The church might not believe them.'

'Four riders with the same story? They'll believe and we must move. What happens to your horse?'

'I told it to chase the priests, so it'll keep going as long as they do.'

'If they lead it to a church keep…. We should draw up a list of your skills, Caliper. I should have said earlier – some priests can detect exploits from afar, so you may have rung an alarm.' She glanced down. 'Are your leftover sticks safe?'

'I've had no problems.'

'Here's one the right length.' She stooped to grasp a straight branch and tested it with two steps.

'Be careful,' Mitch said. 'If guards spot you using crutches….'

'One of the riders recognised me, so our ability laws aren't a bother. Let's move.'

Caliper stepped forward, but nausea left him staggering, and Phos's image split into two as he lurched sideways. He closed one eye and waited before following the girl through the copse as his spine ground out waves of pain.

They climbed the valley's other side as night

fell. Ahead, the grassland rolled on into a faint green shimmer and an expanse of forest where he might shake off fatigue. Rose scents nuzzled the cooling air as branches scratched the growing darkness. He stumbled over a knot of grass but kept going, and he fought sleep by listing Christina's exploits in his mind. He'd never asked for any fighting exploit; once the priests learned his horse was a toothless threat, their hunting parties would scour this moor. His back grumbled, so he'd not squeeze out another exploit for hours, and like a poacher's footprints on a muddy riverbank, he'd set a path for the church to follow; he'd not one scrap of doubt there.

Chapter 13: your clothes will change colour

Damp clawed at Phos's body. She was thirsty for sleep, but pepper scents invaded her nostrils, and she kept coiling into new positions. The dangling branches wheezed out a pale blue glimmer, and wind set the leaves murmuring as drizzle spattered the ground.

Her thoughts raced. She'd left home with a single-syllable name, and she'd mumbled the words of stepping to herself while Mitch had scoffed, but the words sounded hollow. Growing up meant more than longer names; she had to live through stories and endure their changes.

Leester still beckoned. She knew the path, and Mum would ferret through bushes to strip out berries, and barter for furniture to remake their broken cottage.

Phos sat upright and hunched forward as night air left her shivering, and Caliper's snoring marked out time as his chest quivered in the gloom. His exploit had won them a few hours, but the church would follow, and capture meant she'd never visit Dad's museum or return to Mum's embrace.

Her fingers toyed with a finger-sized twig she'd rescued from the remains of Caliper's exploit. The sprig was soot-coloured but as light as balsa. Before they'd slept she'd pressed her hands against a liss tree, but her fingers had only slid over its dank trunk, and copying the miller's posture had brought nothing. Caliper said he'd rigged up another exploit for protection, and Phos had demanded details, but he'd only smiled and sliced his hands through the air. She'd try teasing out more details at dawn.

Phos mouthed her longer name to herself, but her second syllable felt lifeless and meaningless. She slumped back on the damp grass and stared between the soft glow of the leaves at the vault's blackness. *Vault* – the strangest word. She'd asked Dad why no one called it a ceiling, and he'd said ceilings only made an inside; you'd have a roof outside to fend off rain. The vault had no outside, so it deserved a different name. Sleep came as Dad's face lingered in her mind.

She woke late as misty rays of light stretched past the trunks and branches, and her chest squelched as she rolled onto her side. Liss trees usually trickled vanilla scents into the morning air, but this breeze reeked of compost. The others had breakfasted, and Caliper handed her bread and cheese.

'Do we have plates?'

'Plates?' Caliper chuckled and tossed his backpack onto the earth before flattening it. 'Your plate, my priestess.'

'Are your defence exploits working?'

'Christina helped me bond with our forest, and if these trees smell flesh horses, they'll spit out another stallion.'

'Christina came?'

'She taps into my dreams.'

Phos stared at the miller's overgrown eyebrows. 'What do you sense inside when you're working an exploit? What's scurrying through your mind?'

'You're after the learning, Phos?' Caliper shook his head. 'I could teach you bricklaying or carpentry in a trice, but exploits are a different flavour of learning.'

'How different? Can you teach me?'

'With bricks and wood it's the copying that teaches: my hands follow the boss's hands, and my mind grows around the new skills. Exploits are another world.'

Frinelia sat beside Phos with her hands in her lap, and Caliper leaned back.

'When Christina comes, it's hard knowing if I'm awake or dreaming, but afterwards extra thoughts circle my head. I was a cook for a landlord once and got left in a kitchen full of spices in glass jars every colour you could imagine. Nothing I recognised, but I asked around and got up early to try stuff out, and in the end, I cooked up decent fodder. One day the landlord's daughter waltzed into the kitchen for the first time. She was only six, but she knew what worked. Pinch here, fistful there, and she cooked stuff to make your tongue dance.'

'Natural cook,' Mitch said.

'No learning. The knowledge sat inside her head without any learning, and that's what happens to me after Christina comes.' He paused. 'Not much of a teacher, am I?'

Frinelia sighed. 'I read your file, Caliper, and even wrote part of it; even as a boy you showed talent.'

'Fine, it's not all Christina, but I don't know the explaining. Frinelia has the exploits and words, so she'll make a fine tutor.'

Phos scowled. 'Trees spawning horses versus glowing footsteps? Maybe later.'

'You're best starting small,' Caliper said. Mitch gnawed a crust.

'Did you start by burning dresses?'

'My first exploit was Fire Rising, which wasn't so grand, but on my life, I don't have the wit to explain an exploit's guts. It's like tiny threads spool from my fingertips, and they're roads for my thoughts, though there's nothing to see. Christina might show more if we meet.'

'She'll see me?'

'She's after me, but she wanted my friends too. Not sure you count as a friend with your sour face, but behave yourself, and she might drop new ideas inside your skull.'

Mitch lobbed a crust at Phos's head. 'They

won't fit: her head's full of stupid.'

Three black beetles raced out from under a log to skitter over the bread. 'I keep thinking of Mum heading back to Leester.'

'You want to join her?' Caliper stood.

'Part of me does.' Phos glanced at her feet. 'But if you're right about Christina….'

'I can't be sure, Phos, but I know we're connected, and she's nearby even when she's not touching my dreams. Christina's plans grow like a tree: I can touch the trunk, but there's no finding the roots. What I'm sure of is danger if we stay in this forest now the priests know we're here.'

They packed as daylight surged through the canopy of leaves, and Phos shook a set of twigs from her tunic. Three buttons had snapped off in the night, and the garment flapped in the breeze. Frinelia led them through knee-high undergrowth along an overgrown path.

Caliper stopped and pointed due south. 'If we cut across here, we'll reach the forest edge sooner.'

'I thought you'd not been here before,' Frinelia said.

'This way.' Caliper charged into a bank of ferns. He flicked his fingers, and the fronds parted around him. They followed his route, and a horde of inch-long woodlice tumbled from a log onto the black earth. Phos shuffled her feet to keep clear, and after twenty yards they emerged onto a grassy plain. A broken stone wall stood fifty yards off, and beyond stalks of unharvested barley rotted under daylight. Further on, straggling hedges lined distant fields stretching out to the far southern world wall's stony barrier of hazy blue.

Phos wrapped her hands around her damp tunic. A gravel path drifted between the wall and their forest, a bleached contour that ambled past an abandoned cotter's shack. Far ahead a grey-green mountain rode the dawnward horizon – watery with distance.

Frinelia's voice quavered. 'You should see Morzenthal's hill now; it's still a day's walk away.'

'It's there,' Phos said.

'I wandered this way two months ago, and there wasn't a path, so what dragged this one here?'

Phos stood beside Caliper. 'When do we meet Christina?'

The miller shrugged. 'Can't say. We've never truly met; she sends moving pictures of herself you can see through, and they're twice my height.'

'Whizzy,' Phos said. 'So she's at Morzenthal?'

'Must be. Has to be.' Was Caliper trying to drink the hill with his stare? He crouched, and gravel crunched under his boots.

'This track's fresh. Look, it's flattened this grass.'

'The road's following us?' Mitch prodded the gravel. 'Did Christina drag it here?'

'There's much she won't say.'

Forest on one side and a battered stone wall on their right, and ahead rich grass carpeted a spine of hills rolling dawnward. Two ruined stone cottages grew from the wall, and a rusted plough crouched beside a gaping doorway. Children had played here years ago.

Phos rested her hands on the moss-laden stone wall. It felt warm under the sun's arch light. 'They said roads shifted to freshen the world, and new paths meant new friends or your dad finding new work.'

'No road travels this fast.' Frinelia nudged gravel with her foot. 'But yes, you've heard our approved story.'

'But you can't prove nature works to help us; you pick evidence to fit your ideas. Roads might move for their own reasons.'

'Our words glued society together.'

'But now nature fights us, and your words don't work.'

'I've no answers, nor does any cleric, but clues may linger at Morzenthal,' Frinelia said.

'Can you describe the place, and tell us about the dangerous parts?'

'Imagine a vast drum pressed into the top of the hill ahead. A circular arena lies in the centre, surrounded by stacked rings of curving corridors wider than any barn. People huddle in a tiny fragment of the city – we've brought in plasterboard sheets and curtains to carve out dormitories and living spaces – but most of Morzenthal remains a mass of echoing passages. The carousel circles the arena's base and houses the most perilous exhibits. The elders try to seal the entrances, but the exhibits often escape.'

'Have you been inside the carousel?'

'Decades ago. I saw statues that recoiled at my approach, musical instruments that played themselves, masks that altered your vision, and mirrors that chose what they reflected. Clouds of twittering paper birds sliced my skin until I ran. A handful of exhibits have a use, while others can break your limbs with a stare. What's safe one year is lethal the next, and two or more exhibits may agree to combine into an artefact with unguessable powers. Even sneezing can trigger the exhibits, so tread carefully if you enter.'

'And everything's Christina's size.'

Frinelia nodded. 'Many rooms take minutes to cross, and we've fitted extra steps into many staircases. I've looked into immense shafts that pierce several floors. They're empty now, but many people believe the original builders could fly.'

Phos walked without speaking. Images brewed inside her mind: floating monks polished brass cogwheels while eating from flying trays. She smiled: even retired priests would jot down thoughts and ideas, and she might uncover books or ways to test ideas. Morzenthal meant her world had grown.

Their path curved left to skirt a rounded hill where soil and grass had slipped to expose a scar of white rock. The stone wall gave way to an untrimmed hedge, and underneath, dark green needles spilled over earth.

'Part of Morzenthal still sticks up above ground. Once we've passed this bend, you'll notice the roof and high towers. My ancient eyes will only see blurs.

'Everyone wears out,' Caliper said. 'I used to lob grain bags into carts.'

Mitch frowned. 'The world's ageing too.'

'What can you see now?'

'The hill spreads out, and….' Mitch swivelled his head. 'It's exactly halfway between the world walls.'

'Few notice that detail,' Frinelia said.

'There's stonework on the hilltop, three towers linked by curving walls.'

'You can't spot the fourth tower from here, but there's our destination, a long climb with weak tea at the end. One more thing to spot.'

Caliper shielded his eyes. 'Is the higher grass pale?'

'Grass at altitude is often pasty. Look higher.'

'The vault above Morzenthal is dark,' Mitch said.

A faint patch of grey clung to the distant rocks, and Phos stared – the spot seemed unreachable.

'Is there a link?'

'No one knows,' Frinelia said. 'Our world holds five similar cities, and each shows a similar stain on the vault.'

'You've seen the others?'

'Only Morzenthal still holds people, and the young rarely come, so more rooms fall empty each year.'

'Is there food?'

Frinelia's lips puckered. 'There is a room the desperate call a kitchen, and a substance the daring call food. I won't describe anything, but you'll experience it.'

Their path curled downward into a valley lined with young birches. Golden leaves coated the gravel and rustled underfoot, and she smelt honey. Maroon reeds clustered on the path's left side, thicker at the top, scars of purple against the ghost-white birches. Their travelling road had sliced through several reeds to scatter stalks across gravel, and brick-coloured dust billowed over their bodies. Phos's eyes watered as dust stung her throat, and Frinelia began coughing. Each of her hacking barks spawned the next.

The priestess sagged against a tree trunk, and the others surrounded her while dust turned their daylight crimson. Caliper patted Frinelia's shoulder.

Mitch sniffed the air. 'What's that plant? Has anyone seen similar?'

Caliper picked up a strand and rubbed it between finger and thumb. 'Strange....like...No.... This needs washing off.'

'I've a waterskin, and Phos—'

'No – we need to get underwater.'

'There's a brook further on....' Frinelia's face turned purple, and she slumped forward, but Caliper swept her up and cradled her in his arms. He stumbled and her head lolled back, but he raced forward.

Phos's skin burned. Her undershirt pinched her chest as unseen needles stabbed her lips. Caliper loped ahead, but his feet crushed more of the maroon stalks, and dust rolled across their path.

'Where's the stream?' Half roar and half question. Caliper shifted Frinelia's body to lodge her head on his shoulder. A branch whipped Phos's face, but she kept running as Caliper vanished into the forest. She raced around a tree-lined bend, and the miller stood twenty yards ahead, staring at a black road slicing through the wood and covering their gravel path. No, not a road; the surface slithered. This was a five-yard-wide stretch of stinking tar.

Caliper let Frinelia face the blackness. 'Is this your stream? What happened?'

She rasped out a croak before vomiting out a thin stream of liquid, but Caliper lifted her up again and waded into the sludge.

'Get under, Phos – this might be water.'

Phos stumbled forward but reeled at the fish-head-and-dog-muck stench. Mitch sobbed and toppled face first into the morass, but ahead Caliper crouched and gulped air before easing Frinelia and himself below the surface.

Her skin blistered as she stepped forward, and her feet slipped. The slurry rushed at her to surge into her mouth and nose as she sank. Impossible to scream or think; the black tar trapped and crushed her – no telling where the surface sat. Her lungs burned. Phos shoved her arms forward, and her fingertips rasped the stream's stony bed. She tried dipping her feet, but her arms rose. Too much – slime slid into her throat.

Agony gripped her neck as her collar bit into her and wrenched her upward. Light punched her eyes as she vomited mud, but Caliper clutched her shoulder, and his fingers swept muck from her eyes. Black mud plastered his hair against his skull as he smiled, and her feet scraped against the stream's bed.

'All right there?'

Her skin tingled as gobbets of sludge dripped from her hair. Frinelia sprawled on the far bank, slathered in mud but moving, and Mitch waded towards her using the furrow Caliper had ploughed through the slime.

Caliper slapped her back. 'You'll manage.' His voice squeezed past the muck in her ears, and she followed him to the bank before he eased her up.

'Phos?' Frinelia's voice had recovered.

'I'm better.' She squeezed the tremble from her voice and made herself look at the priestess. 'How's you and Mitch?'

'We're breathing, but we both need washing, and we may not make Morzenthal tonight.' Frinelia raised herself on one arm and brushed mud from Phos's sleeve – the gunk had dried. 'Amazing how this mud changes once it leaves the stream.' She sank back onto the earth and stared upward.

Mitch rattled off questions. 'You recognised the pong, Caliper, so what was that brown dust?'

'It smelt of rotten flesh, and there're stories from dawnward about that dust: you've to wash it off, or you'll stop breathing.'

'And if it won't wash off?'

'Small boys can't ask any more questions.'

Mitch frowned. 'The church says everything has a use, so what's the dust for?'

'No idea. Nothing makes sense now.'

'Look the right way and you'll find the sense.'

Caliper laughed. 'I'm thinking of Frinelia's tiny machines knocking back the cider.'

'Perhaps they're broken,' Phos said. 'Someone made these machines, but why aren't they around to repair them?'

Caliper sat and slid off his boots. 'I've no answers, Phos, but maybe our world's a windmill without an owner. Leave long enough between repairs, and gears strip themselves and sails rip apart. Nothing lasts forever.'

'So Frinelia's broken machines built those stinking reeds?'

'We're writing stories here, and perhaps one story tells the truth, but we'll not know which one. A broken gear will scream, but the noise is an accident. Those reeds can kill, but that's not what they're for; the killing happens because they're broken.'

Frinelia sat up. 'You're thinking again, Caliper.'

'Should I stop?'

'Continue for now. These threats may be accidental, but we owe you thanks: your composure in that murk was impressive.'

Phos watched the miller strip away his overalls to winkle out clumps of earth. He stood and gazed at their path as it wound up a hill. Two kinds of strength flowed through Caliper: strength buzzed through his muscles while passion set him flying into the blocks in their path. She'd need strength to survive, and she'd find it here; Caliper might not be a teacher, but he was a lesson.

Her tunic had ripped around her collar, and she fumbled at the cloth without thinking. Watching a strong man wouldn't make her strong, but together Caliper and Christina might give her a chance at learning, and this journey might breathe life into her second syllable. Doubt lingered – could she trust him – why wasn't he explaining those exploits? Phos stood and followed him up the hill.

Chapter 14: run through falling night

The grass past Torzene gleamed as if the land had stretched after a long sleep, and sweetness lingered on the breeze. Golden-brown beechnuts crunched under his feet as scarlet butterflies hovered before his face. Caliper strode upward. The path twisted but always rose, shepherded between two winding earthy banks glazed with blue-marbled crocuses. No one denied that each muddy step carried him closer to Christina.

'Not too fast.' Phos yelled.

More than mud had touched his hands in that murky stream; a delicate stroking had nudged his arms towards Phos. Their first touch? Exploits coiled inside his body, and half of him wanted to hurtle screaming towards Morzenthal, but he leaned against a beech's gnarled trunk and gazed upward as the others climbed his way. Enough breeze trickled over the banks to set the flowers nodding, and he could dream for a heartbeat. Did Christina keep a similar garden, and did banks of crocuses bob in the wind at her home?

Phos shuffled upward. She'd scraped mud from her face, but her eyes had reddened, and her tunic sleeve flapped around her elbow.

The four continued without words, and Caliper steadied himself to match Phos's trudge. Ahead, the grass lining the path gave way to rich brown soil that waited for plants, and orange blooms looking like roses attacked by a mangle appeared around a curve while copper-coloured thistles swayed in the thinning forest. Mitch raced towards a dark brown knot of fungus throttling a tree, but an angry buzz made him recoil.

'Stay clear, Mitch,' Frinelia said.

'Any idea what happened to your stream?'

Frinelia paused and leaned on her stick. 'With more time, I'd head upstream and investigate, but even with this path, we'll struggle to reach Morzenthal tonight.'

'Nothing lasts forever,' Mitch said. 'Not even trees and streams.'

Phos glanced up. 'You get saplings when the old ones die.'

'Ah, but now we've trees that won't grow straight, and any breeze uproots them. What happens when sickness spreads?'

'No fruit or vegetables.'

Caliper chuckled. 'There's a relief. I hate tubrel: there's no taste.'

'You can stuff tubrel,' Frinelia said.

'Yes, you can.'

'Two days at Morzenthal, and you'll yearn for tubrel.'

Caliper fell silent. The day still promised hours of light, and they'd climbed hundreds of yards, but was this too easy? Feeling Christina's fingers brushing his had left him with a hunger for her voice, but she'd stayed mute since, so was she sharing words with other men?

The path led into a clearing where a ring of beech trees circled a patch of leaf-carpeted grass. Phos tottered towards a tree and slumped onto the earth, and Frinelia and Caliper rested beside her. Mitch walked to the ring's edge to pluck a pale blue flower where six beaded rings nested together to form a hollow ball.

Caliper watched. 'Seen one of those before?'

Mitch shook his head and sat. He flicked the beads on one ring and coaxed out a thin tinkling like metal straws rubbed together. His fingers switched to another ring. After a few moments the boy cracked his fingers and churned out a decent version of 'Cats and Dogs'. Phos combed her fingers through her hair, and two muddy chunks fell onto her lap.

Caliper stretched out on the ground as the beech leaves jostled in the breeze, but the sickly reek brewing from his overalls needed sorting, or no one would sit beside him without the retching.

He'd never seen a henge inside a wood, so Christina wouldn't appear here, even though the woman was built of surprises. Caliper tucked his arms beneath his head as wind stirred the branches above, and the leaf sounds grew into waves of restless murmuring; he imagined her whispers seeping into his mind.

The rustling leaves chimed, and daylight mellowed into a golden blur as if fog had rolled across the sky in a single heartbeat. Caliper jerked to his feet and blinked, but the shimmering light stayed, and the surrounding trees breathed out a whispered hum.

He staggered forward. 'Are yous catching this? The leaves are ringing.' Mitch's music stopped, but the tinkling continued.

Phos smirked. 'Been on the cider again?'

'You're not noticing?' Caliper snatched a leaf from the air, and a tingle screwed through his palm as his fingers squeezed themselves into a fist.

'I'm seeing nothing.'

'Exploits affect your vision,' Frinelia said.

'I've drunk nothing, and I've never seen these blurs before.' His words sounded as if he'd dunked his head underwater. Christina often came when he drifted near sleep; he closed his eyes and slowed his breathing and tried to remember her stroking his fingertips.

Nothing. Only a fishy stench burping from his greasy overalls. The metallic tinkling above faded into a papery rustle, and opening his eyes brought back the world's dullness.

'I can't tell what she's doing, but let's move and get closer.'

Frinelia stood and brushed herself off. 'We've exhausted Phos and Mitch, so Morzenthal may be out of reach tonight. You look shattered yourself.'

'Our clothes are still damp,' Phos said.

'I'm fine. I'm not ill, just....' No word fitted, and he pointed up the path.

Muscles groaned as he trudged forward. Their path drifted up and onto a ridge of grassy hills, like a winding finger stretching forward. Below, the plain showed a net of dark hedges cambering up in the distance to meet the curves of the world walls. Ahead, their path rose over a darkening grassy slope crowned by a thin thread of grey stone, and Frinelia pointed.

'Morzenthal's path, but the city is some way off.'

Phos hugged her chest and stared north. 'There's burning below.' Caliper followed her gaze; a village sat on the plain, and red and orange streamers gnawed a windmill's tower while smoke sputtered from its top. Phos pulled out her father's metal tube and flicked it open before pressing one end against her eye. She sighed and handed him the rod.

Burnished brass with lacquer; the smaller tube fitted the larger without a gap. She showed him how to tweak the device until the windmill's warped picture hovered inside the brass. The tube ate distance, and now the tower looked only a hundred yards away, and flames gouged the windmill's sides as a sail crashed downward. Dust loved catching fire, and millers always guarded against sparks, so what had happened?

The distant fire guttered out, and he lowered Phos's tube as the sun's arch drifted eveward and shadowy pools slithered over their path.

Mitch tapped his boots against their path. 'Still got your torch?'

'I've better.'

Caliper knelt. His overalls and apron spewed out a rotten-fish stench, but he pressed his palms against the gravel. Images of twisting roots trickled into his mind, and his spindly threads rattled through the path. The grass answered, and light burst onto his face, and the glow surged out to turn the road into a gleaming ribbon riding the ridge of hills. If this track touched Morzenthal they'd find their way.

'It's still over an hour to Morzenthal,' Frinelia said. 'Or we could double back and sleep under trees.'

Mitch looked back. 'No, we can't.'

Caliper's strip of light stretched ahead and behind, and below, five specks of light jittered over their track. Church lanterns, miles behind but slinking upward; lighting their path had etched a glowing arrow through the darkness.

Phos moaned. 'Can you snuff out the light?'

'Never learned that one.'

'Any other exploits left?'

'Grass doesn't think, so I've nothing.'

Frinelia stared at the approaching violet-white lanterns. 'We're closer to Morzenthal, but they're faster. I should have silenced Rastersen.'

'You're sure it's him?'

'Their pace has anger – passion and greed too. It's him.'

The lights swayed, and Caliper imagined stamping, leather-clad legs, and cloaks billowing in the murk. 'Hustle, and we'll make Morzenthal before them.'

Daylight drained from the vault, and their shadows lengthened before dissolving into gloom. Rain spattered his face as the slope kept rising, and their path's glow yellowed a fraction. They might drift from the path to huddle in a gully, but they'd freeze, and more priests would scour the hills. Wind needled through his overalls as hail hurtled from the swirling darkness, and one glance behind showed the lanterns closing.

Each turn uncovered another twist of track, but they crested a ridge, and the pursuing lights disappeared. Phos stumbled, and his hand grasped her shoulder. The girl trembled but broke free to lurch forward.

Caliper expected Morzenthal's walls every time

they topped a rise, but the same bitter grey landscape kept unfolding ahead. The gravel light dwindled into a sick glimmer, and he fished the torch from his backpack – the beam picked out flecks of sleet.

'Is that safe?' Frinelia's voice rasped through the night.

'We mustn't lose the path.' They'd escape the churchmen's sight for five minutes, which might let them reach Morzenthal. If the priests followed him inside….

Deeper shadows on his left caught his vision, and he splashed light over a moss-slathered mound of broken stone blocks.

'We're near the city: that's one of our fallen ruins,' Frinelia said.

'What happened?'

'We've lost any records, but these stones fell from height – many are half-buried.'

'They tumbled from the vault?'

'People with decent eyes have checked, but the stone above is intact.'

Caliper glanced ahead. 'So these stones floated?'

'I've heard a thousand stories; wander these ruins, and you'll invent new tales, but no one can tell true from false, since everything but stone rotted centuries ago.'

Phos reeled to her left and crashed to her knees,

and Caliper jammed his torch into Frinelia's hand before hoisting the girl into his arms and squinting ahead into the icy rain. 'Snuff the torch: those priests will reach the ridge any moment.'

'Take care: the entrance is easy to miss at night, and your path is fading.'

Mitch halted. 'We've lights ahead.'

Frinelia gasped. 'There aren't lights outside Morzenthal – did those churchmen overtake us?'

'Can't be. Is this another ruin?'

'No. I know this hill; we're facing the right way, but the outer wall has been dark for centuries.'

Caliper snorted. 'I'm starting fashions.' An upright rectangle of golden light bleared through the rain to hint at stone walls stretching either side. Phos murmured as she faced forward.

'I'd like to think this display is for us,' Frinelia said.

'Are they expecting you?'

'Not for weeks. I visited Torzene to follow your progress and planned to stay longer.'

Caliper wiped rain from his face – did his half-drowned eyes mock him, or did the space inside the glowing frame look like a door? It was three times his height, with square panels festooning the space, two across and three high. A crease ran down the middle, and outsize hoops hung halfway up. He'd seen similar in a mansion. A cart stacked with barrels and rakes sat beside the door.

'How do we enter?' Caliper shifted his grip on Phos's body as she stirred and mumbled.

'Swing a hoop against the door, and if they're awake....'

Metallic clanks rang out, and silver rays spurted from the door's centre as it split open. The two halves juddered outwards, and Caliper squinted as two silhouettes fidgeted in the light. A stone apron stretched out from the doorway.

'It's Frinelia; I'm early.'

A woman's voice rang out, a priest accent, clipped words baked with confidence. 'You've brought friends and half a hill of mud.'

'And you found lights.' Frinelia strode forward with outstretched hands.

'They lit themselves three hours ago; the doors work, and several exhibits are stirring. Even the world map is glowing.'

The other figure held back. 'Not everyone is smiling.'

Frinelia hugged her friend. 'We need shelter, and these doors need closing.'

Caliper stepped inside and onto a polished stone surface. Light burst from patches set into the graceful curves of the ceiling, and a short stairway with huge steps ran upward to a panelled wooden door. His boots scattered mud across the floor, and he blinked as warm air skimmed his face. Phos's eyes opened as water dripped from her tunic.

The woman glanced at Caliper's boots before holding his gaze. Flowing grey hair framed a face with a scattering of wrinkles, and a smile simmered below her skin. 'You need washing and new clothes, and we have both.'

'We'd love the sleeping too,' Caliper said.

Frinelia coughed. 'Shut and lock these doors: we're being followed.'

'Bandits?'

'Churchmen. Much has changed outside. Torzene lies in ruins, and they hold us responsible.' Frinelia glanced at Caliper.

The woman glared. 'You've angered the priests? What happened at Torzene, and how many are chasing?'

'Five or six.' Caliper let Phos's feet touch the floor, but he held her upright, and her head lolled against his sleeve.

The Morzenthal elder drew her cloak around her and fastened the clasp at her neck. 'Six now and six hundred by morning?'

'They're puppeteers, and if they catch us here, they'll ransack Morzenthal, so you must lock them out.'

Wind gusted through the open door and rain spattered over stone as the woman's hands balled into fists.

'Still imagining divisions, Frinelia? No one needs your labels, and don't expect my support for any rebels you've grubbed up.'

'We have two children.'

'Blackmail won't lock these doors.'

'They're exhausted.'

'You will all step outside.'

Mitch's voice echoed over the glazed walls. 'They've crested the hill.'

Caliper glanced outside; lanterns hurtled towards them in a running frenzy, and he faced the elder. 'I've talked with your eidolon and learned her name, and she asked me here.'

Shock silenced the two elders, but one mouthed the single word, 'Eidolon.'

'She's waiting for us, and maybe she's behind your city's waking. Let us in, and there's every chance you'll meet her,' Caliper said.

No exploit he knew could touch these glossy walls, but his hand stretched inside his apron pocket to snaffle his mallet. Caliper focused, and tiny buds burst from the wooden handle and bloomed into lacy white flowers to form a promise and a plea.

'Christina taught me the exploits, and you'll

want the learning that's in them.'

The brittle frowns on the elders' faces turned into stares like hunger, and as a pair, they glided to the door to press their hands against a darker patch on the outside wall. Morzenthal's immense doors groaned and jolted before shuddering back to fill the doorway and block out the frozen night with its running invaders. The slam echoed for a few heartbeats, but even in the gloom, he'd felt the fury in the chasing churchmen's faces, and they'd find tools outside to chip at the stone; he'd only won a few hours of safety.

Chapter 15: beware the breakfast

Her dreams of drowning faded, and Phos woke into a silence where clean sheets draped her body in a pine fragrance. Could Morzenthal's people bottle breath from trees? The nearest wall was a polished stone slab ten feet away. Sixty feet above, a white tiled ceiling wafted out a soft glow.

She coughed, and her hacking echoed over the chill hall as her breath fogged. Two lines of sheetless beds stretched across the chamber, but a low table and a long wooden box sat beside her. The floor numbed her feet, but the box only held her filthy boots and a shapeless overall; she remembered arms peeling her clothes away, though dried mud still glazed her skin. A massive doorway pierced the wall in front, a rectangle capped with a pointed arch; its stone carvings modelled leaves and acorns.

'Hello?'

Another echo, and Phos tugged on the sack-like garment before running her hand across the wall. The huge bricks fitted without mortar as if they'd grown into place, and indigo ridges like veins meandered across the surface.

Two silver-headed women in shawls and black dresses bustled inside and smiled before speaking. 'We didn't want to wake you earlier, but your friends are planning breakfast.'

'Where are my clothes?'

'We kept them safe, but they're beyond washing, and we had nothing your size, so we made new ones.'

Phos stared. 'You've no children?'

'You're the youngest by decades.'

'Young or not, I need washing.'

'We've a new bathing place that started working yesterday. Does that suit?'

Yes, thought Phos, *that suits.* She needed to see Morzenthal work. The first woman shepherded her into a vast hallway, a road stretching from right to left, and a gentle curve showed in the tiled walls; the passageways facing her would lead into Frinelia's immense arena. Statues of bearded men stood flush against the walls twenty yards away.

No, not twenty yards, nearly forty. These statues were giants, standing to attention as they gazed over her head, each twice her size, swathed in togas of carved stone, and each face showed character. The closest figure looked bemused, the next concerned, and a third perplexed, so had the sculptor planned a story? The three to her left clutched books.

An arched canopy of glass panes glowed in the daylight, and two rows of slender stone pillars plunged from ceiling to floor. Carved ridges girdled the pillars to imitate tree trunks. Chestnut and tan tiles traced out squares and diamonds on the surrounding walls, and glossy floor stones used tints of grey to mirror the patterns. A few battered wooden benches filled the spaces between pillars like an afterthought. Phos stood by a pillar and stared across the curving hallway before looking up; lines of arched windows pierced the walls halfway between floor and ceiling to form a second storey.

'Are those wall tiles made of different stone, and who stuck them up there?'

'We wouldn't know.'

'You've never wondered?'

'What's the point in wondering?'

Phos frowned. 'Is that glass above, and do you have clouds inside?'

The women smirked and ushered her forward. She stared at the floor tiles, and stumbled as she realised they formed arrows. How could she spot the difference between decoration and sign? Clouds swirled into every shape imaginable, but they didn't hold secrets.

They passed through another archway, three times her height, and into a curving corridor. Their path became a walkway dangling over an immense gulf, where taut wires made railings, and Phos darted to the edge to stare down onto a path crossing underneath.

Amber light trickled through frosted windows in the ceiling, but cracks crazed the glass.

Doorways appeared, rectangles slicing through the thick stone walls, and green light stole into their corridor from one room. Inside, a glass dome threw tinted daylight over shelves holding rows of potted spiky brown fronds with metallic thorns. Saucers holding red and orange pastes littered a workbench, and brushes poked from glass jars.

'Medicinal herbs,' her companion said. 'It's warmer inside.'

'You're allowed medicine?'

'Churchmen come for treatment.'

Holes gaped above the plants, and bleached patches of plaster striped the walls. 'This room's changed jobs,' Phos said.

A slow nod. 'Change has its place.'

'What used to go on here?'

Another watery smile leaked onto the woman's face, but her silence stretched out until Phos glanced back at the room and up at the glass ceiling.

'Did this place hold books?'

The woman frowned as if Phos had sworn, and gestured her back into the corridor. The three scuttled into a passage with pitted walls and mould-tainted air, and grooves scoured the floor as water dribbled from the sooty ceiling.

‘This stretch has always been shabby, but the leaking started yesterday, which is strange when there’s cloudless sky above.’

‘Do you have libraries?’

‘Why fuss over books? I’ve dusted a few, but they’re full of nonsense.’

Phos didn’t bother arguing. Rastersen’s feet churned through the outside mud as he hunted for entrances, and books might help her learn of hiding places and escape routes.

A mob of toga-wearing elders stamped down the corridor towards them; sandals splashed through puddles. Four syllables old maybe, and they might have shared words with Dad. She opened her mouth, but their heads stayed stiff as they barged past her.

‘Rude,’ whispered Phos.

The corridor opened out into another echoing chamber, crammed with empty glass cases. Thin banners with faded letters she couldn’t read dangled from the glass ceiling, but the women led her through a door on her right and into a room with gleaming walls. A high-pitched hum whistled through the soap-scented air.

‘Here’s our new bathing room. Yesterday you’d never have believed the dust, but now everything sparkles.’

Phos’s overall chafed her hips, and she stumbled

over the slippery floor. Bundles of satin fabric covered a chair, and six cubicles ran along a wall.

'Try the cell beside the clothes, but don't go in dressed.'

Phos tugged her overall over her head and faced a cubicle before entering. Three walls surrounded a stippled floor – she imagined herself standing inside a creamy dice. The corners were rounded as if the stone had flowed, and shallow ridges tickled her feet.

'We wash here? There's no water.'

'Not yet there isn't.'

Phos shrugged, and a warm mist rolled around her. The ceiling stayed blank; water squeezed itself from the air without fuss. She rubbed her hand against her flank, and her fingers glided over skin as dirt streaked the floor and droplets beaded on her palm.

The women smiled. 'Morzenthal has woken. Visit our kitchen and wave your hand in the right place, and clean water flows. Extra passageways have appeared that no one dares explore, and another room copies clothes; you have new garments on the chair.'

Phos walked out, and oil glistened over her skin before vanishing. The chair held brilliant white trousers, a vest and tunic, and her cotton undershirt with a tear running across the left sleeve. White leather boots sat beneath.

'This is my undershirt.'

'No. We made a copy.'

Phos frowned. 'You copied the rip?'

'We didn't notice your rip; we copied the whole shirt. You were sleeping, so we guessed your measurements, though we don't know how to add colour.'

Everything was too large, and her buttons were missing, but leather belts hung from the chair, and they helped wrap the stiff tunic around her chest. The cloth belched out a burnt-leaf odour.

'You'll want breakfast.'

And ten thousand answers, thought Phos. Did Morzenthal heal itself? Had Christina woken the city, and what was Rastersen planning once he'd breached the walls? Knowledge might keep her free, but Morzenthal's stacked corridors and rooms would have her darting between chambers, and Dad's words rang through her mind: trying to see everything meant seeing nothing. Her stomach ached; she'd start with breakfast.

The women sent her clambering down a giant flight of stairs where workers had stuffed dark wooden blocks into the corners, and light faded into a fuggy gloom as a sour-beer stench rotted the air. Five elders waited at the stairway base with crossed arms. Bald heads with stray tufts of faded hair sat on flowing white togas, and each man used the same glare on her as if they wanted her to fall. The two women had vanished, and Phos struggled downward as a block rocked under her feet. Stains daubed the walls, and bundles of cardboard and paper littered the corridor's left side.

These elders were desperate to unlock the city gates, and Caliper's words yesterday had done little beyond wrap a frayed cord around the doors. One man stepped towards her and opened his mouth, and a hand gripped her shoulder from behind.

Phos turned at the touch, but the hand was Frinelia's. The elders still glared.

'They're not happy,' whispered Phos.

'Church and city live together here, Phos; some retired priests can't forget their past. There was tension, but until your arrival they worked together. Many see you as a flaming torch inside a dry barn and call for your expulsion. Rastersen and his thugs bustle outside and demand entrance, and his threats paint a vivid picture. If he enters….'

The sentence swayed in the air as a new stench ferreted inside her nostrils, like rotten cheese stacked in an outhouse.

Phos glanced at the elders still milling by the stairs. 'Can we reach the carousel? It's dangerous, but Rastersen has a coward's blood.'

Frinelia nodded. 'We'll find Caliper; he may be at breakfast. His strength hides from him, but the carousel artefacts might respond to his talent.'

The smell worsened as Frinelia led Phos on, and the bile flavours left her retching. 'Are we visiting the latrines?'

'No. The kitchen.'

Phos halted, and her hand rose to cover her face.

'Did you want breakfast?'

Phos's stomach squirmed as if trying to escape. 'Is that last year's breakfast? Is your nose decoration?'

'I think they're cooking sausages.'

Phos jerked forward and vomited, but Frinelia's hand stoked her shoulder before rubbing her neck. The priestess's whisper drifted into her ear.

'The same happened on my first visit. You won't believe me, but this food is edible.'

A final judder shook Phos's body, and she forced her eyes open to stare at the cloth Frinelia had waiting.

'The food helps you stay thin, and it tastes better than it smells.'

'I've heard better promises. How's it made?'

'There's no farm nearby, so everything's recycled, which means….' Frinelia waited.

Phos winced. 'Is there any food instead?'

'Try waiting until you're dreadfully famished. We could tour the food factory. They've a particular style of cooking: all bendy glass and coloured flames to summon food. Incomprehensible but impressive.'

'Who invented this, and why isn't it illegal?'

'The church believes it owns Morzenthal, and its activities are always legal, though it makes sure commoners never learn of our food factory.'

'It's worried people will copy this?'

Frinelia smiled. 'If you only eat when priests allow....'

'They gain control.'

'Any indoor farms would soften their grip, and hunger makes everything edible. If you're desperate, I'll persuade the cooks to demonstrate their factory.'

'There's Caliper's ghost, the eidolon; she might suggest a way forward.'

'Which means finding Caliper, which means entering the breakfast room.'

'There's danger everywhere,' Phos said.

***

Caliper drew in dust with each breath, and the musty decades coated his lips, but he kept ambling with Mitch down the echoing hallway, and after twenty paces, a fresh breeze brought hints of musk. He stopped, and his fingers ran over an oak wardrobe, one of five pushed against the wall. The wood had darkened with age, and each wardrobe had an identical crack scoring its left-hand door. Battered dressers sat beside a scratched piano, and his fingers coaxed out a few dull thuds from the keys.

A table on the giant hallway's other side held a jumble of children's toys, a box kite, a spinning top, and a cardboard windmill, and Mitch flicked the sails to set them spinning. He'd not seen any children, so who had lugged these trinkets up the hill, and why were the wardrobes identical? Caliper stared down the dusty hallway; the right size for Christina, and the subtle curve would suit her.

Mitch turned to him. 'Still hunting your ghost?'

'I'll never stop.' He'd risen before dawn to prowl the city and flash his torch into darkened rooms and Morzenthal's curved halls, each large enough to house hordes of giants. By mistake he'd woken a half-deaf elder sleeping alone. Caliper had apologised, but the elder had gleefully retold his own sighting and described Christina's hair, her dress, her face and eyes. The man hadn't shared words with Christina, and she hadn't looked at him. There'd been no whispered names, but the elder believed himself blessed. He'd described her rising through the floor before drifting back, and Caliper found himself glancing downward while ignoring the sleep pawing at his eyes.

Caliper tapped the hard marble floor before sliding his foot over a join between two polished stones. The slabs fitted perfectly, and the bricks in the walls were fresh. Did Morzenthal hoard squads of eager masons?

Mitch dashed through a doorway on his left, and Caliper followed into a cramped room where shelves crammed with musty books huddled inside a cage of thick wires. Mitch gripped the mesh and stared as the metal creaked: priests had locked readers in with their words, and these books had escaped the church's fires.

Priests, no escaping the priests; their scratchy letters capered over each doorway. Right now they'd swarm outside and probe for entrances, and Phos needed his muscle. Daylight streamed through the ceiling windows. He beckoned Mitch, and the pair turned back to retrace the footprints they'd planted in the thin floor dust.

'There's a massive hill under Morzenthal, so there must be hiding space below,' Mitch said. 'We're nearer the vault here, and those ruins we saw might float again, so we should explore.'

'I've no ideas, Mitch. Phos has the mind, and we'll talk with her. She's most likely scoffing breakfast.'

They walked without words past a set of empty rooms, and a gaggle of elders eyed them as they floundered down a gigantic staircase and into a low-ceilinged corridor with stained walls, where papers and shards of broken pot ran along one side. The kitchen slung out its own brackish stench, a festering worm grubbing at Caliper's nose and mouth.

The kitchen's tiled hall echoed with chatter; thirty heads' worth of grey hair sat at low tables, and fingers dabbled at plates of steaming brown gunk. Caliper's eyes stung, and he dodged as an elder hefted a tureen of bubbling slop past his face.

Phos and Frinelia sat alone at the hall's far end. Frinelia nibbled a biscuit while Phos stared at her in horror.

Frinelia swallowed, held her breath and smiled. 'Sleep well?'

'Watching you eat is a nightmare.' Caliper breathed through his mouth before sitting.

Mitch coughed. 'Shouldn't this stuff smell of food?'

'It's never seen soil.' Frinelia held her biscuit up towards one of the ceiling's glowing patches. 'It's brewed, after a fashion, but barley isn't involved.'

Caliper faced the four Morzenthal elders and grinned, but they never blinked.

'They're brewing now.' Frinelia sipped syrup from a jar and tugged a saucer holding a dollop of maroon sauce towards her. 'The food factory needs two masters, but the senior brewer disappeared while searching for herbs a week ago. They're training a new assistant, but it takes time.'

'Everyone's staring,' Phos said.

‘Fear makes everyone look like an enemy, and Morzenthal’s council meet soon to decide how to handle the priests gathering outside. A friend of mine will argue my way, but others are desperate to please the church, and Rastersen knows how to threaten.’

‘You’re sure it’s Rastersen?’

Frinelia nodded.

‘Will the council hear us?’

Frinelia lowered her voice. ‘It’s uncertain. They’ll make no decision until noon, but stay ready, and learn the city’s layout.’ Her finger dabbed the maroon sauce, and she drew on her plate. ‘Morzenthal’s corridors form rings around the central arena – that’s one level below us – and the carousel circles the arena. It’s lived in, but not by humans.’ Frinelia gazed at Caliper. ‘If Rastersen breaches the walls, the carousel may become our best chance.’

Caliper glanced at Phos and Mitch. ‘What do you think?’

‘It was my idea,’ Phos said. ‘Danger for us means danger for him.’

Frinelia scrubbed her fingers through her drawing. ‘Here’s Minasteryde, the senior brewer, and should things settle, we’ll ask about the food factory.’

An elder squeezed through a pair of swinging green doors, a smile etched on a plump face under a crescent of silver hair. Frinelia waved but Caliper felt a push. Another shove tipped him back before pitching him against the table. Chunks of plaster crashed around him, and plates smashed. The room jolted, and Caliper swayed as screams pierced the air. Phos yelled at Mitch to climb under their table. A metallic juddering hammered through his body, and screams became howls as the shaking stopped.

Shock could block pain, and he slid his hands over his chest, but he was untouched. A heap of bodies twitched to his right, and angry shouts rang out. Were these toga men blaming him? A short-haired elder woman crouched over the brewer and called his name while shaking his shoulder.

Caliper squatted beside Minasteryde and listened. No movement or breath; blood trickled from his mouth, though his peaceful smile lingered, and Caliper touched the woman's shoulder.

'I'll check the kitchen.' Caliper stood as Phos tore strips from a bundle of reeper cloth and threw them to Mitch. The door stuck fast until he shouldered it open, and he burst into a room of upturned chairs and tables. The floor was a sea of shattered glass glistening in twilight – dirty rags stopped daylight leaking through skylights – and a dull green smear had grown over the walls. Caliper's eyes streamed as he walked inside, and glass crunched underfoot.

Windmills shared a single design, so any miller

could rebuild any other windmill, but this fatal shaking had destroyed something unique, and knowledge had died. Frinelia entered and gasped.

'No, not here. This is....'

'Any stored food?'

'What was that shaking?'

'I heard telling of a small Outland town wrecked by shaking, but your church killed the tale,' Caliper said.

'I know nothing.' Frinelia clutched the door, and Caliper's foot nudged a broken flask. This glass factory had sat unchanged for decades: grime still glued three flasks to an upturned table, but grey dust circles showed where others had fallen.

'Food reserves?'

'Only a few weeks,' Frinelia said. 'How's Minasteryde?'

'Dead. Did anyone else know the brewing?'

Frinelia fell silent. 'People help, but we've few records.'

'At least your stink is clearing, but keep those elders out.'

'Stop the panic?'

'No. Well, yes, but we've clues here. There's a line of shards on that floor, so a tube's fallen from the desk. You've a round flask beside the round table, and its underside is sooty, so we search for the burner that sat beneath. Understand?'

Frinelia's shoulders sagged.

'These elders need you, so go find notes or pictures, and ask if people kept diaries. Check bedrooms, and talk with anyone who worked here, like cleaners or caretakers. Get their words and fit them together. You'll manage, and I'm sure Mitch'll show his skill here.'

Frinelia paused before turning and leaving, and Caliper studied the glinting wreckage. Back in his windmill he'd learned the best place to store each of his tools, the right weight for a sack of flour, and which changes in the windmill's heartbeat meant trouble. All remembering. Now he stared at the broken glass and wrote his own memories of the rubble, clues to let him wind back time.

He might scrape the scowls off those toga-wrapped elders and get them working his way and keep those fleshy priest fingers away from Phos.

Caliper jerked as the door twitched. 'Stay out.'

'It's Phos. We need to go.... What the...?'

'Grab the door and keep the others out. Where's Mitch?'

'He's outside. He's fine, but we must see the arena.'

'We need food, even this crud, and this factory needs a rebuild.'

'I've done jigsaws, but....'

'You'll stay by the door, Phos, and stop anyone entering.'

The girl's fingers trembled as she studied the ground. 'Will this floor give way?'

'What?'

'Three elders came up from the arena; the floor there cracked open, and there's light streaming from below. We need to explore.'

Caliper rocked back against a chair. Had this shaking exposed Christina's home? 'Yes, maybe your hole in the ground needs a good watch.'

'I'll go,' Phos said. 'If you're planning to rebuild, try sniffing the glass; anything smelling of food comes from the end of the line.'

'Aren't you the useful girl? Now go see what's hiding underneath.'

She turned and slid through the green doors. Had the shaking cracked Morzenthal's walls? Would Rastersen's puffy face come searching? His candles wouldn't surprise again, and there'd be tens of guards with blades. Caliper's fingers itched for a weapon, but these elders were strangers to the fighting, and he sat alone with the shattered glass.

Chapter 16: it's uphill all the way down

Phos's boots slapped against stairs as she raced upward. An elder's hands snapped at her sleeve, but she swerved away. She hurtled along the curving inner side of Morzenthal's main hallway and hunted for a passageway while gasping for breath. A long corridor opened on her right, and Phos surged down the empty passage as her stamping feet echoed across the walls.

Daylight beckoned, and she burst from the corridor onto a ten-yard-wide curved balcony circling the walls of a vast drum-shaped chamber. Above, a domed ceiling stretched over the arena, and a ring of windows pierced the creamy stone to flood the space with amber light. A metal band circled the dome where it met the walls. Eight sets of stairs curved into the arena like notches evenly spaced around a plate, and Morzenthal's elders had planted wooden slabs into the stair corners to make them human-sized. The arena's floor sat twenty feet below, an immense disc carved from Morzenthal's buttery stone, but a black scar gouged the centre where several slabs had fallen. Ten elders lingered nearby and watched wordlessly as flecks of light erupted from the gap.

The floor was a cork for an immense bottle, and she scrambled down. One wooden block wobbled, but she slapped her hand against the curved wall. Her body jarred as she missed the final step, but pain would wait. She strode forward and into the huddle of elders.

Light poured from the breach. Coloured streaks quivered upward like darting fish and streamed towards the dome; normal light only showed when it struck solid material, but these beams tinted the air. Six steps brought her to the gap's edge.

These remaining stones stayed in place by gripping each other, so a single step might send her plummeting, but she had to see below, and she tapped her left foot on the floor to edge forward.

'Miss, you can't approach – we don't know it's safe.'

'Not knowing isn't safe.'

'You can't stay there.'

Phos inhaled before glancing down into a confused riot of colour, and her body recoiled. No meaning in the chaos below. She closed her eyes. Did the mind need digesting time?

There'd been an abyss, a swollen maw of darkness surrounding distant towers and streets. Glistening beams had smeared colour across her face: violet one instant before shifting into a rich blue and through to turquoise before sliding back to violet. Immense stone slabs had drifted in the air below to bathe in the soft light.

She'd watched toy blocks roll in soapy water,

and the motion below looked similar. The rolling blocks shared the floor's buttery sheen. Those stones had fallen, and the rays had snared them, so would the light hold her if she jumped? Part of her demanded she leap forward, but questions froze her body: this light might not treat teenage girls like stone blocks.

Phos faced an elder. 'Do you have anything to throw?'

The elders looked blank, and their mouths stayed half-open.

'Never mind.' Phos slipped off a belt and squared her boots against the hole's rim. She'd not been dreaming; those stones twisted through the air, and Phos held her coiled belt above the gap and opened her hand.

For a heartbeat, the belt fell, but it slowed as if sliding through treacle before stopping beside a slab, and the leather strap uncoiled. Phos breathed out and let the rays caress her hand. Did her fingers weigh less? The need to hide still made her tremble, but she couldn't trust the light yet.

She folded her arms. 'Do you people know a way down?'

'There's no space below.'

'There's space now.'

No reply. The elders might waddle closer if she kept goading, but even seeing the void might not convince them. Again she squinted past the tumbling stones; far below, a dazzling ring of violet lanterns ringed a square set of black pillars.

A shrill yelp echoed around the arena's walls, followed by a soft thud. Frinelia had misjudged the stairway, but the priestess hauled herself up and bustled closer.

'Step back, Phos: the shaking might return.'

'There's more Morzenthal – come and see.'

'Will you ever listen?'

'I bend rules, but it's not me holding the stones up – this light's doing that.'

Frinelia eased behind Phos and glanced over her shoulder. 'How's this happening?'

'Caliper turned wind into light – maybe he knows. Or Christina.... Whatever.... We must explore.'

Frinelia clasped her shoulders and tugged Phos back. 'Let's keep you secure.'

Phos blushed, and her heart raced as her mind filled with ideas. Ribbons of light danced upward and frolicked with daylight, and were these blue rays designed to reach the vault and its dark patch? 'We move lanterns to shine light where we want – they're a tool – so can this light let us fall like feathers?'

Frinelia's fingers massaged Phos's shoulders. Huge archways pierced the arena walls, eight dark doorways staring at her, sealed by heavy canvas. The carousel, another path, but Frinelia followed her gaze and sighed.

'Not there, Phos. Make the carousel our last choice.'

'Then downward. Where's Caliper?'

'With Mitch. They're trying to rebuild the food factory, but there's too much damage. More churchmen arrive each hour.'

'I have an idea, but we need our miller.'

***

Caliper grabbed a pole from the kitchen floor and knocked down the rags stuffed into the kitchen skylights. Daylight leaped inside to scald the green stains slathering the tiled wall. Grey puddles had covered the floor, but they'd dried into wrinkled stains, and yeast smells filled the air. He'd scraped a corner clear and stood there with a surviving beaker.

Glass shards carpeted the rest of the kitchen, and Mitch sketched on a table's dust as an elder whispered behind him. Words became pictures of pipes and flasks, and Caliper's stomach rumbled as hunger dished out its own class of sickness.

The elder fell silent, and Mitch stared around the kitchen. 'I know what's needed. Two flasks did three jobs at once, but they're smashed, and so are their spares. Can your exploits shape glass?'

Caliper put his beaker on a shelf. 'Nothing I have touches glass.'

'Should I get Phos?'

'No. I'll find her. She'll throw herself anywhere she finds.'

'She's got motive with those men outside; they're hammering at the doors.'

'You'll hunt for more glassware,' Caliper said. 'Our elder friends might have overlooked a few pieces, so follow the dust.'

'I'll be fine, but watch your step.'

Tens of guards and priests mustered outside, and too many elders were willing to take the church's side, but if he kept the girl close they might find new hiding places or a tunnel out to the moor. Caliper loped through the hallways and asked for directions to the arena. The echoing cavern left him blinking, but Phos and Frinelia stood out from the cluster of elders. He clambered down, and the girl ran towards him as Frinelia strutted behind.

'Caliper, can we find rope?'

'Rope?'

'You know rope: thick string.'

Frinelia's hands made fists. 'No, Phos – this is insane.'

'What's your game, Phos?'

Phos hopped from foot to foot. 'You can't repair

the food factory, can you?'

'Too much shatter,' Caliper said.

'There might be glassware underneath.'

Frinelia gasped. 'This is madness, Phos; you're wrapping reasons around insanity.'

Phos faced Caliper. 'Rope,' she said. 'I've seen it done: you tie rope around a man and wrap the other end around a pillar to lower the guy.'

'Done it many times; nothing beats it for fixing a windmill's outside, though most times it's me letting people down. But there're questions waiting, Phos: what if our rope breaks or I lose my grip? What if we can't pull you back up or the rope snags?'

Frinelia crossed her arms. 'We are not debating this.'

Phos blinked. 'What if those priests break in?'

'We're responsible. I mean, I'm responsible since your dad.... There's a reason adults don't let children run riot.'

'You took risks when you destroyed your windmill, but the risks brought you here, close to Christina....'

Were sparks flying from the gap ahead? Caliper studied the shifting streams of colour; Christina always brought him light against the darkness. He crept towards the edge and peered down to watch Phos's slabs still spiralling in the beams, and he let the glistening pulses stroke his face. Was Christina watching?

One step back and half a nod to Phos. 'If you're content, I'll not stop you.'

Frinelia gripped Phos's elbow. 'I will. Putting yourself in danger is your choice, Caliper – endangering Phos is not.'

'So she holds the rope while I'm lowered – would that work?' Caliper squatted beside Phos. 'No arguments; we use the safest knots and kit you out the best way we can.'

'Is this eidolon addling your mind? You want Phos to sniff out your ghost?'

'Find a way, and I'll travel myself. Christina's on our side. If she's underneath she'll not want the harm touching Phos, and we might find glass in the darkness.'

'Perhaps Christina owns a glassware shop – flasks the right shape and cheerful shopkeepers to shine your boots. Sniff reality for one moment, Caliper – there's only dust and danger below.'

'You've heard the hammering outside, so nowhere is safe now.'

'The sooner I go the sooner the food factory gets repaired,' Phos said. 'We need strong rope and strong people.'

Caliper chuckled. 'There's my work sorted. I

saw henger rope above, and it'll hold ten times your weight without stretch.'

Frinelia stroked Phos's hair. 'You're sure? What if there's more shaking?'

'I'm not waiting here.'

Should he break into the carousel and rifle through its danger to find Phos a weapon? Sweat trickled over his forehead, and he screwed his eyes shut, but he still felt Frinelia's glaring – a scouring tendril of blame.

***

Phos glanced up as three middle-aged women in aprons appeared on the balcony to chat with elders, and their whispers echoed around the arena. To her right, Frinelia sat and clasped her knees while glowering at Caliper. Mitch lay flat beside the hole and pushed his head over the edge; he'd agreed to watch the descent and shout if trouble came. Caliper sat to swathe her in his rope harness, one loop for each leg, and another hugging her chest. Fibres squeaked as his brawny arms tugged at the rope, and an image came unasked of Caliper pinching seeds between thumb and forefinger to feed a wren.

He took two steps back and spread his arms. 'Can you twist at the waist and move your hands?'

She demonstrated. Phos's arguments held firm in the silence, and Frinelia said nothing. Mitch had created space in her backpack, and Caliper slid the torch into her belt.

'Your weight will knit the henger fibres together, so don't panic over any creaking. Feet first all the way, keep gripping the rope, and always know your position. We'll lower you gradually, but shout if you need a stop or if you need studying time, or—'

'I'll shout – I get the idea.' Phos pulled at the rope clutching her waist. 'Glad this doesn't go around my neck.'

'The hole's edges are smooth, so the rope won't fray, but Mitch will watch, and I'll anchor the rope. You ready?'

'I'm ready.' Phos sat and dangled her legs into the gap – had those stones slowed? No need to tell Caliper.

He crouched behind and whispered. 'I'm hoping you'll find a way to Christina.'

'You've a message?'

'Tell her…tell her where I am, and tell her I'm waiting.'

'That's all?'

'There's words she's not spoken, and she said the truth would leave me screaming, but she promised more telling later. Tell her I never panicked when Frinelia spoke of the tiny machines, and tell her we need to keep fat boy Rastersen outside.'

Phos nodded.

'You're after escape paths for us and glassware to rebuild the food factory. Don't get distracted unless—'

'Unless Christina. I'm ready.'

'I'll take up the slack, but wait until the rope grips, and grasp the edge and push.'

The shimmering rays streaked past her head, and Phos stretched out her arm. Below, the stones rolled like leaves in still water, and she blushed as she pushed forward.

She plummeted, and her sight blurred, but Caliper's harness tightened to force out a grunt. The leg loops seized most of her weight before the creaking rope inched her towards the lumbering stones, and the light dazzled her until she looked straight ahead. Dim ghosts flickered in the gloom, a figure on a rope, faint reflections against the darkness. She twisted her body to see more copies of herself. Glowing mites danced like fireflies through the air.

Frinelia's voice struggled down; stonework ate the words, but arguments held their own signature. The rope creaked again, and Phos sank past a rolling stone slab and stroked the surface: ordinary stone, but fresh scratches marred its sides. Its spinning had slowed into a crawl as if the light beams were building a cradle for the blocks.

Frinelia's shouting didn't stop Caliper's gentle lowering, and rope bit into her tunic, so the light didn't hold her – good thing she hadn't jumped. Had the shaking triggered these beams, or had the rays stroked the arena floor for centuries? Could she harness the light to build houses or shunt livestock between fields?

She tilted forward, and the rising beams played across her eyes. She squinted, but the colours still dazzled with their slow rhythm, violet through blue to green, and her breathing matched their pulse. Stone dust coated her lips.

'Can you talk, Phos?' Distance withered Caliper's bellow into a reedy whisper.

'I'm fine, so keep lowering.' Her rope swung and her reflections vanished, but ghostlike panes of glass and corners winked into view further off. Each foot of descent showed more as her eyes adjusted, and frost-covered cubes hovered in the distance as if a drunken giant had slammed glass dice into unseen walls. Ribbons of colour streamed around her, and looking up showed her rope as a brilliant streak of light threading upward.

Her descent paused: Caliper might be resting. She twisted to her right as sparks flitted over the edge of one cube, and she swung through the air like a pendulum's bob.

Phos glanced down; the floor looked closer. A

grid of black pillars sat below, an indoor henge with razor-sharp corners. Lanterns glistened in between the pillars. Her rope creaked again as she swung, and bile rushed into her gullet.

Again, Caliper lowered her, and she skimmed above a black-edged pillar five yards wide. Its edges glinted like black steel. Her path didn't shift when she flailed her legs, and another drop left her swinging three feet from a stone as her rope thrummed.

'Caliper – land me elsewhere.' Grit dulled her voice into a limping croak, and craning her neck back showed the gap above as a dwindling smear of colour only visible because her twitching lifeline pointed that way. Phos spat to clear her mouth.

'Caliper!'

No reply.

The rope hauled her back towards a pillar, and she pushed her foot forward as the corner passed inches away.

The lanterns flickered for a handful of heartbeats before dying, and Phos blinked as blackness swallowed her. Had her trespass triggered an ancient trap? Phos scrambled for Caliper's torch and flicked life into it; silver rays fanned through grime. Images flashed past, the pillar's stone gobbling her light, crystalline pools like eyes sitting on a metal floor, distant shards of her reflection winking at her.

Colour returned as the lanterns below pulsed crimson, a bloody heartbeat, and Phos swung back to the henge. Noise grated above, and Phos leaned back. Overhead, the hovering slabs had shifted to line up with the gap and rose to repair her ceiling.

Her rope harness tightened, and pain gouged her body as she hurtled upward. Caliper had to be hauling the rope, as fast as he could, but she'd never reach the gap before it closed, and those immense stones would crush her lifeline. Phos scrabbled at her knots, but she'd risen too far to fall, and her torch slipped to clatter onto the floor.

The ropes stopped squeezing, and she fell: Caliper had realised her position and was playing out his rope. The ground raced upward, and Phos relaxed her legs before her feet slammed against metal, but she toppled onto her flank, and pain lanced through her body.

Frozen metal: the sheets stole heat from her tunic, and her breath fogged the air. The henge pillars loomed over her like unblemished ingots of night, and Caliper's torch threw her shadow over the coal-coloured stones.

Phos struggled to her feet and winced. New shadows flickered around her body as a bright bead fizzed through the shrinking ceiling gap to plummet towards her, and sparks cascaded from the candle, a gift from Caliper, a memory of daylight. Light above dwindled into three narrow cracks before winking out, and her rope writhed like a dying snake before coiling over the floor.

Caliper's candle tumbled, and glints of light picked out a giddying array of cubes coating the walls. Her cavern had a funnel's shape, wide above but sloping to embrace the henge, and the cubes on one side had spilled across the floor. Blurred shadows loomed against their frosted sides. Caliper's candle smacked into the ground five yards away and spewed out more sparks.

Chill wormed through her boots and frost stung her cheeks as the metal rang under her feet, so maybe this floor worked as an alarm. Leester metal was rare, a tool treasured through generations or a precious family ornament, but here it did the work of stone. Caliper's flare popped with a final spurt of sparks, and Phos grabbed her torch.

Dust squirmed around her and recoiled as she stretched out her hand. She untied her harness. The crimson lantern light pulsed to vomit out shadows and show glimpses of the crystal cubes and black pillars. Caliper couldn't reach her here; Christina couldn't live here. She'd brought no water, and the bitter air mixed with stone dust to knife her throat, and her pain ramped up each time she swallowed.

Chapter 17: ancient light

Caliper stared at the rope's stump and ran his fingers over the crushed fibres, but he'd never meet Frinelia's stare. He glanced at the polish and smoothness of the restored floor stones, which gleamed as if the stonemasons had just left. The women and elders huddled on the balcony peered at him without words, and Caliper stared at the archway ahead, the carousel's sealed door. A few elders wandered behind him.

Mitch stood. 'Morzenthal's half building, half animal. Shame we can't train it.'

'You may imagine my thinking, Caliper.' Frinelia's voice curdled the air. 'I'll not speak, but make finding Phos your goal.'

'At least Rastersen won't grab her,' Mitch said. 'And no one expected the city to heal itself. Can we ask Morzenthal to open passages or send Phos a message?'

Caliper dropped the rope. Phos's words had crafted a glass, and he'd squeezed inside, but regret could wait: keep busy and new paths might open. 'Frinelia, what's changed since your last visit?'

'I've been away, so don't ask.'

'Can you ask the elders?'

'I'll check the libraries, but you'll stay here.' The priestess swept to a stairway.

Caliper turned to the elders. 'Have yous seen

those repairing rays before, the ones cradling the stones?'

A plump elder wearing a pale blue cowl stepped forward. 'I remember one carousel exhibit; no one's touched it for years, but it sprays out blue light of every shade imaginable.' The elder paused. 'In normal times, we would demand you undergo rigorous training before entering the carousel. In normal times....' The elder patted Caliper's arm and pointed to one of the arena's arched doorways and its brown canvas seal.

'No, Terelian,' another elder said. 'They can't see the carousel: the church won't forgive you.'

Terelian whipped around, agile for his bulk, and faced the other elders. 'Those thugs outside won't respect your toadying; don't sink to their level.'

'They're churchmen.'

'Are they? Without Torzene their clothes are rags. Give them what they want, and they'll keep taking until we have nothing.' Terelian turned back to Caliper. 'Through the canvas. Follow my footsteps; don't stare at any statues; and touch nothing – especially not the birds.'

Mitch frowned. 'What birds?'

'Follow me.' Dark grey canvas stretched over the archway, but Terelian stabbed the fabric with a dagger and sliced through the cloth. Mitch tugged a leather roll from his pocket.

‘A fat man at Morzenthal; that’s scary,’ whispered Mitch.

Caliper chewed his lip. The blue light had rotated the stones before the crimson beams had heaved them back, so light made a tool, and tools meant toolmakers, builders with skills outstripping those of any craftsman he’d met. Had any builders survived, or was hope misleading him?

Terelian pushed the sagging canvas to one side and stepped into the gloom. Caliper and Mitch wandered into a chamber of old-book smells washed by a dim cousin of daylight dribbling from a patch on the ceiling. Daylight was ferried through Morzenthal along unseen paths. On their left sat a set of low tables holding boxes of coloured crystals. Dusty leather books were piled over warped shelves to their right, and a sweeping set of giant stone stairs descended into a morass of crushed display cases. Shattered glass formed a sea between the cabinets, and outsize knitted dolls dangled from the broken cases as if they’d died while escaping.

‘Don’t stare at the figures,’ Terelian said.

An intact case held leathery heads daubed with shreds of orange paint. The next case contained wooden feet dangling from wires, and a set of black held beads threaded on strings. Battered metal horns spilled from two wooden crates at the foot of the stairs. Behind, wooden pipes pierced a black cloth bag. An outsize violin leaned against a stained plasterboard sheet. Paper sheets and sticks littered the grimy rugs scattered over the floor, and two more oak wardrobes huddled beside the far wall – again with the same crack in the left-hand door.

'Is this safe?'

'No,' Terelian said. 'Most figures have barely shifted since I was last here, but if you hear twittering or see tiny flying birds, tap my shoulder.'

'How many of those wardrobes did yous make?'

'We made nothing, but they kept appearing here, one each day for three months. Younger men than me hauled them across Morzenthal. We think they're safe, but anything left inside can disappear.'

Caliper and Mitch followed Terelian down the vast staircase, and the elder crept forward while staring at the floor. The carousel stretched both ways to form a hundred-foot-wide passage embracing the arena's core. To the right, stacks of cartwheels teetered beside a giant human skeleton forged from rusting iron bars, and beside the outer wall a full-size dinghy with a dusty red sail perched on four wooden rollers. Patches of light glowed in the arched ceiling to drizzle a ruddy glow over the hall.

Footprints snaked between piles of debris where broken gardening tools mixed with shattered pots and carved models of running dogs, and the paths vanished into dusk as the carousel's curved hallway swept to each side. Huge alcoves studded the walls like smoothed-over doors. Model birds dangled from the ceiling to dot the gloom with metallic blue splotches, and stained tapestries hung beside them to twist in unfelt breezes. Movement to his left – had that statue of a young woman twisted his way?

Terelian stopped and scanned the ceiling before leading them between cases, and glass crunched underfoot to spray out a reek of camphor. They passed displays of intricate model boats carved from dark brown wood, but Terelian showed them scars where priests had ripped away labels and plaques.

'Priests, always frightened of stories, always coming with chisel and hammer to destroy. We've hidden many of the labels and stories that lived here, and if the church has truly lost power, we'll restore these tales.'

The elder padded over a twisted path and stopped before sniffing the air. Terelian edged closer to a statue twice his height: a man swaddled in white cloth with a mirror-like ball for a head. The elder bowed a fraction before turning aside.

Further on, a plinth held a miniature liss tree. Another unfelt wind rattled its leaves, and Caliper saw through the trunk the same way he saw through

Christina's body. Mitch stepped onto the plinth and wafted his hand through a branch. The whole image collapsed into a blizzard of glowing dots before knitting back into the original tree.

Terelian gasped. 'Boy, rein in your curiosity: I have no desire to pluck your remains from my toga.'

New glass cases appeared, larger versions with metal rims. One held a model house on stilts with golden foil wrapping its lower half. A tiny ladder had been fastened to a leg, and the upper half was a chaotic scramble of grey facets surrounding two tiny windows. A glassless case held a revolving ball covered in deep-blue paint with green and brown blotches. Mitch rubbed the ball but yelped as a sharp crack ripped through the air, and the sphere kept turning.

Terelian turned to Caliper. 'Does he ever listen?'

'He might one day. Mitch, stow your hands for now,' Caliper said. 'Where did these exhibits come from?'

'Everywhere: nearby, the ocean coast and forests, even the Outland – the glass mountains made a treasure vault and a thousand years of portering.'

'How long have you been here?'

'Almost twenty years.'

Mitch's eyebrows lifted. 'You enjoy Morzenthal's food?'

'With sufficient practice, one develops a taste,

and there are techniques for eating safely. I would provide instruction, but one suspects time is lacking.' The elder stopped and held up his right hand. 'What can you hear?'

'Nothing, not yet,' Caliper said.

'The years have dulled my hearing, so keep listening. Any high-pitched chirping means we must stay still and silent – even your boy.'

'Oh, he's not mine.'

The thicket of cases ended; a swathe of grey carpeted floor stretched ahead.

'Here's your item; well, two items.'

Two bronze statues stood past the carpet: a naked, muscular man stood to gaze at his outstretched hand, and his fingers almost touched another statue, hovering ten feet above the carpet.

'Are there wires?'

Terelian grinned and shook his head.

Each man was Christina's size. Caliper stood underneath the flying man, and half expected the metal to crush him, but only a faint quivering showed in the smooth bronze.

'There's a stepladder, so try touching the flying man.'

Caliper climbed and stretched his fingers upward, but the statue slid up and away. Mitch whistled.

‘You mentioned blue lights,’ Caliper said.

‘You’re standing in them.’

Tiny pinpricks of blue glowed on the standing man’s fingertips, the same shifting colour Phos had braved. Coloured threads linked the statues. Other beams rose from the man’s toes, faint as a candle at noon, and Caliper shifted to watch light stream from his own chest.

‘The beams travel through anything, though night improves the spectacle,’ Terelian said.

Mitch reached for the standing man’s elbow. ‘Will this help Phos?’

Caliper frowned. ‘I’m seeing art: light holds our flying man where the artist planned, so it’s designed. The arena had its design; the shaking broke the floor, but Phos’s light restored the design. I’m thinking we shift this standing man into the arena and make the designs argue, and the arguing might knock the floor slabs away.’

‘I don’t think we’ll be shifting either of these statues. Not before the priests arrive.’

‘I’m not leaving Phos.’

‘No one is, but we need new thinking.’

Caliper gazed at the passageways twisting further into the carousel’s curve; masts and boxes and glittering necklaces spilled over the paths. ‘There’ll be tools here to break stone, and we don’t stop searching.’

Terelian winced. 'I appreciate your urgency, but you haven't had your limbs broken or your skin flayed by these exhibits; they may wake at any moment. Injuring or killing yourself will not aid the girl.'

'You two head back to Frinelia and help her search, and I'll handle the risks here.'

'Nah. We'll both search here and make it fun.' Mitch unfurled his leather roll.

***

Metal clanked under Phos's thin boots, and frost glittered ahead. She pointed her torch at the ceiling but saw only a dim blur. Sense said to wait until Caliper ripped his way towards her, but blurs pressed against the sides of the frosted cubes ahead, and her footprints should show Caliper where she'd gone.

She shivered. Grit coated her mouth, and trying to spit left her croaking in pain. Could she drink the ice coating the floor? Phos's torch splashed light over the cube, six times her height and now close enough to touch. She stroked its side, and the nearest wall dissolved into fog. Mist churned around her wrist, but she felt nothing, so she inhaled and stepped forward. Grey fog blinded her, but another step carried her inside.

Dull yellow light flickered over the room. Dust smothered the floor, and the air was warmer – even brackish. A colossal bed covered in grimy sheets huddled in a corner, and a bedside table held books looking like sawn-off planks. Two upturned chairs sat below a large table covered with plates holding furred scraps of food, and to her right an immense cabinet with drawers ran along the wall. Something rested on the top, too high for her to see. A single line of footprints crossed the floor, each print twice Phos's size, and the footprints led into a stone cubicle filling the far corner.

As a child she'd wandered inside her parents' bedroom to stroke their outsize bed and wrench open the wardrobe doors to peek at the huge shoes and trousers; the strangeness had left her breathless. This furniture dwarfed her too, but she stepped forward to prod the bed.

The blankets had decayed into tangled fibres that crumbled under her fingers. The corner cubicle mirrored the washing space above, and Phos dashed inside, but the booth stayed dry – a crack stretched across one wall.

A simple bedroom, space to rest for a few days, but no one would live here, so had these people flitted like bag-hauling pedlars?

A chair let her see the cabinet top: a scratched worktop crusted with dried-out stains, two enormous rusted pots crammed with spoons sat next to a dip in the worktop – a sink. Bottles crowded the far side, and Phos grabbed one, lighter than glass and paper-dry. She scrabbled through drawers for a sealed container or maybe a mouthful of water, but she found only giant teacups stuffed with yellow mould.

Other cubes would show the same time-chewed rooms. These people had had a kitchen each – maybe they had enjoyed living alone. Phos climbed onto the chair again. They'd cooked here, so how had they drawn water? Her hands shook as sweat dripped onto the filthy worktop.

Dad had muscled water from their garden pump, and she'd grumbled while hauling buckets. He'd silenced her by describing how the largest churches pushed water through pipes. These builders shifted stone with light and built homes from mist, so they'd never lug water by hand. She scoured the cupboards below the drawers and squinted at the join between cabinet and cube wall, but no pipes showed.

The shower upstairs had painted her with water. Phos scraped dust from the sink and pressed her palms against the inside before circling her hand around the curves. Nothing. Phos closed her eyes and wheezed.

Didn't cooking need clean hands? She touched the surface to the bowl's left, and a muted pulse stroked her fingertips. She pushed harder, and a pea-sized silvery ball flashed into place six inches above the sink and hovered before warping into a pencil-thin stream that spattered over the sink's dust. No time for caution; she cupped the icy stream and drank, and she kept dipping her hand into the stream to gulp the water until she panted for breath. Close enough to water, anyway – she filled a bottle.

Phos tapped the right side, and the water drained away to claw at the dust. She sat on the bed. The sheets crumbled to waft threads across her tunic as she prised a book from the table, but her fingers burst through the cover as the pages shredded. The next volume held together, and she coaxed it onto the bed with both hands.

Its cover was bleached beyond reading, but her fingertips eased a page free. Solid blocks of text filled the pages, stained with age, crammed with letters sprouting extra curves and neater than any handwriting. Phos recognised a few words, 'lift', 'access', 'return', 'mass', but extra letters grew inside the words, so unpicking any meaning would take ages.

Movement. The dust specks hovering in the air quivered before streaming towards the wall opposite the one she'd entered. The bed creaked and shifted, and Phos lurched as she fell towards the wall. Her hands gripped the bed, but its sheets burst into powder. She flailed and snatched the headboard, but the whole bed frame tilted and tumbled towards the wall – the floor –

and she fell.

Blackness. Phos's arms and legs froze – she couldn't breathe, but release came without warning. She fell again and her feet smacked into wood – skittling noises echoed everywhere. Her chest and face slapped into a rigid floor, and she slid several feet before stopping, but pain slashed across her legs.

Some force made you fall; they'd never taught her its name, but it misbehaved here – down had shifted. Frost needled her face, and her fingers traced gaps between tiles as another crash echoed on her right. Blinking showed nothing, and weight pinned her legs, and this air was a bitter syrup of tar and mildew.

One heartbeat had shifted her an unthinkable distance and thrown her to fall into this frozen darkness. A faint whistle shivered against the silence, and Phos heaved herself upright as timber slid off her legs. Her bruises screamed, but she sat and stretched forward, and her fingertips scraped her torch's rubber body.

She'd fallen into a bloated schoolroom. A sweep of glossy blackboard filled the wall ahead, and overturned chairs and small tables sprawled around her. The bed frame had fallen through the blackboard before shattering itself over the far wall, but somehow the blackboard was still intact and glossy. Green and brown stains flowered over tan plaster walls on either side, but a few posters still dotted the room, and two huge doors punctured the rear wall.

The desks and chairs facing the blackboard were her size, but centuries of frozen gloom had gnarled the black wood into hard ridges. Graffiti had stretched down here; alien letters scratched the tabletops.

The walls held shelves, rough planks stacked on bricks and bowing under normal-sized books, though the falling bed had scattered volumes over the floor. Phos stumbled towards the nearest shelf, but her torch flickered, and its glow faded into a fluttering violet bead before struggling back into a frail yellowed trace too faint for reading. Light; she needed light. She barged through the desks to the blackboard, but her fingers slid over unbroken glass, and she stepped back. Bitter air stung her nose and fingertips as the torch dimmed again.

Mum had dragged her to church services, where light flared from dangling lanterns when priests groped behind their altar to make them glow. Teachers enjoyed swaggering into lessons. Phos rushed to the back doors and felt for a chair. She climbed up and scraped her fingers over the bricks as her torchlight died.

One brick twitched, and light rained on her. The ceiling lanterns showed as spots of brilliance flush against the ceiling – enough to show ink on the posters clinging to the walls.

She walked over while clamping her hands under her arms against the frost. Brittle paper flinched under her fingers, but faded marks scored the sheet: two figures, one twice the other's height, more diagram than art, lines and shaded patches hinted at faces stripped of character. The large figure's hand rested on the smaller figure's shoulder, and faint lines suggested folds of cloth hanging over their chests, but age had bleached out any fine details, and any lesson stayed hidden. Was the large figure a teacher?

Half the next poster sat curled over the floor, but Phos studied the paper still stuck to the plaster. A large curve, like a ball's upper half, filled the top, and faded ink sketched out an oval underneath the curve's left side. Tiny blocks notched the ball's left side, like an ear. Animal? Plant? An infant's artwork?

She unfurled the fallen roll and winced as it cracked, but the torn edge matched the wall poster, with more lines and a mess of curves. The outer curves made a circle, and two ovals winked at her to bracket the centre, each taller than wide, not a child's scribbled face but a painstaking diagram. A brown tint touched each oval on the side nearest the ball's centre.

Phos gasped. If she sliced through a ring, she'd see two ovals, and her world was ring-shaped. Carpenters carved models of their world, but this worked for posters; a long-vanished artist had drawn a slice through her world. What did the outer circle show? She sipped icy water while shivering. Someone had scrawled a bowl shape under the ball's left side.

Another poster showed a jagged grid of boxes, each holding one or two craggy letters, and Phos thought back to the cube rooms stuck to the vast funnel chamber outside but couldn't see any link. The last picture showed a man standing beside three spindly liss trees. Arrows traced paths between human and tree and back again. What was the message? Humans planted trees, and trees bore fruit? Humans cut timber and gave – her thoughts juddered as frost clawed her hands, and pain stopped her thinking.

Scuff marks covered the floor before the back doors, and Phos would follow even if she was centuries late, follow before the frigid air silenced her. She pulled and pushed at the door handles, but the metal sucked warmth from her hand. She tugged her tunic sleeve over her hand to make a glove, but the door stayed as rigid as iron. Pounding the rigid wood only made a muffled thud. She spent a scrambled minute searching for discarded clothes or rags to swaddle herself, but found nothing. Phos crouched beside a wall and slid her numbed hands inside her tunic as her breath fogged. Caliper couldn't hear her or find her, so would this frozen silence end her journey?

***

Caliper imagined his hand slapping the sculptor's back. They'd share a crisp cider beside a tavern's fire, and he'd ease questions into their chat: who had taught him the statue-making? What skills let him chisel feelings into metal? How long did he spend watching people? A metallic echo of the artist's story had survived these dark years; the flying man planned an urgent voyage, while sadness squatted on the standing guy's face.

Night trickled into the carousel's hallway as the ceiling patches dimmed, and Caliper sensed the piles of exhibits inching closer as dust thickened around the bronze statues. The rays streaming from the arena's scar dwarfed the frail glimmers here, so these frail threads couldn't punch through the arena's floor. Caliper stepped back and stared along the curved hallway, at the bronze masks grinning at him from the glass cases, at the clay pots shaped like bloated feet, and the child-size porcelain dolls staring from a cabinet. Hadn't Frinelia mentioned exploits marrying themselves together to spew out new creations? Did a key lurk inside a half-buried box?

Caliper peered down the carousel and gazed at four wooden mannequins. They startled into life and shambled closer, slow but certain. Their spindly fingers twitched. Five minutes, and he'd need to scarper.

'Don't let the mannequins touch you, and watch out for the birds,' Terelian said.

The elder ushered them deeper into the carousel. Four dog skeletons jerked into life as Caliper passed. One sniffed his knee and followed for ten paces. Terelian hissed warnings as they passed an alcove of eyeless bird models on strings. Dim light glinted from the blue sheen of their flapping wings. Further on, a three-foot crystal cube perched on a table, and dark brown grit filled the bottom quarter. Caliper ran a finger across one edge and recoiled as tendrils of sand leaped against the cube's top before collapsing. He pressed both palms against the smooth glass, and the crystal vibrated as grit fountained upward. If he imagined separate piles the sand divided for him, but sand wouldn't free Phos.

The mannequins lumbered around the curve and shuffled closer, and Caliper squeezed past a teetering hill of musty jackets to face a doll's house like a toy version of Leester's thatched homes. Four-inch figures glided through rooms, and one stumbled downstairs as if drunk while a couple danced by the twisting flames of a tiny log fire. They never noticed him, and watching revealed their pattern – a repeated play without story.

They stumbled onto a bare stretch of stone floor, and Caliper slumped onto a narrow bench beside a wardrobe and a lantern hanging from a pole.

Morzenthal's carousel museum stretched ahead, a thousand-yard-long maze of risk; any key could hide anywhere. Terelian sat beside him and rattled through stories of injuries the museum had caused, and Mitch stood in front to lob questions Caliper couldn't answer. Even if he broke through the stones, how could he lower himself? What if Phos had wandered? How could they stop Rastersen?

'No excuses: we keep trying.' Caliper lurched to his feet and brushed his fingers over stacked trays of brooches and necklaces, and onto a sickly white mask shaped for people his size.

Terelian gasped, and Caliper's vision blurred as distances swelled around him. He looked up, and Christina's image glided through a stack of crates. Her satin robe drifted around her as the mounds of exhibits seemed to shift further away. Terelian's fretted prayers sounded as if they'd travelled a hundred yards, and Caliper heard a distant twittering.

Christina gazed at him. 'We must hurry.'

'We never have time together, but I know you're close. Have you seen Phos, the girl who came with us?'

'You must travel below to reach me. There is….' Her image and voice both faded for three heartbeats before returning. '…white mask renders the newer walls transparent. Time has blocked many paths, but breach the barriers, and you'll find me.'

‘What’s she saying?’ Mitch’s voice had become a high-pitched, metallic rasp.

‘I wear the mask?’

Christina drew closer and crouched before lifting her hand to hover one inch from his cheek. ‘The mask will help you find my physical form. We’ll be together, and….’

He’d expected her sudden vanishing, but air still hissed through his teeth as his world repainted itself in brown and grey.

Mitch stepped where Christina’s image had stood. ‘What happened? Was she talking?’

Caliper nodded and touched the mask. Was it wax? Turning it over showed space for eyes and nose. He pressed the mask onto his face, and it writhed to clamp onto his head. Chilled iron gnawed his skin as its eyes lined up with his.

White fog everywhere. The mask hummed, and he staggered as pain lanced through his skull and his sight faded to black.

‘Not helping,’ Caliper said.

‘No one tells me anything either,’ Mitch said.

Silver lines stroked the darkness as a dew-spangled web reached across his vision, and Caliper steadied himself. More lines appeared to suggest walls and ceilings, and turning showed corners capped by curves, the arches of another alcove. The mask saw through the carousel's clutter. As Caliper stepped forward, the lines dragged through space as if he wandered through a model, and the display picked out a chamber lurking behind the wall. A sealed room wasn't a way forward, but these alcoves had been doorways.

Shouts and clattering footsteps pealed out from around the carousel's curve. The mannequins had drawn near, but now elders hauling tarpaulins raced up behind them. Orders barked out, and the elders threw the canvas over the wooden mannequins before tugging the fabric back. The wooden bodies skittled to the ground, and an ashen-faced Frinelia stumbled towards him.

'We saw the eidolon,' Frinelia said. 'She didn't speak, but she wafted through the arena wall. Did you see her?'

'We spoke,' Caliper said.

'Why did I leave you, and what did she say?'

'Just a few words. She didn't mention Phos, but I have to travel below.'

'Did she give directions?'

Caliper explained; his mask's slow pace meant he'd never explore everywhere, and not before Rastersen broke inside.

Frinelia clasped her hands before her. 'How can I help?'

'You'll know Morzenthal's books, so is there

some class of map for the carousel?'

'The carousel changes, and new walls appear, so any map will be dated, but let me search.'

The mannequins rattled and twitched under the canvas, but Caliper strode to the next alcove and slipped the mask over his face. Another dead end. Mitch shepherded him to the alcove beyond, but again only a sealed chamber sat behind, and the silver lines took longer to refresh. One alcove showed a nest of tiny passages he'd not fit his arm into, and Caliper's shin barked on an iron trolley; tears smeared behind his mask. Terelian followed.

Another alcove. Caliper gasped: the silver lines hinted at a sloping passageway. He ripped his mask away and slapped his palm over the stones.

'Can this wall move?'

Terelian shrugged. 'Yesterday I'd have said not, but now….'

'Do you have hammers or pickaxes?'

'I've seen gardening tools, rakes and trowels, but anything heavier needs grubbing out.'

'Get grubbing out.'

Dusk pooled around the clutter as the patches above darkened, and a crate beside him rattled. Mitch scraped one of his lock picks against a join, and Caliper ran his hands over the stones, smoother than any work he'd touched before.

Minutes passed as light faded into a stagnant twilight, but three elders returned carrying tools, and Caliper chose a two-handed hammer. One blow smacked a fist-sized dent into the stone, and another deepened the hole and splintered out chunks of rock.

'Watch the wall,' Mitch said.

Caliper paused as sweat trickled over his face. His jagged rent softened and shallowed as the stone healed, and his hammer slipped to the floor.

Mitch coughed. 'This wall is original Morzenthal, so it heals.'

Drum sounds boomed through the air, and dust sprinkled from the ceiling as Caliper turned to Terelian.

'I'll investigate.' Terelian hurried off.

'That's your friend Rastersen.' Mitch squatted on a wicker stool. 'He wants to meet Phos. Most likely he's not so fond of you, but he still wants to meet.'

Caliper craved the peace that came when thinking wasn't needed, but outside, fearful puppets with broken strings listened to men with easy answers, and Rastersen would terrify men before offering them a crumb of safety. Caliper picked up his hammer.

'There's other alcoves, and one with worn stones,' Mitch said. 'Maybe the healing's broken there.'

Caliper followed Mitch.

'Look, these stones aren't level.'

Caliper squinted in the gloom. Workers had

hoisted each block into this wall; some foreman had demanded this wall blend with the carousel, but the difference showed. Morzenthal's stones looked perfect, but this forgery showed overlaps and gentle twists in the joints; men had sanded one stone back, and a crack had split another. Good work, but it jarred against Morzenthal's clean lines, and imperfections meant humans.

The distant booms quickened into a mechanical heartbeat. Caliper winced as he slid his mask on, and the silver threads reappeared to reveal another inclined hallway Christina's size.

Footsteps behind, and Terelian's voice glided into his ears. 'You've twenty guards and priests milling outside like worker ants, and they've rigged up a battering ram to break the front door while others hunt for entrances.'

'Can they get inside?'

The drumming paused before returning, louder now.

'The other entrances are hard to detect, but they exist, and many in the council call for unlocking.'

Caliper frowned. 'Can you find me lanterns and rope?'

'What if Rastersen breaks in?'

Caliper said nothing and swung his hammer.

Chapter 18: shadow of the future

Frost numbed her fingers, and she couldn't stop shivering. The time-scoured plaster walls and posters spun around her. Phos stumbled into a bookshelf, and splinters jabbed her palm as books tumbled onto the floor.

Cracks ran through the shelf. Without thinking, her thumb slunk into a gap, and a four-foot spar split away to clatter at her feet. She picked up the ancient wood. The rod had the age-baked hardness of rock.

Teachers always sent her away before they used levers, but she'd played enough to learn, and she jammed the spar into the gap between the doors. Phos thrust sideways, and the doors squealed. She strained, and the left-hand side sprang open to flood brackish air over her as Phos hitched her tunic back into place and stepped through.

The doors led into a vast curving corridor, a mirror of Morzenthal's passages. Sculptors had moulded the wall's plaster into a forest of trunks, and their crinkled bark rose into veined carvings of curling leaves stretching onto the arched ceiling ten yards above. Light filtered through the leaves and reminded her of daylight trickling through the wood where she'd played, but wasn't the ceiling stone? An illusion, a memory of walking outside; glowing greens and golds bathed the air as her boots tapped over the stone tiles.

Clumps of dust daubed the floor, and a stagnant-pond stench filled the air. Her breathing sped up, and she leaned against a wall as sweat poured over her face. Thousands of tons of earth piled above her, and half-broken machines were probably tinkering with her body, but didn't learning always travel with danger?

Another sip of water eased her throat, and ahead a door had toppled onto the floor. Phos paused before looking through the doorway. Scraps of light sneaked from the corridor but showed nothing. She sensed a vast cavern ahead, but darkness swallowed her torch beam, and the space ate her shouts.

Back outside, and Phos sidled past dingy green streaks that had dribbled over the outer wall, and an insect crawled into a crack beside a carved tree. Another doorway loomed on her right, and she stepped inside and into a short passage.

Yellow light burst from a high ceiling, and Phos stepped back. Below, three or four hundred red fabric seats formed rings around a distant circular stage. Stuffing spilled from several chairs, and ceiling tiles had fallen, but even with the decay, this theatre would welcome questions; the circling seats meant you'd see other students learning.

She returned to the curving hallway. The dust grew into small dunes stamped with footprints. Had she completed a circle? No. These were builder prints – twice her size and still sharp. The trail started inside a drift, as if someone had jumped into the dust. Phos tried leaping over the drift, but even her gangling legs were too short, and she'd never avoid leaving prints.

Another room appeared on her right, its double doors gaped open, and she entered. Three heartbeats passed before white light slammed out an eye-gouging blaze, far brighter than the sun's arch. Phos winced, but the glare faded. She'd wandered into a vast wedge-shaped room with beige walls and a high ceiling. Shelves ran along the sides, and each held arrays of identical boxes brimming with folded white cloth. Headless wooden bodies stood motionless on her right. In front hunched three black metal machines looking like insects slobbering over food. Wrinkled crimson sheets hung over chairs, and drawers dotted a cabinet beside her. The ceiling crackled as beige flakes drifted down.

Phos wandered forward. She might be wrong – her old learning might fool her here – but wasn't this a tailor's room? Doorless wardrobes crammed with white jackets stretched into the distance. She stood on tiptoes to unhook a jacket, and dust showered away as soon as her fingers touched the satiny fabric. She stroked an arm, and the tunic quivered. Other cabinets held trousers and boots. Her current clothes scratched, and how often had she hitched up her trousers? She paused. Had she heard rustling?

Phos undid her belt, and her old trousers slipped to her ankles. She shrugged on a clinging one-piece that had to be underwear, and pulled on new trousers. The waist gripped her, and the legs ballooned before shrinking to coat her legs with a pearly fabric. The new jacket hugged her body before fastening itself with a faint sigh, and an instant of pressure at her waist gave way to a solid hug as the jacket and trousers fused.

Smaller cubbyholes sat inside the cabinets, stuffed with what looked like hands without bodies. No, not hands, rigid gloves with metal rims circling the wrist. She snatched one and fitted her hand inside, and the gleaming white gauntlet shrank. Part of her wanted to tug it off, but she waited. The glove knew when to stop, and her hand felt as if she'd dunked it in paint as she flexed her fingers under the glossy fabric. The metal rim snuggled her wrist as if forged by a master silversmith. She picked at the metal, and it resisted for a heartbeat before peeling away. Boots behaved the same way, and she stowed her old ones in the cabinet.

An outfit whiter than any carpet of lilies; Phos's fingers stroked the seams and ran two fingers along the metal collar ringing her neck. Back home a tailor would labour for weeks on this suit, and no suit-maker had ever touched this gleaming fabric, so Morzenthal meant she should learn like a child, learn by prodding and poking anything in reach. Dad wasn't here to guide her from danger, so she had to take care.

These rooms hung off the ring corridor like beads on a bracelet, and each one might house a trade. She imagined indoor fields bustling with machine servants, and breweries wafting yeast and barley through the air. Villagers might work without sweat and curses; there'd be time to read and sing and act, so why had people left?

The next shelves held upside-down fish bowls that threw back curved reflections of Phos's face, and they'd fit over her head while the metal rims they sat on would link to her collar. She snatched one up – far lighter than she'd expected. Light flickered, and a shower of white flakes fluttered past; a bowl might protect her head, but she needed to listen.

A grinding, growling roar bled in from the corridor, and Phos glanced ahead; cabinets stretched to the far walls, but she saw no exits. Had she woken those wooden dummies? No. This rumbling came from the entrance.

Phos squatted behind a cabinet and focused on breathing through her nose, but chiming noises bustled through the doorway with their own rhythm, like a heartbeat of tiny bells. She poked her head out as a squall of glistening dust specks shimmied at the doorway and billowed forward. Metallic specks tumbled in squirming patterns she'd never follow, but after a few heartbeats, the swarm tamed itself, and the dust circled a blurred central point. Dim shapes congealed inside the storm to form spinning bars, spiralling wires and a curving net, a mad dance where everything pivoted around everything else. Shapes collided and merged; each collision pealed out a soft clang.

Hints of something solid emerged inside the cloud. A pair of rigid columns sprouted from the ground. Above, a growing frame of curved rods appeared, a skeleton's ribcage hanging in air. Twice her size, the right size for this room, these swirling motes might rip through her body, but she stood up; Grump's cane and Rastersen's clammy palms could stay in the past.

The cloud rippled like a swarm of bees chasing a fresh target, and dust rushed into the ribcage. Its ribs grew into a solid chest like she'd seen on statues, and arms sprouted from the sides as the blocky outline of a head appeared. This was a blurry sculpture, like a rough carving of a giant human. The leaden surface crawled as more dust smacked into the figure.

Phos inched forward and raised her arm, but the statue's limbs stayed still, an empty house waiting for life. Features coloured the head; closed eyes and mouth brought a quiet imitation of personality. Hands too, blocky models of wrists and fingers. Back home, delivering a statue took three men with a cart and exciting swear words, but here they delivered themselves, which was impressive even if she couldn't tell the gender. No clothes and nothing to hide, though a thin mist still rolled around the limbs as metallic specks stung Phos's cheek.

The statue stayed static, and Phos stepped forward. Three ceiling lights died, and shadows reared around her. She flinched as an intense hissing filled the room.

The body softened and swelled as a long robe condensed across the metal, belted at the waist and tight enough to show breasts swelling into place. Dust danced over the eyes and cheeks as the mouth widened and the lips filled, and shoulder-length hair framed the face as if life waited for a signal. Flesh-coloured patches burst from below to sweep over the grey surface, a flawless peach no paint could match, and dark blue ink flowed over the robe and hair.

Phos didn't know the word, but humans showed a quality; they shared it with dogs and cats but not with spiders or fish. Humans knew if actions helped or hindered, and humans crafted their own future. The quality lived here; she wasn't alone.

The twisting head made her gasp with its perfect

mimicking of human muscles, and the figure's robe flowed as the arms rose. Eyes opened, and a half smile flickered as its hand swept to its face, and the statue blew over its fingers. The arms glided like a dancer's, though they were thicker than Caliper's thighs.

The figure gazed at Phos, and its head tilted a fraction.

'I've done this a dozen times, and I'm still surprised when it works.' A lilting voice where calm tones dripped with precision. 'I trust I didn't startle you, Phos. Materialising before people seems rude, but I didn't know your exact location.'

Phos's mouth hung open. Now even her own name sounded strange.

'You're the first here for centuries,' said the figure. 'I hope you're managing.'

'It's fine. I found water.'

'Water, yes, good. My name is Christina – you've met my friend.'

'Caliper mentioned you.'

'I asked him to come, but projecting outside is difficult: so much has broken.'

'How do you know my name, and Caliper's name, and who are you?'

'Caliper understood a slice of your world's workings, and you've seen his exploits.'

'You've watched us?'

'He learned a few secrets from me, but I couldn't say much: even he has limits.' Christina held out her arms in welcome, and her sleeves flowed to follow the motion, an almost perfect illusion, though her lips never quite matched her words. 'My room awaits, so will you join me?'

'Is it rude to ask what you're made of?'

'I'll explain later, but my room may offer more comfort.'

Outside, and the corridor blazed gold and green like a forest's sunny day, and Christina strode forward before checking herself and walking at Phos's pace. They walked for minutes past several blocked doorways.

'You appeared from a cloud; is that normal here?'

Christina chuckled. 'I've spent centuries alone, so my actions are always normal. I spent my last century in my mental form, but voices without bodies can terrify people, so I changed. It's fun to scuff my feet on carpet.'

'Caliper mentioned ghosts.'

'My image travels, but few see my face, and fewer hear my words. I sought to talk, but I only ever frightened the villagers. Our world decays, and each projection hurts more, and these days I cannot tell where my image appears.' Christina paused and looked upward a fraction as if thinking. She knelt, and her hand touched Phos's shoulder as their eyes met. 'I have a task for you that will test your mind and body to their utter limits, but I believe you will find the strength.'

Phos stared into the pale blue discs of Christina's eyes and the intricate tracework of lines ringing her irises. 'Can I take Caliper?'

'Of course. He's trying to rescue you.'

'I thought he might.'

'We spoke earlier; I wanted him to reach me, and he still might, but your arrival alters everything, and I must protect you as far as I can.'

Christina rose and sauntered forward, and Phos fell silent. Questions brewed inside her, and all of them fought for her breath.

'Here we are.' Christina's willowy body swished into a high chamber shaped like an upturned wine glass. Silver light drifted past paper streamers dangling from the domed ceiling. Two curved sofas surrounded a low glass table, and pictures dotted the walls to show the forests and grass of the world above. One image showed golden leaves cascading from an elm in a gentle breeze. Phos gasped. Moving pictures – was this a window?

'Please sit.'

Cushions crinkled beneath her as a musky fragrance wafted past, and Phos breathed out as she settled back into the couch.

Christina's robe shifted into an emerald green and rustled as she crossed her legs. Her hair turned auburn. 'Caliper is trying to reach us, but he has centuries of decay to struggle through, and for now our link has broken. I sense a thousand questions inside you, but let's start at the beginning. I will go slowly, but tell me if you need rest. I know of several beginnings, but one involves everyone; you have some of the facts, but you need a story.'

Phos swallowed and cleared her throat before gazing at Christina's eyes – a blue taken from the clearest lake, quiet on the surface, but untold currents surged below. 'Teachers say our world never changes, but our apples taste bitter and the trees stink. Are the teachers wrong?'

Christina's eyes never blinked. 'I dreaded telling Caliper this story, but you have less to unlearn. Your teachers have lied, but watching the world will teach you the truth.'

Phos nodded. 'I've seen ancient books where trees have different shapes, and the trees on the carvings outside were shorter than ours, and I think they were older than anything in books. How did everything start? My father said I came from a seed, and plants and trees come from seeds and acorns. Why isn't our world the same?'

'Every world has a start, Phos, and our story begins there.' Christina's robe faded into a spring forest's pale green. 'Your distant ancestors lived far above your world. Their learning would astound you: they travelled hundreds of miles in an instant; their voices carried over immense distances; they could heal the most appalling injuries; and if they spoke of their desires, the earth spawned what they wanted.'

'And they created us?'

'Stay seated.'

Christina stood and approached the wall behind her before lifting both arms. The room's walls blurred before melting into the floor to expose a velvet blackness. The chamber's light faded, and Phos gripped the sofa cushions as Christina's image became a silhouette.

A silvery sphere winked into view on her right. She couldn't tell its size or distance, but the ball looked like a slow-spinning marble coated with a world's skin. Mountain ranges pocked the surface, and darker flat patches looked like seas.

'Your ancestors lived on this surface.'

Phos stood. 'No walls, no vault, and curves everywhere? Nothing overhead?'

'Nothing to protect them; their sky was too open. War came, and their enemies curdled daylight into a poison savage enough to kill anyone outside.'

‘They poisoned the sun’s arch?’

‘Not the sun’s arch, Phos: the sun.’

‘The sun? The….’ Phos played with the word. ‘This came before the sun’s arch?’

A second, featureless gold sphere appeared further off to throw a curved shadow over the silver ball. The golden ball inched around the silver, and its shadow crept over the model mountains.

Phos held her breath. ‘This creates night and day? Our sun’s arch mimics this sun?’

‘Is this too much for you? Would a pause help?’

‘You can’t stop now.’

‘The sun let people grow crops.’ Christina paused to choose her words. ‘The poisoned light withered their fields, and weapons cracked open their homes to let wind howl over the land. Night came, and everything froze, their food, their air, their bodies.’

‘They poisoned sun…light?’ Phos swallowed. ‘Are we safe?’

Christina nodded as golden light brushed her hair. ‘People sought darkness underground, but poison would stain their fields for centuries, and their shelter needed food. You must sit.’

‘I don’t need a break.’ The two spheres faded, and now their only light leaked in from the open doorway. A delicate mist bunched around Phos’s shadow.

'The survivors rebuilt an ancient mine and used their skills to create fields and lights underground, and they believed themselves safe. If you're ready, I should show you.'

Phos looked to her right, and a disc coated in green and brown patches floated in darkness. Phos stepped to her left; the disc was a bowl stood on its side.

'That's not our world.'

'It's part of your history. The war became one of sabotage and disguise, and this reforged mine was their first attempt at hiding. Imagine a bowl stamped into soil and covered by a plate.'

'Their first attempt?'

Christina stepped forward. 'This became known as the First Enclave. Your world lies underneath, and it was called the Second Enclave.'

Phos's cheeks flushed in the darkness. 'There're fields and buildings inside the bowl, and roads bunching at the centre.'

'Villages and towns, together with fields for crops.'

'Those fields near the rim look like cliffs.'

'There's a force called gravity that lets you fall, and the First Enclave's makers twisted it to their demands. Reach the First, and wherever you stand, the force tugs you towards the ground, and after time, it will feel normal.'

'So we're not surrounded by rock?'

'I tried to spread the truth, but only Caliper heard my voice. Shall we continue with this flood of learning?'

Phos blushed. 'Yes, I'm ready.'

Silver light drifted from overhead to pick out Christina's hanging streamers.

'War had devastated the surface, but people had started families in the First, and for decades the crops were rich and succulent. They hoped to stay underground until the poison above faded, but within fifty years their soil turned rancid and their crops withered.'

'Did the sun leak in?'

'No. Waste built up. Nature couldn't endure being crammed into such a tiny world. People knew this from the start, and they'd created tiny machines to ferry food between plants and cart away waste or cure new diseases.'

Phos gasped. 'Tiny machines?'

Christina's eyes studied Phos's face. 'Imagine a windmill turning wind and grain into flour. Now imagine a windmill your size, and now imagine one a tenth that size.'

'Like a toy?'

'Now imagine one an inch high, a tiny windmill

with gears and sails and grindstones, but it still works. Think of a smaller version, the size of a grain of wheat, and now one a tenth that size, next one so small you could stack a thousand inside an inch. Imagine one a thousandth that size, but again, the windmill still works.'

'Toys for tiny children?'

'Your world's builders made the tiniest blocks of matter dance to their music; they made machines like windmills, waterwheels, looms, ploughs, distilleries, any machine required, and their machines talked. A tiny loom might ask a tiny delivery cart for more wool.'

'Frinelia had a story….'

'These tiny machines brought life to the First Enclave, and newer versions support your world.'

'They're not called tiny machines, are they?'

Christina smiled and walked around the sofa before sitting. 'None of my pupils had your thirst, Phos. They're called nanotechnology, or nanotech, as small as anything can be.'

'Are Caliper's exploits part of this?'

'Some people could command hidden nanotech functions. I thought the ability lost, but both Caliper's parents had skill, and your miller has talent beyond imagination. He shapes the world as a potter shapes clay.'

'I should demand lessons.'

'I have never described the nanotech to him; he's strong in mind and body, but he's passed the age where learning is easy.' Christina paused. 'Half of me expected you to run away screaming.'

'It explains what I've seen, and true stories have their own weird flavour; no one invented this. What happened in the First?'

'Their nanotech couldn't remove the waste piling up, so the builders granted their tiny machines new powers. Still more plagues attacked their crops, and the builders became desperate. They absorbed nanotech into their bodies to ward off illnesses and taught the machines how to read minds. At first this worked: the skilled turned stone into metal or glass, and fashioned new plants or powerful medicines.'

'What went wrong?'

'The human desire for power never wavered. Before, people had debated with words, but once nanotech entered their bodies, any arguments drew weapons from the ground – talking weapons that redesigned themselves. Ambition spilled blood, and over time humans passed more and more control to the machines until the nanotech worked only for itself, and it claimed the First. Poison still coated the surface, so the builders clawed deeper and built a new enclave. Failure forced lessons into their heads, and they made your world far larger and with gentler machines. Even so, there was no staying in the First; they sealed its nanotech inside.'

Christina leaned back on her sofa and gazed at Phos's face. 'The builders created this city to house the engines that shaped your hills and mountains, and carpeted them with plants. Your people were born here.'

'My people?'

'Nurseries, classrooms, dormitories and play areas – everything your size.'

'My size?'

'My builders made me their size. Larger humans needed potent nanotech, but they designed the smaller people to survive with gentler machines, and they work inside you now.' Christina's dress flashed a vivid crimson and shone like foil as a black belt emerged to cinch her waist. 'The surface poison lasted longer than anyone expected, and the Second Enclave needed to last thousands of years as your kind kept the human fire alive.'

Phos twiddled her hair.

'The Second's nanotech couldn't keep the First Enclave people alive, but a few survived their final catastrophe and clustered by the entrance to this world. We became parents to their children, and for centuries, we projected our images into their countryside to teach farming and fishing; how to sow seeds or carve wood.

Even ancient history – stories from America, Asia or Africa. Over time, our machinery here faltered, and by *machinery*, I mean constructs like me' Christina paused. 'You look tired, Phos. Would a short break help?'

'A nap? No, thanks. You talked about friends?'

'*Constructs*, *friends*, two words for one idea. There were nine of us and sometimes I murmur through their names. Isabella, Sophia, Charlotte, Emily, Michael, Peter, Emma. We laughed while sharing stories and remembering friends. But over those centuries our bodies failed, and one by one my friends slowed before stopping forever.' Christina glanced downwards. 'I spent most time with Gwendoline. Like me Gwen was a construct, and we worked to educate our adopted children and illustrate their world's workings. She lasted for centuries, but one day I came here to find her sitting where you are now – sitting without moving. I touched her arm, but she never twitched or breathed, and her eyes stayed blank. I laid her beside the other constructs, and the last five thousand years won't have touched her. There's been little reason to materialise since, but here I am, hoping to carry out a construct's final duty. I couldn't tell you why I've lasted seven thousand years. The First's machines lasted decades, and the Second's until now.'

'Until now?'

‘You have evidence.’

‘Dying plants and stinking trees?’

Christina nodded and rested her hands on the sofa’s cushions. ‘No one can make an immortal machine, but the builders let their creations breed. For thousands of years, child machines in the Second copied their parents, but each birth added errors. Now the machines are unsure; tree branches twist back into their trunks, and leaves die as soon as they bud.’

Phos brought her legs up and sat cross-legged on the sofa. Her life was an inch-long thread on a thousand-yard tapestry, and fatigue closed her eyes, but she forced them open. ‘The First failed, and the Second dies, so is there a plan?’

‘I have half a plan, and maybe a direction,’ Christina said.

‘Do we tunnel down again?’

‘We lost the talent. You must revisit the First Enclave with an argument.’

‘Do I climb the world walls?’

‘No. There’s a direct path. Once I realised the Second was dying, I called people here, but only Caliper approached.’

‘And you got me.’

‘The rim of the First Enclave’s bowl touches the surface, and that’s where the builders forged our nanotech. Reach the rim, and you’ll see vast maps of the First, where the builders planned their work; the First Enclave used to listen for instructions.'

'Used to? Did it stop?'

'I'll write an instruction package, an argument, take it to the rim, and the First might listen and understand. Orders won't work, but we may persuade the nanotech to recreate the Second's tiny machines.'

'So this map room works like the tiny huts workmen use when they're building houses?'

Christina nodded. 'I can create the package, but I can't touch the First. A light you can't see cascades through this city. It holds me together, but I can't walk where it doesn't reach. Take friends and learn the secrets we've forgotten. I've seen you scurry beside your miller; I've seen you ask questions and run tests, and you've rediscovered ways of thinking we should never have lost. The new thinking may help you survive.'

'May?'

'The First must have changed beyond recognition, so you'll face unimaginable threats, but you must leave before dawn, and there's no time to plan. Learn once you're there, and your new way of thinking will help.'

'Who designed the first tiny machine, and can we forge our own tools in the First?'

'Time has ripped up many records, and my mind

stutters. It forgets, and recalls events that haven't happened, but I know the First's machines have the strength to rip your body apart. Avoid the nanotech until you reach the map room. We erected barriers to protect the Second, and I must weaken those barriers to let you enter the First, and the nanotech may take advantage. I'll take you back to the upper city and help you break through the vault, and I'll write the argument to persuade the First's machines, but before any of that happens, I'll need your permission.'

'What?'

'Humans built me to teach words and numbers to children, to clear furniture after lessons and comfort the fretful. I can do more, but my powers festered unused because my body scared my creators, and they demanded I wait until a human standing beside me gave permission. I hoped Caliper would come, but in extreme times, I can accept a child's orders.'

'Your lessons must have been fun.'

'I can reset this city to its ancestral design and make it a place where journeys start and end. Materials and people shuttled between here and the First, and your permission will rebuild the path.'

Memories of Leester's classroom surged through Phos; she'd seen hands weave threads into vivid pictures of crimson roses – talent could conjure worlds from nothing.

Phos sat and her suit crinkled. ‘How did people appear on the surface? Was there a seed?’

‘There’s much my builders kept from me, and they never expected me to hunt knowledge. I can’t prepare you for the First’s dangers, and you must work out the rules.’ Christina played with her sleeves before looking at Phos. ‘I need your permission to restore this city and the pathways.’

‘We called this place Morzenthal.’

‘Morzenthal? Fascinating. Do I have permission?’

‘You’re asking a thirteen-year-old for permission? What if I refuse?’

‘We stay here while I create food you’ll hate, and we wait as our world dies.’

‘That’s not what humans are for; you have permission.’

Christina’s eyes closed, and she sighed, and her chin lifted as her breathing stopped.

Phos stood and trotted around the table. ‘Christina?’ No sleeper looked this silent; the woman’s neck was as ashen as Dad’s unbreathing face. Christina’s hands twitched and her fingers vibrated before life poured back into her body, and a harsh rattle escaped.

‘Don’t try that yourself, Phos.’ A metallic taint clawed her voice.

'You've reset the city?'

'The process has started, but the walls in upper Morzenthal will take several minutes to shift, and most areas won't alter until all humans are safe.'

'Most? Those elders won't expect change.'

Christina pursed her lips. 'We must avoid suffering, but small shocks can stimulate. Your next journey awaits. It will start difficult and get harder, but there is little choice.'

The floor trembled as Christina ushered Phos into the corridor and turned right. The grassy shades of a summer's morning flitted over the carved leaves above, and Phos scurried behind. Christina gestured at a room as they passed. 'The first Second Enclavers were born without mothers, but with more time, we could visit the machines that nursed them.' She glanced at a mossy patch creeping over the carved corridor wall. 'Some equipment still works; some doesn't; and some misbehaves.'

A yawning doorway twice the size of the others appeared to their left. Lights flared as they entered a circular room where desks and chairs faced outwards, so these pupils had stared at their blackboard walls – now mildewed slabs of curved black glass. Christina's fingers grazed a sheet, and the ceiling dimmed as the fungus sloughed from the glass. White blotches glowed on the walls and swelled into scrolling letters as images of spinning apples and pears floated into view.

Words groaning with distorted letters, words married to pictures, fruit and animals, trees and houses, the bones of an ancient lesson. Most desks stayed lifeless, but a handful repeated the blackboard's words.

'I used to teach here, but until now I couldn't bear to enter.' Christina's voice quavered as the glass blackboards mirrored her words.

'You knew my name, so can you see what's happening outside? I must see Mum.' Phos's words scratched themselves over the glass, a fiery-red invasion.

'Are you certain? You've no time for distraction.'

'She's my mum, not a distraction.'

'Will you help her if she's in danger? Delay means not seeing the First.'

Phos blinked. 'You said you couldn't act without human permission, but does it work both ways? Do you take orders?'

Christina raised her arm. 'Take my hand: I need your blood.'

Phos peeled off her glove and clasped Christina's fingers. Papery skin rasped against Phos's palm.

'She's alive, and I'll show you.'

Fresh images welled over the walls, dancing

shades of grey, and the picture moved though it looked as if an artist had carved it from grainy wood. Three women chatted without sound as fabric twitched behind them.

'There's no one I recognise,' Phos said.

'I'm seeing through your mother's eyes. Your mother talks to people inside a tent, and they're using lanterns. Is your mother's name Shelaker?'

Phos nodded.

'I'm reading lips; they used her name in a rude joke, so don't worry.'

'I can't see Mum's face?'

'Not unless she uses a mirror.' The pictures faded and Christina faced Phos. 'Your world is dying, and reaching the First means leaving now, so we must speak to Caliper.'

'You two have history. Are you luring him? He mentions you, and it's like he's praying or…well…I'm young, but I know a little about men, so seeing as you're twice his height and made of dust specks glued together by light aren't you promising what you can't deliver?'

'I only have words, Phos; even if they stretch across our world, they're only words. Yes, I gave him false hope, but reshaping Morzenthal needed human permission.' Christina stared upward. 'Maybe I used hope as a tool, as a weapon, but everyone's interests stayed deep inside what Gwen called my heart. Can you see?'

Phos perched on one of the tiny chairs. 'How will you tell Caliper?'

'With great care. Will you look for your mother?'

'No. Finding her means dying with her.'

'The First?'

'The First, and the surface,' Phos said.

'We'll visit the centre henge and travel upward. You're wearing most of the required suit, but you missed the helmet.'

'Those bowls I saw?'

'You need your own air, and I'll transport the equipment you need. The men outside mean we must leave at dawn. I'll tweak this wall to let us pass. It shouldn't admit children, but decay makes rule-breaking easier.'

'These blackboards are broken? I fell through one earlier.'

'Are your hands tingling?'

'Oh, shut up – I'm nervous enough.'

'We've no other way; I'll enter first and you follow.' Christina paused. 'Your passion for learning will help you survive the First Enclave, but it will also bring danger. I can't tell how the new world has changed or how Caliper's talents will affect it, but go gently, and find a balance between researching and prodding.'

Her words scrolled across the blackboard but scattered as Christina strode into the dark glass. Phos closed her eyes and followed.

Blackness muzzled her. Was she hanging in space? Breath wouldn't come and her heart jammed, but the world reappeared in a blink, a cell like the one where she'd refilled her water bottle. Christina strode through the far silver wall, and Phos followed. Back now, into the clanking cavern of echoing footsteps, and the black henge waited ahead. Her coiled rope still sprawled over the floor. The lanterns sitting between the henge stones drizzled out a purple glow too feeble to reach the ceiling.

'How do we climb?'

Christina's feet scuffed metal. 'I'll build us a road. I can follow you to upper Morzenthal but no further.' She paused and stroked a henge pillar while looking upward.

'What do these stones do?'

'They house raw material for our climb.' The pillar hissed as smoke coiled upward. The lanterns hurled out a red glare, and the air above rippled as if rising from a blaze.

'Is that nanotech?'

'No. The machines are invisible. You're seeing

their effect on the air.'

Phos arched her neck to follow the rippling smoke as crimson light glittered over the distant glass cubes. A rhythm seized the beams, and each pulse built the glow until light scalded her eyes. Vibrations left her feet aching and her teeth chattering as a ruddy glow stroked the ceiling.

Christina's eyes closed, and her limbs locked like a statue's, but something smoothed the pillar's corners. Four streamers burst from the wall cubes overhead; filaments of red and gold spiralled into the centre and braided themselves into a pulsing ring above the henge. Cracks ripped through the screaming metal floor, and jagged black ridges burst out around the stone pillars, but Christina never moved.

'Christina? What's happening?'

The ring overhead swelled downward to touch the floor, a vast tunnel of light, a writhing cage. Smoke poured from the pillars, and the fumes pounced into the brilliant ring of filaments as the cage widened at the top to make a funnel. A low rumbling left Phos breathless. Half her mind demanded she plunge her hand into a beam, but she stood still.

A grinding noise rang out from Christina's body, as if a plough had scraped a stone. She shuddered as smoke curled from her left fist, and her eyes opened.

'We're set, but don't try returning to the

classrooms.'

'Problems?'

Christina stared at the charred stump of her hand. 'Both Morzenthal and I are ancient, and changes hurt.'

Where had Christina's thoughts drifted over these silent centuries? No wonder she'd talked to Caliper.

Christina sighed. 'Only Caliper listened.'

Coincidence, or did Christina sense her thoughts? Phos stared. 'He never stopped saying your name.'

'He's unique. At first everyone heard us, but the fourth generation were mostly deaf, and the fifth utterly so. Caliper is a….' Christina's face froze for a heartbeat. 'There's a problem. I asked Caliper to find me, and he's broken a wall and uncovered an old path.'

'Can we meet halfway?'

'I can't message him now, but my changes make his path lethal. We must stop him travelling, and he may not hear my voice, so you must tell him.'

'I won't forget, but how do we climb?' Gold and scarlet streamers still raced around to wrap them in a glittering cone.

Christina stared upward. 'This web holds our carrier field.'

'What's a carrier field?'

'I'll show you.' A pearly fog foamed around their feet, and Phos jolted upward. Pressure thrust against her soles as the fog stretched out to the funnel's sides.

'This will raise us, but keep away from the sides.'

They rose an inch every few heartbeats, and Christina tapped her feet while looking at the ceiling. 'Frinelia knows more than she's told. Her church bathes in secrets, but ask her about the Heresies. People believed the nanotech would create cities for itself. If so, you must avoid those cities, but you must also learn to live from the land.'

'What would these cities look like?'

'I have no idea.'

Phos frowned.

'The last records I saw of the First spoke of slender black glass spires rising from the ground, coils of plant life worming inside the towers, and carts wheeling outwards from the city as if exploring and claiming. The towers changed as the survivors watched; branches sprouted from the trunks. Ahh, why is this field so slow?'

'These wonders, the metal creatures and new ways of travelling – even broken they're breath-stealing. Why are they locked away? Most villagers sweat to set food on their plates, and they've no time to think.'

'There's your answer,' Christina said.

'You mean, work stops us thinking? Is that the church's goal?'

'Remember Frinelia's word?'

'*Puppeteer?*'

'You didn't fall into your current state; people desperate for control pushed you. I've watched priests teach each other how to operate medical apparatus or library systems or viewing platforms, and the priests wince as they touch the controls, but if they control food and medicine, others dance to their tunes. They're terrified of commoners rising to their level.'

'That's why they cage books?'

'We might open a cube festooning these walls and haul out devices to fashion clothes or mine the earth, but your priests seek to ration free time – commoners shouldn't have time to think.' Christina crouched in front of Phos. 'I would teach you everything I know of the First and its tiny machines, but my knowledge is thousands of years old, and we have no time. But you've learned how to learn: you've asked questions and developed ideas.'

'I ended up with a million ideas and no idea which was true.'

'I've seen you test your world, Phos. The belt you threw into the light, your work to find water, the way you prised open the classroom door. You can develop ideas, test them, draw conclusions and test again – and each test brings the truth closer. You've rediscovered an ancient way of learning and a method impossible to hide, a light for every world. Use it in the First; refine it, and the Enclave may yield its secrets.'

'What does Frinelia know?'

Christina stood and stepped back. 'She's risen far, but part of her knows she'll never breach the church's inner circle, and in part that's why she seeks revenge.'

'For her daughter?'

'The histories she's uncovered have helped her stitch together a story that doesn't stray far from the truth, so keep her talking.'

Vibration deafened Phos and she looked up. The red light bathing their ceiling had vanished, and so had the arena's floor. Only a yawning black gulf showed above, but shouldn't she see the arena's covering dome?

Their milky disc spread out as the funnel widened, and they glided through the space where stones had rolled through the air, and up into the arena. The old floor had vanished to leave a ring of stone circling an immense hole, and their motion slowed until their disc sat flush with the ancient stone floor. The throbbing pulse faded into a growling murmur before silence returned.

Wind buffeted her face, and the air held the damp chill of outdoor nights. The domed roof had gone, and the metal band she'd seen now formed a rim around a circle of night, but the vault stayed unseen. Their arena stood empty, and Phos called out to let her voice echo around the curving walls.

Christina clapped her hands, and silver light cascaded from her body. 'This disc will rise at dawn, and if you and your friends are on board, it will lift you to the First. At dusk it returns here, but I can't stop it repeating the journey tomorrow.'

'Rastersen,' Phos said.

'He will follow. Passion burns inside him, and he believes your talent may oil his path to power.'

Phos nodded.

'He sees you as a resource, but he also sees himself in you. He plans to steer you past the obstacles he endured, and use you to strengthen his hand.'

'No. I'll find my own way.'

Christina smiled. 'I hope you will, but we must find Caliper.' She breathed in while staring at the arena's archways, where elders had torn canvas seals from two of the doors. 'Do you know where everyone is?'

'I've been away,' Phos said. 'Can't you sense Caliper yourself?'

‘My vision here is poor, but we must find him.’

Phos darted towards an archway but stumbled with fatigue. Caliper had braved the carousel. She slapped aside the canvas and hurtled down the steps, and Christina followed to scatter shadows over the piles of exhibits. Three dolls knocked on their glass case as she scurried past. She tripped and fell against a stack of three bloated wooden heads. Their lips parted to hiss at her, but she darted away.

Lanterns bobbled in the distance. She entered an open space; two elders argued beside a tall glass case like an empty coffin, but they looked up at Christina and fell silent. A single elder stood four yards away beside a lamp, leaning on a single crutch, young for Morzenthal, with only a scatter of grey in his hair. Christina drifted towards him, and he collapsed backwards into a chair.

‘Sir, have you seen the miller, Caliper?’

His eyes flickered to Phos before he pointed down the hallway.

‘There’s our path.’ Phos ran forward and collided with a display case, but sounds drifted from ahead: metal bit into stone, and bricks tumbled as men’s cheers bounced from the walls.

Elders had brought lanterns here and shunted the display cases aside. Glass shards carpeted the floor. Caliper stood gripping a sledgehammer, and he’d punched a yawning fissure into an alcove's back wall. Elders swarmed behind him, but gasps rang out as they saw Christina.

Phos's throat was raw, her mouth papery, but her story needed delivering, and she elbowed herself through the elders. Christina held back.

Caliper stared into a dark tunnel, and his lantern threw light into a sloping passageway.

Phos smirked. 'Where are we headed?'

Caliper kept facing the tunnel. 'The stones trapped Phos underground, but they found plans, and this passage runs below.'

'Does she still need rescuing?' The room swirled around Phos as sweat trickled over her forehead.

Caliper stopped breathing, and his head swivelled towards her; his face was red.

'How long…how long have you been…?' He closed his lips as his swear words fermented. 'I've spent hours breaking through, and you….'

'Have you finished?'

'I've not even started. I've not….'

'Don't use this passageway,' she said. 'There's lots to say, but that's most important. There's something else, and someone else.'

'Christina is down there.'

Phos shook her head and turned. The miller's gaze followed her raised arm, and the now silent

Morzenthal elders shuffled to clear his view. Phos couldn't read Christina's face, but a set of wrinkles vanished from her robe, and a few wisps of her hair straightened themselves.

'Hello, Caliper,' Christina said.

Chapter 19: grasp the circle's end

Christina's arms rose from her sides, and peach-like tones flushed across her face as her crimson robe shone like dawn against the gloom. Still twice his height; her image blurred as if he stared through a sheet of ice, but now she wouldn't disappear. Christina tilted her head a fraction as brown hair framed her face, and hints of silver light trickled from her dress as if she were a lantern swaddled in gauze. The rays picked out the dust he'd knocked into the air.

The elders parted around Christina. Most stared, but five knelt to bow their heads, and Phos stayed still.

'Christina, I….' Could he stop his staring?

'Do you understand me?'

Christina's words dripped into his mind like leaves landing on still water, and he nodded.

'Good to see you alive, Caliper. The path behind isn't safe.'

Should he read anything into the way she pressed her lips together? 'You came and brought Phos.'

Christina took one step forward before pausing. 'There are two stories. One you may not believe, but the other….' Her mouth twitched, but her eyes never blinked. His gaze darted to the carousel's shadowy tapestries and the elders swarming Christina; they looked like crumpled paper dolls. Phos stood apart. Her lips formed words, and her broken syllables skittered against Caliper's ears.

Caliper frowned. 'I'm only hearing you, Christina.'

'I'll adjust.'

Phos's voice pierced the murk. 'Is everything all right? Should we wheel you somewhere?'

'Can Phos hear me?'

'Yes, Phos can hear you,' Phos said. 'There's a cloud linking you two.'

Colour oozed back into the crowding elders, and creases grew on Christina's robe as she stepped back and faced the crowd.

'Can everyone understand me?'

The elders gasped, and one elderly man fainted. The distant hammering returned as a demand booming across the carousel.

Christina raised her arms. Her left hand was a clotted mass of grey ash. 'I sense questions everywhere, and answers will come, but let me spend time with your miller. Tomorrow you may not recognise your city, so prepare for change.'

A smile; her gaze touched him again, and the world around Christina blurred and darkened. 'No one will hear us now, and we'll rejoin Phos later.'

Christina turned, and the elders scuttled from her

path as she marched into the exhibit stacks. She squeezed between two bronze statues her size, and her arm knocked over a frame strung with beads to scatter the balls over the floor. Caliper glanced back; Phos stood beside a gaggle of elders and stared, but worry stained her face.

Christina strode into a shadowy stretch of the carousel, and a stack of painted masks chirruped as she passed before damping themselves into a hushed murmur. She paused beside a small plinth holding a small statue, six inches of bleached porcelain with arms stretching upward, and Christina's fingers caressed the tiny hands. Mist still tainted his vision, and he remembered a day decades ago, returning from school to his mother's lifeless body, and having tears turn his world into running streams of light. Christina had stroked the statue in the same way he'd reached for his mother's hands.

Caliper blinked and followed. How often had friends grumbled about him being single and churned out stories of couples fated to meet? Had his earlier rejections cleared his path to Morzenthal? He stared at the back of Christina's head and the folds of crimson rolling over her shoulders, and memories of her face let him ignore her height. This sleeping museum doled out privacy in its darkness, but her dress ladled out enough light for him to follow.

'Does your arm hurt?'

'Don't worry.' Christina drifted into a clearing and gazed at a carved stone pillar before swinging around and dropping to one knee to hold her stump towards him. 'I sacrificed my hand to reach you, but now we're together, I'll reset.'

Mist swirled around the stump to breathe a fleshy hue into the soot, and the stub flowed into a new shape as a flicker of pain shivered across her face. Her hand grew back to share her face's colour, and Christina's fingers made a fist before relaxing. A gouge now ran across the stone pillar. Was *reset* another word for 'healing'?

She stretched out and draped her hand over his shoulder. He flinched but stayed standing. He might drown himself in the patterns etched into her eyes, crinkled bands of pale blue circling her pupils. Her full lips parted as she drew in a deep breath.

'We've talked and grown closer than I thought possible. I've worked with thousands of men, but you've occupied my thoughts like no other. You've sacrificed your home and faced danger to reach me. You deserve honesty, and I should be honest with myself.' Christina swallowed and he held his breath. 'We're different forms of life, which makes us different people. Your freedom of thought gives you the strength to pick this world apart and even reshape it. You're seven thousand years younger than me, and you have skills I can't imagine, ways of thinking I can't comprehend, and I have a few talents you don't.'

She released his shoulder and her features blurred: her skin dulled as her nose and mouth broadened. Christina's fine brown hair shaded to black and shortened, and for three heartbeats, a young boy with a cheeky grin knelt in her place before the features swirled back into Christina's face.

'I'm not my appearance; none of us are. My vision changes when we're together, so a cord links us, but I am nothing like the human women you've met. Everything adds up to one thought, Caliper, one conclusion we can't escape: we can't be together.'

Christina clasped his shoulders. 'I'd explain further, but we lack time. I've given Phos a task that will tax her beyond imagination. She is clever and brave, but her recklessness scares me. Passion carried you here, and passion is precious, but can you change its nature? Can your passion protect Phos?'

The carousel's artefacts spun around him, and words clotted in his throat.

Christina's grip tightened a fraction. 'The exploits bend to your desires, and you've faced danger without flinching. Now everyone, including me, needs you to become a travelling guardian and a hand gripping the reins. I regret the deceit, and I'll never wipe the bitterness from my mouth, but I cannot be what you seek.'

Was he swaying and plunging into a lonely future of silent days? Sweat prickled Caliper's forehead, but he'd damp down the anger and show strength while gazing into Christina's eyes.

Christina pursed her lips. 'Can I explain another way?'

'No. It's fine.' Christina's words still scraped his mind. Would future days see him slapping his own face in fury at the way he'd fooled himself? No need to burden Christina with guilt, and even now she showed none of the twitching impatience that had needled other women.

Those slender fingers slid over his overalls' sleeves and onto the sides of his chest – a gentle hug in the darkness.

Could he change the colour of his passion? Keep the fire, but make it serve as a guardian? Might Christina change her mind? Change was hard; brew cider, and you'd turn an apple's crunching freshness into a silky froth, but a single slip would rot whole barrels into a sour mass of stench, and people were harder work than cider.

'Have faith in yourself, Caliper. Give children paint and paper and ideas, and they'll surround you with fabulous artwork. Teach Phos your exploits, and help her paint this new world. I'll send you suits; they're tough but not unbreakable, and you'll attract attention, so take care.'

'Can't you come?'

Christina shook her head. 'We may learn new ways of talking. Your mind is a beacon, and I see you even when miles of rock stand between us. No one can replace Phos's father, but you'll make a strong guardian. You must.'

'Did you watch her father die?'

'Outside Morzenthal I'm only an image and a voice, or I'd have stopped the madness. We must hurry: your friend Rastersen goads priests and guards into breaking Morzenthal's gates. He hopes to kill you, and he'll tear Morzenthal apart to find Phos. He's convinced he can mould her into a young version of himself.'

Caliper frowned. 'How do we travel?'

'A carrier field, a travelling disc, will cover Morzenthal's arena and rise at dawn. It will pass through the vault before sinking back at dusk. You must ride it this morning, but the priest's men will follow at dawn tomorrow, so you have one day to put distance between you.'

Christina's steady breathing had to be a trick to bring comfort, but she drew a deep breath as she grasped his hands. A squeeze, a careful smile, and a papery warmth stroked his hands.

'Phos will wait for you, but I must delay Rastersen and let you board this morning's disc. I may need to change my form again, so expect the unusual.'

'Let me find Phos,' Caliper said as a coarse grinding rumbled through the carousel's hallway to force a shiver through his body.

***

Phos faced the elders swarming before her. Their shadows leaped across the carousel walls, and she squinted into the dark maze where Christina had led Caliper. The ceiling lights had faded, and the mumbled drizzle of elders' questions stopped her thinking. Hammering still rang around the hallway.

The elders' questions were toothless, and she doled out answers. Christina's origins, her history and what she knew of the elders, and one toothless man asked how her robe changed colour.

Terelian whispered in her ear. 'They'll keep this up for hours, so say if you want rest.'

Phos's suit crinkled as she raised her hand. 'I'll answer later, but now there's preparation.' She expected protest, but the elders hushed themselves; having adults follow her orders left her dizzy. No time to sleep, even when fatigue clawed at her, and she borrowed a lantern to traipse through the carousel.

Movement flickered ahead as Caliper squashed his body between a glass case and a huge drum, and his shoulders slumped as he saw her.

'She told you,' he said.

A quiet nod, and Phos pointed at a low bench swaddled in thick canvas. They sat side by side, and Phos raised her leg onto the bench to face Caliper. Her lantern dished out a puddle of golden light among the teetering stacks of debris.

'We're always searching,' Phos said. 'I keep thinking our world came from a single seed.'

'Mitch told me.'

'Might be a stupid idea, but the idea keeps pestering me, since our world has to start somewhere. Maybe it's the searching that's important.'

'You fail at one task, but another slaps itself on your plate. Christina said she'd given you a job and you'd need protection, though I've nothing of the details.' Caliper glanced at her leg. 'You've fierce new clothes.'

'We need these suits and helmets for air. We'll need Frinelia for knowledge and Mitch for scampering skills, and Christina said she'd send equipment. And most importantly, we need you.' Rastersen's hammering paused – had Christina silenced him, or was he shifting his men?

They shared stories of the carrier disc and the

world above, and Caliper settled back on the bench to rub a finger over Phos's sleeve. 'What would your dad say about you leaving behind your tunic?'

Phos studied his face, the matted hair and rebel eyebrows on a face calmer than she'd expected. She touched Caliper's sleeve. 'What would you say?' Hugging always felt alien, but her hands found his waist and shoulder, and after a few moments, his arms enveloped her. No wallowing, only eyes showing the vivid blue of cornflowers, holding a deep peace she'd never copy.

'Your disc is our best hope for escape, but if Rastersen breaks in, I'll do my best to shove him outside.'

She closed her eyes and tried imagining Christina's map room, but the rim might stretch for miles, so what should she hunt for? She had no choice: if she missed the disc, Rastersen's hands would seize her and shape her into a servant.

Footsteps. Enough warning to unwrap her arms. Mitch crept into their space, holding a glass tube, and a whiff of Morzenthal's food followed.

'They said you'd returned, Phos, and we've pipes and flasks and crates sitting on the arena now. Touch the pipes, and they're like metal, but you can see through them. I'll remake their food factory. I've samples to work with here.' Mitch held out a sooty-green slab. 'I'm sure I can brew more, but you'll never believe the ingredients.'

'Don't want to know,' Phos said.

'It's brewing, except they use—'

'Don't tell me. I need sleep, not purging. Have you tried this stuff?'

'It's weird, but you'll survive. Hold your nose and don't chew.'

Phos snapped off a corner and closed her eyes before opening her mouth, and the slab vaporised into a bitter mist of rotten yeast. Mitch chuckled as Phos swallowed and shuddered.

'Now she needs water,' Caliper said.

'Try more food; it's amazing how your mouth adapts.'

'We've work, Mitch – important work,' Phos said.

'Isn't food important?'

'We'll only need a few days of food, so focus on our needs. And after eating your food, I'm not hungry.'

Mitch grinned. 'Should I bow or polish your boots?'

'You're needed, Mitch. You can fix stuff before anyone knows it's broken, but we need to prepare. Make a list of what Christina's stowed on the arena's disc.'

'We need food, water and shelter,' Mitch said.

'And air.'

Mitch tilted his head. 'Where are we heading?'

'We're delivering a message to an older world. It might heal our land, and it's our only way to avoid Rastersen.'

'Elders visited the roof. They're saying it's worse outside. There's smoke and shaking, and the landscape's tearing itself apart.' Mitch nibbled his khaki slab.

The lantern faded, and the stacks of boxes behind began clicking as the air grew damp. Two columns sat ahead; carved leaves wrapped the wood, but in the half-light it looked like vines had sprouted from a pillar. Caliper stared ahead with his hands in his lap.

Darkness had always been a time for questions. She'd lain in her hammock and asked herself why sycamore seeds flew and why trees offered berries to birds. Each question spawned a thousand answers, but would testing let her sift through the chaff and find a single right answer? Could she test a thousand ideas?

'Why do people expect me to handle this?'

Caliper turned to her with a watery smile and stretched. 'You're best placed to take this challenge. Where's Frinelia?'

'She's sorting through your arena boxes,' Mitch said. 'I've peeked, and we've suits like the one you're wearing. Tools, rope, knives, stuff to build a cart, and weird cloth; it's stiff at first, but imagine a different shape, and it changes. Mitch nibbled a corner of his slab. 'Where are we going?'

'Frinelia for now.' The three ambled past Caliper's shattered alcove and hauled themselves up the steps. Out on the arena, the elders had unearthed lanterns that lobbed violet-tinged beams from the balconies and onto Christina's creamy disc – scattered now with crates. Phos shivered as her shadow danced ahead in the undiluted night air.

Frinelia hunched over a brown box, and she peeled the top away before glancing up. 'They said you were safe; I was asleep when you arrived.' A hug and eye contact. 'And you met the eidolon.'

'We've loads to cover, but Christina said I should ask about the Heresies.'

Frinelia gulped. 'She's listened to us?'

'You've heard of the world above – the First Enclave?'

'I've never heard that name, but….'

Phos stared. 'You knew about it?'

Frinelia rested her hands on the crate's edges. 'There were a hundred stories saying different things. Mist can make a barn look like a church, and these tales made a thick fog.'

'But you know these stories.' Caliper leaned

against a crate. 'Journey with us; come and freshen our air.'

'We still face peril from our anarchic miller who dangles small girls into the unknown, but I'll come, though check with me before touching any ropes. I seem fated to miss the eidolon – where is she now?'

Phos ran her hand over a crate, smoother than any wood, and she smelt apples even though the box stayed sealed. 'She's fending off Rastersen and writing instructions for our journey. How's the food factory, Mitch?'

'They have enough spares to rebuild now, and if they can't slot the new pipes together, I'll return in…well…. How long's our journey?'

'A few days.' Phos kept her voice level.

'We'll return before their stocks run out.'

A rumble echoed around the arena's walls as metal clashed with stone, and Caliper pointed at the crates. 'I'll shift these so nothing's near the disc edge, but you mentioned suits?'

'In these boxes – they grow to fit.'

'I never found clothes that fitted, and making my own led to disaster.'

The four peeled open the cases. A copper cable sat coiled around a fist-sized drum. Gleaming pliers and hammers and coiled springs snuggled inside a foam-filled case. Light seeped over the grey vault, and Phos's eyes smarted.

She dug out a jacket for Caliper. The shining fabric writhed in her hands but stretched once his outsize hands gripped the collar. He sniffed the material and winced, but undid his overalls. She wrapped the jacket around his chest, and the fabric sealed itself around his body. Mitch held up a set of boxy backpacks, and again the material grew to fit them.

Frinelia gasped. 'Your chest, Phos – are you bleeding?'

Red marks welled over her suit, and Phos slapped her hand over the fabric, but this wasn't blood; unreadable letters surfaced across her jacket. Stripes circled her sleeves and legs, and Caliper stared at his arms as deep-blue squiggles appeared.

'Someone wants to identify us.'

Phos lifted her left arm and stared. 'Who's watching?'

'No idea, but Christina's eyes are strange, and perhaps she wants to tell us apart.'

'Who would mix us up?'

'You don't know Christina,' Caliper said. 'Or perhaps you do.'

Phos and Caliper sat on separate crates and gazed at each other.

'It's fine, Phos – I don't think you're crazy.'

'Christina promised me a package.'

‘She’s keeping Rastersen out until the disc rises, and she won’t fail.’

‘Can she write this package if she’s fighting him? Dawn’s coming.’

Tearing sounds ripped through the air, and stone barked against stone as rumbling shook the floor.

‘The front gates,’ Frinelia said.

‘Have they broken through?’

‘Can’t tell. I’d suggest reconnaissance, but if our priest has breached the walls….’

Caliper picked up a rake as Terelian clambered up the curving stairs, and other elders drifted from the balcony. Light cascaded from the vault and cast shadows as Phos helped Frinelia dress herself. Turquoise blocks swooped over the priestess’s front. Mitch’s suit mixed red and yellow, and he scratched at the letters, but they dodged his fingertips.

Screams bowled across the arena’s walls, and Phos snatched up a knife. ‘There’re vicious tools in the box beside you, Caliper.’

‘Nothing for fighting, though I saw one item….’ He darted to a crate.

Daylight pounced through the open ceiling, and Phos stared at the balcony. Vibration lapped her feet, and silver streaks swept across the disc. She fell a quarter inch as fog squirmed over her boots, and Caliper and Mitch glanced downward as the crates juddered. The disc crawled upward, but it would speed up, and how could Christina reach them?

The remaining ceiling crept closer as pink fingers of daylight trickled across the vault, and Phos shuddered. Fine scarlet filaments burst from the disc's edge to climb through the ceiling's ring and form a gossamer tube weaving upward. Mitch reached for a strand, but the thread danced away before snapping back.

Movement came below as a scatter of red raced onto the balcony, and Christina stormed towards a stairway and stopped at the topmost stair to peer at their rising disc. Phos stepped forward – should she meet her halfway? No. She'd never scramble back onto their platform. Three priests in black capes burst from a doorway ahead of Christina but stopped dead as she raised her arm. Christina's hand pulsed for a moment before bursting into a cloud of fog, and a silver hoop scythed through the air to hum towards Phos. A hundred yards away, but Christina's aim was near perfect. One step left, and Phos scooped the ring from its path.

She held a six-inch ring of hammered silver as wide as her thumb, a model of the Second Enclave. A parting gift; the heavy argument dragged down her arm.

Christina faced the priests, and she towered above them, but without warning, her hair and robe bleached themselves a sandy off-white, and her figure collapsed like ash after a fire as powder flowed over the stairs. Caliper gasped and darted forward, but their disc was only ten yards from the remaining ceiling; the red filaments etched their road into the air.

Mitch pointed. 'Your friend.'

Rastersen loped onto the balcony, and his men surged around him, but he stared upward at Phos. She shouldn't have been able to see his eyes at this distance, but her body froze, and she couldn't turn her gaze away until their disc slid through the ceiling and out into the wind-scrubbed sky above Morzenthal. For a heartbeat, she saw herself standing beside Rastersen to shelter behind his strength, but her guts twisted and she blinked – servants never asked their own questions. Her escape was temporary: she hurtled towards danger she couldn't avoid, and Rastersen would plunder Morzenthal for weapons.

Mitch faced her. 'This disc returns tonight and rises tomorrow, right? We have one day until he follows.'

They kept rising, but the disc's milky edges turned glassy before curving upward to form a bowl, and the sides stretched higher and curved above their heads to wrap them inside a raindrop with a flattened bottom. The outside of the arena's sliced-off dome appeared below, circled by a ring of rain-flecked stone pierced by windows, and Morzenthal showed as a set of stone rings stamped into the rolling moor. Smaller domes squatted on the outer ring, and ten black-robed figures clustered on the roof to stare as Rastersen had. Four towers formed a diamond around Morzenthal's circles.

The sun's arch sat dawnward, a last dawn lighting their way. Dregs of night still blurred the plain, and the world's floor bowed away both dawnward and eveward. The world walls were sharp in the chilled air, and the threads gripping their raindrop thickened as Phos stared out – strange to think of a cage offering freedom.

Phos slid Christina's hoop into her backpack before grabbing a helmet from a chest. 'We'll need these.'

Caliper had stayed silent since Christina's body had turned to powder, but now he stared upward. No grief there, so did he still sense Christina's mind?

He turned to Phos. 'The First's tiny machines have more guts than ours, and if I summon a horse up there, I'll get a stampeding herd or worse. Weird times.'

Phos grinned. 'Weird stuff happens because you're here.'

'Why do I travel with you?'

'Because you're curious, but you're right about

the exploits. We think before speaking.'

'And think before arguing.' Caliper's hands fumbled over a helmet he'd wrestled from a case. Their glass raindrop rose without judder, and they'd have a few minutes before the vault arrived.

'What about these Heresies?'

Frinelia's shoulders sagged and she settled on a crate. 'There's a lifetime of learning to share. I can rattle off a thousand stories, but too much gristle wraps the meat, and many tales must be false.'

'Keep watching when we arrive, and say if you recognise anything.'

Mitch pressed his hands against the glass walls. Below, shadows ran from the rolling ridge of hills they'd climbed to reach Morzenthal. The river dawdled through squares of farmland, and clouds blanketed the eveward lands to cover Torzene's scar. A few hours of freedom might lie above, but danger sat everywhere, and Rastersen was already preparing to chase.

Chapter 20: stairway of raindrops

Phos stared through the glassy walls at the curved ribbon of green hills and patches of forest lying below. The Second Enclave had been home, but each tree she'd climbed and each blade of grass she'd rolled over now faded into green smudges. The upward push against their feet eased. Crimson fibres still clutched their raindrop, but Phos imagined snapping threads and plummeting, and she flicked her head back to stare at the vault's dark patch. Depth showed inside, so was it a tunnel? Others had ridden the air this way: builders had glimpsed a world they couldn't survive while visiting children they'd have to abandon, and her fear echoed their grief as everything led to stillness and hushed breath.

Caliper sat with closed eyes and clenched fists as his suit markings flowed into fresh patterns, and his chest showed a set of zigzags that might have been ferns. Their pearly disc glowed to make silhouettes of their feet, and bitter air stung her cheeks.

'Helmets on, everyone.' Phos slid a glass bowl over her head, and her hair untangled itself. The helmet jostled against her collar before sealing. Her air tasted of hot metal until a whispered breeze welled around her neck and tousled her hair.

Mitch copied her. 'How do we speak?' Mitch's

words were sharp, but they'd picked up a buzz as if bees swarmed in his throat.

'As normal – our helmets pass on our words.'

Caliper hefted a helmet onto his head, and his hair scrambled over his face before settling into a thick cover for his scalp. His beard twitched before calming itself into a combed shadow of itself.

'What's happened to my hair?'

'You nearly look smart,' Phos said.

'I'm not supposed to be smart.'

Their disc slowed as the vault approached. The raindrop lined up with the tunnel, and the dark grey ceiling lowered itself over their heads. One last glance at the green and brown blurs below, and the tunnel walls slid around them. Rock squeezed daylight into a slender ring that narrowed until darkness fell.

A cradle escaped. Mitch flicked on a torch, and faint speckles glinted on the encircling walls as they climbed. Danger sat everywhere; one wrong touch might snap her fingers, but not learning would kill. Even sitting and waiting might be lethal.

Her body sagged, and she stumbled as sweat streamed over her face, but she grabbed a crate. Mitch teetered to his side, and Caliper peered at her.

'You playing with these suits, Phos?'

'Not me. Do you feel heavy?'

'It's not that big a change, so are you

managing?'

Phos nodded. 'Christina mentioned gravity; it pulls us down, but something's cranked it up.'

Frinelia groaned. 'I'll need two sticks.'

Phos stared upward but saw nothing but blackness. 'Builders made this place for themselves, not us, and walking will be tough.'

Their disc crept through the tunnel, and their underfoot light faded as the beam from Mitch's torch slid into darkness.

'There's glinting far off.'

An immense faceted pillar stood miles away, a vertical column of crystal, a ghost against the night, and cracks criss-crossed its surface where a colossal shard had splintered free. Glowing rubble hovered in the darkness beside the pillar, and Frinelia stood and gripped Phos's shoulder.

The humming deepened as their disc eased upward. Again the tunnel shrouded them for a few moments before they rose into a forest of ladders and rusting iron girders mangled into corkscrews. Spars and grids like waffles had crashed together to build a ragged hedge circling their raindrop. Far above, square lanterns spat out harsh white rays. Pools of shadow squatted beneath buckled metal sheets, and anyone peering from the wreckage would see their bodies. Walkways snaked between the debris to form rubbish-covered paths for people Christina's size.

'I've read about this chamber,' Frinelia said. 'They stored food and raw materials here for their final move.'

The raindrop's sides vanished, and the milky glow underfoot spread out onto the warehouse floor. Mitch flicked his torch beam over the wreckage, and huge shelves gleamed in the distance.

Phos whistled. 'This is a warehouse?'

'I've seen drawings of trolleys carrying crates. What can you hear?' Frinelia's voice quavered.

'Only your voice.'

'I imagine these machines failed thousands of years ago, so we should be safe.'

'You're sure? Most of Morzenthal still works.'

Phos's suit clicked and chirped as ripples flowed over her jacket. Caliper stomped up behind her. 'Do you sense the voices, Phos?'

'What?'

'The tiny machines. They're listening as they were back home, but they're listening harder now, and they're stronger, so be careful what you think.'

'What do you mean, listening harder?'

'You can't feel them listening? They're there,' Caliper said.

Mitch ambled onto the surrounding floor and towards a walkway.

'We're at the bottom of Christina's bowl, and we fight up to the map room,' Phos said.

'Fight?'

'If needed. Don't walk too far, Mitch.'

Mitch stared ahead. 'Can we breathe this air?'

'Christina thought not, and we can't risk—'

Mitch gripped his helmet and flexed his neck, and the seal hissed.

'Mitch, no.' Frinelia heaved herself forward as Caliper leaped at Mitch, but the boy wrestled the globe from his head. Frinelia and Caliper froze with their hands stretched out.

The boy's face flushed as he smiled, and his voice sounded fragile. 'Funny air: all thin and icy.'

'Put your helmet back on, Mitch.' Frinelia struggled to keep her voice level. 'Everything I've heard says this air won't keep us alive. You're needed – you're part of the team.'

'Let's save the suits.' Mitch's breathing sped up, and his face shaded into an angry red. He buckled and bent forward before crumpling sideways onto the metal, and his helmet bounced over the floor. Caliper leaped to catch the bowl, and he swept back to Mitch in one fluid movement. His hands slid underneath Mitch, and a three-inch lift let Caliper slot the helmet back over the boy's head. One faint click, and Phos darted forward to wrap her hands around Mitch's torso and peer into his face.

'Mitch? Mitch?' His eyes opened.

Frinelia's foot prodded Mitch's leg. 'Did we learn? Breathing this air is like eating grass – it won't kill, but it won't keep you alive. We're not supposed to be here, so secure your helmet.'

Mitch knelt and coughed. His hand clutched Phos's arm as she helped him sit. 'It's quiet outside – not like Morzenthal.'

Caliper popped the covers off two crates. 'Let's stick together and get to work, except you, Mitch. You can help by sticking your arse on the floor.' He lifted out a set of wooden boards, poles and wheels. Everything fitted together to shape a basic cart. Straps hooked onto the cart's front, and Caliper slipped a black leather harness over his suit.

'Want to stick your backpack on the cart, Phos?'

'I'll wear it for now.'

Caliper tugged the cart before tapping a small hammer against a wheel. 'It's fine. What we need goes on the cart.'

Sweat flooded Phos's forehead. 'Right now Rastersen is scouring Morzenthal for weapons and suits. We don't know what he'll find, but if we learn the First's ways, we have half a chance.'

Caliper tossed blankets over the crates stacked on their cart. 'Best chance we have is outrunning him.

This nanotech, whatever we call it, it's all risk. Even with Christina's help, I blacked out on my first time, so let's put distance between us.'

Phos stepped off the disc and her boots clanked. Six passageways spread out from the centre, littered with broken bottles and crumpled boxes. Fire-blackened girders surrounded each passage.

'We'll take this corridor and aim for the rim,' Phos said. 'We're at the bowl's bottom, so any direction works.'

Rusted sheets rested against a girder. Her boot nudged one, and it shattered to spew metal shards across the floor. They passed the litter and the burnt ironwork, and Mitch's torch picked out shelves. Fifty feet of brown crates towered above, with identical spaces between the boxes. Dust braided the floor, and Caliper pulled his trolley midway between the walls. Every few tens of yards they'd pass yawning, dark gulfs where alleyways snaked into the ironwork. Perhaps First Enclave survivors had clawed out homes inside this beehive, and answers might swarm on these shelves – you didn't need cooks when walking through orchards. Phos looked behind; they'd stamped footprints across the dust.

A table stood on their left without legs – a floating sheet. Phos waved her hand underneath but felt nothing. The sheet warmed her fingers but wouldn't budge more than a few inches. No dust touched the surface, but hundreds of cogwheels and spindles hovered above the sheet, and she prodded an inch-long coiled spring.

'Leave them, Phos: we must hurry,' Caliper said.

The spring drifted across the sheet like a pebble on ice, but once past the edge, the coil tumbled to the floor. Three nudges showed the pattern: gravity didn't reach through the sheet, but push anything past the edge, and gravity remembered. Was gravity like light? Was this sheet a curtain?

'Can we fit the sheet on the cart?'

'Will it help you run faster? Let's keep moving.'

'Bet we can break this if we work hard,' Mitch said.

'Leave it.'

Copper foil had spilled from a fallen crate. Phos reached for a sheet. The feathery material coated her hand to wrap each wrinkle in her glove. A faint glow still wafted from the floor, but the ground had buckled, and the tottering crates on her left creaked as she passed.

No thirst or hunger now; perhaps the suit fed her and kept sleep at bay, but Rastersen would pillage Morzenthal for similar suits.

Grey-green mottling infected these shelves; five-pointed leaves like ivy drooped from the shelf edges. Phos stroked the leaves, and the heavy cold of iron leaked through her gloves, so these couldn't be plants. Had a builder tied fakes here, or had nanotech tricked these girders into growing like plants? Buds showed further along the shelf. More leaves festered further down. Vines and branches sprouted from shelves, and whole gantries had collapsed; her girder crumbled under her fingers.

'First Enclave nanotech,' Phos said. 'Seeds landed here by mistake, and their plans worked on the metal.'

'But metal isn't soil, is it?'

'It isn't in our world.'

'You and your seeds, Phos. Let your mouth rest.' Mitch flicked a leaf.

Frinelia's fingers traced the crumbling girder. 'We mustn't linger.'

Phos gripped a leaf and tugged it towards her.

'Don't touch: we don't know how this spreads.'

'Just looking.' Something squeezed her left sleeve.

'Your arm, Phos, look at your arm.' Caliper grabbed her shoulders and hauled her back as vines burst from her sleeve and curled along her arm. She ran her right hand over the tendrils, but new shoots budded between her fingers.

‘How do I shake them off?’

‘I’ve exploits for clearing weeds, but these aren’t plants.’

Phos’s hands itched and her suit pulsed. Flecks of light surged across her helmet. Thicker vines sprouted from her forearm, and her hands shook.

Caliper’s hands clamped her left arm, and she held still as his breathing slowed. ‘I’m not used to metal, but this stuff thinks it’s ivy.’

A few of the thinner wire vines withered, and their leaves shrivelled. Her suit hummed, and she sensed a net of threads scrambling through her sleeve, streams of energy. Was the nanotech obeying Caliper?

Syllables flowed into her mind; even delivered without breath, they held the miller’s throaty ruggedness. ‘Not working, Phos. I’ve not enough. These roots are stuck fast.’

New visions swept into her mind: a thousand tiny metal hairs squirmed into her sleeve and tried to rip open her suit, and each one stood fast against Caliper’s threads.

She’d grown up knowing how to grip and lift, but these metallic plants were alien, and she had to learn again. Phos let her mind nuzzle Caliper’s threads, and his design was clear. Frost killed plants, and their miller planned to copy a harsh winter morning, but ice never hurt metal. She tapped into his threads and remembered visions of flames melting wires as her mind poured the idea of burning into Caliper's exploit.

Their miller yowled and staggered back, and the vines slithered from her arm to slump onto the floor. The invading creepers had bleached her suit's arm white, but her swirling red letters grew back – quiet tattoos of victory.

Caliper clamped his hand under his arm. 'What did you do?'

'I thought threads were running through my suit – was that your exploit?'

'Was that you with the burning? Hold your hands back, Phos: these exploits will have your arms off.'

Mitch tapped his foot on the floor. 'After attention, are we, Phos? Are you going to prod everything we find? This strangeness will eat us.'

Phos scowled. How could she learn when a single touch dragged poison into her suit? 'I'm sure ignorance won't help.'

'Maybe so, Phos, but don't hoard your learning.'

'I'll share, but wait until we rest.'

Caliper coughed twice before stepping into his harness to heave their cart forward, but he paused and stared.

'There's green light flickering ahead.'

Rays trickled down the passageway and picked

out veils of scattered dust. Bushes of metallic leaves curled around the buckled struts ahead. Whole sections of shelves had collapsed to scatter crates across their path, and the boxes had burst to scatter wonders over the dust, suits Christina's size, curls of metal that might be tools; coils of rope and dusty black balls spilled from ripped black sacks. Contorted vines had stripped out several shelves, and dense thickets of iron leaves erupted from the ground.

'How do we pass?'

Caliper inched up to the leaves. 'We can't cross these without touching them, but let me.'

'Caliper, no.'

'There's no staying here, but keep your burning thoughts ready.' He stepped into the dull grey plants. Phos held her breath, but his boots stayed clean. No shelves left now; thorny grey bushes sprouted from tangled girders, and the remaining struts had buckled and twisted like branches while a few crushed crates perched above.

'We're almost outside,' Phos whispered.

Green light flooded the walkway, and creepers dangled from the ceiling and chimed as Phos brushed against them. Tiny boxes clung to the vine, two-inch replicas of those left on the shelves, and Phos wanted to check inside but pulled her hand back. Trees had ripped through the floor to turn their corridor into a fighting mass of trunks – a nightmare indoor forest.

She prodded a tree trunk. Nothing happened, and she let her palm slide over the bark, unlike anything she'd climbed, smooth metal mixed with wood's heartiness. No space for the cart, but Caliper lugged the crates to the moss-littered floor and plucked the wheels off their axles: he'd shoulder through this thicket and rebuild on the other side.

Alien trees with branches like cones festered on each side, and the roof opened into swirling fog as grey light seeped onto powdery soil. End of the warehouse, but a welter of skewed trunks and gnarled branches stretched ahead as if three forests fought over the same space. Every trunk was doused in green moss.

Mist stopped Phos seeing far, but the trees dipped ahead, so did she stand on a hill? Sharp chirps and twitters ripped through her helmet and built into an angry climax before fading and restarting. To her left a green swathe of grass ran to her right and dodged past trees to slither into the fog.

'First Enclave,' Frinelia said. 'Caliper's bringing the cart through one piece at a time. Stay close.'

Mitch trundled down the grassy path and let his hand slide through the stalks.

'Not too far, Mitch. We've no idea what's outside, and if that grass copies the ivy….'

The boy stopped, and his whisper drifted into

Phos's ears. 'Look here.'

She followed, half expecting her suit to burn as grass whipped her thighs, but Mitch knelt to scrabble at a patch of bare earth and pointed at two gnarled brown sticks rising from the soil. 'These were legs.'

'Legs for what?'

'Legs for builders, bones, the things inside people's legs.'

'Oh, yuck.'

'People died here – maybe several.'

Frinelia appeared behind, wielding her stick. 'Can you work out how many?'

'I'd need to dig, but there's at least two buried here. Their bones broke before burial.'

Mitch stood and soil spilled from his gloves. The forest was thinner here and the mist faded. Ahead lurked distant treetops and a grid of hedges surrounding olive-coloured fields. This world's slope was obvious: they stood at the bottom of a vast bowl, and fog churned above to form a lid they'd need to pierce.

Tiny coloured squares slid from left to right across her helmet. Had the ivy poisoned the glass? She needed to investigate, but Rastersen's arrival left her lacking time, and he'd chase her to the rim of this deadly classroom.

***

Caliper's stomach lurched as the fog melted: he wasn't staring at a hill but a basin's inside, a vast crock lined with forests and fields and snaking hedges forming an impossible green wave poised to crash over his body. Three mist-wreathed columns showed ahead like vast skewers piercing a bowl. Dense forest bracketed him, but a swathe of grass stretched forward.

Caliper lowered his head as grass curled around his legs. Screeches rattled through his helmet, shrieks of confusion and sickness, as if someone was torturing birds, and Christina's words still scythed through his thoughts.

'Stay close, Phos,' he said.

He looked up; the girl's legs twitched as if she was trying to run in every direction at once, and she tossed her head back with laughter as Mitch impersonated one of their teachers. There'd been a fiery courage in the threads she'd braided into his thoughts, but danger too: those exploits had hissed like snakes fighting for release. He staggered against the cart.

This world was Phos's playground, and she'd started to dish out orders; she needed protection, and he had to argue back more. The girl snapped off a thorn sticking out from a shrub.

'No exploits for now, Phos – we need speed.' He leaned forward to goad the cart, but the grass snatched at his wheels. 'Try planning our route.'

Phos pointed up and ahead. ‘Those were roads. If we follow one we’ll approach the rim.’ She glanced at his cart. ‘Can we avoid leaving tracks?’

Caliper shook his head. ‘I’ve known trackers to learn from single footprints, and Fat Boy won’t come alone.’

‘We can’t outrun him, can we? Found much, Mitch?’

‘I’m sitting on a graveyard, but there’s not much to learn: the skeletons are jumbled, and soil’s seeped into the bones.’ Mitch held up a warped iron blade, a crude scimitar that looked like a blacksmith’s hangover. ‘They made flying discs and bowl-shaped worlds, so why use swords?’

‘Couldn’t trust their nanotech.’ Phos glanced upward. ‘Perhaps we shouldn’t trust nanotech either, but we’ve no choice.’

Their path sliced through a dense patch of gorse crusted with golden flowers, and into a square field lined by tangled banks of trees and shrubs. Wind rumpled the dry grass stalks, and a gap in the square’s far side held a faint trail that curved upward into a distant grid of hedges.

‘Someone planted these trees centuries ago,’ Mitch said.

If he studied this greenery long enough he’d imagine plants locked in a slow battle for water; brown ferns punctured olive-coloured banks of moss, and stunted elms erupted from straggling bushes of unpruned purple flowers. Work for a thousand gardeners.

She pointed up and to their left. 'There's a ruin ahead with walls inside a circle. Our route runs nearby.'

Caliper glanced upward at a church-sized scar of white stone resting on parched grass.

'Rastersen will follow,' Caliper said as he shut his eyes.

'He'll track us wherever we go, but the ruin might hold builder nanotech,' Phos said.

'Terrifying.'

'It looks like it's nailed to a cliff now, but when we reach the ruin, you'll think this place is vertical.'

If he kept his eyes lowered he could imagine himself trundling over a flat plain even if the cart struggled. Phos watched with pursed lips, but at least having her stare at his wheels meant she wasn't running off. Another heave, and he tore the grass strands locking the wheels.

'Need help, Caliper? Those wheels are ornamental.'

'You can try clearing the grass, but that's an ongoing job. We need every box on the cart, so I'll manage.' Caliper sneezed. He'd never clean his helmet's insides, but the droplets vanished.

Their path squeezed between two wizened hedges, but a bundle of livid green vines laced between the two thickets to block their way. Thorns bristled over the creepers, and in the hedges, a squad of pallid flowers swivelled towards him.

'Still got that knife, Phos?'

'Don't you have an exploit for clearing weeds?'

'The one I tried earlier nearly ripped my head off, so we'll stick to the knife.'

'It's blunt and we've twenty vines here. Try an exploit; start easy and build up.'

The creeper was the thickness of his thumb and ringed with thorns, but his hand darted towards the vine. Caliper paused: again her orders had seized his hands. Shouldn't he deny Phos for her own safety?

Phos's hand clasped his elbow. 'We'll be half an hour cutting these, which is time we can't waste, and I've seen your talent.'

A four-inch stretch of vine lacked barbs, and his fingers wrapped the creeper. Caliper closed his eyes and remembered the dry brittleness of autumn leaves.

His hand spasmed and clamped the vine. Caliper's eyes opened, and he stepped back. The vine followed for a pace before crumbling. Fiery glints cascaded along the creepers as they burned from inside. The burning raced into both hedges to guzzle branches and flowers, and ash spilled from his glove.

Smoke coiled upward, and the hedge on his left slumped as glowing flakes climbed into the air. A sigh lisped from the charring twigs and leaves as smog billowed on both sides. Heat seeped through his suit, but after several heartbeats, the fire sputtered into a hollow silence. Flames had charred a tree trunk on their left, though its leaves now shone a slick green as if drenched by rain, and mounds of smoking ash lined their track. One curled vine still poked above the cinders, but he'd demolished huge chunks of greenery.

'Look what you've done,' Phos said.

Again her words had made a glass for him to crawl inside, and he'd brewed a headache worse than anything earned in a tavern brawl. Smoke still climbed, and tiny dark blue dots glided around the grey plumes. Caliper's backbone growled and his head lolled forward. He sagged onto the cart as Phos stared at a stretch of unburnt hedge ahead.

Plants twitched there. Fronds grew longer and thinned, and leaves became barbs – could a hedge brandish its fists?

'The hedge is changing. Let's move closer,' Phos said.

'Stay away and listen for once. If we study everything, we'll get nowhere.'

'Just look, Caliper.'

'I am – it's a hedge.'

‘What’s your helmet doing?’

‘Helping me breathe?’

‘Watch the hedge.’

Swear words usually bought him silence, but Phos wouldn’t know half his curses. ‘Remind me never to travel with you again. What are you gawping at?’

Phos’s voice became shrill, and she stepped forward. ‘Are any symbols showing on your helmet?’

Caliper grunted and hobbled towards her. ‘My head’s been shat through a rat’s arse, so don’t think I’ll save you with another exploit. Stay away….’

He stopped. Glowing lines and squares roamed over Phos’s helmet to pick out targets on the hedge. A warning for most but an invite for this girl, and Caliper swore inside. Protecting her had become harder, and his promise to Christina had withered into empty words.

Chapter 21: weight from the past

A clump of ferns twitched before Phos, and a red triangle flared over her helmet glass to veil their sprouting leaves. She tilted her head, but the triangle anchored itself to the thicket's image, and alien writing scrolled underneath. Caliper's yelled complaints stopped.

Phos stared ahead. 'What's showing on your helmets?'

'I'm only seeing you and the vegetables, but your helmet's colouring itself.'

She spun around and her helmet cleared. 'Frinelia, what are these suits? Why were they built?'

'I know one story. Parents pleaded to meet their children as their old world crumbled, and these suits helped the farewells linger even as their air turned sour. There were—'

'Everyone behind me,' Caliper shouted. He dashed to their cart and slotted a curved blade onto a pole to make a scythe before rushing past her to face the hedge. Phos turned back to the hedge, and the red triangle reappeared, but now the symbol scurried towards her across the rippling grass, and a thin tentacle reared up from the ground. An angry red maw hurtled towards her face.

Caliper swung his arms, and his blade snicked

through the tentacle, and the corpse shot past her shoulder to crash behind her. Blood dripped from the scythe's wound, and her red triangle faded as Caliper kicked the limb.

'That red on your helmet, Phos, makes a warning. Learn the signs and shift yourself next time; you'll only learn if you stay alive.'

'I didn't know red triangles meant danger.'

'You do now.'

Her cheeks flushed. How long would this school day last?

Mitch pulled a pole from the cart. 'Why did only Phos see the warning?'

'I focused on the hedge and the triangle came,' she said.

Frinelia coughed. 'You didn't use a special hand movement or turn your head a funny way?'

'She's always twitching,' Mitch said. 'We called her Phos the fidget.'

'Try concentrating, Mitch.'

'Let's line up behind Phos and copy her walk.'

Frinelia cleared her throat. 'We will proceed towards the ruined building; we can rest there and prepare for tomorrow.'

Caliper struggled into his harness and strained at the straps. His breathing grew a ragged edge as he faced Phos. 'Stay close and watch for red triangles.'

They stepped into a wide expanse of grassland where gentle hillocks swelled under the rippling plain and patches of dusty red soil breached the wiry grass. An hour of silent hiking passed, but the ruin only inched towards them as brick-coloured dust smeared their legs. A lane of sickly grass wound towards the ruined house, where two walls trapped a bare patch of earth, and Caliper nudged the cart to keep it on the path.

Phos glanced upward. The flying dots had vanished, and the bowl's cloud cap had risen to show strings of silent hamlets dotted around the curving world; hushed and barren clumps of stone houses sat beside derelict barns. Spiderwebs of paths linked the villages, and ahead three immense spires thrust upward from the rolling landscape like canes stabbed into the earth.

Caliper's breathing rasped through her helmet, and his straps slackened. He bent over and gripped his knees.

Phos paused. 'Need a breather?'

He wordlessly gathered the straps in his hands and squatted on the cart as his breathing became a harsh rattle. The words *Loosen your collar* bubbled up in Phos's mind, but she sat beside him.

'Has this happened before?' Frinelia's voice kept calm as Caliper shook his head. Phos curled her fingers around the miller's glove, but his wheezing sped up, and she squeezed.

How had Caliper described those threads? Could she reach inside his suit? She closed her eyes, and her memory fed her a dim profile of his stooping body and brawny arms, but her mind's fingers slipped over his image as if she chased snowflakes. Spiky letters and dashes flashed over her helmet as she glanced at the ruined house, but Caliper's eyes closed, and he clenched his hands as his body shook.

Nothing but the slow waving of the grass before them; centuries of silence ignored their trespass.

Caliper spluttered and his breathing stopped. He lurched forward and gripped his helmet as his face turned sallow. Two blue symbols winked into place at the top left of Phos's helmet, blocky human figures linked by curving lines, and tiny green letters like numbers slid over Caliper's helmet in reply. One moment his sweating face rocked beside her, and the next fog filled his helmet. He still panted, but a quiet calm slid into his breathing, and his fingers sprang away from his helmet.

'Phos? Frinelia – are you there?'

'You're snogging a cloud.'

'Tastes mushroomy,' Caliper said.

'But you're better?'

'I'm enjoying these suits.' His nose and beard reappeared as his helmet's green symbols folded into nothing.

'Little worlds,' Frinelia whispered.

Phos slid her hand over Caliper's sleeve. 'You're wearing a Caliper-shaped enclave. We still need this map room, so can we help push the cart?'

Caliper grinned while strapping his harness back on and hauling the cart forward. The wheels squeaked, and Phos nudged a box to stop it falling. The plain rolled ahead as the cart trundled over cracked soil and threw up red dust. Grass stalks curled around a wheel, and she snatched a single stalk. It looked like wheat, but symbols appeared on her helmet: two garishly painted and twisted ladders tangled around each other to form a story she'd untangle later.

Movement flashed as a bird hovered thirty feet above. Its feathers shone like a rainbow dipped in liquid metal. Deep-blue wings shaded into emerald at the tips, and a turquoise shimmer flowed across its body as Phos's hand rose in welcome – the bird was almost Caliper's size.

Mitch stared. 'Are we dinner?'

'It's curious; it's not seen humans.'

Caliper tugged the cart leftward, and their bird followed. Its underside turned pale, and those metallic wings flapped at the same rate as her heartbeat.

The ruin drew near, and Caliper sped up as the grass thinned. The surrounding wall showed now as a circle of twenty fluted pillars twice her height, and a ramshackle drystone wall reared up just outside the pillars. Had someone scrambled for protection with rocks?

Inside, two rough plaster walls linked to make an L-shape while a third smaller wall stood apart. Dark green moss stained the sides, and gravel filled the ground inside. Lines of flat stones linked the corners, but replace those pebbles with proper walls and you'd outline a house. A rickety shelter clung against the short wall, a scramble of mismatched plasterboards and nailed-on planks. Phos picked at the lichen scabs slathering its front.

The cloudy day faded into blue twilight, and Phos closed her eyes for a few heartbeats. Her suit had stretched out her waking hours, but fatigue fermented inside her body. The bird veered towards a spire and climbed into the sky.

Mitch stood astride the flat line of stones. 'Used to be a wall here till someone nicked it.'

'The walls left don't have windows,' Phos said.

'Perhaps those stolen walls were all window, you think?'

Mitch had stolen her thought, but she stared at the shelter. If tiny machines granted your wishes no one would teach stonework or bricklaying, but what happened when the nanotech stopped listening? Had the survivors bashed together this hovel while brawling for bread? The remaining walls could hold two builder-sized stories, so had thieves ripped out the floor and stairs?

'Notice anything about the shelter, Phos?'

'It's all rush and spit?'

Mitch chuckled. 'You're not paying attention. People our size built that door.'

Phos grimaced as Mitch peered inside.

'Let me go first – we might find relatives,' Caliper said. He squared up to the door, and light blue letters flickered over Phos's helmet as his feet crunched over sand. His breathing tickled her ears, and after a few heartbeats his voice buzzed. 'Come inside but take care.'

Caliper's torch splashed light over two cloth-swaddled chairs huddled in a corner. Two human skulls perched on each seat, and bones littered the floor and mixed with withered fabric strands. Her boot clinked against a curved metal sword with its point sheared away, and another half sword lurked behind a skull.

Phos scooped up the sword stub and gazed at the clean cut; rust-coloured letters flowed across her helmet to circle the weapon. She twirled the sword and the characters followed.

'How do you summon exploits, Caliper?'

'Careful, Phos. The First isn't for beginners.'

‘Remember your breathing trouble? Rastersen is fast, and he won’t come alone; he won’t underestimate you again. Can you handle him and his guards?’

Caliper stayed silent.

‘Can you teach me? We might need to fight, and your exploits could give us an edge.’

‘It’s not a skill I can teach, Phos. My knowledge sits in my head, and there’s no explaining.’

‘But you call the exploit – it doesn’t just appear. Teach me the calling.’

Doubt flared in his eyes, and his hands twitched before he bent to grab the other sword.

‘If we weren’t up against this man….’ He shook his head. ‘I’ve no skills in metal, but you’ll start with closed eyes. Can you think of a sound you only notice when it’s gone? Like a dripping pipe or a creaking bed – a sound that seeps into your mind without bothering your ears.’

Phos nodded.

‘Hold your breath and listen for those murmurs, but keep your mind alert. Grip the sword in your left hand and push it forward, and now open your right. Don’t open your eyes, but imagine threads rushing from your right hand’s fingertips and into your target, and you’ll feel the iron’s bite chill your hand. Now draw your right hand back a fraction – a fingernail’s width. You’ll sense tugging, and sounds will trickle into your mind – do you hear the silence end? Eyes closed, Phos. Your left hand's gripping the sword, so let your right hand play out those threads.'

'There's weight in my right hand.'

'Left hand holds the target while the right studies shape and texture. Rock your left a touch, and learn the weight and balance. Use the right to stroke the texture, and learn the sword's strains and flaws.'

Phos screwed her eyes shut, and a memory crashed into her mind as if she'd remembered a long-lost doll. Hard to tell if she was seeing or remembering, but notches scarred the sword's blunt edges, and hairline cracks scoured the blade. The handle came from a far older weapon.

Caliper's voice arrived as a distant whisper. 'Your left hand should feel the heft. Swing the sword to learn the movement, and let your body reach into the blade, but keep those eyes shut. Does your hand know the weight?'

'It's there.'

'That's a mould for your thought, the idea of a sword. Now here's the fun – ask a question.'

'What?' Phos squeezed her eyes together.

'Ask your sword what it looked like before it had the slicing.'

Phos hesitated. 'You're saying the sword knows its original shape?'

'You've seen seeds, Phos; they spit out plants and trees. The plans wait inside. Go on, ask your question.'

Phos chewed her lip.

What was your original shape?

'Keep those eyes closed one moment, Phos, but you're grand. Your helmet's answered your question. Fine – have a look.'

A shock of colour came as she opened her eyes, and a set of giddy heartbeats passed before she understood. Her left hand still held the cropped sword, but her helmet had thrown washes of colour over her right hand: a sword's portrait, a perfect curve of blade. She flicked her right wrist, and the helmet's colours shifted to follow as if the sword were real. Her fingers wrapped a handle she could only see on her helmet, though weight nagged her right hand.

'So I can see what the sword was. It's great, but does it help?'

Caliper shrugged. 'Maybe the villages further around the bowl held tricks.'

'We're short of time. You mentioned seeds, and if the sword is a seed, can we ask the seed to grow again?'

'Not now, Phos: I've had buildings collapse on me trying that.'

'We need weapons, and these exploits need

understanding.'

'Don't.'

'Stand back.' Phos closed her eyes and inhaled. The ghost sword still filled her right hand.

'Don't, Phos. No….'

Can you grow back?

A harsh crack rang out and her feet jarred. Her hand dipped, and her grip on the invisible sword almost slipped, but her eyes snapped open. A whole blade nestled in her right hand, and a jagged foot-wide hole gaped in the stone floor. She scraped the new sword over the ground, and it clanked like metal.

'Slow down, Phos. You stamped a hole in the earth; you could have hacked off your foot.'

'Does that always happen?'

'You've made iron but you've lost stone, and it all has to add up. I should have told you earlier, but your rushing….'

Phos slid the blade against one of the chair backs to whittle away a sliver of wood. 'The suit boosts my skills.'

'You remade a sword, but will it help?' Mitch took the sword from Phos's hand. 'Rastersen has worse.'

'This world takes instruction, and its skills become our defence.'

'Why can't my suit do this? Can we swap suits?'

'Keep breathing, Mitch; I'll try another exploit.'

'Watch it, Phos,' Caliper said. 'Too many exploits will frazzle you – take one bite at a time.'

Phos smiled, and ten steps carried her back to the line of pebbles linking the two walls. She closed her eyes and let her mind cast out its threads, and new memories soaked into her thoughts. Phos saw days where plants draped themselves over the plaster walls, surfaces flaking over the endless years, and centuries of emptiness scouring the house's delicate mechanisms. She pushed the memory back in time, and new images flowed across her mind. Panes of glass had linked these plaster walls, and a crystal roof blurred the evening sky. Shimmering ghosts flickered across a floor filled with chairs and sofas, a day's motion crammed into a few heartbeats. Her question was ready.

Can you grow back?

Nothing. Only the faint crinkling of her suit. Phos opened her eyes, and a faint haze tinged the outside grass.

'Look at the shelter,' Frinelia said. The hut's timbers had jutted past the line of stones, but the ends had sheared off to litter the soil. Caliper lobbed a stone between the plaster walls, but it bounced from the air, and Phos slid her fingers over a smooth surface she couldn't see: nothing like glass, firm but not cold.

'It'll keep the weather out.'

‘Did you just lock us in?’

‘Not deliberately.’

‘Ah, so long as it’s an accident,’ Caliper said. ‘Can you accident our way out?’

Phos spread her palm over the invisible wall.

What can you do?

A storm of blue letters swarmed around her fingers and swept across the sheet before finger-sized squares settled above the alien symbols like an invitation.

Phos’s fingers dabbed one square, and the writing flowed into fresh patterns. She touched another, and another, and a fourth before the blue symbols winked out and her hand fell forward.

Caliper chuckled. ‘What did we learn?’

‘We’re learning how the house works, and that’ll help us understand the First. The builders didn’t drag carts behind them, so we find out what they used, and we’ll move faster and learn how they defended themselves.’ Phos blinked; her vision blurred. ‘We also need rest.’

‘That’s all?’

‘That’s enough for now.’

Other skills waited for her, but right now Rastersen and his gang were tearing through Morzenthal’s libraries. Elders would reel from his threats and bring him books, and Phos’s arms and neck ached as the walls swayed around her.

***

Fog wrapped their house as daylight dribbled away, and nearby trees scratched at the growing night's mineral sheen, but Caliper pressed his palms against the window and lowered his face to hide the pain scuttling across his spine.

Phos stood beside him and danced her fingers over the shapes she'd conjured. Frinelia dozed against the short wall as Mitch juggled three pebbles.

'You want us to stay here tonight?' Phos's voice stayed faint as her gaze stayed fixed on her symbols.

'There's a maze of hedges past this house, and my scythe's no help in the dark, and we need rest.'

'My reckoning puts us a fifth of the way to the rim, and Rastersen will move faster than us. There's something here about travelling.' She tapped the window.

'There's no travel without sleep, and I'll never sleep in this suit.'

'If I change the air, you can peel your suit off,' Phos said.

'Change the air? Do I carve "Be careful" on your helmet?'

Phos's hands capered, and symbols curled around her fingers before jumping onto her helmet while Mitch rasped a stick over the wall to spray plaster over his suit. Caliper's brief schooldays had mixed punches with punishment, and they'd never help now.

He pointed at the twirling letters. 'Can you read that scribble?'

'These pictures mean furniture.' Phos tapped the icons. 'Table, chair, light, and there's a place to watch stuff happen elsewhere. They're ideas, but these ideas can become real.'

'What?'

'I think, and my suit listens to me and talks with the house. Thoughts become real.' Phos's cheeks flushed pink beneath her glass helmet.

'It's late, so can you wheel out some beds?'

'Tweak gravity, and we might not need beds.'

'Phos, beds work, but your fiddling….'

'We'll never outrun Rastersen, but imagine using gravity against him.'

'You're teaching yourself gravity?'

'I've a way to learn,' Phos said. 'Seeds grow when they're watered, so seeds have instructions inside that say, "Sprout when there's water."' Phos's fingers flicked a group of four symbols, and they glided over her window like marbles before grinding to a halt. She pinned one letter with her index finger and dragged it over another. The two symbols shook for a heartbeat, and a curly squiggle sprang out. 'Breaking open a seed shows us nothing: we can't read the instructions, but what if you change their world? What if you swapped the water with cider?'

'Funny use for cider.'

'It's worth trying. Start with an idea. I don't know.... You say cider gets the seeds drunk, so they can't read their instructions. Try growing seeds in cider; if the plants come up wonky, your idea might be true. Do new tests with new liquids; each test might hint at what's inside the seeds.'

'And if your seeds don't grow?'

'You can say cider stops the instructions and kills the seeds.'

'Or puts them to sleep,' Caliper said.

'I'm not expecting answers to come tumbling out, but if learning's hidden, this gives us small steps towards the light. It works no matter what books the church burns. I got stuck for ages because I could think up tons of ideas, but if you rank your ideas and test the best ones first....' Phos traced blue lines over her window, a plan of their house. She coaxed out another blocky symbol before jabbing her finger at a spiral inside a box.

'This controls gravity, and it'll let us sleep in mid-air.'

'The cart has blankets. Warm, thick blankets.'

She nudged the spiral towards an empty corner

of her map. He could grab her arms, but he'd never bind her all night. 'Leave it, Phos: you're tired and light's failing.'

Her hand flicked another letter, and their ceiling rained a white glare, but she still shunted her pictures. 'I'll only affect the corner; I'll take care.'

'You don't know the word.' Their room quivered, and Caliper turned as dust and gravel fountains spewed from the far corner's floor to rattle against the ceiling.

Mitch lobbed a pebble into the gushing dust, and the stone rushed upward to clack into the ceiling. 'Want us to sleep up there?'

'Needs adjusting.' Phos twirled two overlapping symbols and glanced back.

Caliper sighed. 'You're a menace. Put it back before it spreads.'

'Leave it, Phos.' Frinelia rapped her stick against the floor.

The corner's light faded, and the girl strode forward to thrust her hand into the dust plume. 'It feels light but I'm not sure.... I expected blue light....' She stepped into the corner and faced him.

Mitch's voice rang out. 'Check your letters.'

'What?'

'They're spinning.'

Light dimmed, and the square of roof above

Phos burst open. Stones sprayed upward into darkness, and her arms flailed. Her body tilted backwards before rising. Her eyes closed and her mouth hung open as her limbs hung at her sides. Frinelia screamed as Caliper lunged forward. He planted his feet outside the corner and grabbed her knees – too slippery. His hands slid over fabric; without his grip, she'd hurtle upward into the night. Caliper's fingertips won a frail grip on her left boot, and Phos dangled in the air with outspread arms. She shuddered as her head rolled back.

'Caliper, what's—?'

'Stay still, Phos. You blacked out. Don't move.'

Tension shivered across her body, and the girl's arms thrashed. He tugged at her boots, but her floating body was stuck in the air. Caliper heaved, and her body pivoted around her waist to tip backwards, but his fingers slithered off her boots, and he clutched emptiness. Phos fell and slammed onto the floor as gravel pinged around her.

'The symbols,' Mitch said. 'I stopped them spinning and put them back as they were.'

Frinelia knelt and clutched Phos's shoulders. 'Can you hear?'

The girl twitched and raised her head before rolling to her left. 'The symbols must talk to each other.' Dust spilled from her helmet as she glanced up; her work had bitten a square hole through their ceiling.

She paused. ‘Good work, everyone.’

‘You complete arse. What does acting the maggot teach you?’

She looked away. ‘I learned we’re sleeping on blankets.’

‘No more tampering tonight. This world’s tagged us as invaders, and right now it’s working out the best way to kill us, and it won’t need your help. At least talk before trying new tricks – do we agree?’ He crouched to touch her shoulder – replace a gearwheel’s stripped teeth, and one stubborn stump always argued against sliding out, but sweat, and it would spring.

A silent nod. ‘I ran too fast. Should I fish bedding from the cart?’

‘Sit and recover. I’ll grab blankets and food.’

‘Thanks for the rescue.’

Frinelia stood with her hands clasped behind her back and stared at the square of dark blue stamped into their ceiling; light still trickled from the remaining roof. ‘No one wants to punch a hole in their ceiling, so these machines have broken.’

‘So we leave them alone. I’ll get our stuff.’ Caliper walked to the window and stopped. ‘You’ll draw me a door first, but take care.’

Phos gazed at the window’s letters. ‘The people here wouldn’t have walked to the window every time they needed work done, and there’re traces of….’ She closed her eyes and raised her arms. Her fingers fluttered, and she pushed her palms together before easing them apart. A scribble of lines and pictures flickered between her hands.

Phos brought change like a summer storm, but confidence didn't mean wisdom, and he should speak more – shield her until she could train herself.

'Didn't we agree you'd stay off the exploits? Rastersen's coming to play, but try easy stuff first.'

Movement outside. A feathered scramble jolted onto the ground ten yards away, and a twilight-coloured body glinted in their house light. The bird stalked closer, and its wings licked the air for balance as its icy eyes stared into his.

Chapter 22: travel as the ancients

The bird ran its gaze over Phos before studying the rest of their room and stared at the damaged corner for several heartbeats. The animal's wings swished as its head held steady, and blue feathers hugged its torso to suggest muscles.

Phos flicked a symbol onto the house map, and white lines scored the glass to suggest a doorway. She stepped into the night. Caliper followed, but she wanted to approach alone, and flicking her hand sealed the doorway.

She neared the bird, but Caliper banged the window, and his voice rasped through her helmet. 'Open this door, or it's going arseways.'

The animal hopped sideways as if blocking the path to their cart, and its head twitched. She raised one hand, and the bird's talons pawed dust.

'Don't face him alone, Phos. Christina asked me….'

Phos pressed her hands together to create another crystal slate. Icons burbled up to describe their air, and the bird scanned the writing before snapping its gaze back to her. Caliper still yelled. She'd learn little here, and she retreated – one touch opened the door.

Spittle flecked the inside of the miller's helmet. 'How many times, Phos? You said you'd watch your rambling.'

'We must learn.'

'What does prancing with birds teach you?'

'There's learning everywhere, so keep calm.'

'What would you learn if it sticks its beak through your helmet?'

'We don't know it's violent,' Phos said.

'I promised Christina I'd protect you – should I stick you on a leash?'

'I'll choose my path, so don't threaten me.'

'You need threats if you don't listen.'

The floor cracked and hissed, and Phos's fingers juddered and curled themselves around cool metal as weight dragged at her left hand. A dagger nestled in her grip. Its curved handle swept into four inches of blade. Caliper gasped, and Frinelia raised her hands and scuttled forward.

'Drop the knife, Phos.'

Phos raised her hand. The dagger's edges glistened. Its handle had grown around her fingers, and its birth had ripped another gouge into the floor.

'If the world hears a threat....'

Caliper met her gaze. 'And hunger breeds threats.'

Mitch tapped his foot over the floor's scar. 'Couldn't they make food that way?'

'We saw fields, so this exploit couldn't make

crops.' Frinelia stepped towards Phos. 'Can I hold the knife?'

Phos let the dagger clatter to the floor. She'd never considered stabbing Caliper, but these machines had waited over silent centuries, and they'd leap at the slightest murmur.

'I need to handle my temper – we all do.' Caliper stared at the dagger.

'I'll seal the room and freshen the air; we can sleep once we're out of our suits. Just hope our dreams don't spark off any exploits.'

'With luck, the builders considered dreams.'

'But their machinery's broken.'

'The cart has bedding,' Frinelia said. 'If we persuade our bird friend—'

Mitch pointed. 'It's gone.'

Phos and Caliper glanced at each other, and she redrew the door. Scattered claw marks scuffed the dust as darkness rolled against their house. Not a glimmer showed elsewhere, so their light would beckon anyone inside the bowl.

Caliper snatched a crate from the cart as Phos wandered back inside to flick symbols over the windows. She closed her eyes, but icons still flitted through her mind. They needed beds, but what thoughts worked here – *rest* and *chair*? Her eyes opened, and a fresh icon winked into place. She dragged it over her map, and a hum droned out behind as a six-inch-high plinth squeezed up from the floor, big enough to hold bedding. She brought up another platform, and half a minute of stroking the window repaired their ceiling.

Frinelia stared. 'Can you create pillows?'

What were the words – *clothes* and *sleep*? *Soft* and *bed*? Wrong words: her body jolted as if bees had crawled into her suit, and three more guesses brought another three shocks.

'No matter. We'll manage,' Frinelia said. 'I can't imagine your words, but can you enrich the air and let us remove our suits?'

Phos tinkered with the icons, and fresh symbols spouted from her fingers. The window's pale letters set out thoughts of wind-scoured skies and muggy days, and pastel tints swam into a faint rectangle where a delicate violet on the left shaded through green and into a harsh red. A fine black line sat in the red, but thinking of shelter nudged the line into the safety of the green – a colour borrowed from the Second. Soft tones breathed warmth into the ceiling light, and the plaster walls shimmered for an instant before reappearing as smooth sheets of beige.

'I think it's safe, Mitch. Fancy testing the air?'

He unsealed his helmet, and she studied his face before peeling her own suit away. Caliper blushed as she slipped off her undershirt, but he dug out water flasks, and they freshened themselves.

'These suits mean we don't need water, but I miss the drinking, and if we find a lake, I'm gone,' Caliper said.

Phos wrapped a blanket around her as Caliper handed out bowls and segments of boulmer fruit, which glazed her lips with a chilled tartness. She cradled the dish and covered it with a plate. Tomorrow they'd aim for the rim, and if a plate covered this bowl-shaped world, they'd have to squeeze their way past and find a home for Christina's argument, currently resting snugly in her backpack. Phos dimmed their lights as Frinelia lay beside her, and she drifted from calm rest into a fitful sleep.

The mist outside soaked the black night. Everyone in this world had slept at the same hour, and she imagined their single room as a square bubble clinging to the world's curves. Images of Christina and Caliper skittered through her dreams, and one open-eyed spell left her imagining the nanotech planting thoughts into her mind. Sleep returned, and images of the First Enclave's creation drifted past: outsize humans rode self-hauling carts that knitted trees over brown dunes. Her dreams roved over milling crowds, thousands of frightened people racing towards fresh swathes of grass and trees. She searched their faces, but each one held an alien fleshy fullness; the trees were squat and dull. Her vision rolled over the shallow hills dotted around the bowl's distant edges, but the rim rolled for miles, and fatigue tainted her dreams.

Phos woke. Dawn's blue light rinsed the floor, and the symbols daubing the windows had faded, though they brightened as she focused. The plinth underneath her bedding had moulded itself around her body.

Mitch stood beside her. 'The room's learning: the gravel's turned into paving stones, and you should see the spires outside. I noticed something yesterday, but my dreams added more.'

Phos blinked: waking hadn't cleared away her dreaming images. Caliper restacked their cart, and she glanced around their room and slid on her suit before sealing the door. No sign of birds, but rolling grassland wrapped their house as the world's curve climbed into the grey bank of clouds.

Crackles and a blizzard of shrill rattles scythed through her helmet, and she winced. Phos tapped her helmet as a sudden burst of hissing gave way to a man's drawn-out sigh.

'Is someone trying to speak?'

'You're making a real impression, Phos: we see your tracks.' Rastersen's oiled confidence flooded her mouth with bile. She imagined Rastersen's breath brushing her ears as his hands gripped her shoulders.

Caliper scowled. 'Who is this?'

'Ah, our brilliant miller. Your candles won't work here, so my guards will ensure Phos and I can talk without interruptions. We're closing the distance between us as we speak. I believe Phos's lively mind has dug up the truth of the hard landing, and I'm sure she now realises how limited our options are. Only one path remains.'

Phos waved the others into silence.

Rastersen cleared his throat. 'You and me, Phos. I'm sure we had the same reaction on hearing about the oncoming famine, but vomiting never changes much. I drew myself a picture, a creaking oak with ten people huddled on one rotting branch, and I imagined a rising gale screaming at the tree. If everyone stays, everyone falls; everyone's memories will wink out as if no one had lived, and our children remain unborn ghosts.'

She swallowed, and her hair felt greasy.

'If our ancestors had uncovered our future earlier, we might have sought different paths, but our world rots, and only one way is left. I have a future laid out for you. Join me, and you'll sit among the survivors.'

'Or we'll find another branch.'

'Control is vital, clay is shapeless until it meets a potter's hands. You'll see once we meet; I'll hand you forbidden books, and we'll walk through libraries you can't imagine. You've woken the machines here, and your work may save more lives, but we must work together.'

'Come and catch me. How are you finding these suits?'

'Somewhat snug. Our ancestors may have been a touch smaller than us.'

'Their suits are different,' Phos mouthed to Caliper. He nodded.

'We see your house, Phos, so stay where you are. Should your miller behave, I'll let him go, and won't that be nice?'

Another question that didn't need an answer. Phos pressed her palms together and spread them. Her glass slate showed a curved grid tracing out the First's bowl, and four yellow dots pulsed beside the warehouse. Could she harness the tentacles lurking in the hedges?

'Still listening, Phos? You seek challenges; their friction creates heat, and heat allows growth, and isn't that why you chased the windmill's light? Our new world offers both refuge and challenge.'

Frinelia hissed before falling silent.

'We need your talents. My world changed when my second syllable came: I thought knowledge would fall into my lap, but I had to memorise hymns and prayers, and learn meaningless rites, because no one understood my desire to learn how the world worked. Perhaps marriage means the same for you, but if I tell the world of your talent, we'll avoid that trap. Join us, Phos.'

What books had he touched? His Torzene office had squatted on the ground floor. Was he luring her with a lie, or did his parents hold secrets? She couldn't unclasp her hands, and she stared at Rastersen's dots and at the light green band linking him to her. His words about marriage mirrored her thoughts, but she couldn't forget his clammy palms. Phos looked up; sweat matted her hair, but Caliper sat on the cart to set his eyes level with hers, and he held out his palms.

Phos's fingers twitched as the yellow dots marking Rastersen's place surged her way. She slid a fingertip over the green connecting line and dissolved it.

'He won't hear us now, but we must move. Did you hear him say his suit can't grow? Is it an antique?'

'Let's hope he lacks your talent,' Frinelia said.

A faint grin touched Caliper's face as he buckled on his harness. 'Will his helmet show the same squiggles as yours?'

'No idea, but he's learning, and we can't hide.' Phos paused. 'What did he learn as a priest?'

Frinelia shrugged. 'His father was adept at manipulating the uneducated and inexperienced, and

Rastersen's seminary provided practical lessons in bullying and control. This chaos has unshackled his talents.'

'He was a quarter priest, so what does he know?'

'Rastersen had books he shouldn't have, but I couldn't say what lessons they held. He knows how to learn, and this madness unlocks every imaginable secret.'

Phos chewed her lip. Caliper's threads could snare plants, and Rastersen's words tugged her the same way. Would she freeze if they met again? 'We have to shift.'

'Let's visit the spire.' Mitch pointed ahead. 'See, those plants at its base look dirty. Someone's drained their life.'

'It's on our way,' Caliper said. 'You've seen the cart, though – it'll take hours.'

'Rastersen won't have a cart, but we've another way to travel,' Phos said.

'Don't tell me – you're talking with our world.'

Phos stooped and ran her hands over the wiry olive grass. Tension raced through her arm and mind, and she crouched beside a sandy patch as her suit sprayed images of speed over her helmet. Not a cart but the idea of a cart, an idea with warnings. Did birds feel the same when they chased worms?

'Stand behind me.'

There, a borrowed ghostly memory of waves riding over sea – no, not sea, dunes surging over desert. She saw images of boats cresting hills of sand as plumes of white dust sprayed out. More pictures flooded her mind, a sharp overhang showed at each boat's front, and walls tapered up from the sand onto wide flat decks.

Caliper stared. 'What are you planning?'

'Saving your shoulders: the builders didn't haul carts around, and nor should you.'

Phos's boots crunched over dry soil as she trickled her threads through the packed grains. Dad had stacked crates in the darkness of his shed, and she'd gone exploring when she was small, reaching up and inside to stroke curves and corners, wondering what hid inside. Now her touch flowed through the sand's quiet dark to trace out surfaces – packed sheets of tense powder quivering to hear commands. Phos raised her palm and wobbled upright as her threads flowed. Her mind carved sand, and the bare soil below cracked open as dust grains knitted together and wormed upward. Dirt splattered her helmet.

Mitch stepped back. 'Is this your doing?'

'I suggested an idea, and the sand's organising itself.'

'What's coming?'

'They used to travel this way,' Phos said.

White jets of sand hissed from the ground and braided themselves into twisting columns of dust that rose twenty feet above her before arching back towards the earth. Sand bounced from an invisible surface, but enough stuck to form a platform at eye height, tapered to a point at the front and square at the back, and a pillar jutting from the front might create a place to steer. Sheets of sand climbed upward to meet the deck. The boat formed a gleaming wedge with arching facets sliced into the hull, and its curved sides reminded her of breaking waves. Ten yards long and four wide, and lacking sails and masts, but a hunger for speed crouched inside the craft.

'Lovely,' Frinelia said as the last sand plume died. 'Can you conjure sea as well?'

'I can't say how it moves, but it's for travel.' Darkness had wrapped this seed for thousands of years, but it had sprouted once she'd shown it light. Had the builders ordered new boats for each journey?

Mitch stroked the boat's walls. 'How come only Phos can do this?'

'Can you imagine one Phos fighting another Phos? Perhaps the world picks one person to grip the talent.'

'Perhaps the world makes mistakes. You need to pass on your learning, Phos: if we know more, we can help more. Might even help you.'

'Let's get the boat shifting.'

'Always with the delay,' Mitch said.

The sand had listened; the boat was human-sized but lacked entrances. Another memory fluttered, and stroking the boat's side showed her a hairline gap. The wall quivered, and a section snicked out into a hingeless door – a slab of compacted dust. More beige sand flowed out and settled into a short flight of steps linking boat and earth.

Caliper slapped the hull. 'How does this work?'

'No idea.' Layers of sand listened underfoot, and flashing coloured squares painted her helmet, but she'd focus and shift this boat.

'Be careful,' Caliper said. 'If these machines have gone deaf….'

'The spire's miles off, and the rim even further. The cart's good, and we'll take it with us, but it's slow.'

Caliper's fingers grazed the sand wall. 'Let me test this.'

'You do that, and I'll work out the movement,' Phos said.

Caliper hauled himself up the steps to pace the deck. 'Seems safe, though I can't tell much.'

'It's just a beached boat,' Mitch said. 'Raising it is brilliant, but apart from playing sailors….'

'This is different.' Phos joined Caliper. The

packed sand felt springy under her boots. 'Stack our crates and the cart on the boat, and we'll head for the rim. The spire lies on our way, but even with the boat, we can't dawdle.'

Mitch grinned. 'Maybe we'll meet your world seed.' Tiny yellow letters capered over his helmet, too small to read.

'What are those letters?' Phos asked.

'Only just turned up; can't read 'em yet. How will we recognise the map room?'

'Christina didn't know what it would look like, so our search starts when we reach the rim.'

The bowl was at least ten miles wide, and she'd seen how a circle's outside was always just over three times the distance across, so there'd be acres of searching as Rastersen chased. Three birds pockmarked the sky ahead, a graceful check on their position.

'Still with us, Phos? The boat's loaded – whatever we call it,' Caliper said.

'Just watching birds.'

Phos walked to the front, where the deck narrowed into a point. Sand had sprayed around her to form low walls, and she approached the pillar, a column of scrunched-together sand at the front. Any driver would watch for rocks and hedges as they steered the boat, and her hands searched the sand-white stem. Faint hollows opened beneath her fingers, like those she'd stroked on age-yellowed piano keys. Ahead, a hedge lumbered over a scrambled ridge of bleached rocks. Another hollow house sat beyond, and Mitch's twisting spire lurked in the middle distance.

Caliper helped Frinelia up the stairs and onto a raised platform running along the walls like a bench. Phos closed her eyes and gripped the pillar. Her suit clicked but said nothing. No reins on this boat; sand-strangled grass surrounded them to choke off any escape.

She'd seen pictures of boats cresting storms on the inland sea and labouring up hills of water before plunging into foam-flecked canyons to heave water out of their way.

Impact slammed into her stomach like a giant's punch. Spittle sprayed inside her helmet, and yelps burst from Frinelia and Mitch. Their boat had charged forward six inches before grinding to a halt. The deck now tilted, with Phos at the lowest point. She didn't drive this boat; she had to shift sand around the hull.

Again she stroked the pillar, and her threads explored the boat's shape. The packed sand of the boat's hull pushed against the free dust outside, and the craft's weight crunched the soil. Dad had described the Second Enclave's sea, and the spray escaping the restless power of the rolling waves, but would his words work here?

Their boat eased into a crawl as life flowed through their craft. The hull sliced through a shallow dune, and waves of dark red grains rushed into the boat to slide under her boots before hurtling back into the earth. Slower than walking but easier on Caliper; his crates gripped the deck as their house crept past.

Caliper raised his voice against the grinding. 'Knew you'd do it, Phos.'

'I always wanted to see where the land met the vault.'

'Even back home?'

'I wanted to see everything back home – even stuff that didn't exist.'

She felt a streak of damp sand on the boat's left, soft and yielding. The doughy patch would skew their path, but her senses surrounded the stretch, and she whispered out a command.

Hold together.

The boat stayed upright to slip through the ring of stone pillars circling their house, and now the surrounding drystone wall stood ahead. Its weight bruised the sand, but circling around would cost time. Phos crunched the boat through the wall. The boat juddered, but its hull smacked the flat stones aside, and a wave of tremors stole her breath as the boat rollicked forward.

Grass and shrubs blurred on each side, but their

boat gobbled the vibrations and calmed itself. Phos glanced back as their house fell behind, and their hull scratched a faint trace across the sand as two birds kept pace.

Minutes passed. Her head throbbed, and a remote chunk of her mind showed people in suits like hers, people wrestling with glistening black snakes coiling over their legs. Images came of humans cowering in glass houses from swarms of crimson dust. Did memories drift in the air here and wait for visitors? Were machines still listening?

New icons flashed on her suit, shimmers of messages she couldn't understand, but speed meant a morsel of control. Stumpy elm trees and rambling thickets drifted past, and broken stone ruins dotted the landscape. A cone of dirty cloud, like an upside-down mountain, billowed far around the bowl's curve; sheets of dust laced with dark green streaks curled through the air, and she imagined tumbling hedges. White spray spouted from the cone's centre before collapsing back like a fountain's jets.

Mitch pointed. 'I said those gravity blockers can break.'

Phos nodded.

Pain shredded her spine without warning. The threads she'd woven through their boat snapped, and too late she sensed a tear ripping across the boat's hull.

Their craft tilted left and skidded from the back as the pillar ripped itself from her hands. She crashed against the floor, and her suit stiffened into a rigid shell. Two crates smacked into her as they stuttered to a halt.

Had Rastersen's mind wormed its way here? Phos gasped for air; each breath brought him and his hands closer. She tried to sit up, but her suit clamped fast around her limbs: a cage, a prison.

***

Phos's body sprawled belly down by the boat's pillar, and her palms pressed against the boat's tilted deck. Mitch tended to Frinelia; sweat beaded over the priestess's ashen face.

'You all right there, Frinelia?' Caliper asked.

A single nod. Phos's head bobbled, but her limbs hadn't shifted. Caliper shuffled her way and fought the sloped deck by fixing his gaze on the grass plain surrounding their mangled boat. Grey cloud seethed above to cap their bowl as the single spire loomed ahead.

'Can you hear me, Phos?'

The girl's limbs rocked and her suit fabric flexed, but he heard nothing. Caliper stepped over her legs and knelt before sliding his hands under her chest to flip her over. Her face appeared, a flushed mask of panic, and her lips moved without words.

‘Phos…what’s the…?’

She blinked; her head shook; her limbs struggled against the rigid suit; sweat plastered her coppery hair against her skin.

‘What’s happened?’ Mitch’s voice warbled with panic.

‘There’s no telling: I can’t hear her words. The boat’s damaged, so let’s take her to the ground.’

The sloping deck twisted his muscles, but he hefted her body into his arms and staggered upright to inch down the slope. Phos’s outstretched arms and legs left him fighting for grip, but Mitch took Phos’s feet and helped Caliper slide her body onto a dusty patch of earth, and she stopped struggling.

Caliper sat beside her helmet, and Phos stared back; she’d stopped trying to talk.

‘Can I get tools from the boat?’

‘Hold back a while, Mitch.’

Frinelia stared from the deck. ‘What better weapon than one that paralyses distant enemies?’

‘Is this Rastersen’s work?’

‘It has his stink; he fantasised about taking prisoners.’

‘Can we block his tentacles, whatever they are?’

Phos’s eyes darted to one side and her fingers trembled, and Caliper found himself clutching her hand as his helmet crackled.

'Caliper?' Noise blurred her voice.

'Phos, you can talk?'

'Speaking this way is difficult – it's meant for emergencies. Something jammed my suit, stuffed it full of cords.'

'So you can't move?'

'They're getting tighter. I've prodded the suit, and there're a few exploits I can use.'

'On your suit? You're using exploits on your suit? You need it to breathe….'

'Try stepping back,' Phos said.

'If you don't make it, there's no point in me moving.'

'Rastersen's not left me much. He knows how our suits are built, but the builders added a few exploits late on, and those still work. I'm serious about you stepping back.'

'You're sure?' Caliper squeezed her fingers, and an image of coiling emerald cords seeped into his mind. 'We won't have the talking.'

'Six or seven paces. I'll wave when it's done.'

Caliper paused before releasing her hand and backing away. The soil rippled underneath her. Tiny waves flitted over the sand, and the surrounding blades of fine grass sank into the soil. Her suit fabric turned silvery for a heartbeat before worms of ochre dirt corkscrewed from the earth to snake over her chest, and the swelling earth pushed her up a few inches.

Frinelia's voice slid into his helmet. 'Is Phos doing this?'

'She's trying to free her suit.'

The ground calmed; the soil snakes dissolved into powder, and Phos's hand twitched. Caliper loped forward.

'Not enough,' Phos said. 'I've one exploit left, but it's risky.'

'How risky?'

Phos's eyes watered. 'This exploit examines and resets the suit, but you're not supposed to wear the suit when it happens. I won't be able to breathe while it's working, but it might clear Rastersen's cords.' Her voice wavered. 'Get back, Caliper. Get right back, and don't ask if I'm sure.'

'You're sure?'

'If I could throw mud….'

He released her and his helmet fell silent. Caliper trudged back to the boat and steadied his breathing before running his hands over the gouges exposed in the boat's hull. Mitch scrabbled at the boat's pillar.

Frinelia reached for his shoulder. 'What's she planning?'

'Something needing space. What does *reset* mean?'

'She shouldn't....'

Ground trembled underfoot. He swung around, but his vision blurred. A flickering duplicate of Phos's spread-eagled suit stood upright above her as a ghostly crimson light brewed around the image.

Mitch stood. 'Which is the real Phos?'

'She's still on the earth – the picture is standing.'

'Who'd want her picture?'

'I recognise the light: our healing machines spew it everywhere,' Frinelia said.

Searing white seams ringed the knees and elbows, and a flash of violet light sent Caliper staggering back against the boat, but he shielded his eyes and squinted.

The suited vision had vanished, and now a hairless red-tinged mannequin stood above Phos's motionless body. Bundles of packed maroon fibres suggested slabs of flesh, and eyes bulged from their sockets as the limbs twitched.

'I've seen this image; it's the human body without a skin,' Frinelia said.

Caliper stared. 'Phos's body? What are they...?'

'Someone's studying her.'

'She's even uglier on the inside,' Mitch said.

Another purple blaze stung Caliper's eyeballs, but now a skeleton glowed above Phos's feet, and the skull and ribs jostled as if trying to escape. Meaningless scribbles and lines flickered beside the ghost before the vision faded.

Only Phos left now, still splayed on the earth, and beyond her body the grass stalks waved in the breeze he couldn't feel. Two elm trees scratched the air in the near distance, and far off the spire seemed to watch them.

Caliper darted forward and plucked Phos's hand from the soil. Sweat drenched the girl's face and she gasped, but her eyes opened.

'I had it wrong, Caliper. It didn't work. The suit uses the same word for itself and our bodies. I thought the exploit would examine the suit.'

'But it looked at you – unpleasant for everyone.'

Phos thrashed her limbs but the suit only rocked. 'This taught me some builder words, but my skin burns like stink. I don't know any other exploits, and that priest's coming.'

'We're here for you. Can Mitch drive the boat?'

'I'm trying but the boat won't answer,' Mitch said.

Phos's mouth opened but closed again as tears pooled in her eyes.

Caliper let his helmet hover a few inches above hers. 'If the priest sends you trouble, it proves the suits talk to each other. Will you hold that thought, Phos?'

‘Talk?’

‘Remember the iron leaves we scrubbed away? Yesterday we worked together, so let me look inside your suit.’

Phos winced. ‘Don’t, Caliper. Rastersen’s cords want to spread, and they’ll infect you.’

‘There’s one plus of you being bundled up, Phos – there’s no taking your orders.’

Caliper released her fingers, and her hand flapped for his, but he gripped her shoulders and closed his eyes before pushing his threads into her suit. The priest’s invasion had forced bundles of emerald cords through her fabric, and the enemy braids reared up like a cat spotting a mouse as his threads eased forward. Phos’s limbs writhed under the choking cords, he felt her choking, and her pain ripped a blood-red scar into his mind. Each foreign rope came from a knot of pulsing energy squatting in Phos’s chest piece.

Caliper thrust his filaments forward. The green braids snapped back, but enough of his threads reached the central knot, and he jabbed memories of winter ice through his fingers.

Phos’s bindings shattered, and fragments of Rastersen’s cords swarmed through his gloves and into his own suit to cluster around his wrists and elbows. His arms locked solid, but Phos stirred. She sat, and her hands gripped his wrists to thrust fire through his suit.

The invading green braids writhed and charred into soot.

Caliper's eyes snapped open as the girl smiled back. She heaved herself to the side before gingerly pushing herself onto her feet.

'I owe you, Caliper; I was wrong to doubt.'

'We'll have to manage your scampering now, won't we?'

Phos glanced at the boat and the gouges ripping through its hull. She teetered forward as if learning to walk again, and her hands brushed against the boat's rough scars.

'We have to manage Rastersen as well. He's learning faster than us.'

Chapter 23: the wrong-colour answers

Soil crunched under Phos's boots as she craned her neck back. The birds drifted around Mitch's spire, and her helmet painted brilliant red rings over the trunk. Standing grey stones circled the spire's base like a necklace, and olive-coloured creepers bunched around the trunk.

Their boat still tilted. The powdery earth gripped the broken hull, and Phos remembered the moments before their crash: supple fingers of thought had curled into her threads to topple their craft.

'Rastersen's learned about the boats, so did Morzenthal's books mention them?'

Frinelia sank back on the boat's benches. 'Pretending to be a priest is hard, and I only won the full cloak four years ago. I've only read our most notorious works, but there are rumours of guidebooks. He's only had a day's reading, so perhaps we worry too much.'

'But his parents had longer.' Phos paused. 'I expect they denied him nothing.'

Caliper peered upward. 'We have bird-shaped friends – is your suit calling?'

Phos followed Caliper's gaze; thirty birds circled above, like teachers watching pupils, and her helmet coated the tower with golden flecks. Mitch darted towards the spire.

'Where you going, boy?' called Caliper.

'Watch him, will you? I'd order him back, but we should examine the boat.'

Phos ran her hands over the ragged crevices Rastersen's thoughts had torn into the hull. The sand underfoot twitched and rose into the air. She told the grains to fill the gouges, but her boat wasn't listening, and the new sand fell back.

'Rastersen's serious about meeting: he's locked our boat into a new design, one that won't move.'

'Can you make a fresh boat?'

Phos grimaced. 'Yes, but he'll know I'm building, and he'll interfere.'

'Can you learn what he's doing and fight back?'

'I can find out where he is, but that won't help.'

Caliper shifted his feet and gazed at the spire's base. 'We should see your fat boy Rastersen at work. Ever use the henges back home?'

'What do you mean, use?'

'So you've not used them. They're more than stones; they're houses for exploits.'

Phos blushed. 'What sort of exploits?'

'All sorts. There's one that shoves your vision ahead of your body. Takes practice, but it's your man for watching priests. But exploits here are fierce, so we tread slow and careful.'

Mitch's breathing wheezed through her helmet. Phos turned to see him approach the spire and pick his way around crumbling brown slabs of tilted earth.

'Stay close, Mitch, and watch those birds.'

'These stones match those near Ferstus,' Mitch said.

'Wait for me, boy, and keep your paws off them stones.' The miller cantered to the spire with clenched fists. 'The henge stunned me last time, but if Rastersen's boatbuilding, we'll not want the waiting.'

Phos followed. The spire loomed overhead and reeked of strength and age. The ground at its base made a crazed jumble of broken earth. Mitch reached up to unfurl a creeper from the spire.

'Don't upset those birds.' Caliper lumbered over the broken ground towards the nearest standing stone. She imagined the immense spire tipping over to crush them, but she focused on the stones, weathered slabs twice Caliper's height and daubed with moss.

Phos scurried beside him. 'Need help?'

'Are you fine back there, Frinelia?'

'I'll survive – you chat with the stones.'

They reached the stone, and Caliper's fingers brushed the rock, but he snatched his hand back.

'What's the sensation?'

'It's more like remembering a dream, but squeeze your mind and you can nudge yourself somewhere new.' Caliper flapped his hand through the air as if shaking away pain. 'Can you show me your man's whereabouts?'

Phos tugged a crystal slate from air. The four dots had travelled further than she'd expected: four yellow spots hovered in a dark field of green near their house. Phos spread her hands, and the image swelled to show both Rastersen and themselves.

'Grand.' Caliper faced the way they'd come. 'I'll work myself there and learn what's playing.'

'Can I help?'

'I can't carry you on my back: exploits don't work that way.'

'We know these suits talk, and two can carry more than one. Remember the metal ivy.'

'We do that and there's double danger – what if we're both knocked out when Rastersen shows his arse?'

Phos pointed at the grey slab. 'How do these stones work?'

Caliper sighed. 'Your mind's still growing, so I can't let you play here.'

'We've shared everything so far, and if I can take pain off you, I will.'

'And you'll be having the learning, won't you?'

'I'll help. Our suits can divide the sensation, so send a quarter my way – a tenth or whatever. It'll ease our path while I study.'

'Our talking always ends with you having your way, Phos, and why's that?'

'Must be my radiant smile. At least show me how you start with the stones.'

Caliper shook his head and paused. 'Imagine there's a mind waiting inside the stone; you can have the talking without bothering about words, and you can borrow its eyes. Don't knock me off course, and don't cut your own path.'

'Do we hold hands?'

'I reckon so, but I've never taken passengers.'

'It's all about testing,' Phos said.

Caliper tried to run his hand through his beard, but his hand struck glass. 'Stay calm and look ahead, and avoid new buildings – they'll rip your mind apart. Expect trouble too: my first time with the stones left me fierce sick.'

Frinelia coughed. 'Be careful, Phos. That's Caliper, not a thing. We only have one Caliper.'

The miller breathed in before slapping his hand against the mossy stone, and Phos offered her left palm as a gloved invite. His fingers wrapped hers; his eyes closed; and after a few heartbeats her vision faded to grey as Caliper's slow breathing echoed through her body. Did she taste regret as well? Did Christina's words still roll through his mind?

Her stomach churned and sweat beaded on her forehead as blackness swallowed her world. Now a hundred hands seemed to hoist her into the air and buffet her body into motion. Phos's vision returned; two figures in white suits held hands before a standing stone. Again hands wheeled her around, and her vision blurred before settling into a steady ramble: grass hurtled beneath; there stood the scratch their boat had etched into the parched soil. Caliper carried her vision ten feet above the earth. An urge for speed nipped at her, but words wouldn't come. Hedges appeared ahead and rushed below in a smear of dark green as their path banked to their left.

More elm and oak trees dashed past before their hurtling juddered to a stop. Four men wrapped in glinting suits of red metal stood at the far end of a field, and three blue-feathered birds hovered above their heads. A rip laced through the landscape beyond the men, a torn page where land flickered against air, and she tasted blood as fear infected her mind. Was Caliper struggling? Phos tried backing off, but the exploit nailed her vision into place.

The red-coated figures jerked like stiff-limbed dolls. Their helmets were metallic globes clutching a curved glass window. Four men: one pointed while three squatted to glide their hands over earth. Rastersen's orders greased the air.

Pain lanced through Phos as the flickering rip grew. One man waddled forward, and coloured shards tainted his helmet window as his arms hacked the air – an order to tiny machines.

Caliper's temper rang out as a bitter tang of frustration tinged with loss, but in one heartbeat, his mood changed into a wordless fury mixed with a needle-sharp aim: a plan. Dirty sand boiled around the leader, and he toppled sideways before flailing at the soil. One bird landed beside Rastersen to claw his neck, and another swooped to slam into a stooping worker and rake a squall of coloured talons across his back. The last bird thrashed its wings and rushed straight at Phos's viewpoint, and the flickering rip raced towards them. Jumbled shadows of cubes and pyramids surrounded her before blackness smothered her world.

Where was her body? Where was this pain coming from? Was she screaming? The skin on her legs burned, and did hands grip her waist? Blinking showed nothing.

'Phos, answer me. Are you there?' Caliper's voice faded before returning, but he sounded miles distant.

'What's happened to her?' Frinelia's voice had recovered its quiet fury.

'The birds – where are the birds?' The words scalded Phos's throat as she spoke, and she sprawled on the grass before jerking herself into a sitting position to flail her arms forward. Her hands bounced off glass – a helmet?

'I made them see threats, and they bowled over your fat priest and buggered his boating plans, so we've bought time,' Caliper said. 'I can't do that again – not for hours. What can you see, Phos?'

'Everything's black.' Phos blinked and shook her head. Her suit chirruped but darkness still smothered her.

Caliper clasped her shoulders. 'Can you see nothing?'

'If you've cost Phos her sight….' Frinelia's voice faded.

'I've lost sight before, but it usually only lasts minutes.'

'Usually?'

'Don't spend your days scrabbling for the worst, Frinelia: you'll go sour. Mitch, grab Phos's hand: she's safest on the boat.'

Red-hot wires screwed themselves into her scalp, and her hands shook as her suit writhed around her body, but any pattern stayed hidden. Mitch's fingers threaded through hers, and he drew her upward; his hands steadied her as she walked.

'Your helmet's growing letters,' Mitch said.

'And I can't read them.' She had to prune away

the panic, but blindness meant they'd never find the rim, and Rastersen would recover from Caliper's sabotage. Phos rubbed her gloves against her helmet, but nothing broke the darkness, and Mitch's fingers sought hers again.

'Your symbols are glowing green, and my helmet's showing pictures,' he said.

'The boat might help me, Mitch, so steer me there.'

Her hands stroked the boat's sides; Rastersen's rips still clawed the smooth curves, but she heaved herself onto the deck and steadied herself against the slope.

'Where's the stem?'

Mitch embraced her waist and nudged her forward. Her fingers fell into the familiar niches, but the boat wasn't listening.

Mitch paused. 'Can you teach me the steering?'

His suggestion made sense – being the only pilot left them vulnerable – but Rastersen's words still tugged at her mind, and Mitch had heard them as well. What was showing on his helmet?

'The basics, Phos,' he said. 'Start and steer.'

The boat trembled as Caliper slogged on board. 'We didn't do more than scratch Rastersen, and right now your fat boy is repairing our damage. Mitch is right; we must shift.'

Phos gripped the stem and bowed her head. ‘No matter who steers, this boat still needs repair. Take me to the hull.’

Frinelia’s voice squawked inside Phos’s helmet. ‘There’re thirty birds swarming above – is that your work, Caliper?’

‘Everything’s my fault. I’ll take you, Phos.’

The hull wriggled under her touch, and bands of vibration clamped her wrists as she sensed the boat yearning to speak, but her blindness broke the links.

Mitch’s hands clamped her shoulders, and she shivered. A faint curve hovered in front of her, the darkest grey against black. She shut her eyes but the curve remained – no, not a curve: a crescent, a globe. Phos slid her left glove over her helmet, and the crescent flickered. ‘Close your eyes one moment, Mitch.’ The curve blacked out before emerging again. Mitch took a few more directions until Phos realised the blurred shadows of grey and black were what Mitch saw.

Phos tottered upright, and her own body unfolded before her, all gangle and stretch. Mitch nodded and her stomach churned, but she gulped down several breaths and pointed at the boat.

‘Stare at my left hand, Mitch, and keep staring wherever it goes.’

Colour leeched back into her borrowed sight,

and she saw the cracks running through the hull. Phos bent, and sand frothed under her hands again. She remembered the gliding motion plasterers made when repairing walls. Sand surged from the ground and into the gaps, and the boat trembled as the dust stayed to fill the gouges resting in the sand. Caliper's work had stopped Rastersen's fiddling for now.

From Phos to Mitch to the boat, the link was feeble and slow, but the boat listened. Yellow letters danced across Mitch's helmet – too blurred to read. *Maybe words of healing*, thought Phos, like the signs she'd seen when Caliper's suit had healed him, though hadn't those figures appeared in green? She'd ask once they'd paused – once she had time for breath.

***

Caliper watched colour drain from the girl's face, and her matted hair had lost its copper sheen. Phos's hands wafted through air as sand packed itself into the hull. Mitch smiled, and his eyes darted over the tiny yellow letters scrolling over his helmet.

Phos's voice croaked out. 'I think the boat's steerable now, and we should press on. Mitch, lead me to the stem, and keep your eyes steady.'

'Don't worry.' Mitch stepped behind Phos and caressed her shoulders before nudging her up the stairs. His hands flitted over her arms, more exploration than needed, and Caliper stepped forward but stopped himself. This wasn't a boy's groping; shapes cascaded across both their helmets, so Mitch was dipping into Phos's knowledge. Frinelia sat near the pillar and watched the pair.

Phos stooped to scrabble at the boat's stem. Mitch grinned and whispered to himself as new letters snaked over his face. The boy squatted to stare at Phos's fingers.

Phos pressed her fingers into the stem's hollows, but her eyes streamed with tears. 'Can you stare ahead, Mitch? Focus on the earth before the boat, and I'll work the stem.'

'Those words on your helmet, Mitch,' Frinelia said. 'Who are you conversing with?'

'I'm not conversing, Frinelia – I never converse.' Mitch's head shook a fraction before he faced forward. 'It's not just Phos who sees the magic.'

Frinelia glanced at Caliper. She opened her mouth but stayed silent.

Caliper stepped behind Mitch and squinted at the yellow letters. Was the boy chatting to the birds? Hadn't Phos mentioned ancient machinery lingering in the First? Had it woken for Mitch?

The boat jolted forward a few inches before grinding to a stop.

Phos sighed. 'You looked away, Mitch. Don't

get distracted; concentrate on the soil the boat's about to touch. Try again?'

'Sure.'

Caliper turned as movement flickered; birds glided behind, pursuing streaks of blue. The boat quivered and shifted forward, and Phos shuddered.

One bird broke from the flock and raced forward to storm towards their boat with oiled wings, all beak and outstretched talon. The animal surged past Phos's shoulder, and the boat quivered as Mitch winced, but after three heartbeats they picked up speed.

'Those birds aren't as charming up close,' Mitch said.

'Shift us forward, you two,' Caliper said. 'I'll set up the scythe.'

Thirty birds knifed through the sky to chase, their blue bodies black against the sallow cloud capping their bowl. The flock jostled into a horseshoe of pursuit to wrap their boat; their slow-pulsing wings let them keep pace. Mitch fixed his stare ahead, and Phos swung the boat leftward to face the rim, a distant goal Caliper couldn't imagine. Bile leaked into Caliper's mouth as his fingers fumbled with the scythe's blade. One nick meant death.

Chapter 24: the past can catch fire

Sand grated underneath the hull. Phos's teeth rattled, but colour seeped into what she saw of Mitch's shaking vision. A sea of emerald grass stretched ahead, and a blue-grey band slid from the mist to stretch from left to right.

Mitch's head snapped to his right, and her sight blurred before focusing on two smears of blue. The birds were overtaking. She urged their boat leftward and stumbled as rock scraped their hull. Her hands slid from the stem, and the boat slithered to a crawl. More streaks of blue rattled past, and Phos toppled sideways and smacked into the deck.

'Mitch, is there a way through the birds?'

'They're coming closer. They're—'

A hard jolt rocked the deck as a bird slammed into the side. Phos scrambled upright and shoved her hands back into the stem's hollows.

'We need speed.' Frinelia's voice sounded faint.

Phos blinked. Rastersen's damage still tainted their boat, but Mitch's vision fixed on a sprawling ridge of hedge ahead, and she heaved the craft towards the streak of dark green – she'd run their boat along its length for cover.

'See any red triangles?'

Yellow words still caked Mitch's borrowed

vision, but the writing blurred like ink over damp paper. Another crash knocked her forward, and three birds with outstretched talons scudded her way. Phos slowed the boat, and the animals crashed into the hedge, but crackling sounds itched against the boat's side. Her borrowed sight failed, and blackness swallowed her, but Caliper's feet thumped on the deck behind as the boat juddered to a halt.

'There're green scribbles on your helmet, Phos; it's a right dance there.' Caliper's arms held her steady, but grit scoured her eyes, and she sealed her lips to hold the scream inside.

Sight returned in a tempest of dazzle – not Mitch's blurred imitation but her own. Her hand rose to her helmet, and she blinked as those birds hovered thirty feet away from their stalled craft to avoid the hedge. Red triangles swarmed over the thicket and crept closer, and Phos seized the stem to grind the boat forward. They'd run out of hedge in a minute, but moving might ward off those tentacles.

Caliper laid his scythe on the deck. 'Keep it slow, Phos.' He jumped out to lope between the boat and hedge. 'I'll handle any tentacles, but stay close. Keep turning and don't be predictable.'

'Are we ever?'

Caliper snatched a vine as he ran, and the triangles juddered his way. A knot of stunted elms forced her to swing the boat rightward, and he disappeared behind the boat's rear. She'd lost her armour, and two birds skimmed towards her before rearing up with their talons at head height. Phos threw herself down to let the pair hurtle a few inches above the stem. Mitch hurled a stick, which clattered off a bird's body.

She hauled herself up, but a heavy blow cuffed her back, and colours stormed over her visor. The boat tilted as an invader boarded. She remembered talons and beaks as snapping noises rattled around her helmet, but hands steadied her body.

'Keep the boat shifting, but stay low.' Caliper scooped up his scythe as the swirling helmet colours faded.

'Are you burning shrubs again?' Phos pushed the boat forward.

'Everyone needs hobbies, but stay near the thicket.'

Gouts of smoke spiralled into the air, and one glance back showed the hedge's red triangles winking out as the birds retreated ten yards.

'What happens once the hedge burns out?'

'Keep circling. I need Frinelia's words,' Caliper said.

She curved their boat into a slow loop as black smoke boiled from the thicket to give a few heartbeats of shelter.

Caliper returned, panting. 'No time for practice, but we've a way forward. Head for the rim.'

'The birds will catch us.'

'I've learned a new trick.' He crouched and fiddled with his boots. The smoking hedge fell behind, and the birds raced to ring the boat. The blue-grey band drew closer, but it was minutes away, and the unbroken grassland left them naked.

'Go slow,' Caliper said. 'Keep going straight, and give me your permission.'

'Permission for what?'

'This.' He touched her shoulders, and her suit shivered as it linked with his. Caliper's thoughts rippled past her body, through the boat and into the sand underneath, which seethed like boiling water.

'What's happening?'

'Frinelia sold me a fierce tale, so we'll have fun. Take a left when your feet tingle. And that's no road ahead.'

'How do you know?'

'It's not just you with the exploits.'

Her soles tingled as the boat's hull scorched the grass and smoke spewed behind. Frinelia had burned footprints into grass after Torzene, and Caliper had twisted his own strength into her exploit. The birds veered away another twenty yards, and she tugged the boat leftward to spray out an arc of smog.

Phos stared ahead. 'If that's not a road….'

'Ever seen the sea back home?'

'Will we float?'

'This place makes dreams real,' Caliper said. 'Imagine you're riding a boat, and you'll smell the salt.'

The band rushed closer, and Caliper released her shoulders as the boat sped up. The sand beneath had been a constant nag, like a tight shoe, but now it vanished, and her senses snapped back into their craft. Phos understood: the earth had dipped away, and their speed had spewed them into the air. They flew before smashing into water, and she tumbled to the deck as spray spattered over their suits. The boat glided through sea before drifting to a stop. The birds watched from the bank.

Frinelia stood and clutched the rear wall. 'Will they follow?'

Caliper stood beside her. 'Living in spires means they're not fond of the ground, and they'll not enjoy the swimming.'

Phos wiped water from her helmet. 'How did you know smoke would scare them?'

'Go tread on the undergrowth by the hedges; it's yards thick, and fire would clear it, so you're sure they've not seen smoke. They only attack in numbers, so they're cowards, and cowards never manage the strange.'

'You guessed, didn't you?'

'It worked, so stop wailing.'

Frinelia slumped onto her seat. 'Cross this belt of sea, and we'll reach the rim.'

Phos grasped the stem and let her threads explore, but the water stayed dead. Shallow waves chopped at the hull, and she closed her eyes to force out her senses as the boat hung in an expanse of nothing.

'This is only water; it won't answer. We've no wind or sails.'

Five hundred yards of ripples stretched to the dim shadow of the far bank, where mist clotted above a grey beach. The bowl's far side arched above her with its dim blurs of brown and green, and the ocean band scratched a belt around the world.

Fog rolled ahead, more wall than cap, a plate covering the bowl they'd climbed, and a yellow-orange glow simmered behind the mist. Gravity still stuck her to the ground. She imagined herself standing inside a swollen tunnel, but unlike the Second, the First had an exit.

'Reach past your limits,' Phos whispered.

Writhing bundles of energy flitted between their hull and the quiet mud six yards below; fish and eels nosed back towards their bobbing boat, and Phos sensed a rollicking wriggle of muscle and nerves she couldn't place. She shuddered: these were creatures without tools or fire; their sea made a prison where every child copied its parents.

The water wasn't listening, and Phos raised her arms to waft threads through the air. A whispered breeze pinged dust against her helmet. Did the boat hold memories of sails inside its machinery? She'd seen rigged masts in books, but wasn't a sail just a billowing surface? A few thoughts told the boat to wring out a slab of frosted glass, a massive crystal slate. It sprouted from the deck like a sail twice her height, and symbols capered across – maybe signs for wind and speed.

Air gusted around her body as the sail caught the dusty wind, and the boat drifted towards the distant beach. Mitch's mouth moved without words as letters slid across his helmet. He frowned and shook his head but glanced at her before looking away. She stepped his way. Questions festered inside her, but tremors rippled under her boots, and sand spilled over the boat's inner walls as cracks ploughed across their deck. The left wall slumped outwards into the sea, and Phos dashed her threads through the deck to explore the hull. Fresh wounds had hacked through the sand, and she rushed out a single plea to the grains to hold together, but they stayed silent.

'Wonderful. Our boat can't handle the sea.'

The dissolving boat still fluttered forward, and

heat came; not the sweaty pleasure of summer but an oven's swelter. The builders had shaped suns to their needs, and their boat's drifting had thinned the fog to unleash the light. The boat shook, and Phos sensed a black crevice chewing through the hull to spit out smaller cracks. She scrunched her eyes shut and flicked threads deep into the boat with one message.

Pour yourself into the large crack.

Two pulses trembled against her feet as she sensed grain knitting to grain, and their boat tilted upright again to bustle through the choppy waves.

Ahead, silent ripples lapped a slope of grey sand, and a shallow hill climbed into the mist. Clouds cleared to show an immense wall standing ahead like a plate balanced on its edge, a vast mottled yellow-orange disc, a cover over the First Enclave's bowl.

Frinelia's head drooped towards the deck, and green symbols flickered around her helmet while Mitch crouched and looked back at the land behind. Sand crunched beneath their hull, and Phos stumbled forward; they'd butted against the far shore. She jumped over the wall into shallow water before wading shoreward, and coarse sand gritted against her boots as she stumbled onto the beach.

Flat stones pocked the sand, and Phos kicked one over – no trace of moss or lichen. Christina's argument weighed down her backpack and waited for action, but where were the builders' tiny huts, and where was Christina's map room?

She padded up the short slope. At the top, jagged boulders squatted on a flat desert of gritty sand while rocks threw shadows towards her. Ahead, the yellow disc glowered, but she glanced sideways: the First Enclave's bowl curved up and away on each side. Ten miles of curving landscape arched over her head, a band of beige sand, and rocks looked as if they'd been glued to the curling strip of barren dunes.

Mitch squatted beside her and dug his hands into the gravel as Caliper hauled boxes from their boat. Frinelia had escaped the crumbling boat and perched on a crate.

Ahead, a sharp thread of black divided the sandy ground from the glowing disc, so did the desert stop before touching the disc? Phos tried spreading her thoughts, but her threads withered the instant they touched the dust.

Caliper climbed up and stared forward. 'I'll set up the cart.'

'Use the boat's remains as a base, and we'll travel light,' Frinelia said.

'Christina said the map room stood past the rim.' Phos stepped forward, and dust scattered over her boots. Mottled patterns covered the false sun, and each pace brought new shapes over the horizon; if the disc was a plate, there'd be space between plate and bowl.

Grains of sand skittered against the back of her helmet and raced past her before jamming solid in the air. Ripples churned across the sand, and her boots buzzed. Caliper swore as several boulders shivered and sank into the desert, and gouts of oily syrup welled upward into puddles that linked into a slick pool to block their way.

Sucking noises echoed inside Phos's helmet, and symbols blared warnings: this oil was hotter than boiling water.

Caliper faced her. 'Your work, Phos?'

'Not me. I can't touch this land.'

'Stay back.'

Black mud surged from the slick's centre to pile into a six-foot column, and grey stains burst across the pillar's head before oozing down. New icons flared onto Phos's helmet, and curving letters flowed beneath images.

Mitch backed away. 'Do we run?'

'We're being messaged.' Phos inched forward, and the pillar flowed into a new shape. Globs of the tar slumped from the top to leave a rough globe, and a gap appeared at the base to promise legs.

Caliper gasped. 'Is this how Christina appeared, Phos? She said she'd find new ways to talk.'

'It's different, but….'

‘Stay back,’ Frinelia said. ‘We don’t know….’

Another swarm of grit rained against Phos’s back before hurtling into the oily statue, but the ooze swallowed the grains. Corners emerged from the shivering muck, corners linked with hard facets to suggest shoulders and elbows without flowing robes.

‘This isn’t Christina. I’m sorry, Caliper,’ Phos said. They shared a glance, but the statue’s head tilted, and one of its legs slithered forward half a pace without leaving the ground.

‘Rastersen knows we’re here.’

Phos stepped to her left, but the statue treacled forward, and its head twisted to follow. The priest wasn’t inside, but his mind infected this ooze, and her body froze.

‘Odious man, but he doesn’t lack brains,’ Frinelia said. ‘Can we outrun this statue?’

Rastersen’s dark pool had flowed over ten yards of desert, and Phos inhaled. Memories of his gripping hands pinned her legs to the ground, but she closed her eyes and forced her left foot four inches sideways. She turned before her body could regain control and opened her eyes to scurry forward. Stones skittered from her boots. She’d curve around the pool to restart their journey, find a way to bring the others.

The tar pool surged forward as she ran, racing alongside her, and new oily waves splurged ahead as rocks sank into the dissolving sand. Could she borrow Caliper's swear words? Phos paused: the congealed statue was a hundred yards away, but Rastersen's smile still clawed her mind.

'I should contact him,' Phos said.

Caliper snorted. He unstrapped his cart and walked to her. 'That's your plan? Smile and ask if he'll let you pass?'

Frinelia picked her way across the rubble. 'You'll never trick him, Phos: he's spent years working on girls your age.'

Phos stared back. 'He's all boast, all snot and vomit; you saw him snivel. I need to learn how he's running this exploit; he's learned packets.'

'Yes, more than you,' Mitch said.

Phos frowned. 'He shows off, which helps us – he let slip his suit was too tight. Besides…. Well, there's no besides – talking's our only path.'

Caliper reached Phos and touched her shoulders. 'You're sure?'

'He's heading our way now.' She raised her hands to create another slate. 'No one speaks except me.'

Dust scudded over the tar pool as the others' helmets stayed quiet under the disc's yellow light. Desert beckoned on the other side of Rastersen's boiling grease, though frost glinted on the distant rocks.

A map etched itself onto her crystal slate, the First's bowl, and the picture contracted to focus on three yellow dots. Rastersen had lost a man, but he'd reached the spire.

Frinelia touched Phos's wrist. 'Words can't be unsaid, so think before speaking.'

'He knows our position, so there's nothing to lose.' Phos twisted her hand until an emerald thread snaked from the dots. Her helmet hissed and she swallowed.

'Will you give us the pleasure of your company?'

Silence. She imagined his tongue running over those overfed lips, and her heart beat several times before his voice gasped out.

'Phos, you returned.'

'Enjoying the extra world?'

'It's fascinating, Phos. I imagine your fabulous mind is swooning here. The sights, the potential, the learning: every step is a lesson. But each step brings danger. Think how your boat dissolved, and remember the birds. Even the air is unbreathable….'

'How did you learn that?'

'Research, Phos. Frinelia may mention the church's work in recovering lost knowledge, if she stoops low enough to open her mouth.'

Frinelia scowled, and Caliper slotted his blade

onto his scythe.

'I feel the urge to meddle with every artefact here, Phos; the same call runs through your fingers, but take care. Learning is a frost; ice makes each blade of grass glitter, each leaf easier to see, but the same frost burns the fingers of the curious. Wait until I reach you, and I'll keep you safe.'

'You lost a man,' Phos said.

'Don't step into the black river – we tested it well.'

'We've not lost anyone.'

'Yet. Ever imagine running away from school? I'm sure the thought came, but you stayed because you knew you couldn't survive without your parents. Your bravery matches your intelligence, but meddling with this world is perilous: one scratch can kill.'

'Up here learning grows on trees.'

'And trees are lethal. Come to me, Phos: as you see, I've learned how to work this world, and I can protect you. Frinelia clings to her secrets.'

'He's lying,' Frinelia mouthed. Phos turned away.

'You continue to impress and educate, Phos. I thought myself immune to lies, but you almost persuaded me you were a simple schoolgirl. Have you chosen your second syllable?'

'Chosen long ago.'

'It's well overdue. I share your need to learn. Study with me, Phos; we'll break open barriers and study the healing machines and learn stories from forbidden books. I'll guarantee you a place among the survivors. Imagine the status and influence; imagine others handing you rare manuscripts and fighting to run errands in your name. No more teachers and priestesses spreading falsehoods.' Rastersen paused. 'I can't uncover your world seed, but I can help your search. You only need to wait for me.'

Phos pressed her lips together; she'd hardly mentioned the world seed.

'I was your age a few years ago, Phos, desperate to learn more than school allowed, and I believed the world would spill learning into my ears. But my teachers ignored my talent and bundled me into the seminary. And like marriage the seminary meant an end to learning. I won't let that happen to you; someone with your talent should never be a servant, so I'll show you forbidden libraries and remove all barriers to learning.'

Her face flushed crimson, and Phos turned her back on Caliper. She flicked at the lines on her crystal slab until only a single yellow thread linked her and Rastersen.

'Can I trust you?'

'You've learned by testing, so come and test me.

If I'm lying you'll outwit me.'

Caliper thumped Phos's shoulder, and she faced him. His face erupted into a storm of gagged fury, and spittle sprayed over his helmet.

'Where are these libraries?'

'There's a living city, another version of Morzenthal, buried inside the glass mountains of the Outland, impossible to reach without help, but I'll ensure safe passage. Unguarded libraries, banks of plants growing under man-made lights, places where the wise fashion potions and forge new metals to recover our histories.'

'Are there others my age there?'

'A handful. We never ignore talented commoners, but we never expected brilliance from females. Let our mistakes become our teachers. Nature has rules to govern the falling of stones and the howling of wind, and even the flow of water. The ancients knew these laws and became strong through obeying them, but we've forgotten much. Help us rediscover; create tests for us; help us rebuild those ancient machines. There is your prize, Phos: take charge and write our future.'

'What does this place look like?'

'The ancients' architecture has its own distinct flavour of domes and pyramids. It's like where I stand now, the station below the spire. Don't tell me you missed the place. The walls here display our world in exquisite detail and let us tweak the land.'

'You're seeing a map – you found a map room?'

'Join me, Phos, and be here when I open this world, a new refuge. We'll work together. You should see this chamber: the images here make it hard to believe I'm underground.'

Had he stumbled onto Christina's map room? She closed her eyes and her shoulders stooped.

Rastersen's voice continued like drops of rain – a patter of words flooding her mind. Caliper fumed a few paces away.

'We're similar, Phos,' he said. 'Blessed with an urge to learn but imprisoned in a world where people ration knowledge.'

Phos stayed silent.

'Like you, I used to fume at our world walls, but our world moulds us like clay. Understand your limits, and you'll learn about yourself. I understand your need to grow; I've felt it myself, but uncontrolled growth can harm – wine can become vinegar, and bread can sprout mould. Wait for me, Phos. Stay there with your friends, and we'll make sense of this new world as we learn together. I know the best path for you.'

Phos turned; wind carried dust over the shimmering oil pool, and the fine grains dirtied the slick before sinking. The black grease quivered as if waiting for Rastersen's orders, and Caliper stepped in front of her, hands on hips.

Her eyes closed, and rows of uncaged books swam before her, painted landscapes dancing in their frames, hushed explanations of exploits and demonstrations of ancient machines, but a memory of a slim man wearing a waistcoat emerged. Dad had given her words to use when hearing a story, a way to tell truth from lie. He'd tinkered with his waistcoat buttons before fixing his stare on her. 'Demand details, Phos. Dig deep and ask who, what, where; ask the why behind the why. A truth teller only needs memories, but a liar's story will wither when you drag it to a place they haven't written.'

Phos gnawed her lip. 'This living city, this glass mountain library, what's it called?'

The tiniest delay came – a sliver of time thinner than the fastest heartbeat – before Rastersen fired back a single word.

'Montressel.'

A tiny pause might throw an arrow astray, and even inside Phos's suit, the lie stank. 'Is Rastersen your real name?'

'I'm not lying: I don't know. Can we agree that our world dies and our society must change to survive? Even your talents won't save everyone.'

Phos flicked her fingers over her crystal slate –

Caliper should hear.

'Still there, Rastersen? I once thought I could invent a new tree, and I stuck willow bark over an oak, but the bark peeled off after three days, and your story falls apart for the same reason – your words don't match your heart. Most priests have no problem getting wives – perhaps it's the money or the robes – but you changed worlds to chase me. Why is that? Can't you control women your age?'

'Limits, Phos, remember the limits. There's still my black river….'

'A baby in a cradle has limits, so do we stop babies growing? I always pestered Dad for looser reins, and he loosened them as far as he could, and that's how I learned, and why I've survived. I broke both the rules and the walls; I made my own path.'

'Phos—'

'Who leads your survivors? You want worship, but you're only ever worshipped by the young.' She sliced her fingers through the slate's green lines.

Regret snared her fingers for an instant: she might have learned how he'd brought oil to the desert and what secrets he'd squeezed from Morzenthal. Now she'd have to win knowledge by herself.

Caliper smacked his face against her helmet. 'Complete arse, you are – what was that speech?'

'Not much.'

‘Why cut us out?’

‘I needed focus, and he can’t listen now.’

‘Thrash out agreements, did you, Phos? His statue’s shunting our way, so what happens when it arrives?’

‘How much did Rastersen learn?’ Frinelia clutched Caliper’s arm.

The ground softened, and heat flared beneath Phos’s boots as Rastersen’s pool grew. Caliper’s scythe clattered to the ground as his arms circled her waist, and a long pull dragged her from the foaming tar. Her feet scrabbled onto sand.

‘This way.’ The miller snatched his scythe and backed away. Everyone darted behind him, and he lobbed a fist-sized stone into the pool. The tar swallowed it.

‘Rastersen’s showing off,’ Frinelia said. ‘His parents chose his toys, and now he wants control.’

‘And there’s more than one sort of control.’ Phos stared over the simmering grease; ice glistened over the far side’s rocks. ‘We must cross this pool.’

The ripples covering Rastersen’s pool faded as the others waited. She breathed in and let her senses flit across the tar.

The priest’s exploit swarmed over the sand; a creeping mass like a thousand maggots scurried from the distant desert to skate over tar before returning.

Phos's threads hoisted one of the tiny creatures into the air. This wasn't an animal, but a bundle of thought reeking of Rastersen, a mechanical slave circled by a fine chain with instructions to pilfer warmth from the other side's sand.

'Phos, you need help?'

She shook her head. The creeping machines mirrored Rastersen's gait, but people changed their minds, so could she infect these devices? Her thoughts thumbed inside its body to plant an idea.

Change your goal: smear cold onto the black tar, and tell others.

Change rippled through the herd. The swarm shifted as waves of machines surged forward to dump desert frost into the oil, and a dull white bloom smeared across the tar. Perhaps you couldn't make heat, but only shift it between places.

'Getting there,' Phos muttered.

Mitch pointed. 'Is that ice?'

'Oil ice perhaps.' Phos nudged her flock into a two-yard-wide strip, and the pale tongue reached their side. Caliper prodded the scythe's pole against the path and grunted in relief.

'Let me go first.'

'It's worse than boiling below,' Phos said. 'We'll only have moments.'

A few creatures changed back to shift heat from

the tar to her strip, and black holes appeared in the waxy solid. Rastersen's fingers were busy.

'We need to go now.'

Caliper nodded and dropped the scythe before stepping onto her bridge. Clumps of waxy debris stuck to his boots as he hustled to the far shore. Frinelia strode behind while Mitch skated over the tar.

Phos swallowed and rushed onto the bridge, but walking meant she had to release the machine creatures, and her feet punched through the crust. Thick tar spattered her ankles. Had her feet caught fire? Another lunge, and the fatty tongue dissolved to pitch her forward. Her helmet slammed onto sand as gloved hands gripped her arms to haul her onto the far bank. Burning agony stung her legs before fading.

Caliper coughed. 'We've got you, Phos. No panicking allowed, but keep moving: the pool's growing.'

Phos's fingers formed fists on the frosted grit, and she jumped up. 'The man keeps learning.'

'You sound impressed.'

'He's impressive and disgusting all at once.'

'Is he better at exploits than you?'

'He's showing off – he wants us cowering.'

Frinelia pointed ahead. 'We should move.'

Phos nodded and brushed tar gobbets from her suit. Rastersen's words still rattled inside her; if they met again, he'd have new arguments.

'I looked ahead,' Mitch said. 'The land's peculiar: it folds away.'

'Stick together, and check for footprints or wheel marks.' Caliper pointed at Phos's backpack. 'Still got Christina's present?'

She nodded: the hoop's weight tugged at her shoulders. Each step saw more of the disc's mottled patterns rise into view. A fine black thread divided land from sky, and one last step made her certain. A gulf stood between the parched land and the luminous yellow disc ahead; the plate covered the bowl without touching the rim.

Phos lingered before sitting and inching herself towards the brink while holding her breath. She'd seen cliffs before, creased slabs of jagged rock wrinkled with grassy clumps, and she poked her head over the edge.

Phos recoiled. She should have seen stone sweeping down, but no. There'd been a gritty desert littered with pebbles. Old worlds failed her, but if she'd scrawled a map of this land over cardboard and folded the top half away from her, she'd have made what she'd seen: the builders had folded the desert.

Phos raised her head. She'd reached the rim of the First Enclave's bowl, and now she sat at the bottom of a vast ring of sand, a ten-mile-wide tunnel sweeping over her, but if she stuck her head past the edge again, she'd stare onto a circling plane like the brim of an upside-down hat. Mitch squared his toes against the cliff edge and chucked a stone forward. It curved through air before jerking into a new arc, and she heard it smack against sand.

'Be careful, Mitch.'

'Funny word coming from you. It's fine. Look.' He leaped forward and pivoted in a scramble of limbs to land feet first on the cliff face. His feet stayed hidden, but now he seemed to grow from the cliff. Agility became flesh as he walked – forward for him but downward for Phos.

Frinelia's voice trembled. 'Can we follow?'

'You'll be giddy for a moment, and everything's lighter this side, but it works the same.'

Phos gripped the corner, and gravity swirled across her fingers. One world stopped and another began. She shut her eyes and scrabbled across on all fours. Her stomach lurched as icy sweat pricked her forehead, but her left hand clutched a small rock.

'What can you see, Phos?'

'Not sure yet, so don't rush.'

Her eyes opened; if she ignored the last minute, this world would look normal. A parched wasteland stretched ahead, though slender grey pyramids clustered in the distance. They'd walked onto the rim surrounding the bowl. Phos stared left and right at the expanse of flat desert. The pyramids formed an unbroken ring to circle the rim. The glowing disc hovered above like a vault of scalding light. Morzenthal's buried schoolroom had shown their world as a ball, and now she stared at the world's underside.

Caliper and Frinelia swapped words as they shuffled over the corner. Phos stared ahead; points of light glittered and trickled among the pyramids, cubes maybe, and ribboned spirals hung above as if roads had fled the ground, though time had bitten gaps from the strips. The overhead disc's glow faded into a dull grey above the pyramids, as if the builders had only planned light for the First.

Caliper whistled. 'This is the surface?'

'We're underneath the surface,' Frinelia said. 'I've seen drawings of these towers.'

'No windmills or trees, and no apples, so they'd have no cider. What about eating and breathing?'

Phos asked her suit questions, and red lines splurged onto her helmet.

'This air is thinner than the First's, so best keep wearing our helmets.' She'd aim for the pyramids. Afterwards she'd not know her direction, but she'd keep everyone shifting. 'Poison killed the plants here, so we're near the surface and the map room.'

What was Rastersen seeing now? Did he stand where she should stand? Was he waiting for her to despair and turn back?

'About this map room,' Caliper said. 'Every man wants the easy walk into work, so he asks to live near his job. Sure if we find their bedrooms and living space, we'll be close by your special room.'

'We don't know how they travelled; Christina mentioned them moving like lightning.'

Caliper gasped and stared at Phos.

'Caliper?'

'She's back,' he said. 'Christina's talking.'

Chapter 25: a staggering sweep of feathers

Caliper screwed his eyes shut and tried to build sentences from the garbled syllables, but his own heartbeats deafened him. Hissing coated the words to swamp any meaning, but he'd never mistake Christina's deep tones and the way they left him dry-mouthed.

'You're sure it's her?'

Caliper raised his hand and Phos fell silent. Murmurs darted past his ears: '…your idea…travel forward…the dome at…care. ..' Christina's voice died, and he opened his eyes. The parched wasteland stretched before him, the distant pyramids looked like teeth, and light seared his eyes as his suit tightened around his chest. He'd promised to keep Phos safe.

'Christina said travel forward, and she'd heard my idea – don't know which.'

'Hope it's a good one,' Phos said.

Frinelia stepped forward a few paces and stared at the pyramid city as dust billowed around her boots to stain her suit. 'I've seen these towers before – two of our exhibits throw images over the carousel's outer wall. Once a decade, you'll see a wall crumble.'

'Have you seen this section?' Caliper asked.

Frinelia shook her head. 'I think this city rings the First Enclave – it's vast.'

‘Thirty-one, thirty-two miles,’ Phos said.

Caliper’s stomach churned. Christina had mentioned a dome, but even the sliver of city ahead would eat up a year’s searching, and the fat priest learned more of this world with each heartbeat. He stumbled forward. Had Christina changed her mind?

They walked in silence, though Phos stole a few glances backwards. Ahead, a six-foot dark grey wall split the desert from the pyramids, but three ramps ribboned up from the dusty plain to arch over the barrier. Phos pointed at the nearest sloping road, a builder-made wafer of rock rising into the air between two sloping glass towers. They reached an apron of smooth grey, like stone poured out to smother the desert, and Caliper’s feet rang out clack-tap sounds.

‘Let me climb first.’

Caliper’s shadow skittered ahead as the road rose. It creaked under his weight, and the grey crust cracked as they shuffled over the wall. Slender pyramids stretched ahead, silvery monuments pocked with dark patches like doorways set flush into the walls, and the towers stretched halfway to the night-coloured ceiling.

Back home, pyramids were church-haunted monuments of shadowed fear that squatted like dead beetles on the ground. Here twenty tapering monoliths cast back a pearly glow, and the sky in between was etched by hovering roads and curving wires. Below rested a sea of bleached stone cubes, cowering houses sharing walls, nothing the same size. Narrow walkways slunk between the blocks. Bare holes pierced the walls, and dust had crept inside, though a few houses held faded tints of blue.

Mitch dawdled beside them, and tiny yellow words crept over the boy's helmet.

Phos touched Caliper's elbow and pointed at the nearest pyramid. 'There aren't any stairs, so could the builders fly?'

'No idea, Phos.'

Frinelia tottered ahead. 'We only saw scattered pictures, so little here makes sense.'

'We need the map room,' Phos said. 'Look for links, and imagine what the builders thought. If we can't reach the pyramid doorways we search what we can.'

'There're flower beds and benches below,' Frinelia said. 'They had time for gardens.'

Withered grey stalks traced out ancient banks of flowers, and benches sat beside dust-covered paths. Crescents of brown earth scythed the dusty floor where a long-dead gardener had carved a rose into the earth. Couples had walked here while sharing words.

'Christina never mentioned this place – did she hide details?'

'She's never been here,' Caliper said.

One pyramid's outer wall had slumped to uncover six floors teetering like a stack of plates, and grit showered from the scar. Ahead, three glass cubes hung over their walkway as if nailed to the air.

Christina hadn't mentioned winged builders, so how had workers reached the pyramids? He strode to the nearest cube and pushed his hand against the frosted glass, but the pane wouldn't budge.

'Like the Morzenthal ones.' Phos caressed the glass as squiggles flooded her helmet, but she didn't flinch. 'Why is it hovering here?'

'Is it waiting?'

'Perhaps it's built for travel, like a cart waiting for a traveller. If it's still listening….'

Caliper tapped the glass. 'Like our boat?'

'These are more basic.' Phos slid both her hands over the cube, and icons winked into place. 'You pick your journey and enter.'

Frinelia frowned. 'We step inside this cube? Everything here is derelict.'

'We can't climb these pyramids.'

Glowing pictures rippled over the cube's glass, and Phos pointed. 'Christina mentioned a dome, and one of these destinations looks dome-ish.'

'Dome-ish?'

She flicked a dark red square set inside a half-circle, but the cube didn't budge. Phos jabbed other symbols and sighed as her free hand formed a fist.

Mitch stared. 'Can't you get us inside?'

'I'm trying. I walked through Morzenthal's cubes, but this came earlier; it's solid.'

Caliper tugged a bar jutting from the cube, and a door swung open. 'Remember handles?' He stepped inside, and his feet slipped over the glass floor. Two yellowed builder-sized benches ran along the cube's sides, and tracing his finger across the fabric raised puffs of orange dust.

'Your move, Phos.'

The girl darted against a glassy internal wall, a cat toying with mice. The floor shook, and Caliper stumbled against a bench, which spewed orange powder over him.

Frinelia brushed dust from his helmet. 'You have a talent for destruction; people might pay to ensure your absence.'

'But you're staying with me.'

Phos smirked. 'We learn more when you break stuff.'

'Your dome still needs finding.'

The door closed, and new symbols spilled over the wall to stack themselves into a grid, but gaps broke the pattern. Phos's hands caressed a red square, and grating echoed through their box. The cube jerked upward ten feet before trundling forward, vibrating as it crept over mounds of rubble. A curved wall drifted below, and another. Caliper imagined himself creeping like an ant over a tree stump's rings, so had this city grown into place? Gloom filled the air as they drifted away from the shining vault.

Phos pointed ahead. 'Dome-ish.'

A stained and buckled bulge of metal poked above rubble. Beyond the dome, a black wall swept from ceiling to ground and stretched left and right like a stage curtain; the brim circling the First Enclave ended here. Their cube stuttered and sank towards a black patch like a door's shadow wrapping the dome thirty feet above ground, and the vibration built into a jaw-shaking rattle. Jagged rocks inched below. Whining burst out from their box, and it shuddered to a stop in the air, still two yards short of the inky square. Phos chased the wall's symbols, but the icons died, and her hands slumped to her sides.

'There's nothing left. Can your exploits build a bridge?'

Caliper shook his head. 'I'm best with plants, and this place is dead. You've nothing?'

She shook her head and drummed her fingers against the glass. 'People flew here, and my suit shows railings behind the patch, so it's more than a wall. Can we jump?'

Caliper pushed the door open and scooped a metal chunk from the floor before chucking it forward. Their patch gobbled the ingot. 'Fine, but is there a drop the other side?'

'The builders wouldn't put doors above a drop.'

'They did this side.'

'No. There was a walkway here.' Mitch pointed at rubble covering the ground.

'Wonderful,' Caliper said. 'We can't stay here.'

'Let me jump,' Phos said.

'You fall, and we lose our lantern-headed girl and her exploits, and I'll be the guy who let it happen. I've a three-yard run, and if I time it right….'

Curled letters capered across Phos's helmet as her fingers twitched, and Caliper remembered squirrels scuttling up trees. Her energy made his promise to Christina a burden, but going first might shield her.

'Shift this debris and give me a run,' he said.

Mitch kicked four metal brackets through the door, and Phos bent the seat brackets out of his path without effort.

'I'll describe what I see, Phos, which might help you work out the builders' thoughts.'

Frinelia gazed at the floor. 'There's no space – you'll never build up enough speed.'

'I did the barn-to-tree jumping business as a boy.'

'Five hundred years ago,' Mitch said.

He'd need a dancer's balance, and dancing always made him vomit. Caliper jammed his shoulder against the cube's frosted windows and twisted his body to manage the burst of energy needed. If he tore his suit….

A silent count, and a final breath, and Caliper launched himself. His final step set his left foot too far forward, but he flew with rigid limbs and into the patch, and his eyes stayed open as blackness swarmed him. His boots skidded over metal and he fell face first. A bar smacked his helmet as his body jarred to a stop. He sipped air and tried sitting, but his palm scrabbled over the floor before he gripped a post.

Caliper's helmet grudged out a sputter of light, which splashed over a far wall and a distant domed roof. His suit clicked and his chest ached – he tasted metal.

'Are you there, Phos?'

His suit hissed; silence would goad Phos into jumping. He'd slid against a set of railings, and he gripped the bars and hauled himself into a wary standing stance as breath whistled through his mouth. He'd crashed onto a gently curving walkway with a floor built from fine strips of woven metal. Caliper faced the black patch.

A storm of white-suited limbs bowled into him.

His back struck the railings, and he teetered but clutched the bars.

Phos struggled upright as rainbows rippled over her helmet. 'Are you safe? We waited as long as possible.'

'You waited half a heartbeat, you arse. What if I'd fallen? You'd have splattered over my ribs.'

'My suit showed you standing.'

'Didn't stop you smacking me, did it? And how the bollix did you jump?'

'Not sure. I think the suit boosted me,' Phos said.

'You jumped when you weren't sure? Madwoman, you are.'

'Can't have you having fun alone.'

'You near knocked me off this ledge: the floor's icy.'

'Did I invent a new sport?'

'Stop the comebacks, Phos; listen. We need Mitch and Frinelia and light.'

'These suits shine – look.'

Glare seared around his face and Caliper winced. 'Cut that out: you'll blind me.'

Phos splashed her light around the dome's black metal. Her head dipped, and Caliper gasped before gripping the railings and stepping rightward.

'Did we dream the last few hours, or have we

changed size?'

Their walkway circled a vast bowl, a cartwheel hovering over a cauldron, though this cauldron was a hundred yards wide and fifty deep. A blue band curved around the bowl's top. Below, dusty green lines sketched squares over an olive-stained centre. Spires skewered up from the surface, and white specks littered the bowl.

Phos sauntered along the walkway. 'We've an up-to-date model of the First. I can't see our tracks, but they'd be tiny.'

'I've made models but never entire worlds. Is this your tiny hut?'

'Map room. Has to be. Christina's argument belongs here.'

'The model's up to date.' Caliper shivered. 'Can we reach this bowl?'

'The walkway surrounds the model; I expect the builders ordered changes from where we're standing. My suit shows bedrooms and kitchens nearby. You're trembling.'

'My arse is freezing.'

'Your suit should only hint at the chill – give me your hand.'

Phos's fingers drifted over his palm before clasping his wrist, and she stared as fresh icons slid over his helmet. 'Your suit's damaged. Did you knock it?'

'This idiot girl chucked herself at me, so yes, it's had a knock.'

'I can trick your suit into warming, but it'll need tweaking each time we move.'

Phos laced her fingers through his, and two human-shaped symbols glowed on her visor as warm air bathed his arms and legs. 'It's fine for here – let's explore.'

'Mitch and Frinelia might help, sc can we find planks?'

Metal creaked underfoot as they searched the walkway. Tools littered the path, and Caliper's foot brushed outsize hammers and spanners. He bent to stare at what looked like flower heads cast from silver. Beside stood a pile of wooden rods curled into knots, and coppery foil wafted in the thin air as his feet passed. One knobbed baton vomited green syrup as he knocked it with his boot, and a silver wedge squirmed into a ball.

Phos's lights swept over banks of dark metal cabinets set back from the gantry. Caliper strained at the handle but nothing gave. He stopped when his ribs ached. A second cabinet burst open and spewed out ropes, trays and metal rods, and a huge stuffed toy dog bounced from his helmet.

'The builders had children.'

'Yes, or we wouldn't exist,' Phos said. 'The builders filled the cabinets, and the contents shifted afterwards, so was there shaking?'

'Can't tell, but there're wooden beams here. Stick enough over the gap, and we'll trundle Frinelia across.'

The beams were lighter than any wood, and Phos helped him slide the planks through the black patch. Caliper paused and stuck his head outside; his teeth rattled as light clawed his eyes.

Mitch stood in the cube's doorway, and Frinelia leaned against the bench's remains.

'Did you miss us? Never mind – we've some class of bridge.'

Phos heaved a plank through the black. It smacked his arm, but he gripped the wood and thrust it at the cube's doorway, and they laid eight planks side by side.

'Do you need towing, Frinelia?'

'Make room, Caliper. I'm neither decrepit nor obese.' Frinelia ushered Mitch away and tapped her foot on the bridge. Caliper guided her and Mitch followed.

'The floor is slippery, but I think I can touch the main lights.'

Light flickered fifty feet above and flowed into a yellow ring above the walkway. At the far side of the circle, a raised stage sat on eight stubby stilts – space for a leader to order changes. Crates cluttered the platform's left side, and a wall lurked behind the stage, pierced by an unlit corridor.

Phos picked her way over the walkway debris. Broken boxes had spilled out builder-sized masks and helmets dripping with black grease. She kicked a tarpaulin and its fabric shattered.

Mitch and Caliper pressed themselves against the railings to stare, and Mitch pointed. 'We came near that village, and it's showing what's there now, but if I dig through the model, will a real hole appear in the First?' More words scrolled over his helmet.

'I expect it's the other way around, but the link's complicated,' Phos said. 'Machines are waking; the builders might have changed the First Enclave's air from here.' She hauled herself onto the platform to face the bowl, and three rectangles of light sprang into life before her. Lanterns flickered above, though several stayed dark.

Drag enough musicians into a room, and you'd need a man to keep order, but Phos had arrived with her twitching fingers.

'Take it slow, Phos.'

'Christina's argument should fit here.' Phos stroked one panel before dashing to another, and their walkway buzzed. Dust streamed from the dome and ceiling as her fingers slid over the rectangles of light, and letters flickered into view for a heartbeat before vanishing. She played these glowing instruments her way, her hands following rules he'd never fathom. Knowledge became dance as she leaped between the slices of light.

Phos's body froze, and she stared at him. 'You're hearing the voice?'

'Rastersen?'

'No. Different. You can't hear it?' Phos cocked her head. 'It's angry.'

'You've upset someone you've never met? Very Phos of you,' Frinelia said.

'I tried to see how Christina's argument fitted – I found stories inside the light, and I was close when the voice came....'

Her voice faded, and Caliper remembered her cringing before Rastersen.

'The voice said it would stop us, but it sounded like someone reading out words.'

Mitch stepped behind. 'Is the voice coming from Rastersen's underground station?'

'I don't know. Does anyone else hear voices?' Panic tainted her speech. As if in reply, a voice trickled into Caliper's helmet, a whisper carried over a thousand miles of breeze, and Christina's breathless words slunk into his mind.

'Caliper – do you read me?'

'Christina?'

'Aren't you two lucky with the voices?' Frinelia said. 'Mitch and I should mime.'

Caliper raised his hand as Christina's voice struggled through the crackling.

'We've little time: your priest manipulates the nanotech. The builders made his suit for war, though it's older than those you wear.'

'What's he after?'

'His suit lets him sense Phos's actions, and his own lust for learning pulls him closer. The birds in the First Enclave answer his calls. He takes risks and learns fast, and….'

A shuddering noise rasped through his suit.

'Christina? Christina?' Could he wring words from silence? Caliper wheeled around, and Phos waved to him from the platform. Her mouth moved but he heard nothing.

Frinelia sniffed. 'Is our situation deteriorating?'

'I don't know. Maybe.'

Phos cantered along the gantry towards him and raised her hand to make five fingers of invite. He clasped her fingers, and her voice buzzed through his helmet.

'Rastersen's damaged my suit, so you won't hear me unless we touch.'

'You'll need both hands to work those lights,' Caliper said.

'I'll work on the panels and raise my hands to speak.' She grimaced. 'Christina said builders made his suit for war, so what's coming?'

'I don't know.'

'You are so completely, utterly, wonderfully hopeless. Every time, Caliper, you never fail.'

'At least we have warning. Where would an attack come from? Can we close the patch?'

'We can move back,' Phos said. 'The corridor behind the platform must run behind the huge wall we saw outside.' She squeezed his hand. 'We use Christina's argument before we leave.'

'You're still curious, but shouldn't we block the door?'

'I'll do that, and I'll work out how the argument fits. The argument might slow Rastersen.'

'I left the scythe behind. What's your voice saying?'

'It's stopped, but it gabbled about infections. Are we the infection? Whatever. I need to sort out the argument. I'll find you if we need to talk.'

Phos slapped her backpack onto the stage and fished inside to hoist out the hoop, a memory of Christina in metal. She set it on the platform before rushing back to her glistening rectangles. Signs and coloured splotches stormed under her hands, and three spinning circles formed rainbows before her.

Any attack would come through their dark patch. Caliper ripped open a packing case and rummaged through stacks of black metal ingots. Underneath sat a vast toolbox he couldn't budge. Stacked boxes sat on higher shelves. He tugged one forward and swerved to avoid its fall. It burst to spill out brass rods a yard long and blunt at both ends. He heaved one upward, but the mass would only slow him.

Another box crashed down and spewed out thin grey rods, chill to the touch and longer than his arm, with enough whip to let him hope. Again Christina's words stroked his ear.

'Did you…the birds are heading towards…breathe different air…together….'

'That's not enough.'

Frinelia coughed. 'Christina again?'

'Any word on closing the door, Phos?' The girl hunched over her windows of light, and her hands still scythed the air. Caliper glanced at Mitch and Frinelia. 'Those birds are approaching, so tell me what needs clobbering – you'll never meet a miller who can't fight.'

Mitch stared at the walkway and the black patch. 'They're smart animals, Caliper, and the walkway's a circle, so what if they burst through the patch and split up?'

Worry dirtied Phos's face as pictures of curving landscapes swam through her lights. A necklace of brilliant dots sprang over the bowl. She lifted her arm, and Caliper galloped towards her platform and gripped her hand; her voice burst into his helmet.

'Rastersen's learning like lightning, but he's not touched your suit – let me see how it talks.' Phos snatched his other hand and closed her eyes. Ripples surged across his suit for a heartbeat before her eyes snapped open and she tugged her hands away. 'Can everyone hear me?'

Caliper nodded and Phos pointed at the bowl.

'Those are the underground stations. They create new air and push out water, and they need to see Christina's argument. If they agree with her ideas, they'll forge new nanotech for the Second – we have a chance.'

'About this door, Phos…' Caliper said.

'I'm pretty sure I closed it, but it needs testing. This world will change too.'

'Should we worry?'

'Change may help us, since the birds are part nanotech; their bodies switched when this world changed, and they can't breathe our air.'

Mitch stepped up behind Phos. 'Find another way: we can't kill those birds.'

‘They’re animals,’ Phos said.

‘So are we.’

‘We can talk to each other and write words and learn from what happened centuries ago. I never met my granddad, but I know what he learned about repotting plants. We learn why things happen. We show plays and play music and tell stories. The birds can’t.’

‘The birds might do more on their spires,’ Mitch said.

‘Our world changed, and we acted and escaped. We learned why it was dying, and we have half a chance of healing it. How would animals react if their world failed?’

‘They’d die.’

‘And there’s the difference: learning means surviving the storm. I don’t know; maybe these birds can link with the nanotech here and adapt, but we must use the argument.’

Phos and Mitch stared at each other – had they argued before? Caliper shunted crates into a barrier.

‘There’s one path,’ Phos said. ‘Our house grew windows that held back the air, so can we make larger windows to house the birds in their spires?’

‘How do we shepherd the birds inside?’

‘Birds in the Second nest in trees at night, and it might be the same here.’

‘You don’t know that,’ Mitch said. ‘You make

stuff up and pretend it's real.'

'Yes, I make stuff up, and that's why we're not choking on smoke in the Second. One man was the first man to imagine a house. There was a first forge and a first windmill. Thought creates worlds.' Phos returned to her gleaming squares of light, and her hands raced over the twisting shapes. 'I don't know how to build windows big enough, but we can try, and we need to use Christina's argument.'

'How do the birds manage between you changing the air and you building these windows? Hold their breath?'

'It's our only plan,' Phos said. 'Not knowing everything doesn't mean you sit on your backside.'

Caliper slid a crate into a gap to finish his wall and turned. 'I could have mouldered on my arse in my windmill while our world rotted, but I came with you lot. Given our games in the muddy river and those tentacles and our scrapping birds, I might have made the right choice; sometimes you've no option but change. If a tool's wrong for the job, change your tool – we use the argument.'

'They built the Second Enclave to last,' Phos said. 'They built the First for speed, so it's a spinning top and always ready to tumble. The birds may die even if we do nothing.'

Mitch coughed. 'I still say we talk.'

Frinelia pointed. 'Here's your chance.'

Caliper and Phos turned together. A bird's head poked through the black patch. Its feathered skull twitched and glistened as it studied their room, and the animal strutted forward as a second bird appeared.

'Phos – the door....'

A third entered, and the trio swaggered left to pluck a path over the walkway's debris while staring at Caliper. Hunting birds could tear rabbits apart, and these birds were huge.

'Phos?'

'I'm trying. I thought I'd closed it, but....'

A fourth creature stepped through the patch and barged into the others. As one, the animals unfurled their wings. Phos froze before pawing her lights.

'Behind me.' Caliper raised the rod he'd found, but the flimsy wire quivered. He'd stacked enough boxes to block both approaches to the platform, but the birds strode forward, and their eyes never left his. He'd never raise an exploit in this metal cage, and if they used the other gantry....

Caliper drummed out a rhythm against the floor with his stick. Their bodies paused before surging towards him.

'Back, you buggers' he roared. Ten feet away, and his fragile boxes wouldn't stop a child. 'Phos, tell Fat Boy to call off his pets. Mitch and Frinelia – keep back.'

The lead bird raised one wing and sliced through a box. Their wings worked like razors; fine for harvesting, but they'd slash his suit open and leave him choking, and leave Phos helpless. The animal's neck pounced through the gap it had carved, but Caliper lunged forward and stabbed his rod into the bird's throat. Blood gushed out as the animal screamed, and its head flailed back. He twisted the rod free, and the bird's eyes glazed over. It slumped, and the other birds shimmied back.

'Keep working the door, Phos. We need it closed. You two find me a club.'

These birds would out-think any tavern brawler; they'd not repeat a failed attack. Razor wings and spear beaks, cold stares flicked between them and Phos. If the birds split up, he'd never shield her.

The two rear birds launched upward and wheeled above the bowl towards Phos. If he rushed to her side, he'd leave the front animal free.

'No, no…. Hide, Phos; don't let them get close….'

She scrambled under the platform and lay flat. Her sheets of light winked out as the two flyers swooped onto the stage to rake their talons over the metal before jumping from platform to floor and scratching underneath. Phos slithered away from the edges.

Rattling came from behind; his bird had knocked three boxes from his wall's top, and its blue-coated body barged through the rest. The animal's beak smacked into his helmet. Caliper heaved his arm forward, and his rod pierced the animal's feathered neck. The stick shattered, but the beast screamed and recoiled, and he waded forward to seize the bird's throat.

They wrestled as a furious roar fountained through the bird's neck. Its legs kicked, and those razor wings tried to envelop him, but he stayed close and swore as the beak cuffed his helmet again. No chance of throttling this beast: muscled slabs ran under those feathers. He stumbled over the first bird's body, and his enemy bucked and screamed. Caliper and the bird swung around as the other two animals clawed the metal from Phos's platform.

Mitch rushed forward, and Caliper's bird lurched at him, but Caliper hauled the animal back as pain raked his chest.

'Get back, Mitch.'

'I found a blade.'

The bird writhed, and cramp screamed through Caliper's fingers. 'Give me the—'

A dagger glinted in Mitch's hand, and the boy slipped the blade into the bird's neck. A desperate squirm almost ripped the knife away, but the bird's throat rattled, and their fight became a gentle lowering as the three sank to the floor. The beast's wings quivered as blood dripped through the floor's metal grille. Pain growled over Caliper's left arm.

Mitch handed Caliper the tiny dagger, and Frinelia scrabbled through a crate. Phos still hid under the platform though her two birds had peeled half the metal away. One jumped to the floor to scratch for her body, but she twisted her legs away.

Tavern rules were painful to learn but hard to forget, and tavern rules said get a bigger weapon. Metal shards littered the floor, sharp and impossible to handle, and the box's rods had skittled through the gantry floor. He grasped a wooden pole but it crumbled.

'Here, Caliper.' Frinelia lobbed a ball at him, and he snatched it from the air, a tangled mass of sliding fibres, a net. He raced towards Phos's platform and let the net dangle from his hands and rammed it over the bird's head. The animal screamed, but mesh pinned its wings.

'Not met nets before, have you?'

The bird scraped its head over the floor, and its wings flailed. The other animal glanced up but returned to ripping Phos's shield. This net had been plant life once, and tension surged through Caliper's fingers. He gripped the fibres and let his threads caper. Heat flared across the mesh, hot enough to brand the bird's feathers and sear his netting fast. The animal bellowed and shook as the net tightened until the fibres squeezed silence from its body.

'Any more nets?'

'None left,' Frinelia said.

The last bird stopped to stare, its eyes twin beads of vicious skill. A year ago Caliper had spilled lamp oil during a tavern scrap, and a slippery floor meant you didn't need to fight standing. His fingers gripped Mitch's blade – a flyer couldn't be armoured everywhere. He ran forward and jumped and flew feet first until his back crashed onto the floor. He slid forward to hurtle between the bird's talons.

Blue feathers streaked above as he coasted over the freezing metal, and Caliper raised his arm to slice into the bird's belly. His hand shook as the bird roared, and blood splattered over his helmet. His body ground to a halt as the bird collapsed behind him. He'd done neater slaughter jobs, but this would do.

Caliper breathed out as pain lashed over him. Something held him back, but he didn't need to rush.

'Caliper?' Phos clutched his hand, but her voice sounded distant. His answer wouldn't come, though he had a memory of having won somewhere, even if the victory had brought him this suffocating cloud of darkness. Too much to remember.

Words coasted past, spoken words he could only follow by clearing his mind. Any memory of meaning faded the instant new words arrived. Hands raised his head and fluttered across his suit. Questions poured over him, and answers pooled in his mind but stayed unspoken. Nothing relieved the crushing weight pressing on his chest; nothing helped him breathe.

One thought lingered in his mind: a steady beacon in a howling gale. He'd kept his vow to keep Phos safe even as her words streamed past him, and Christina's face turned to his as a smile danced on her lips. Despite those endless years of rejection, he sat beside her now – the one who always returned to speak with him. Caliper couldn't follow her words, but he'd never forget the richness of her tones. Now they played deep inside his mind, a voice that would never leave, soft words from the one woman who had never forgotten him.

Chapter 26: the tipping edge

Phos wasn't sure when the moment had arrived. When had she realised her panicked words weren't being heard? When had she known their suits weren't linking? When had she admitted she'd lost Caliper?

Tears came unbidden. Memories hurt; his face and his voice's deep burr, his ease in lifting the heaviest burden, even his smile. Pain came with each thought. He'd often sat with his head bowed, thinking through what she'd said while waiting for words to come, but now any silence would spawn memories of his silences.

Caliper's body rested on the woven metal floor, flat on his back, arms resting at his sides and his open eyes pointing at the ceiling. Blood spattered his suit, but the droplets faded into pink before vanishing. Phos gasped as the inky-blue curves and rings on his arms and chest narrowed and disappeared; her fingers clutched his wrist, but his suit returned to its satin blankness.

Frinelia sat on Caliper's other side and splayed her hands over his chest as if hunting for any fleeting signs of warmth. 'We should have fought alongside him, Phos, given him a moment's rest.'

Phos glanced at Caliper's last target; the bird glared as its wing twitched. 'We're still not safe: it's trying to rise. Do I use Caliper's knife?'

'No. Let me: taking life needs poise; everyone leaves a mess their first time.' Frinelia uncurled Caliper's fingers to take his blade. She glided forward and stooped to slash the bird's throat without breaking step, and blood vanished from the blade.

Mitch stepped back from Caliper's body and mumbled as yellow words streamed over his helmet.

'You did everything possible, Frinelia: none of us could fight, and your net was almost enough.'

'He deserved more.'

Caliper had told her to hide, and she had, but he'd also told her to close the door, and she'd answer his last wish even with her numbed legs. She stood and walked past Mitch on her way to the platform's remains, but stopped as her name flickered across the boy's helmet.

'What are those words, Mitch?'

No answer. The boy shied away.

'Mitch, who are you talking…?'

The question carried its own answer: Rastersen had watched over her shoulder as she'd studied the First. Phos seized Mitch's arm. 'Where is he? What did he promise?'

The boy turned towards the black patch and shrugged her arm away.

'Don't turn away. What's been said?'

Mitch wheeled back, his face beaded with sweat.

‘I didn’t expect the birds would…. I mean, Caliper was….’

‘Is Rastersen following us here?’

Mitch stared at her. ‘You have the talent, but you miss the big picture: your skills might let more people survive the hard landing. Wouldn’t your skills help your mum?’

Phos stayed silent.

‘You wouldn’t listen; you wouldn’t stop your rush into this unknown, and others need you. Rastersen thought your suit might touch the nanotech in the Second.’

‘If there was an ounce of truth in that Christina would have said. Rastersen just wants a stage to stand on, an apprentice.’

‘You must believe, Phos: I didn’t expect Caliper’s death.’

Phos glared. ‘When’s he coming?’

The patch flickered, and a nightmare pushed inside their cavern, a metallic red human shaped shell bristling with ridges and fins, a savage corruption of theirs – a war suit. Rastersen floated through air and landed on his feet on the other side of the map bowl. Again she remembered their horse ride and those thighs surrounding hers. Her muscles locked.

The priest stood, hands on hips, his helmet a metal globe with a reluctant glass window to frame his face. His eyes drank in the scene. Five heartbeats passed before his boots began to clank against the metal walkway, and he picked out a route towards Caliper's shattered box wall.

'A pleasant surprise, Phos. One might think nature insists on our meeting.'

'Where are your friends?'

'Why describe them as friends?' Rastersen paused. 'They'll arrive soon.'

Frinelia stood beside Phos as Mitch tottered towards Rastersen. 'How did they die?'

'Didn't you own a cloak, Frinelia? Maybe I shouldn't fret over badges of rank: our world's changes make symbols meaningless, and Phos has learnt that only strength matters.'

Rastersen's feet made a slow drum beat as he approached. Frinelia raised her knife as he shouldered past Caliper's stacked boxes, but his arm flicked out, and she collapsed backwards as if punched in the stomach. Rastersen strolled forward and stamped his foot onto her chest. The priestess's suit froze, though her head still twitched.

'Strength comes from giving orders when orders aren't needed, frightening people into serving, forging weapons from whatever you touch.' He turned to Phos. 'And that requires learning, and that's why you must follow me. Think of knowledge, Phos, the power to learn and follow your desires.' Rastersen pressed his foot down, and Frinelia's suit quivered.

Phos stayed silent.

'You're without options. I'm reluctant to carry you under my arm, but we will return to Morzenthal, and work together to control our new world.'

'Remove your foot, Rastersen,' Frinelia said.

He pressed down again, and Frinelia groaned. Phos glanced behind; he'd bowl her over before she reached the dark corridor, and the black patch led to a leg-breaking fall.

'Your suit dances at my command, Phos.' Sweat dripped over his face, but his arms rose, and her suit lurched to the right. She staggered sideways before stumbling and crashing onto the metal floor. Pulses wriggled over her limbs – had he fastened hooks into her suit to make her a puppet?

The clanking floor chilled Phos's body, but thoughts flashed across her mind. She'd linked with Caliper's suit and seen the mechanism carrying his voice – a pair of cloudy jewels covered in facets. Rastersen's meddling had appeared as a tangled web of green cords, and the same web now throttled her entire suit to make it shudder with fever, but she stared back.

Phos's vision split into two views: the left side showed Rastersen's crimson suit striding closer, but the right revealed two pulsing beams of emerald light, glistening spirals pouring into her suit, an infection gnawing her fabric and coming from coils in his wrists. A week ago seeing two sights at once would have left her vomiting, but now the spirals made a path for her vision. She imagined salmon leaping through surging water, and her suit gnawing his wrists.

Rastersen jerked back as her suit softened, and her vision snapped into a single image. Agony screwed through her spine. Again her helmet showed emerald light lancing towards her, but she snuffed the priest's rays out. She thrust out her arm to flick out her own beams, but his suit swallowed the splashing light. Phos scrambled upright to face Rastersen.

'Stay as you are, Phos – no more exploits.' He plucked a loop of rope from his waist. Frinelia's knife had vanished; Caliper's net had turned to ash; and Mitch slunk towards her.

Phos held her breath, but her eyes never left Rastersen. The map bowl shared the First Enclave's shape, and if it echoed the First's landscape, it had to hold nanotech. She darted towards the bowl. Rastersen lurched at her, but his suit twitched and he stumbled. His metal glove scraped her shoulder, and she shimmied clear.

Mitch's arms snapped out to block her path. He only had to delay her for an instant, but she pointed at his legs to web his thighs with emerald beams, and he teetered before crashing to the floor. Phos ran towards the walkway's inner railings and leaped. Her left hand gripped the topmost bar, and she swung up, and her feet cleared the metalwork by three inches. For one instant, she hovered over the bowl before falling. Beige smears raced past, and the ground scraped her body as her helmet ground against the model world. Phos's suit stiffened, and by accident she tumbled onto her back and slid to the centre before juddering to a stop halfway down the bowl.

Nausea rolled through her body, but she pushed herself upright. Rastersen gripped the guard rail and leaned forward. The reflections washing his helmet buried any emotion, but a smile lurked in his voice.

'No escape, Phos. We've much to learn.'

She'd ploughed a furrow through the hedges and fields covering the model landscape, but tiny fireflies swarmed over the damage to knit fresh model grass over her gutter.

Rastersen dangled his rope over the rail. She might crawl up the bowl behind, but his swollen hands would grab her the instant she climbed the walkway's inner railing. How had the builders rescued fallers? Had the nanotech dissolved trespassers, or had builder children dared each other to jump?

The priest's red suit whined, and he rose into the air. His body slid forward before descending into the bowl – too graceful for comfort. Rastersen's feet touched the bowl's landscape five yards away, and his suit rippled like water before smoothing itself.

'We'll work together on leaving the map, but your spirit needs governing.' His right hand held the rope towards her. This invite would become a flurry of limbs before he'd pin her elbows behind her back. Mitch stared from above, and she stepped back.

'You sense what links us, and part of you resists, but our wishes must be tempered by understanding what is possible. We're joined; we both seek to learn; we've both carved our own path. Imagine us working together.'

'I'm imagining you lying to me. I'm not your staircase.'

'You still need persuasion, Phos, I understand. Watch.' He flicked his rope, and the loose end whipped through air to coil around her right wrist like a demented snake. Phos's free hand snatched at the rope, and she tried stepping back, but Rastersen hauled her forward as her feet stumbled.

How had Caliper burned his vine? Her suit only showed a lifeless cord stretched taut between them, and the model plants below couldn't speak. She needed metal or rock, and no matter how deep she probed she felt nothing. The priest tugged his rope, and she reeled forward another step.

'I've learned more than you, Phos, and I can ease your path. Tread in my footsteps, and you'll run where I've walked.'

The line clawed into her wrist as Rastersen jerked her forward. She almost fell, but he skipped forward to snatch her waist, and his hands raced up her sides.

'Are we running out of escape routes?'

Phos's eyes closed themselves, and images skidded through her mind: Caliper weaving branches into a horse and braiding ribbons of light into Morzenthal's hills. He'd have exploited this priest by charming grass and trees, but she needed metal. Memories faded, and Dad's gentle smile drifted into night as Rastersen's smirking jowls loomed before her. A contrast: Dad had nurtured her, while Rastersen sought to force her into a pot of his own design, marriage by another name; she'd become his servant and his puppet.

Phos stared at his shining red helmet and the sweated face crammed in its cage, and a fresh thought burst through her like a shock of freezing water. Caliper had said how thinking made dreams real, and her body relaxed as a smile crept onto her face.

'You always ask the wrong question,' Phos said. 'Try asking why I'm not scared.'

'Humour me – why aren't you scared?'

‘Courage comes from what’s in my hand.’ Phos snaked her left palm up and let it hover before Rastersen’s helmet.

‘You’re brave because your hand’s empty?’

‘An empty hand is a question, and questions create knowledge, and knowledge means freedom. Not your freedom – mine. And I’m brave because you brought me metal.’

Rastersen’s visor fogged and shattered as his helmet and chest piece crumbled into flying shards. Phos’s fingers bent around a dagger formed from red metal and glass – a child of the priest’s suit.

Rastersen’s face flushed, and his mouth gaped as air howled out. His hands snapped over her neck and squeezed. Her suit collar scrunched around her neck, but Phos thrust her dagger forward to pierce his throat. A hissed scream burst out, and blood sprayed over her helmet. Rastersen’s arms flailed back, and his body twisted before slumping to the ground. She waited for his body to stop twitching, waited until she was certain she’d sliced this puppeteer’s strings.

‘No one stops me learning.’

Her fingers ached, but she still clutched the dagger, and blood dripped onto the world.

Frinelia’s voice wheezed through her helmet. ‘My suit freed itself – what happened?’

Should she announce her second syllable now?

Frinelia might play the priest again, and Rastersen's blood could serve as ointment. Wasn't killing meant to change you? Weren't you meant to wither with guilt? Perhaps it didn't count when the prey killed the hunter.

'What's happened to Mitch? He's not moving. Can you climb to us?'

'One moment.' Phos crouched, and Rastersen's suit twitched and settled into the bowl as the map digested his remains. She glanced at her feet, but her boots were untouched: the map knew the difference between living and dead.

Frinelia appeared at the railings, and Phos stepped forward. Now she wasn't falling, the model First's own gravity held her to the ground, even as she shuffled forward. She was almost horizontal when she stepped across the model belt ocean. The dizziness left her gasping, but she sank to her knees and edged forward until she could grip the railing's base and slide her hands upward. The topmost bar felt cool and secure, and she heaved herself up and over until her boots clanged against the metal floor.

Frinelia stayed mute. Mitch still struggled against his suit, but her webbing held fast. The glowing waterfalls on her stage reappeared as symbols flowed over her helmet. Caliper had wanted the black patch closed. Phos stepped onto a shred of platform the birds had left and studied the lights. No need to rush now:

like a tossed coin, the patch would either be closed or open, and switching symbols changed its nature. She glanced up and the patch vanished.

Frinelia sat on one of Caliper's crates. A watery smile trickled over her face, but her shoulders stooped and her eyes closed. Mitch's head still twitched, and his mouth moved without sound.

Five steps let her perch her backside on the boy's chest and gaze at the domed ceiling as she prodded his helmet.

'I'll let you speak, Mitch, but I can leave you here, so choose the right words.'

His gasping splutter filled her ears.

'I never lied, Phos.'

'You showed Rastersen our position. You led his birds to us, and Caliper died. Your work and your fault.'

'I didn't see you winning. You kept scuttling into the unknown, and you shared nothing. Rastersen had details, and he promised me—'

'Promises, Mitch, that's all he was, and I know what drove him.'

'You dangled these exploits and never explained. Shouldn't learning mean sharing?' Mitch squirmed against his suit, but it stayed rigid. 'Rastersen was right when he said we can't live here.'

'Remember the air we made; remember the

windows and tools, and let me show you my new dagger. This place is a blank sheet of paper, and we should start writing. Or I should – not sure you have a place.'

Frinelia's eyes opened.

'Phos, let me—'

'Shut up, Mitch. Caliper stood in my way lots of times; I got angry, but his interfering kept me alive and let me learn. Rastersen wanted to stand in my way, wanted me as a puppet, something to control and make him look strong. He'd have stopped me learning, but learning let me win.'

'You kept your learning secret, Phos. Rastersen said he'd show me the underground stations. He sent pictures, and helped me wake my suit. If there was a chance to help the Second and soften the hard landing, shouldn't you have taken the chance? I would: people should share knowledge.' Mitch paused and chewed his lip. 'Even my dad might have listened to me.'

'Rastersen rots in the bowl now. Remember him saying his friends were coming? Let's see where they are.'

Her hands parted to create a slab, a glance back at the First, free from yellow dots.

'He either killed the others or let them die, and it's us three now. Do I make it two?'

Frinelia stood but left one hand on the crate.

'Enough, Phos.'

'Mitch killed Caliper.'

Frinelia stepped forward. 'Rastersen had a genius for learning triggers: you hushed your voice while speaking with him, but I saw your face. Didn't he tempt you with promises, and weren't those promises almost strong enough to snare you? Don't condemn Mitch because he wasn't born with your strength.'

Phos's eyes flicked to the far wall, and breath rattled through her throat. Beyond sat the First, and far below, their home and her father's body, and Caliper's shattered windmill.

Frinelia touched Phos's shoulder. 'Ever wonder how they make puppeteers? There're a thousand recipes, but most start with fear. Scare people; make them believe they're in peril, that strangers have caused the crisis, that they'll only find safety if they treat others like animals. Hate greases that path. Rastersen's death was just, but master your anger, and do not become what you fight. At least wait until you can think again.'

Mitch stopped flailing, and Phos stood to turn her back on him. She could copy Frinelia's elegant slashing and settle her mind for a day, but what if she enjoyed Rastersen's game of threats? Drink turned good men into shambling wrecks where cravings blotted out memories of families; feed her anger now, and she'd spend her days fighting to control others instead of seeking this world's secrets.

'No more worries about saving these birds,' Mitch said.

'What?'

'They attacked Caliper.'

'It's not so simple,' Phos said. 'The birds knew Caliper couldn't stop two attacks, so they divided, and if birds think like us….'

'Your windows held back the air, and we can build shelters.'

'You hated that plan.'

'Can you let me move? The plan might work – the birds acted like Rastersen's henchmen.'

'Henchbirds.'

'Whatever,' Mitch said. 'If we'd learned more, the birds might have fought for us. Use Christina's argument, and build your windows, Phos; they'll give the birds time.'

'What can you bring, Mitch, and can I release you?'

Crackles flew around Phos's helmet – had Rastersen's guards arrived?

'Can you hear me, Phos?' Distance mangled Christina's voice. '…aliper? We've lost our connection, and his suit is silent.'

'He fought. He protected us. He….'

'You're safe now? You're safe but Caliper fell?'

'Yes.' Phos swallowed.

Silence, time enough for a machine to grieve. Christina's voice returned – clearer but drenched in sadness. 'Press my argument against a screen. It'll ask the First to rebuild the Second's nanotech, but I need your permission.'

'Will this affect the First?'

'Yes, but I wrote my argument to consider the First's desires. I hope it agrees with me, but it may see the birds as more important.'

'We made plans.' Phos outlined her ideas to Christina.

'The First senses your thoughts, and I believe it understands. We can hope it listens, but these changes will take several days.'

Phos picked Christina's hoop from the platform and held it against the centre screen. 'Let's start, Christina. You have permission.'

Words to change two worlds, words to free people – should she demand a fanfare? The hoop quivered before dissolving into a cloud that streamed out and downward into the bowl. Was the nanotech already burrowing into the First and working out ways to freshen the Second's air, and would the trees near Leester grow straight and stop stinking?

'We tell the church to stop its hard landing,'

Phos said.

Frinelia nodded. 'I'll find contacts. We'll need strong proof, since many priests won't appreciate food growing everywhere.'

'Let's have them visit here; they'll tell stories with their own words.'

'There'll be months of chaos back home.'

'Best time to change minds.'

Mitch's voice leaked into the silence. 'Phos, can you release my suit?'

She struggled to a crate and closed her eyes. Each heartbeat complicated the world; each story was a fine thread, but time tangled each braid into a massive knot. Could she manage without Mitch, and should she forget her world seed?

Christina's voice returned. 'This link can't last, but there's ancient machinery above that won't fail. I see changes: hills emerge in the First; waterfalls stream over cliffs; and domes grow around the spires – a thousand facets of glass strung together. The First won't abandon its birds, and we must hope it won't forget us, but avoid the bowl for the next few days.'

'Can I see my mother?'

'I'll find her,' Christina said.

'Do we wait here for days and days or keep climbing?'

Frinelia smiled. 'For you, Phos, that's not much

of a choice.'

'There's a timeworn path towards the surface. It rises through several floors, and I sense a primitive version of the carrier field you rode with me. There are chambers far older than Morzenthal or the pyramid city, filled with scraps of life and energy, but seek solid versions of the screens you've touched here. I'll keep watching….' Hissing scrambled her voice. '…will seem primitive…earliest…the outside world….'

Christina's voice faded, and Phos paced towards Mitch's suit. Their eyes met before he glanced away. Dust trickled onto his body.

'Do we take you, Mitch?'

'Rastersen's gone and my helmet's clear, so don't keep looking for threats. And there's something missing from your searching: you miss details.'

'Such as?'

'Remember the rough shelter in the glass house? Someone built it for people our size. Remember the spinning icons that changed gravity and Rastersen's helmet writing?'

'I saw the writing,' Phos said.

'And you did nothing because you never saw the link. I'll be your eyes and ears, and notice what you miss – no one is good at everything. Perhaps I'll find your world seed. I'm sorry I scoffed, and you're right, Caliper saved us all. I'll never forgive myself for his death.'

Phos's boot pressed onto his chest, and her threads flooded through Mitch's suit. The bindings she'd wrapped across his limbs made an emerald net, and its strands shifted as the boy struggled. The net could stay, but she'd slacken the cords a little; if Mitch played with puppeteers he should expect strings.

Would she enjoy having him dance to her tune? Phos paused. Had Rastersen become Rastersen by wanting others to obey? Would she end up hurling out needless orders to earn the same reaction? And how many times had Rastersen burbled about a link between them? She damped Mitch's green webbing into a dim glimmer.

Phos stepped back. 'Get up.'

The boy paused before drawing his knees to his chest and rolling to one side. The floor clanged under his feet, and he faced her with hunched shoulders.

'Walk towards me.'

One step, and another, and another – was he smiling? His eyes met hers before twitching away.

'Keep going, Mitch.' Phos brightened the webbing, and his suit stiffened to send him toppling forward.

'You wanted me to share learning, Mitch, and there's your lesson – your suit is mine. Yes, you can notice things, and yes, you can come with me, but cross me again, and you'll hit the ground – gravity is a bitch.'

Mitch struggled up and scowled before sitting beside Frinelia, and Phos grimaced back. With practice, she might shape his suit into new forms and watch him wince, but she should stop herself climbing the stair; Mitch could walk in front, but she'd also watch herself.

'We climb, and talk with Christina,' Phos said.

'More climbing.'

'Everything gets older as we climb.'

'Am I speaking to Phos, or Phos's curiosity?'

'We'll face storms of questions when we re-enter the Second, so we need answers. Where did the builders come from, and is Christina telling us everything?' Phos picked her way around the torn metal cluttering the floor and stroked Frinelia's shoulder. 'Will you come?'

'I can't run again, Phos.'

'We'll help and we'll go slow.'

'No, I can't leave. This is where my anger stops. Revenge is a wild beast I've ridden for too long; I've seethed and fought when I should have listened, and it stops here. I'll spit out my regret.'

'I don't understand.'

Frinelia clutched Phos's hand. 'You're young; you won't know the words, but our customs cover a child's death. The mother stands watch beside the body for a full day.'

'"'Staying to ease the passing,"' Phos said. '"'Staying to let the silent know they are loved, and to bring peace to the speaking. The passing of the days will bring an easing of the pain to hold the passing years in their courses."'

'You know the words.'

'I've read the words of passing, but I'm not sure I know them, not as you do.'

'My daughter, Phos, my reason to live. Her last breath lingered on my cheek for an eternity, but when her eyes stilled, I couldn't look at her face: my trust in the church meant I'd failed her, and I couldn't give her watch. They buried her without me while I buried myself in work, and it took me years to scrape together enough strength to visit her grave.'

Frinelia stared upward.

'Part of me wanted to strike the church that day, but I knew time would sharpen my anger. I controlled my fury. Each day, I learned more of the church's ways, and each day, I won more power. I told myself stories of a day of revenge, a day drawing closer with each heartbeat. But I paused. I lingered and dallied and found excuses. I told myself I needed more strength and one more exploit. I waited until my hair turned grey and my skin wrinkled, and still I waited even as our world withered.'

Frinelia tottered to Caliper's body. She bent and

sat beside his head, and her fingers stroked his helmet. 'I'd have delayed forever if Caliper hadn't appeared. He destroyed his home and risked torture because he loved, so why did I loiter? He shamed me into action: a miller showed strength when priests failed.'

She threaded her fingers between his. 'He wasn't what I planned, but he was what I needed, and I must let the silent know they are loved. Caliper isn't my son, but he brought me life and let me act, and now he's with my daughter.'

A few steps carried Phos towards Caliper's body. His expression stayed set under glass, his eyes open as if searching.

Frinelia bent her head. 'I'll stand watch with him; it may be enough to still my anger. Keep talking with Christina, Phos, and find your world seed.'

'What do we take?'

'Leave it to me,' Mitch said. 'You never know until you lack.'

Phos reached inside her backpack for her ruined doll – a memory wrapped in frayed linen. She placed it on Caliper's chest and took three steps back before pausing.

'We'll not go far, Frinelia. We'll find a small room where we can change out of our suits, and we'll find you. We'll rest before we re-enter the First.'

'Would anything keep you here, Phos? Even if I

recounted stories of dangers above?'

'No one's been past this point for thousands of years, and if I'd always taken the safe path, we'd never have met.'

Frinelia nodded. 'Knowledge is the only thing we ever truly own, and if you seek more learning, you're right to voyage further. Take care, Phos.'

Phos embraced Frinelia before walking with Mitch into the corridor behind the stage. She paused and looked back at the wrecked platform and its torn metal sheets. Frinelia's hunched figure nestled beside Caliper's body, a mute end to their conversation. This parting meant she'd have to survive without Frinelia's wisdom and without Caliper's strength.

Chapter 27: numbers as high as you like

Mitch strode into the shadowed corridor behind the stage. She caught up and her suit lights blinked on. This floor sounded hollow, a wafer-thin bridge over unseen space. It creaked and swayed under their feet, and her lights skittered over the gaping holes piercing the corroded floor. Empty spaces yawned each side as their walkway became a ribbon bridging a black gulf, and rusty poles stabbed the bridge's edges – too far apart to stop humans tumbling into the darkness. Mitch grabbed a pole and leaned over the edge.

'I didn't bring a rock. Do you have one, or can you shine your lights?'

'Aren't your suit lights working?'

'You've got the touch, Phos.'

'Here.' Her hands snaked across his waist as her mind brushed the filaments weaving through his suit. A simple tweak flooded his helmet with light.

'Stop it.'

'Stop squirming.' Metal creaked underfoot as Mitch bucked back, but she dimmed his glowing lights.

'Can't see much,' Mitch said, and Phos pointed ahead.

The metal ribbon screeched as they walked. Phos remembered playing with egg shells, but ahead the walkway slotted back inside a corridor. Fog licked at holes in the walls, and smaller walkways branched left and right to create pools of darkness that swallowed her light. She had Mitch walk ahead.

'Watch for holes in the floor.'

'We continue?'

'No other choice.'

Shadows danced ahead as their lights caught tears in the walls; buckled sheets of rusted iron thrust jagged edges into their walkway. Time had bitten metal from the path's left-hand side to leave a ten-inch-wide strip of pitted floor above the blackness, and Phos took the lead with Mitch clasping her shoulder. Beyond, the path emerged into a colossal space, a bloated version of Morzenthal's arena.

Remote walls of tarnished silver circled them as if they'd stumbled into the bottom of a mile-wide well. The floor was a buckled, rust-stained disc, and five caves dotted the walls like shadowy pools. Gloom shaded the far sides. Hundreds of yards above, a dark circle gobbled their suits' lights.

Phos edged forward onto the disc. Centuries past, an immense column had crashed to stamp a chasm into the iron. Her helmet showed twisted wheels tangled with cables below – damage enough to stop their journey.

Mitch kept clutching her shoulder. 'Even for builders this place is huge, but does this chamber touch the surface?'

'Hope so, but I'm not sure how we climb.'

Parallel lines scraped the rust, cart tracks, but any cart would be twenty feet wide. She imagined monstrous horses hauling immense carts, but this world forged weapons from rock and boats from thinking sand, so she needed fresh thoughts. The far wall was twenty minutes' walk away, and wheeled boxes sat where wall met disc.

Her suit twitched, and her helmet rushed her vision forward. Phos staggered but stayed upright; now she seemed to hover a hundred yards from the carts. Their wheels sagged as if they'd melted over the floor, and dents covered the sides, but iron chairs still studded the topsides and waited for builders.

'This disc lifted heavy machinery, but those carts shunted light loads.'

'Wonderful, Phos, but look again at the floor. Who made those footprints?'

Weren't those rust patterns random? No. Mitch's finger pointed out a blurred lane winding into a cave, a route worn by ghosts from past centuries. Her suit etched faint lines above the cave entrance – a narrow tube skulked behind the wall.

'There's a tiny shaft inside the entrance, which might help us climb.'

Scars ran across the wall, and faded signs she

couldn't read plastered her helmet as she studied the entrance. They shuffled over the battered metal until they reached the cave. Inside sat a tunnel with a gentle incline and rough chiselled walls. The passage ended in a grey iron door scrawled with faded yellow letters. A central wheel invited her hands. It resisted for a moment before grating into a reluctant rotation, and the door scraped open one inch.

'We're going the right way.' Phos and Mitch pulled, and red triangles splurged over her visor as the door jammed into the ground. She gritted her teeth, and her suit gripped her arms to lend her strength. Vibration hummed through her hands, and one final tug burst the door open.

They'd found a tiny cell with walls made from woven metal. Someone had escaped from the inside by heaving apart the walls. Buttons covered one side; not the cube's glowing icons but discoloured paintings daubed onto yellowed squares. She looked up, and images of cables trickled over her visor.

Phos stroked a square but felt nothing. She pushed harder, the square shunted back, and their door snicked shut. Four more pokes did nothing, but she pressed the topmost picture, and their cell scraped against the metal outside. New red triangles sprang onto her helmet as they rose.

Mitch crashed against her. His arms skated over

her chest, and Phos toppled against a wall and raised her hands – was he stealing skills? She stared, and his eyes glinted for a heartbeat before a sheepish grin soaked his face.

'Crowded in here, isn't it?' He backed off, and his hands sank back to his sides. Phos checked his webbing; nothing seemed askew, but she watched his hands – one of Rastersen's exploits might linger in his suit. Their cell jerked and paused before crawling higher, and metal scraped metal as the buckled cell walls scoured the shaft.

'Up again – isn't variety fun?' Mitch said. 'Why not use Morzenthal's blue light?'

'Builders made this first and learned more as they dug. Their world was dying, and getting in trouble teaches more.'

'That's why you always kicked off at school.'

The box rasped against the shaft again, and Phos's teeth ached from the shaking. Their walls wouldn't answer her suit's threads; nanotech bathed the First, but this machinery had a morgue's quiet. Nudity didn't bother her, but this silence meant nakedness. If it stopped here, she'd be trapped with this boy and those hands.

Fog clotted across Mitch's face, and he flapped his arms as cloudy streamers followed his fingers. Frost pricked her neck, and breathing pulled frozen daggers into her throat, but Phos's visor threw new symbols before her eyes, warnings of scalding heat outside her suit, hot as any forge. The cloud hid Mitch, and her fingers burned with frost.

Why was her suit freezing? Was it hearing lies? The fabric should fit the outside temperature – she'd seen the mechanisms, and she'd nudged Caliper's suit into matching the map room's chill – but this writhing fog confused it, and spots of heat blistered her back. Phos couldn't avoid the fog, but she could make things simpler and tell her suit to overlook the outside and stop trying to adapt. Her helmet whirred as warmth slunk through her limbs, and Mitch shivered at her touch.

'What's happening?'

'Your suit thinks this fog is white-hot when it isn't.'

Their helmets touched, and her hands circled his waist again. Her thoughts lingered in his suit as she reset his heating. She checked his webbing, still untouched, but bile surged in her throat.

'You'll survive.'

The fog drained through the door, and her whole suit swelled to constrict her body. The rasping sound faded even though their cell still climbed - had her suit gone deaf? The box doddered to a halt, and Mitch faced Phos.

'Will the door open?'

She pressed a button, but nothing happened. She stabbed each picture, but the box stayed dead.

'Fancy brute force?'

Phos stuck her boot against the far wall and set her back against the door. She strained as Mitch pushed alongside. The wall buckled, but their door shuddered open three inches, and a final heave bought space to squeeze out.

Her suit lights shone over a vast circular room with a domed ceiling. Rows of desks had lined the walls, but chaos had scattered the tables and chairs, and broken glass littered the floor. A black slab perched on a desk, while others had fallen and splintered, and wires trailed over the frost covered floor. Time had peeled panels from the walls to expose segments of glittering machines. Scraps of paper clung to the slabs and desks.

Mitch's words broke the silence. 'Can we raise Christina?'

Phos called but heard nothing. She prodded a black slab, but her threads slid through it. She lumbered forward and found a new gait to handle her swollen suit, and symbols swam across her helmet. The symbol for air bumped into the symbol for nothing.

'There's no air,' Phos said.

'There's always air – you can't have no air.'

'Does the fog hold it back?'

‘It’s hard to test for no air, and no, I won’t undo my helmet.’

Phos had felt weight waiting to crush her in Morzenthal’s underground. Walls still enveloped her, and her suit still swaddled her body, but now a sense of release fluttered inside her chest, like the joy you’d feel in a freshly unchained dog.

No windows anywhere; the dark blue ceiling curved gently, but she imagined panic-fed builder people gouging strips from the wall panels. Phos strolled past an upturned desk and stepped onto a pair of bodies. She gasped but Mitch stayed silent. Taller than any human, builders wearing bleached overalls; their facial skin had stretched and dried, though their hands touched to form a caress lasting through dark centuries. The man was bald, but grey hair still curled across the woman’s face.

‘They’re not wearing suits, so there was air here once,’ Mitch said.

Phos held her breath and stepped over the man’s legs. Ahead, ice-covered metal ribbons and wires spilled from the walls to fray into a thousand threads. Two huge doors stood to the side, and she ran her hands over the left-hand door and tapped the metal to learn its thickness. It teetered, and she lurched back as it toppled away to slam against the ground.

Vibration shook her suit, but she’d heard

nothing. Did this room gobble sound, or did sound need air? She'd test later. The other door stayed frozen.

Phos wandered over the fallen door into a hallway like she'd seen in the larger churches, and she turned her head to light the walls. Builders had created rooms to fit their bodies, everything their size, and they'd etched delicate traces of honeycomb patterns across the silvery walls.

'To your left, Phos.'

She squinted. A faded green circle sat beside a blue, and other shapes lurked alongside, and a few moments of thought helped her understand. A map, the centre blue circle marked the room with broken desks, and five other areas grew from the centre like petals.

Mitch pointed. 'A home needs four places: sleep, eat, wash and play. We've six circles here.'

'Work? School?'

'Blue is the work bit. School, I hope not: there might be homework.'

'What's the brown shape at the top right?'

'Where?'

Mitch couldn't see her letters, but she pointed out a thin black line scratching upward to a brown square, a road touching a target. Did these domes support the brown square, and had it come first?

Her helmet drifted pictures over the map's circles: a misshapen bed hovered over one circle, and another showed a knife and fork designed by a drunk.

'Sleep and eat,' Phos said.

'What?'

'My suit's showing symbols, and the green circle shows a tuft of grass, so it's for growing.'

'What grows without air, and why build farms indoors?'

'We find out.' An image flashed over the brown square at the road's end – a tiny house on stilts. 'This whole site is hardly bigger than our school, so I can't believe it's where everything started.'

'Still hunting your world seed?'

'There'll be whole cities up here.'

'Remember Christina and Frinelia, and your mum.'

The hallway led into another chamber, holding vast wheeled tubs and racks of shelves shunted against the walls. Phos grabbed the edge of one tub and stood on tiptoe to peer inside; soil filled each vat, but grey strands laced the earth like the ghosts of plants, maybe wheat – Caliper would know. Her helmet displayed stalks of living gold swaying in an unseen wind. Curiosity flitted through her mind, and her suit's vision focused on a single grain. A century's learning sat inside this image, and she recognised a handful of words as her helmet showed two linked spirals twisting through space to form a twisted ladder.

'Not enough for a loaf,' Mitch said.

'This is for learning, not food, and our wheat is different.'

'Did they try growing plants without air, and are these the original plants?'

'Perhaps they changed this wheat into ours to let it survive the Enclaves.'

Mitch laughed. 'Did they build your world seed here?'

'Mocking again, Mitch?'

'You're a fountain of bizarre, Phos, but thinking our world squirted from a seed is fierce weird.'

'There's lots I don't understand, but this hall seems simple, and it's older than either Enclave. If the world seed exists, it's close.'

They passed barrels cast from a buttery, smooth material, and split-open sacks spilling out olive-coloured grains. Mitch poked at a wall of pulled-out wires and twisted boards decorated with glittering square bumps. Above, an array of upside-down bowls hung from the ceiling to face the soil tubs.

'Those were lights like our sun's arch, but they don't move,' she said. 'Where did the plants come from?'

'Who built the builders, and is your knowing a need or a want?'

Phos focused on the green webbing circling

Mitch's suit and nudged him forward. 'This isn't a hobby, Mitch. We learn and survive, even up here, even if our own world changes.'

'Steady, Phos. Don't start enjoying the control.'

Phos examined the door leading into the next chamber, where dust on the floor had mixed with ice. She wandered inside and her face flushed; builders had fitted the plant room around this upside-down rocky bowl, so this dome had come first.

A brother to Morzenthal's carousel; glass cases covered the walls and faded banners coiled over the floor. She approached a table holding a set of rocks. Amber light flickered around her feet and stretched into the distance to suggest a path. Phos followed for a few steps, but the exhibits bewildered her.

One picture showed a First Enclave spire with flaming clouds hiding its base. Another showed cones and cylinders hanging in night air, and a third showed curling lines and splashes of colour. Mitch studied a faded painting etched into glass: a shack built of metal facets and perched on four legs. Hadn't Morzenthal held a model of that house?

Mitch pointed. 'Do we still want a small room?'

Dusty glass panes formed an unbroken cube reflecting their suit lights. The door stuck before springing open.

'Perfect. We'll tell Frinelia when we see her, and

try to contact Christina.'

Phos brushed past two cupboards with ripped-off doors, and piles of paper crammed into a corner. Dust-caked books sprawled over a table, and a black slab hung from a wall. She reached out with her threads, but they skittered and died. They needed gum: the chips on the door meant air would leak.

She creaked a book open. Lists, words, numbers and more baffling pictures; all stories needed beginnings, but time had tossed these words into air. The same spindly house image repeated across the pages, two windows nestled inside a frantic mess of panels, and the building sat on stilts, so had a builder lived on a marsh?

'There're pictures of that all over.' Mitch scraped dust from the glass wall. 'Don't forget Frinelia.'

'I'm not, but we need to seal the gaps around the door.'

His hand brushed hers as they left the room. She flinched but pointed at the museum room's far side. The rocky walls surrounded a gap, a breach, a gulf of utter black.

'Ever seen light being eaten?' She walked ahead of Mitch. Dust furred the cabinets here, and grey flecks coated two flasks sitting on the floor beside the hole.

'Don't take risks, Phos. Frinelia's waiting, and

so is your mum.'

She stepped forward. Walls had always surrounded her – a bedroom, or a classroom, or the world walls, and even the First's bowl made a prison – but this rift meant change. Curiosity had loaned her enough strength to chase fire through darkness, so why hesitate? Both darkness and light could teach.

A muted scatter of glints dusted the ground ahead like gems strewn over a carpet. Another step took her up a shallow slope towards the broken wall – the dome's edges buckled inwards as if a huge boulder had crashed into the dome.

'Surface?' Mitch whispered.

'Surface. Must be the surface.'

Phos strode forward, and through the hole ripped into the wall. One more step, and she was outside; dust crunched under her left boot. More light here – a blue-white shimmer danced over the ashen dust.

Low rolling hills rose on her left – each one a treeless hump of ash, but three metallic domes capped one distant mound. Walking was a struggle, but she jumped forward with both feet together, and Mitch trotted behind and gasped. Ahead, a gold dot flickered just above the ground, gone the instant she looked.

'You're missing the fun again, Phos,' Mitch said.

'What?'

'Look at your boots – we're casting shadows.'

Slivers of night stretched out from her legs and over the dust ahead.

'There's light behind, but I daren't turn,' Mitch said. 'You first.'

'We turn together.'

The upturned bowls they'd left behind sat on the grey desert, but above them shimmered a brilliant blue-and-white disc. No, not a disc – a globe, a glorious blue marble, wreathed with curling strands of white. Seas circled green and brown islands. Distant but immense, quiet and waiting, the globe hung without support.

'What's it for?'

Mitch's question pattered across her mind. She'd always wanted to learn the stories behind each leaf and twig, every whistling gust of wind. She'd driven Dad half-insane with questions, but this globe crouched in darkness as if it didn't need history. 'It's not for anything. It is.'

Did light flicker beside the globe? She stared at the overwhelming blackness surrounding the sphere until her eyes watered, but her suit took control and focused on the seas and islands. Her vision dashed forward until she saw light sparkle over the globe's blue water, and green patches painting the islands with forest. Clouds hugged the curved surface; rivers meandered through deserts and grasslands. Her vision snapped back, and she blinked. The globe wafted out an icy light, utterly unlike Christina's brilliant gold orb. Phos shook her head and stared at the powdered soil underfoot.

A path ran to her left where wheel marks had bitten into the dust. She looked along the path, and her golden fleck reappeared as a mote hovering in the night.

'We explore there and head back.'

'Our world poured out of your gold speck, did it? How far away? No, don't tell me. Walking tells us.'

Her suit said nothing as the path coursed over gentle hillocks in the rocky dust. Phos felt an urge to hurtle towards the hills and cram as many secrets into her mind as fast as possible: what did those other domes hold? What stood behind those hills? Had Frinelia heard of this landscape? She'd compare this world with the First and Second, and learn what instructions lurked below the soil, and she'd learn without controls. Her boots kicked up enough dust to stain her legs grey. Caliper would have loved the mess.

Phos slowed and stared upwards. No clouds – not even the memory of clouds. Faint points of light speckled the vault. No, not a vault: an absence, an open sky, an end to walls and a velvet promise of freedom. With time, she'd learn how to fly, and without priests only sleep would slow her. She flicked her fingers to clear the webbing in Mitch's suit.

She remembered counting at school; teachers had doled out enough words to let her reach a thousand, and she'd asked how you counted higher, but they'd spat out those angry words that said they lacked answers. She couldn't explain why she needed to count more than a thousand, but why did anyone need limits? At night she'd created fresh numbers to let her count forever, and they'd find work up here. Phos kept walking.

To her left two huge carts squatted beside the hill domes as if waiting for entrance – their builder sized seats sat open to the air. The hills were smooth, maybe built from sodden clay, but this world seemed arid - had an ashy rain smothered any ruggedness?

'We're close,' Phos said. The point of golden light showed now as a solid block, thirty yards away, wrapped in ripped and wrinkled golden foil. Splayed out legs raised the platform off the ground; the whole artefact looked like a battered four-legged spider. The foot of each leg was a bowl, pressed into dust, and one leg had a ladder attached. A black funnel sprouted from the block's underside to point at the soil.

'That's the bottom half of the museum's house – I thought it was a house, but….'

'The ladder's not our size. It's for builders.'

They drew closer. A tall glass fence circled their platform, but sections had shattered, and a two-yard-wide gap let them enter and approach the block with its angled legs – scraps of gold foil clung to the metal.

'This was an exhibit. You could look but not touch, don't you think, Phos?'

'Builders walked here.' Huge footprints littered the dust as evidence of a lumbering dance performed thousands of years ago. One remaining section of glass fence sliced through a footprint. 'The dome museum was ancient, but this is even older; the museum celebrated this table, and they wanted it shielded. Oldest thing we've found.'

A small four-wheeled cart sat nearby with two dust-caked metal seats, and boxes and cables dotted the dusty surface. Their road ended at the cart.

'Builders lived in the top half, and that's gone,' Phos said.

'Where?'

'Think hard and stories come,' Phos stepped forward and stroked the ladder's lowest rung before pointing at the globe above. 'Anyone living there would see us hanging in the sky, like we see them. Did they wonder who lived here? Did they travel here all those centuries ago?'

Mitch pointed at their block. 'This is like your boat?'

Phos nodded. 'A flying boat, maybe. I see two sets of footprints. We've seen models of the top half –

you might fit two builders inside. Imagine builders voyaging from the blue globe and landing here to create our world. Perhaps they returned in the top half, but they left their mark.'

Mitch blinked. 'Like seeds?'

'Seeds have instructions inside, and maybe these builders had instructions. It's a story Mitch, you don't have to believe it, but stories can explain.' Phos patted the ladder. 'Perhaps this seed didn't sprout, but imagine them sending later and larger ones which stayed and built more.'

'Why did they come?'

'Why does a baby leave a cradle?'

'So, was this house your world seed?'

'Let's find out.'

'After we help Frinelia and find your mum. There must be an end to your poking at stuff.'

'No,' Phos said. 'I hate endings.'

A word from Kevin.

If you enjoyed Lightmaker do leave a review at the place where you purchased the book Reviews help me build a presence and let me publish more. Amazon's review page is at: https://www.amazon.co.uk/review/create-review/listing

Thanks to members of Oxford Writing Circle for guidance and support. Special thanks to Danni and Annabelle Parker, Jay Aspen, Helen Moulford, and Brigid Allen. Development advice from Hal Duncan. Copy editing by Leonora Bulbeck. Proofreading by Nick Hodgson. Cover design by Vince Haig.

Visit my personal website and blog at https://kevinelliott.space. Sign up for my newsletter there to learn more about the thinking that went into Lightmaker, the influences on the novel, and learn about my future writing projects. If you can't see the link Google its title: 'Where's my Flipping Tea?'

Follow me on Facebook: search for 'Kevin Elliott – Author', or on Twitter @kevelliottspace

A Nebula Radian ebook.

First published in Great Britain in 2020 by Nebula Radian.

The moral right of Kevin Elliott to be identified as the author of this work has been asserted by him in accordance with the Copyright, Designs and Patents Act 1988.

All the characters in this book are fictitious, and any resemblance to actual persons living or dead is purely coincidental.

All rights reserved. No part of this production may be reproduced, stored in a retrieval system or transmitted in any form or by any means, without the prior permission in writing of the publisher, nor to be otherwise circulated in any form or binding or cover other than that in which it is published without a similar condition, including this condition, being imposed on the subsequent publisher.

Copyright © Kevin Elliott 2020

Printed in Great Britain
by Amazon

49346335R00303